SLAVES IN THEIR CHAINS

KONSTANTINOS THEOTOKIS
which fled to Corfu after the fall (
ennobled for service to the Venetiaı
maths and science, but as a studen
abandoned his studies and moved   ...ₑd to a
Catholic Bohemian baroness conside   ....ɪan himself. On reaching
his majority he married her in Prague, despite the disapproval of his family,
and took up residence in the dilapidated Theotokis country seat in the
north of Corfu. Here over the next two decades he immersed himself in
philosophy, Sanskrit and European literature, and in addition to the powerful
Naturalist fiction about Corfu's aristocratic and peasant life for which he is
chiefly remembered, produced a distinguished body of translations – from
the *Mahabharata*, the Greek and Latin classics, Shakespeare, Goethe, Heine,
Flaubert and Bertrand Russell.

In 1897 he organized a group of his retainers to take part in the Cretan
insurrection against the Turks. During a year at Munich University in 1908,
he became more deeply interested in marxism as an alternative to nationalism
and on his return to Corfu helped found a local socialist club. In the lead-up
to the Great War he endorsed the pro-Entente policies of Greece's liberal
prime minister Eleftherios Venizelos.

Theotokis's taut, dramatic village stories often turn on violated honour
and, like his two novellas *The Convict* (1919) and *Life and Death of 'Hangman'
Thomas* (1920), explore folk customs and morality, while his socialist views
are more evident in his short urban novel *Honour and Cash* (1912). The
longer novel *Slaves in their Chains* (1922) is his most personal and ambitious
work and artistically his finest. Theotokis died of stomach cancer at the age
of fifty-one.

J.M.Q. DAVIES attended Greek schools in Salonica and read Modern
Greek and German at Oxford before pursuing an academic career in
English and Comparative Literature, teaching at the Universities of Alberta,
California, Melbourne, Darwin and Waseda. His publications include a
monograph on Blake and Milton, articles on literary theory, and a number
of translations, including Arthur Schnitzler, *Selected Short Fiction* (Angel
Classics, 1999), *Dream Story* (Penguin Classics, 1999), and *Round Dance and
other Plays* (Oxford World's Classics, 2004), and Hugo von Hofmannsthal,
Selected Tales (Angel Classics, 2007).

Konstantinos Theotokis

SLAVES
IN THEIR
CHAINS

Translated from the Greek
with an introduction and notes by
J.M.Q. DAVIES

ANGEL BOOKS
London

First published in 2014 by
Angel Books, 3 Kelross Road, London N5 2QS

www.angelclassics.com

A CIP catalogue record for this book is
available from the British Library

ISBN 978-0-946162-78-9

MIX
Paper from
responsible sources
FSC
www.fsc.org
FSC® C013056

The publisher gratefully acknowledges financial
assistance from the A.G. Leventis Foundation

Front cover image: 'Yannis Kontos on Horseback', detail of a
mural painting by Theofilos Chatzimichail, c. 1920; Kontos House,
Anakasia, Pilio, Magnesia Prefecture; reproduced by permission of the
Greek Ministry of Culture and Sports (Ephorate of Contemporary
and Modern Monuments and Technical Works of Thessaly)

Typeset in 10.5/13.6 Garamond Premier by
Tetragon, London
Printed and bound in the UK by
TJ International Ltd, Padstow, Cornwall

CONTENTS

Introduction

C ORFU, fabled home of the Phaeacian princess Nausicaa who refreshes a travel-worn Odysseus in Homer, with its palaces and ruined forts and cypress trees, has long been regarded as one of the more romantic and sophisticated of the isles of Greece. Its cultural uniqueness was shaped decisively by the Venetians. From 1386 they successfully fortified it against the Turks, keeping it within the Western sphere of influence, created an Italian-speaking ruling class, analogous to the Francophone aristocracy in Russia, accommodated Jewish refugees from the Spanish Inquisition, and covered the island with productive olive groves. During the Napoleonic era Corfu was occupied successively by the French, the Russians in alliance with the Turks, and again the French, briefly becoming the capital of the semi-independent Septinsular Republic, but in 1815 at the Congress of Vienna the Ionian Islands became a British protectorate. In 1821 the mainland Greeks rose against the Turks who had ruled them since the fall of Constantinople in 1453 – a struggle in which Byron famously took part. And when in 1827 the Great Powers intervened to break the stalemate, it was the Corfiot Count Ioannis Kapodistrias who was accepted to govern the fledgling independent nation. It was also Corfu's great (Zante-born) Romantic poet Dionysios Solomos whose 'Hymn to Liberty' would later provide verses for its national anthem.

Under the British, Corfu was ruled by a succession of High Commissioners, assisted by a Senate drawn from the local nobility and an Assembly. And over the fifty years of the Protectorate the island prospered, acquiring a university, a bilingual Greek/Italian newspaper, arcades and palaces, a cricket ground and a network of serviceable roads. Here the neurotically romantic Habsburg Empress Elisabeth would later find refuge, naming her sea-view palace the 'Achilleion' after the Homeric hero, and here the German Kaiser and Europe's high society would repair for recreation during the Belle Époque. But popular though the British were initially, they were undermined as time went on by nationalist Ionian radicals, or *Rizospastai*, who agitated for union with what after

1832 had become the Kingdom of Greece under the Bavarian King Otto. And in 1864, following a report by William Gladstone (who bemused the islanders by addressing them in ancient Greek), the British ceded the Ionian Islands to Greece, blowing up Corfu's New Fortress behind them.

Their departure was a mixed blessing, especially for the old Italianized nobility. Some of them went on to play leading roles in the new, more liberal Greece under the Danish-born King George I, but others found themselves deprived of patrons, increasingly plagued by debts and defaulting peasants and in competition with the rising middle classes. Corfu's university, the renowned Ionian Academy, was closed in favour of the more recently founded University of Athens. And as Greece pursued its irredentist 'Great Idea', or *Megali Idea*, of liberating and reuniting the remaining Greeks of Thessaly, Macedonia, Crete and Asia Minor within a new Byzantium, the Ionian Islands found their neutrality, ostensibly guaranteed by the Great Powers in 1864, eroded by military recruitment drives. By 1923 this foreign policy had led to a costly insurrection against the Turks in Crete (1896–97), two Balkan wars over Macedonian territory (1912–13) and the invasion of Turkey (1919–22), which was repulsed by Atatürk and precipitated retaliatory massacres and the expulsion of the Greeks from Smyrna.

Konstantinos Theotokis (1872–1923), after Solomos the Ionian Islands' most outstanding writer and one of the more colourful and intriguing figures in Modern Greek literature, was well placed to become the chronicler of Corfu's complex multi-ethnic society on the threshold of the modern era. He came from an ancient family that with the fall of Constantinople had fled to Corfu and Crete and by the seventeenth century been ennobled and entered into the *Libro d'Oro* – analogous to Burke's *Peerage* – for service to the Venetian state. His illustrious clan included merchant buccaneers, theologians, the painter Dominikos Theotokopoulos (El Greco), the first president of the Ionian Senate, and Giorgis Theotokis, three times prime minister of Greece. According to his younger brother Spyridon in his fragmentary biography, their father, Count Markos Theotokis, embodied many of the paradoxes of his class and times – an enlightened intellectual, archivist and scholar abreast of modern thought, yet by temperament an aristocrat critical of the French Revolution and bourgeois democracy as inventions of the Jews and Masons, and given to dwelling on his ancestors' achievements in a way that did little to prepare his offspring for the modern world. At forty-five, his bachelor elder brother Alexandros having provided no heir, he married the beautiful, artistic seventeen-year-old Angeliki Polyla (also from a patrician family and niece to Iakovos Polylas, the editor of Solomos's posthumous papers) and sired ten children.

Konstantinos, their first son, known familiarly as Dinos and raised often speaking Italian with his mother, would become the simulacrum of his father and his complete antithesis – proud of his heritage, scholarly, romantic, yet politically liberal and later a socialist who like Tolstoy forfeited his feudal patrimony. Precocious at school, he showed a special aptitude for maths and science, collecting insects, charting the stars, submitting papers on powering balloons and seemingly destined for a scientific career. But once enrolled as a student in Paris he took to living extravagantly, flaunting his titled status and squandering the allowance his doting uncle Alexandros had secretly mortgaged the family estate to provide. Abandoning his studies after only a year, he fled to Venice to escape a flu epidemic and there fell in love with and rashly proposed to Ernestine von Malowitz, a cultivated Bohemian baroness almost as old as his own mother and a Catholic. Summoned to Venice to rescue him from this 'embarrassment', Count Markos alerted her to his son's difficult character and modest expectations, but she insisted that her young suitor was honour-bound to keep his promise. So after waiting till his majority to oblige his father – doing the rounds of Corfu's high society and writing a novel about Greek bandits, *Vie de Montagne* (1895), in French – Dinos married Ernestine in Prague and took up residence in the Theotokis *archontiko*, or ancestral seat, of 'Karousades' in the north of the island, built originally in 1525 and named after the adjacent village. This remote, dilapidated but idyllic dwelling would remain their home for the next two decades.

Here Theotokis embarked on an ambitious programme of self-education, reading extensively in European literature, studying Sanskrit, and immersing himself in the philosophy of Nietzsche, Schopenhauer and Marx. And over the years, in addition to the powerful realistic village stories, novellas and major social novel *Slaves in their Chains* (1922) on which his reputation chiefly rests today, he produced *inter alia* several allegorical tales influenced by Aestheticism, a Nietzschean rhapsody entitled *Passion* (1899) and a large body of translations – from the *Mahabharata*,

Lucretius, Shakespeare, Goethe, Heine and Flaubert – thus continuing the long-standing Corfiot tradition of keeping Greece abreast of Western culture. Important in helping him come to terms with his Greek identity and decide to write in Greek was his friend Lorentzos Mavilis, an older Corfiot poet and ardent nationalist who would later be killed in the First Balkan War. And it was under his influence that Theotokis mustered a small group of his retainers in support of the 1896 insurrection against the Turks in Crete, quixotically emulating his own heroic ancestors.

Tragedy struck in 1900 when his only daughter died of meningitis, and he and Ernestine became permanently estranged. Hitherto she had put up with living in a village with not much Greek and a violent-tempered husband, and had turned a blind eye to his indiscretions with the peasant maidens – who, as his brother Spyridon remembers, regarded pleasuring the master as a duty. But now she turned to religion for consolation, and divorce being out of the question for a Catholic, they lived parallel lives in the old house. In 1908 in the course of two semesters as a visitor to Munich University Theotokis became seriously interested in marxism as an alternative to nationalism, and on his return to Corfu he helped found a local socialist club, without however becoming practically involved in politics himself. In the lead-up to the Great War his distrust of German imperialism led him to support the pro-Entente policies of Eleftherios Venizelos, the Cretan reformist prime minister and champion of the 'Great Idea', and he served under him briefly as an emissary to Rome. In 1919 Ernestine refused to sign allegiance to the new Czech state, thus forfeiting the Bohemian estates that she had inherited on her brother's decease, so that for the first time in his life Theotokis was obliged to seek employment, as a civil servant in Athens. During his last years he became closer to the married Irene Dendrinou, a poet with whom he had earlier edited the journal *Corfiot Anthology,* and for whom he wrote exquisite sonnets. He died of stomach cancer at the age of fifty-one, his wife taunting him that his suffering was a punishment from God for all the pain he had inflicted on her. To a friend he reflected ruefully that he felt he had at least another decade's work in him.

Writing from outside the literary circles of Athens and not living long enough to see all his work through the press, Theotokis only gradually achieved the posthumous recognition he deserved. With his regional focus, he was overshadowed by novelists like Grigorios Xenopoulos and Yorgos Theotokas, whose realistic fiction about city life was more popular with the expanding urban middle classes. Internationally he was eclipsed by the next generation of prose writers, pre-eminently Nikos Kazantzakis, but also Stratis Myrivilis and Ilias Venezis whose chronicles of the Great War and the legacy of the Smyrna massacre proved attractive to translators. But his decision to write in demotic Greek, as against the archaizing *katharevousa*, or 'purified' Greek, which grafted ancient Greek morphology and vocabulary onto the simpler post-Ottoman language spoken by the people, has helped enhance his standing over the years. The Paris-based linguist Yannis Psicharis in his influential polemic *My Journey* (1888) made the essential point in defence of demotic Greek, that language evolves and purist attempts to turn back the clock are ultimately doomed. But the issue divided the nation along broadly conservative/progressive lines for decades and *katharevousa*, reinforced under the Colonels, was not officially abolished from use in secondary schools and newspapers until 1976 after their overthrow.

Theotokis's taut, dramatic village stories, many of them first published in demotic periodicals between 1900 and 1910, are contributions to the then flourishing tradition of *ithographia* – fiction describing folk customs and morality through which writers like Alexandros Papadiamandis and Andreas Karkavitsas helped define the emerging nation's cultural identity. They are unsentimentally realistic in the manner of Giovanni Verga's Sicilian stories, though carefully plotted in the tradition of Flaubert and Maupassant, and pervaded by a vitalist sense of passion as almost a force of destiny, if usually a destructive force as in Greek tragedy or Thomas Hardy, rather than a redemptive one as in Nietzsche or D.H. Lawrence. Many revolve round violated honour, often avenged with a primitive brutality symptomatic of a culture in which personal or family vendettas were still commonplace.* A number of these stories display Theotokis's talent for satirical humour, but are tempered by a compassionate understanding that shows how close he was to these isolated communities.

The novella-length works too are well structured narratives focusing on humble people, each being given a slightly different inflection by the ideologies and models Theotokis was currently assimilating. *Honour*

---

* An account of the Greek code of honour and how it spilled over into urban violence in both Greece and in America is given by Thomas W. Gallant, *Modern Greece* (2001) – see Further Reading.

and Cash (1912), socialist and proto-feminist in theme, is set in Corfu's quayside suburb of Mandouki, where Greek and Italian are heard spoken in the market side by side. The drama revolves round a factory worker's refusal to bail out her daughter's seducer, a highborn bankrupt reduced to smuggling, by agreeing to his extortionate dowry demands, and the pregnant daughter's resolve to relinquish him and strike out on her own. *The Convict* (1919) is a more psychological tale influenced by Dostoevsky, in which a peasant innocent (nicknamed 'Tourkoyannis' as his harlot mother was first violated by the Turks) is wrongfully accused of murdering his master. Richer as a study of folk mores and Naturalist in its emphasis on the sordid is *The Life and Death of 'Hangman' Thomas* (1920), an often hilarious tragicomedy of lust in old age with grotesque Expressionist touches, which satirizes peasant acquisitiveness and spite and the oppressive power of the collective.

Slaves in their Chains (1922), Theotokis's most ambitious and personal work, is likewise a tragicomic novel but focuses on an aristocratic Corfiot family in decline on the eve of Greece's entry into the First World War. Broadly in the mode of Mann's *Buddenbrooks* (1901) or Galsworthy's *Forsyte Saga* (1922), it also has affinities with *The Leopard* (1958), Lampedusa's sophisticated novel about the Sicilian nobility's waning fortunes after Garibaldi's triumph and the unification of Italy in the 1860s. In contrast to *'Hangman' Thomas* and the short stories, which show a peasant culture frozen in a timeless present, *Slaves* displays an almost Proustian consciousness of time in its portrayal of an aristocracy shackled to past glories and codes of honour, crippled by debt and unfit to survive in a world of escalating change. Ten years or more in gestation – it exists in three successively more complex versions – it is less optimistic than *Honour and Cash*, and pervaded by a very Hegelian sense of tragedy as resulting from the clash of incompatible value systems. In some respects it has all the hallmarks of a realistic Victorian novel – with its Balzacian paterfamilias, its chaste and sinful heroines, and its grand balls and death-bed scenes. But formally – in its compactness and symmetry, its Pre-Raphaelite delight in ornamental detail, its complex use of interior monologues and flashbacks, its musical structure and its deft use of symbolism – it is very much a self-conscious early Modernist work, closer in spirit to Virginia Woolf than to Zola or Arnold Bennett.

Particularly memorable is the ageing, irascible, Lear-like Count Alexandros Ophiomachos Philaretos, a man who has 'never understood the world' he lives in, and is struggling to salvage what is left of a patrimony he has squandered and mismanaged. All the scenes in which he is centre stage – soliloquizing about his woes, bargaining with the Jewish money-lender, blackmailing his elder daughter into a lucrative but loveless marriage, trampling on his ancestral portraits – are intensely dramatic and frequently amusing. And the domestic atmosphere he generates as he rails against his defaulting peasants, his rebellious younger daughter, or the disreputable ancestors of his long-suffering Countess, is very Greek, putting one in mind of Virginia Woolf's essay on Dostoevsky in which she compares his fictive world to a room full of people discussing their private affairs at the top of their voices. But if he lacks the Olympian philosophical detachment of Lampedusa's Prince Fabrizio, likewise reduced to compromising matchmaking, he is not like old Karamazov a buffoon. What makes him in many respects a tragic figure is that he is aware of his own folly, feels humiliated by what he is obliged to do to avert disaster, and yet finds himself – in an almost classical sense – powerless against fate.

Ophiomachos's two eldest offspring – all four still live at home – are the central figures in symmetrically contrasted love triangles, one epitomizing noble, the other lustful passion. Eulalia's dilemma is whether to remain loyal to her penniless consumptive childhood sweetheart, Alkis Sozomenos, or allow herself to be 'sacrificed' – again the classical echoes are unmistakable – to the affluent parvenu doctor, Aristidis Steriotis, to save the family's fortunes. Alkis, who worships her with quasi-Petrarchan fervour, is an idealist and aspiring writer consumed (like his late father, an armchair Garibaldino) by dreams of social revolution and a new golden age. Doctor Steriotis belongs to a more ruthless and pragmatic breed, a point satirized in the subject of his scientific papers – on the genetic affinities between pigs and humans. A firm believer in the social Darwinist doctrine of the survival of the fittest, he is inexorable in pursuing Ophiomachos's daughter, and his quest for status eventually procures him a seat in the Athenian parliament.

The second love triangle centres on Ophiomachos's elder son Giorgis and his adulterous affair with Aimilia, wedded to the wealthy but terminally ailing scholar and aesthete Periklis Valsamis. Giorgis, an elegant *flâneur* like Theotokis in his student days, who has inherited his father's

pride of caste and prejudice against work (his foreign diploma lies forgotten in a drawer), is torn between his patrimonial values and those of his
radical friend Alkis. Aimilia, a kindred spirit to Emma Bovary (translated
by Theotokis) or Zola's Nana (*Nana* appeared in Greek in 1879), is the
obverse of the dutiful Eulalia, whom she despises as a 'wooden saint'; she is
ardent, jealous, demanding, a veritable life force. Her stoical self-sacrificing
husband Periklis, given to philosophic musing and quoting Lucretius on
the soul's fate after death, embodies the Schopenhauerian quietist side of
Theotokis's temperament – and of European decadence.

The deftly caricatured supporting cast present a panorama of contemporary social types – noblemen, bankers, industrialists, poets, loose
wives, charitable widows and aspiring politicians – and some of these
Beerbohmesque portraits and the use of authentic local aristocratic
names like Ophiomachos and Ioustinianis were sufficiently pointed to
have caused offence. Two secondary figures are important structurally in
that they act as go-betweens between the major parties and comment on
events from quite different perspectives. The amusingly wily money-lender
Mimis Hadrinos was based, according to Spyridon Theotokis, on the
alarming figure who visited the Theotokis family in cravat and pointed
shoes when money was needed to pay his prodigal brother's hotel bills in
Venice. Effusive in his protestations of devotion to Ophiomachos while
securing his loans to him by brokering Eulalia's marriage to the doctor,
he epitomizes the modern capitalist spirit of acquisitive self-interest. He
is saved from Faginesque grotesqueness by his moments of fondness for
his master, but the Count's contempt for him is a reminder that Corfiot
society in the Dreyfus era was not immune from anti-Semitism. Giorgis's
enigmatic, ugly anarchist friend Petros Athanatos, who arranges his
assignations with Aimilia, is as cynical as the money-lender but in other
respects his opposite. Part chorus, part fool or (as his name implies)
'immortal' soothsayer delivering home truths, he represents another facet
of Theotokis himself, that of social commentator on his times.* But it is
Alkis who defines the author's artistic aims most clearly when he remarks
on the challenge of creating something fresh and beautiful. In Darwinian
terms, virtually all the characters can be seen as either predators or victims.

---

* His stooping figure and adulation of Aimilia recall the historical figure of the
hunchback Konstantinos Christomanos and his infatuation with the Habsburg
Empress Elizabeth, who employed him to tutor her in Greek.

Slaves in their Chains and the shorter fictional works of Theotokis are of a piece in achieving a high degree of surface realism, but the novel, driven by a Flaubertian urge to make every word count, deploys symbolism much more systematically – not primarily for atmospheric suggestiveness, as so often in, say, Conrad, but as a series of leitmotifs orchestrated on an analogy with music, akin to the Wagnerian technique Mann adopted in his fiction. Old Ophiomachos, for instance, is repeatedly presented adjusting his frock-coat against the chill winds of change and death, while the representatives of Corfiot society are described in much the same formulaic manner each time they reappear. As in Homer, little set descriptive vignettes are repeated verbatim – a streetscape seen from a window suggestive of the world's indifference to individual suffering, or a ruined Venetian fort invoking now a remote ideal, now oppression and enslavement. Variations on a crimson theme occur: Aimilia entertains her lover between scarlet sheets, for instance, and Alkis delivers his radical speech in the red anteroom at the ball. Characters' names are (often ironically) symbolic: the degenerate Alexandros Ophiomachos Philaretos is a 'serpent fighter' and 'lover of virtue', while the implications of Alkis as Sozomenos, the 'one saved', are even more intriguing. As in Mann's *The Magic Mountain* (1924), sickness becomes a metaphor for decadence, and in line with the title of the novel, most of the characters are enslaved by tradition, social convention or their passions and ambitions. Finally, the work opens and closes sonata-like, with near-identically phrased mirror deathbed scenes, each with three women in attendance, recalling the three Marys at the tomb of Christ and the three Norns or Fates.

Given Theotokis's historical circumstances, straddling two centuries and several cultures, divided in his class loyalties, and still refining his novel at his death, the question arises whether the work conveys a philosophically consistent attitude. The Russian literary theorist Mikhail Bakhtin has usefully distinguished between older 'monologic' forms, particularly the epic, which endorse a single ideology, and 'dialogic' or 'polyphonic' forms, pre-eminently the modern novel, which convey multiple points of view.* Is *Slaves in their Chains* ultimately an ideologically driven socialist novel, and if not, how far is it a controlled dialogic performance?

---

* Mikhail Bakhtin, *Problems of Dostoevsky's Poetics*, translated and edited by Caryl Emerson (Manchester University Press, 1984), chapter 3, 'The Idea of Dostoevsky'.

The internal evidence that Theotokis deliberately strove to transcend all narrow didacticism lies in the even-handedness with which he presents the incompatible value systems and mutual incomprehension of the main protagonists. The Ophiomachoses may be representatives of an outmoded feudal order and fatally flawed as individuals, but they are portrayed with some sympathy and their virtues are acknowledged. Conversely, their class antagonists are admired for their enterprise and energy and given their due as to some extent victims of exploitation and contempt, but they are also shown to be crude, ruthless and frequently dishonourable. There are a number of scenes of mutual misunderstanding in which we find our sympathies evenly divided, and poignant use of dramatic irony is made throughout. Incrementally, as the novel unfolds, all the forces at work in society – conservative, progressive, idealist, pragmatic, quietist – and the characters representing them are treated with scepticism and irony. Theotokis's concern to avoid monologic simplification is particularly evident in his handling of Petros Athanatos, whose status as a rational commentator on events is undermined by his slavish infatuation with Aimilia. Like Pierre Bezukhov, the detached observer in *War and Peace* whom he in some respects resembles, he too is all too human. All of which suggests that in this culminating work of his maturity Theotokis succeeded in reconciling the rival claims of marxist-influenced dogma and Nietzschean relativism and producing an early Modernist novel that is genuinely polyphonic. The opening and closing mirror scenes, which involve love, fate and death, the essential coordinates of the human condition, seem to invite us to contemplate the action *sub specie aeternitatis* as a perennially recurrent saga of decline and renewal, bringing things full circle in a way that both the mathematician and the artist in Theotokis must have viewed with satisfaction.

J.M.Q. Davies

Translator's Note

Remarkably for a writer who in Greece is regarded as one of the nation's most distinguished early Modernists, Konstantinos Theotokis has not received the international readership he deserves. This translation of *Slaves in their Chains*, the crowning achievement of his maturity, is the first to appear in English.

In general Theotokis wrote in educated but accessible demotic Greek, avoiding all but a sprinkling of dialect terms and expressions. This was in part a conscious political act on his part, reflecting his socialist leanings and commitment to raising the educational level of ordinary people. *Slaves in their Chains* however is stylistically his most versatile and sophisticated work, and an effort has been made to respect the integrity of his frequently lengthy periods and the varied rhythms of his prose. The range of social types the novel introduces also furnished opportunities to experiment with a variety of oral registers.

The money-lender's idiom, though stylized for comic effect, is earthy and colloquial, and that of the Count no less vigorously idiomatic, especially in his domestic tirades. The parvenu doctor by contrast, whose hawker father's world is evoked by such homely and untranslatable words as *tsarouchia* (rustic pointed shoes) and *kokoretsi* (grilled sheep's entrails), is satirized through his use of the clichés of social Darwinism and the jargon of the medical journals to which he contributes. Alkis's Romantic and Aimilia's Sentimental rhetoric sometimes has a rhapsodic breathlessness which is of the period, but the Petrarchan idiom of anguished hearts natural to a writer whose second language was Italian has been toned down a little. The formulaic descriptions of minor characters repeated each time they reappear, at once a mnemonic device and part of the musical structure of the novel, have been minimally trimmed in this translation. Creating a simulacrum for the banal poetic diction of the court poet's funeral oration was easier than suggesting the flavour of the minister's pompous political discourse using affected *katharevousa*, the archaic 'purified' Greek in official use well into the twentieth century.

Regarding titles, the money-lender's use of *effendi* to address Ophiomachos has been rendered as 'Master' to suggest something of the intimacy of their relationship that 'Count' or 'Milord' would not convey. The use of titles with Christian names, for instance Mrs Photini [Sozomenos] or Dr Aristidis [Steriotis], though still common in Greek, is archaic in English and has not been rendered, except where the money-lender addresses the Count's unmarried daughters deferentially as Miss Eulalia or Miss Louisa. And to avoid confusion, the masculine form of surnames has been used in the case of women: thus Countess Maria Ophiomach*os* rather than Ophiomach*ou* as properly in Greek. Generally the Greek form of Christian names has been retained, even where the English form is common – Petros rather than Peter, Alexandros rather than Alexander. This makes for consistency with the names that have no English form and brings out the ethnic individuality of the original.

As regards transliteration of Greek names, generally beta has been rendered as *v* (Valsamis), ypsilon as *y* (Spyridon), phi as *ph* (Photini) and chi as *ch* (Ophiomachos). Some exceptions have been made, such as with Eulalia and Giorgis, more easily recognizable to English readers than Evlalia and Yoryis, and Hadrinos, much closer to Greek pronunciation than Chadrinos. In the case of non-fictional names like Eleftherios Venizelos, the most widely used spelling has been adopted.

The edition on which this translation is based is *Οι σκλάβοι στά δεσμά τους / I sklavi sta desma tous,* edited by Θανάσης Παπαχρόνης / Thanasis Papachronis (Athens: Grammata, 1991). The main source for the biographical information given in my afterword and notes is Spyridon M. Theotokis's acute fragmentary account of his brother's earlier years, edited by Tassos Korphis and published in Athens in 1983. I should like to extend my special thanks to George Georghallides, Anthony Hirst, Vrasidas Karalis, my publisher, Antony Wood and my wife Poh Pheng for their invaluable criticism and suggestions.

J. M. Q. D.

SLAVES IN
THEIR CHAINS

PART ONE

I

MRS PHOTINI SOZOMENOS was in her kitchen. She was a short elderly woman, already past sixty, simply dressed in black, with a light blue cloth apron round her waist; her pale face was very dry and wrinkled and a tear lingered in her exhausted sunken eyes.

In a corner of the kitchen a rather older woman, her servant, was sitting on a wooden chair in silence, her head in her hand and looking equally depressed.

It was late afternoon. The window was open. Outside, the setting sun had turned the few clouds rosy pink. A light breeze came in, warm and moist, a breath of spring in the heart of winter.

Photini was warming a little soup in a small copper pan. She stirred it with a wooden spoon, let it come to the boil, withdrew it from the glowing coals, broke two eggs into it and as she brought the spoon to her lips to taste, said to herself with a sigh:

'He's in a bad way!'

She turned towards the door and listened, then continued brooding:

'He won't eat it. He can't face anything at all now.'

She shook her head sadly. Her face had the drawn anxious look of a defenceless person numb with fear, who is either unwilling or unable to acknowledge the reality of her misfortune, yet finds the strength to carry on, and the dreaded thought she had been trying to avoid flashed through her mind: this was the end!...

In despair she raised her eyes toward heaven and her lips began to
tremble:

'My darling Alkis! Surely, surely it won't happen! That cannot be
God's will. Why, oh why would He punish an elderly widow like myself?
Couldn't He take me instead? The boy has his whole life before him! Oh!...'

Mechanically she poured the soup into a bowl, stood a moment half
hoping, half fearing she might hear some sound, then holding the sick
man's meal carefully in both hands she finally left the kitchen.

The setting sun came in through the window, flooding the spotless
little room with glorious light. Outside, the hesitant chirping of a bird was
audible, perched on a branch of a lilac in full bloom. From the street came
the rumble of a passing coach and the sound of voices from people sitting
idly in the little café opposite. Everything in the room had assumed a rosy
colour, the walls, the furniture, the sheets, even the pale thin translucent
face of the sick man lying on his back under the sun-warmed bedclothes.

His head was propped up on four pillows. His eyes were hollow
and half-closed. Dark blotches stained his broad fleshless brow. His
cheeks were sunken and his dry lips were scarcely visible beneath his dark
moustache and little beard. His whole expression was remote, and his
fine features bore the marks of suffering, his breathing was shallow and
laboured, like little sighs, and every so often he would turn his head this
way and that to suck in air, his long thin fingers clutching at the sheets.
He seemed exceptionally long lying there in bed and still extremely young,
even though his face looked prematurely aged from the disease.

On a small square table by his pillow were an assortment of bottles,
an unlit candle and two silver teaspoons, and at the foot of the bed was
a large wooden armchair, just then unoccupied.

'Here you are, Alkis,' said his mother, approaching the bed and trying
to smile, 'here's your soup.'

The sick man made no reply. Resting the bowl on the little table for a
moment, she tucked a white napkin under her son's chin, then patiently
tried to spoon some soup into his mouth. But the sick man couldn't
swallow it. His hollow eyes fluttered for an instant, the soup drooled out
of the corner of his mouth and a rasping cough convulsed him. Photini
replaced the bowl on the table, turned her eyes toward heaven a moment,
as if in supplication, then sat down dejectedly in the armchair and looked
across at two other women sitting sadly and in silence.

One was Eulalia. Dressed in a light sprigged frock, her blond head uncovered, she was watching the sick man's every movement, his every laboured breath and cough, with an anxious intensity that betrayed her feelings, leaning over to see whether his lips were moving or his eyes visible under his lids. The other, a tall solemn aristocratic lady from a bygone era, dressed in a frayed old-fashioned black silk gown, her white hair tucked under a little black tulle bonnet, was her mother, Countess Maria Ophiomachos.

For a long time the three women remained silent. Photini watched over the sick man with patient resignation. He was more restive now. He tossed his head about more violently and rumpled the bedclothes with his feet, while his fleshless fingers kept plucking at the hem of the sheet as he sighed and moaned. A crimson beam of light from the setting sun caught a knob on the brass bedstead and was reflected in the mother's haggard face, the timid chirping of the bird could now be heard more distinctly in the room, as it had perched higher in the flowering lilac outside the window, and the street was now bustling with life.

Eulalia sighed as she turned her blond head towards the window and with a sad smile began to listen to the bird singing on its twig, its tiny beak opening and closing as it stared up at the sky. She could hear people talking in the street and snatches of their casual conversation reached her ear with absolute clarity. Finally she turned away and gazed ardently at the sick young man and the two other women. They too seemed to be attending to what was happening in the street.

The sick man whispered something. All three women listened intently. None of them could make out what he was trying to say.

'Still no sign of the doctor,' said Photini anxiously after a while.

'Still no sign,' echoed the other old lady, her face impassive.

Eulalia looked at them but said nothing. Silence reigned for quite some time.

Finally the mother rose again, went to the head of the bed and felt her son's brow, then glancing heavenward with a little sigh, she turned to look for something on the dresser and returned to her seat, pressing her tired lids between thumb and finger.

'Is he feverish?' asked Countess Ophiomachos after a pause. Photini did not say anything but nodded faintly.

'Have they been today already?' she added softly.

'This morning,' the mother murmured.

'And what did they have to say?' she persisted, leaning towards her.

'Alas, anyone can see how grave things are!' replied the mother sadly, shaking her head and motioning toward the invalid. 'And yet I can't help feeling they revive him when they come. Oh, what a night, what an interminable night. The two of us shut up in here... It seems an age!'

She carried on like this, sighing intermittently and raising now one hand, now the other to adjust her neatly combed brown hair, which had lost only a little of its lustre with the passing years.

A groan from Alkis suddenly cut her short. She turned toward the bed, but the ray of sunlight from the brass knob dazzled her and she could not make him out immediately.

She smiled at him however, shielding her eyes with her hand and gazing into his pale face for several moments, then she turned fretfully away towards the window.

Down in the street a cabdriver was cursing his horse in a loud voice and other people were laughing noisily. But her eye was caught by the little bird hopping among the branches of the flowering lilac and looking in curiously through the sick-room window, now and then emitting irregular peeps from its tiny throat.

'Still no sign of him,' she said again after a while.

'Still no sign,' sighed the other woman sadly. A lengthy silence followed.

Then Eulalia suddenly seized the mother's hands in hers, gazed into her eyes, and smiling tearfully said with quiet conviction:

'He'll be cured! Oh, I'm sure he will recover!'

Then she approached the bed.

For a while she stood beside the sick man's pillow, looking sadly down at his gaunt face, which just then looked even more hectic in the last rays of the sun, and shaking her head a little watched his every movement, every twitch of his body, every toss of his head, every tightening of his fingers gripping the sheet, every effort of his sick lungs to snatch a breath. Suddenly her face went pale and her expression became utterly dejected. She looked away, moving her head abruptly and breathing more rapidly, then raising her hand she rubbed her brow distractedly and with a sigh moved slowly over to the window.

As she pressed her forehead against the glass, her eyes filled with tears and despite herself she succumbed to a quiet fit of weeping.

Just then an acquaintance of hers happened to cross the street and unconsciously she registered the fact. Gradually she became more aware of the people sitting in the café opposite, the tall trees lining the street, the little bird reluctant to leave the flowering lilac branch, the golden dust raised by a carriage rumbling past, and the dry pitiless cracking of the coachman's whip. Then she watched the red disc of the sun, now shorn of its dazzling beams, as it sank towards the rippling golden-purple horizon and, raising her eyes to the pale sky, gazed at a passing cloud radiant with the subtlest colours, yet still she couldn't shake off the heart-wrenching sorrow that had made her weep.

By now Photini had risen and joined her. Sighing, she took her hand and squeezed it. Then, herself in tears, she opened her arms to embrace her, her moist eyes full of gratitude. Eulalia fell on the anguished mother's breast and for some time the two women remained locked in one another's arms, both weeping quietly. The old Countess watched them sadly.

They now sat down again next to one another. Photini in her wooden armchair, wiping the tears from her puffy eyes, continued to hold Eulalia's hand in her lap.

'It's been three days,' she murmured sadly, 'since he swallowed anything... no medicine, not a drop to drink... His lips are parched and he hasn't slept at all. Three whole days!'

'It's the disease taking its course!' replied Eulalia, shaking her pretty head sadly as she looked at Alkis.

'Praised be the name of the Lord,' sighed Photini, 'for He ordains!'

'He ordains,' echoed the other old woman, her eyes downcast.

They again fell silent.

By now the sun had set and the sick man's face looked very long and sallow, like that of a corpse. His nose seemed thinner and more prominent, and the moustache and beard which covered his pale lips and hollow cheeks much darker, yet his restlessness had increased and his breathing had become more laboured. He struggled in vain to heave a sigh. The attempt choked in his throat and a violent fit of coughing shook his whole frame, his hands clawing at the white sheets and his legs stirring under the bedclothes, which seemed to lie heavily upon his chest.

The daylight continued to fade and the furniture seemed steadily to recede into the ever darkening corners. The air seemed on the point of congealing and turning into tangible black dust inside the room, where the three frightened women, though unable to admit as much to one another, were anticipating death at any moment. With the sad waning of the day came the extinction of their consoling hopes, and the mother felt a heavy weight upon her heart which grew more oppressive by the moment.

'It's dark already,' she remarked, 'and still no sign of the doctor.'

'Still no sign,' replied the old Countess patiently.

'But he'll soon be here,' declared Eulalia in an anxious voice. 'We won't leave unless he comes!'

'Of course we won't,' affirmed her mother calmly, giving her a gentle reassuring smile.

A profound silence again descended.

The noise in the street had largely subsided. Only the occasional shout could still be heard, as the melancholy twilight descended over all creation. All three women felt depressed and restless in the gathering gloom of the sick-room, which seemed to swallow them up as they gazed in mute anxiety at the sick man, whose head now stood out against the white bedding, looking like some eerie shadow from another world, as only the dark hair and beard could be made out, the face itself swallowed up in darkness.

The elderly servant now came in, shuffling her feet feebly and carrying a lighted lamp. She placed it carefully on the dresser and paused silently a moment by the bed, her arms folded. Then shaking her head she went across and closed the window and with downcast eyes left the sick-room. Outside, they heard her heave a sigh.

Finally, at the very last moment, Doctor Steriotis himself entered the room. All eyes turned to him expectantly. He was a man of about forty, with an already established reputation about town for his scientific learning and ability to work wonders as a doctor. He was still blond, but his little goatee beard was just beginning to turn grey. Of medium height, with restless pale blue eyes, he was wearing a new, elegantly cut black suit.

He paused for a moment at the door and his normally carefree cheerful face darkened suddenly. But he recovered at once and with a smile and an odd swing of his narrow hips came into the room and greeted the three ladies cordially.

'Save him!' whispered the mother at once, clasping her hands.

'Save him!' Eulalia also begged him with tearful downcast eyes.

The doctor gave the young woman a curious glance, biting his pale lip, then likewise looking down murmured to her earnestly:

'If the medicine isn't working, how am I supposed to help!'

Then he shook hands with the two older ladies.

A moment later, looking at Eulalia with a nervous smile, he asked:

'By the way, what are you doing here?'

Eulalia said nothing and did not return his smile. Then he approached the bed.

Standing gravely beside the sick man for a few moments, he held one of the bottles on the little table up to the light, pursed his lips, then drawing his gold watch from his pocket proceeded to check the patient's pulse.

Photini watched him with mounting anxiety. No one spoke. Finally the doctor relinquished the sick man's wrist and, taking a small nickel box out of his other pocket, said with a frown:

'I'll give him an injection.'

'I can't bear to watch!' cried the mother, covering her eyes with her hands. Then suddenly she hurried to the door.

The other elderly lady followed, leaving Eulalia and the doctor with the patient.

It was dark in the little parlour to which the two old ladies retreated and sat down. But soon the ancient servant brought in a little lamp for them there as well. Only then did Photini start weeping softly.

'It's all just the same as it was then!' she exclaimed after a while.

'Just the same!' sighed her companion.

'Ah, it's hard to believe,' the mother continued, 'that it's been twenty-five years already, because the grief has not gone away. It could all be happening now... It was just the same then as now. We went through all this with our first child, before Alkis was born. He was barely six years old.'

'Just the same!' sighed her companion.

Photini felt an irresistible urge to talk. Her present anguish was stirring old sorrows and preoccupations, long dormant in her soul and now painfully reviving.

'His father, God rest his soul,' she went on, 'and my sainted mother-in-law were still alive then. Ah, they already know his fate in the place where they are now! His father used to hold him in his arms for hours at a time. It was a strain because the child was heavy, but he was impatient with being confined to bed. Sleeplessness and pain had made them both ill. But the child wanted to enjoy the daylight a bit longer by the window, and would watch for people in the street he recognized and wave to them, then look up at the sky and wave to it as well. He would gaze and gaze at the light and at the world he loved so much. Eventually his father couldn't hold him up to the window any longer, and kissed him on his feverish cheek and said: "My boy, you're too heavy for me!... Back to bed now, all my bones are aching." They were aching from the effort and all the sleepless nights. It had been a long illness, long and hopeless. Then he kissed him and asked him smiling whom he loved best, his mother or his father, and the child smiled back, having been asked this question every time they played together, and promptly replied: "Both equally!" Those were his last words and his last smile, because after that he lost his power of speech and shortly passed away. And now it's all happening just the same again!'

And with this she burst into tears, overwhelmed with grief.

'Just the same,' sighed her companion quietly, her face impassive.

'His devastated father,' Photini continued, 'came out of the room where he had died looking pale and dazed, and glared at the heavens with anger and resentment. Before our child fell ill, he had claimed he was an atheist and non-believer. Later I would often see him weeping and in prayer. But on that day he was outraged by God's power and cursed Him for inflicting such a heavy blow. Just then his old mother, grief-stricken herself, happened to appear. With a tear of sympathy she said to him: "Alas, my son, don't turn against God in this hour of trial! Bow your head with patience!" The poor man flung himself down on the settee beside the little corpse and wept, burying his face in his hands, and I too wept distractedly beside them, but then his mind became deranged from grief, exhaustion and lack of sleep. You were there too, remember, and now it's all happening just the same again.'

'Just the same,' murmured the other woman, closing her eyes and nodding.

Then Eulalia appeared at the little parlour door, and anxiously observing the two ladies who had suddenly found themselves weeping in one another's arms, announced in a voice thick with emotion:

'The doctor wants to see you.'

The two old ladies followed her to the sick-room in a daze.

Alkis was now lying on the bed without any pillows. The doctor was gravely taking his pulse. For a moment the mother thought with horror that the end had come and was on the point of rushing across to kiss her dead child, and start weeping and beating her breast at the calamity. But with a look the doctor restrained her and said quietly: 'He's alive!' Then correcting himself at once, he added more cautiously: 'He's still alive! But will his poor weak heart hold out?' And he smiled sadly.

Fine beads of sweat started from the sick man's brow as he struggled to draw irregular short breaths. Everyone looked on with beating heart. Suddenly his throat moved convulsively, he opened his eyes wide and started coughing, a strained dry gut-wrenching cough at first which however gradually loosened and became stronger and more persistent. The sweat on his pale brow slowly increased, drenching his whole face and body, until finally he closed his eyes in exhaustion as if about to expire.

The mother was trembling. The other two ladies looked on in a daze. The doctor kept quiet. Suddenly Alkis woke up again and looked about, his eyes restlessly surveying the entire room. Eventually his gaze fell upon Eulalia, who was looking at him with sorrow and anxiety, and he smiled at her with his pale emaciated lips... Then he closed his eyes again.

Everyone continued to observe him with anxious curiosity. The mother's heart was beating fast. The poor woman was on the point of fainting, unsure whether to rejoice or cry and holding her breath with suspense as she watched the doctor's face, the faintest glimmer of hope sustaining her.

The doctor continued to monitor his patient's pulse.

Meanwhile Alkis smiled as from within a dream, then half-opening his tired eyes and looking at Eulalia a moment, he murmured faintly:

'You dead too?... You too? Have I found you once again?'

Then he turned his head away and closed his eyes. He became drenched in sweat once more and his face turned waxen.

'Oh, live!' Eulalia cried out to him in trepidation, her eyes overflowing with tears, while the two old ladies embraced again, likewise overcome by the emotion of the moment.

They began to pray together softly. The doctor gravely prepared another injection.

'He's clearly delirious...' sighed the mother.

'It's the fever,' said Countess Ophiomachos.

'Where are you going?' the sick man now whispered without opening his eyes. 'When you died, I never said goodbye. How swiftly we've
been reunited!'

'Alkis!' said the mother in anguish.

'Alkis!' said Eulalia, equally distressed.

'We've lost him!' cried the mother in alarm.

'No!' said the other old lady, deeply moved.

'He can hear you,' warned Eulalia reproachfully.

'Water,' whispered the sick man.

The mother spooned some unsteadily into his mouth and the sick
man swallowed it.

'He's turned the corner,' said the doctor, smiling. Then correcting
himself at once he added: 'Perhaps he'll make it, there's a chance.' And
he gave Eulalia a curious glance.

The mother stared at him stupidly with a questioning look. She
hadn't immediately grasped what the doctor was saying, and then could
not believe her ears. She was by now so certain that her hopes were quite
illusory and that only wishful thinking had kept the consoling possibility
of his recovery alive within her. The threat of a calamity, one she had been
grimly expecting all her life, had once again loomed so terribly close! She
looked about not knowing what to do, turned her head heavenward a
moment, then with heaving chest yielded to a prolonged fit of sobbing.

Taking Eulalia's hands in hers, she smiled sweetly through her tears
and kissed her on the forehead, then bending over her son she gazed at
his tormented face a while before kissing him too on his perspiring brow.

Alkis meanwhile murmured deliriously:

'In the world of truth!... No one can see our earth from here...'

'Strange ravings,' remarked the doctor. 'He still hasn't emerged from
the religious paranoia people experience at death's door. Science has
explained this phenomenon too... It's the result of cerebral anaemia.'

He glanced at Eulalia to gauge her reaction.

Alkis looked at her too just then, apparently perplexed, but said
nothing.

She, smiling though her tears and clutching her breast imploringly,
again cried out: 'Oh, live!'

The invalid smiled back at her and closing his eyes sank into a profound sleep.

Shortly afterwards the doctor, satisfied with the situation, said goodbye
to the three ladies. Cheerfully he pressed the mother's hand, offering
a few words of hope and comfort, gave Eulalia a strange look, bowed
slightly to the old Countess and left the room, swinging his hips in the
curious way he had.

Photini picked up the lamp and invited the other two ladies to follow
her into the little parlour.

There her nervous excitement after so many moments of black anxiety
and sorrow prevented her from relaxing and she remained silent, as if her
soul needed time to adjust to this great and unexpected joy. She wished
to open her heart to these two women, who had sustained her through
her suffering, without keeping any of the circumstances of her long life
secret, even as far back as the birth of her sick son. And she kept revolving words and phrases in her mind that would do justice to the bygone
scenes she was now so vividly recalling. Indeed she was able to remember
everything she had ever seen, heard or done with absolute clarity... as if
she were reliving each day of her entire life.

Restlessly turning here and there and picking up some object from
the table, she recalled all the harrowing moments, which though past
had not yet been effaced by the great joy that daunted her; then suddenly
she started talking rapidly, recounting to the others anything that came
into her head, weeping, smiling and sighing by turns, and every so often
glancing anxiously in the direction of the sick-room where her son was
now sound asleep.

2

Ever since childhood Alkis had not been very strong. His complexion
had always been poor. He was excessively thin. He had little stamina
and frequently fell ill, his brain often refused to function and he had
the curious air of a child asleep with open eyes. Only gradually over the
years had he improved. Early on the sickly child had been fired with an
unquenchable thirst for knowledge, which each bout of illness seemed
to enhance, sharpening his critical powers as if he were thereby acquiring
experience of life and self-knowledge much more rapidly.

His father, Ayisilaos Sozomenos, encouraged his son's zeal for study and did not pay the least attention to his physical weakness, being privately convinced that his child would one day become a man after his own enlightened heart.

Photini would always tremble when her husband addressed her sternly on the matter of their son's upbringing. And yet Ayisilaos Sozomenos was such a good man! A modest lofty soul with amiable manners, he was far abler than he seemed. He had led a humble orderly life in a municipal office, but as a young man he had studied in Italy and was immensely learned. All his life he had been addicted to books written in impenetrable language, which Photini had often dipped into without understanding a word, and even now she wondered how anyone should want to write such useless works or anyone else want to read them. All she knew was that they were on something called 'philosophy' and that their obscure pages contained an attack upon religion, attempting to prove it useless and harmful to both man and science.

Nowadays Alkis too would often browse in these books, which he could understand, of course. But to her son all this philosophy was just so much hot air. Photini was quite certain it had never influenced his faith, even though like his father he never went to church. Alkis would not be her son if he didn't hold firm to his orthodox beliefs, even though he had spent years abroad. That was why God had come to his aid in his hour of need. In that respect at least, Alkis had not listened to his father, who had wanted to win him over and have him follow in his footsteps.

This was how his mother saw things. Yet she fondly remembered how, for all his peculiar ideas, for all his alarming pronouncements at home where he knew he could not be overheard, for all his secret enthusiasm for revolutionaries, Jacobins, Carabinieri and God only knew what other heretics, Ayisilaos Sozomenos had been a saintly man. Honest at work, quiet at home and devoted to his wife and child – to their first-born initially and then to Alkis – he kept his peculiar ideas to himself, no one in society ever heard a word against him and until the day he died he avoided becoming actively involved in politics. It was only to the adult Alkis that he confided his fondest hopes, his secret yearnings, his conviction that an age of brotherhood, goodwill and happiness would one day come about. A natural modesty, innocence and shyness, and a fear of compromising his family, made him restrain himself and not speak his mind. Indeed, he still felt a stranger in the land that had accepted his family and provided him with a comfortable living, and so he didn't feel he had the right to proclaim his opinions, even though he himself had been born here and loved the place, and his mother was a local woman with a small country holding on the island.

Old Epaminondas Sozomenos, however, Photini's father-in-law, was a genuine foreigner. He too had been dead many years now, and had not been alive even at the time Photini first moved into her husband's home. She had known only her mother-in-law, a saintly God-fearing woman whom she still remembered fondly. As everyone knew, Epaminondas Sozomenos was originally from Cyprus. Blind fate had brought him to these shores on his way home from one of his trips to Italy. While there, he had received news that calamity had struck: the Turks had seized all his assets on his native island, effectively condemning him to permanent exile if he were to escape being put to death. Hitherto a prosperous merchant, he now suddenly found himself reduced to poverty. But he had also studied Greek in considerable depth, a proficiency few possessed in his new homeland but much in demand, as libertarian winds of change had been blowing and local government reforms had recently declared Greek the official language of the island.

So that was how Epaminondas Sozomenos had found himself stranded in this peaceful corner of the globe. He had married not once but twice, producing only one child, Photini's husband Ayisilaos, and thanks to his double set of in-laws and his expertise in Greek, after a period of tutoring lawyers, judges and members of parliament, he had eventually been appointed director of the government printing office. In those days salaries were good and the cost of living cheap. So Epaminondas could afford to send his son to Italy to study law and all those other obscure subjects known as philosophy that his daughter-in-law found so alarming.

There Ayisilaos had got to know the young men who, he claimed, had been planning a general insurrection and the unification of the whole of Italy. To Photini's way of thinking however, all such movements affecting law and order were reprehensible, maliciously courting the destruction of the world, and it was a mystery to her how so peaceable, honest and saintly a man as her husband could have been close friends with those renegade ruffians and remember them with boundless enthusiasm to the end of his days. Photini preferred not to think about it. All she cared to remember was that this was how her son Alkis had come to learn Italian so quickly and early become immersed in the culture of that nation.

He had still been a sickly youth when Ayisilaos first introduced him to the longer poems of Dante, which he himself knew by heart. How his voice would resonate as he recited them! How his eye would flash! And how his son with his sleepy yet responsive gaze would hang on his father's lips, as if dazzled by the infinite beauty being unveiled before him! Photini could still remember it all. She could even remember snatches of the poems herself, since, being young at the time, she had assimilated them too, and because they resembled the church's sacred texts she had believed them. She believed in all the terrifying punishments of the infernal world and the indescribable happiness of the innocent souls in their celestial paradise. She was also fond of music and in the days before her widowhood she would play old-fashioned songs on their ancient piano, which Alkis having no ear would whistle out of tune, or having no voice sing in an excruciating monotone.

Ayisilaos Sozomenos had also been a government employee. Photini still received a modest widow's pension. As a young man, as soon as he returned from Italy with his fine diploma he had secured a position, putting aside the unsettling ideas that doubtless would have harmed him, since a prudent society and the even more prudent members of the government would have been indignant had they got wind of his beliefs, just as Photini herself was frightened by them, even though she was devoted to her husband and the father of her children. And so Ayisilaos had kept his ideas to himself, or at most aired them now and then within the family when there were no strangers within earshot. And so society regarded him as just like anybody else. He enjoyed the reputation of being an industrious and honest citizen, and Photini's father hadn't had a moment's hesitation in letting her marry him, despite never having met the young man personally before. And she had led a contented pious life beside him.

Often Photini would think back with pleasure on her married life, her son's childhood and the firstborn infant of her youth, who had smilingly fallen asleep in the arms of death one day, leaving their home so silent, sad and desolate, even though nothing in it had actually changed. After that her life had assumed a different rhythm, until joy had reawakened in her heart, displacing her mute grief, when she had given birth to Alkis.

But after that her maternal soul was always apprehensive... She would pray anxiously as she watched over the sleeping infant, her whole being suffused with tenderness and a burning desire to protect both of them from the threat of some terrifying new calamity. She became totally absorbed in ministering to the tiny creature, who in her eyes was worth more than all the world, and later her son's poor health and frequent bouts of illness had added to her incessant worries. Fondly she remembered how she had suckled him herself and how later she would put him to sleep beside her, softly singing old songs to him or regaling him with fairy tales, and recalled the child's delight in stories about princelings clad in gold, kindly dowagers and the whole exotic crew of fairyland that perform superhuman feats.

At the same time, in her anxiety over his recurrent illnesses she had not wanted him to learn to read and write too early, but as soon as he turned six her husband, whom the experiences of two successive generations had taught the value of an education, decided otherwise, and refusing to yield to any of her counter-arguments declared that he would rather have no son at all than fail to attend to his upbringing in the manner he saw fit.

At home, for all his mild manners, her husband Ayisilaos's wishes always prevailed. His decision permitted no delay and his son's sickliness did not make him change his mind. From the outset he himself became his teacher, patiently and diligently striving to overcome the child's natural indolence and make his lessons more accessible. Every so often some illness would put a halt to his endeavours, but Ayisilaos did not despair. He tried assiduously to make up for lost time, and to his delight observed that after every illness his son would return to life imbued with fresh gifts and zeal for learning, as if suffering were sharpening his little brain and his childish soul were suddenly expanding.

Photini was still talking when the town clock struck nine. Just then Petros Athanatos entered the dark little parlour. He was an ugly, swarthy young man, but with fine lively eyes. His clothes were shabby and he stooped as he walked, his head bowed and clutching his soft hat in both hands. As he entered the room he noticed the two visiting women, recognized them at once and lowered his gaze bashfully. Then he greeted them awkwardly and turning to Photini enquired anxiously: 'How is he?'

'He's saved!' the mother replied happily, giving him an appreciative look. 'He's sleeping now.' Petros stood there silently a moment, his large unkempt head bowed even further, an ironic smile on his lips, as if he

were regretting his own weakness, then by way of justifying his presence
he continued:

'Mr and Mrs Valsamis sent me over. Or perhaps I should say – Mrs and
Mr Valsamis,' he corrected himself with a sigh, stressing their respective
titles. 'I'd better run along and tell them right away. Mrs Valsamis doesn't
like to be kept waiting, you know.' And he laughed his disagreeable laugh.

Photini urged him to sit down beside her, but he shook his head and
before the three women could say another word hurried out of the room,
his steps clattering noisily down the stairs.

The women again lapsed into silence for some time. Photini got up
and opened the door into the sick-room a crack, then returning to the
parlour smiled and said:

'He's still asleep. He's sleeping like a lamb.'

Countess Ophiomachos smiled too and after a pause remarked:

'Poor Petros, he's so well educated and so poor and he doesn't have
a job!'

'Mrs Valsamis has taken pity on him,' said Photini, lowering her eyes,
'they feel a certain kinship as he too comes from a good family.'

'*Mrs* Valsamis, *Mrs* Valsamis!' said the Countess, biting her lip a little.
She looked at her daughter who had been sitting apart in silence all this
time, her eyes glazed and apparently absorbed in some private dream of
her own.

They again fell silent for a few minutes.

Soon however Photini began reminiscing fretfully again. But now her
words were more obscure, as if she herself no longer quite knew what she
was saying, beyond the fact that her Alkis had eventually grown up and
his soul had then undergone a change.

Anxiously his mother would watch him immersed for hours in his
studies, or talking earnestly with her husband about things she didn't
understand, and sometimes she would find him alone and pensive in
the silence of his study or wandering the streets with half-open mouth
and vacant stare, completely absorbed in his own thoughts, as if forever
chasing some elusive dream. She also noticed how about this time he was
becoming more compassionate. He was deeply moved by human pain and
misery everywhere he came across it, and became ever more conscious of
her maternal solicitude towards him. Frequently she noticed him gazing
at her fondly, forgetting himself in silent veneration. He had prematurely

left off childish games, and some natural shyness or involuntary aversion
kept him aloof from any rowdy amusement. Thus Alkis grew up as it
were enclosed within himself, isolated from the society around him. The
Ophiomachos residence was the only one that he frequented, and the
Ophiomachos children would often come and seek him out. They had
all gone to the same school, and Photini knew that they had been fond
of him ever since. But the two families had been acquainted for much
longer, from well before their children had been born.

Eventually their school days had come to an end, Giorgis Ophiomachos,
one of the Countess's two sons, had left for France and Alkis had spent
some time studying in Germany. Before leaving, Alkis had gone to say
goodbye to the Ophiomachos family in their old house, and with a touch
of romantic grandiloquence had promised never to forget them, gazing
tearfully at Eulalia who, moved herself, had squeezed his hand. And the
memory of the sweet girl, whom once abroad he would imagine as already
a grown woman, had always remained fresh and vivid in his mind, so
much so that when years later he returned home, they resumed their old
acquaintanceship as if they had scarcely been separated even for a day.
Though now of course Eulalia no longer came to play. Time had wrought
its changes, and Alkis by then had become a man.

Then Ayisilaos Sozomenos, defeated by life's battle, had descended
into the tomb, and that first sorrow had proved a terrible ordeal for
Alkis, who realized at once that from then on he would have to struggle
to survive. For Ayisilaos had died a poor man, leaving his son nothing
but his unsullied name.

Now Alkis lived alone with his mother. For the time being they lived
off her small pension and spent their meagre savings. Life was difficult.
But Alkis was a believer in an ideal world, in a century of happiness for
the human race, which would dawn and nothing whatever would be
able to stop. His studies, never neglected despite his physical frailty, now
started to bear fruit. A number of ideas had fired his soul. But then he
had again lacked the physical strength to pursue them, as if the flesh were
unwilling to soar and provide wings for his imaginative flights. This was
when Alkis had fallen gravely ill.

It was already getting late. Alkis was still sleeping peacefully between
his white sheets, and old Count Alexandros Ophiomachos too had now
come past Photini's house to escort his wife and daughter Eulalia home.

He was a rosy-cheeked old man, small and thin, with a full white beard and the thick red lips of all the Ophiomachos clan, and he stooped a little in his threadbare old frock-coat which reached below his knees. He greeted Photini with a smile, and evidently diffident about enquiring further, stood silently to hear what the ladies might have to say.

'Alkis... it's Alkis!' his wife said tremulously, a tear in her eye.

He looked at her in sudden alarm, his heart contracting, and not knowing what to say stared blankly at Photini, who was calmly responding to his greeting. Suddenly he felt himself getting angry with his wife again, and staring at his feet said to her harshly and abruptly:

'You're always expecting the worst, even at home! Always, always!' And after a pause he added spitefully: 'You!'

'He's saved!' she told him, smiling happily through her tears, 'He's saved!'

She tried to take her husband by the hand. But he stepped back a pace, glaring at her angrily before looking down again, then as if determined to get the matter off his chest he repeated, adjusting his old frock-coat as if feeling the cold:

'Always the same, always! It's a knack you have. You always begin by frightening a man to death with your cries and tears and carry on, as if good news had to go through hell first! What a woman!'

Eulalia smiled happily. Her mind was wholly absorbed in the present, she wasn't worrying either about what might yet happen or about herself. The Countess shook her head, looking fondly at the Count, while Photini pretended not to notice their little tiff. Finally the Countess sighed and, indicating Alkis's mother, said to her husband:

'God has had pity on her, the poor kind-hearted widow.'

'God! God!' whispered the irritable old man with a sarcastic smile, glancing on high in mock terror: 'God! – What a woman!'

Then the three Ophiomachoses took their leave of Photini and left the room.

That night Photini slept heavily in her armchair next to her son's pillow. When she woke at dawn, she realized that Alkis's eyes were open and gazing at her tenderly. Joyfully she bade him good morning, then trembling and with tears in her eyes she took his hand and kissed it.

Alkis, evidently still confused after his protracted sleep and unquiet dreams, immediately asked:

'Who was she?'

'Eulalia, my son,' she replied smiling. 'Didn't you recognize her?'

'Yes,' Alkis nodded with a sigh and closed his eyes again.

3

It was afternoon. Count Alexandros Ophiomachos Philaretos, small, stooped and elderly, but with a vigorous white beard and the thick rosy lips of all his clan, was pacing restlessly up and down his study in the ancient overcoat he had worn about the house in winter for years. That day was not particularly cold however.

His study was a large room in a gloomy old house down one of the narrower streets of town. In spite of its four large windows, all on the same wall, it was dark, as if grey dusty air were trapped there, for more recent houses had encroached on all sides of the ancestral Ophiomachos residence, which in former times had towered in proud isolation above humble single-storey dwellings.

Faded curtains and discoloured blinds darkened the room further, the air was dank and heavy, and the worn floors exuded a musty smell of mould and dust. The wall-paper too was faded, shabby and peeling, and the antiquated furniture had gone unpolished and neglected for many a long year, also attesting to this noble family's decline.

Against the wall opposite the windows were two large walnut cabinets full of mouldy books. And roughly in the middle of the room, in front of a low squarish armchair, was a white wooden table protected with thick blue paper and piled high with dusty documents folded lengthwise, many tied with string. In the midst of them were a small portable writing-desk, its once green-beige top now stained with ink, a round zinc inkpot and several pens. Another cupboard and a table against the end walls and one or two queer antique chairs completed the decor of the room where old Ophiomachos now spent his days.

Ranged about the walls were the family portraits, darkened by age and damp, each in its black or tarnished gilt frame: the Ophiomachos ancestors, once noblemen with great power in the land, now forgotten and slumbering peacefully beneath the earth. Some were clean-shaven with white powdered wigs, others wore gold-braided uniforms, an early one was clad in armour. A few female portraits were among them, beautiful proud women with serene smiles on their thick lips, and there was also a curious picture of a stylized tree with unnaturally curling branches, sparse foliage and small dark blue medallions with names inscribed in white. This was the Ophiomachos family tree.

Quiet prevailed inside the house. Only the sound of a carpenter could be heard smoothing his planks with a plane in the street.

That afternoon the old man was again pacing restlessly up and down, chain-smoking the thick cigarettes he rolled himself and chewed down to the middle, and every so often he would glance at his gold fob watch hanging from a nail above his chair, then at the ledger lying open among his dusty papers, and sadly shake his head. He was expecting someone.

'He'll come... He's bound to, he always shows up about this time,' he said to himself. 'And where am I to find the money, a colossal sum like that?...' He raised his hand to his brow as if to fend off all the cares besetting him, and for the hundredth time bent over the huge ledger and studied it attentively.

'Fifteen hundred francs are due today,' he sighed. 'Where are they supposed to come from? Where? And if only that were everything! But it's not been three weeks since I renewed the last IOU, and now this one's fallen due, and in a month there'll be another. Where on earth am I to find the money, either today or for next month? I'm ruined! It's a lost cause!' And as he said this to himself he ran his finger down the lines and columns in the open ledger.

'Indeed it is!' he went on, resuming his brisk pacing as if to escape the immediate business that was worrying him most. 'We'll never find the money. Where's it to come from, for God's sake! There won't be a drop of oil this year. The land-owners won't even have enough oil to grease their hair with. What a curse the oil is. Especially when one has no other revenue... Everything depends on oil! But even if the olives were to grow the size of melons I still would not be free of debts! Alas, we Ophiomachoses are destined for disgrace and it's all my fault!'

Flushing suddenly, he looked first at his family tree then at each of the portraits of his forebears – the aristocratic ladies with their ample bosoms and polite superior smiles, the knight in armour who under the Venetians had fought against the Turks in Crete and the Morea, the men in white wigs and gold-braided coats, all looking down at him indifferently from their tarnished black and gilded frames – and before he knew what he was doing he shouted at them angrily: 'You are all to blame!'

Then with a gesture of exasperation he turned his back on all the portraits and after a pause continued to himself: 'I've managed things all right so far! So far? Well, more or less! Though even my wife is now beginning to smell something fishy. It's no good continuing to hide my troubles from her. Nevertheless, I've not yet had to sell off anything. Nothing important, nothing people would get to know about – so nothing to speak of! And yet my houses are all doomed, even this one here – I might as well write them all off. Every one is mortgaged to the hilt. And what about our olive trees out in the village? No, they at least are unencumbered, just as my father left them to me. But our country residence has gone to rack and ruin, it's now beyond repair! And I go on giving myself airs, pretending I let it decay deliberately because I don't like living in the country, and acting benevolently towards the peasants by letting them pay their way out of their obligations, or purchase the olive trees close to their homes. Now even they have got wind of my predicament. And all this just to cover everyday expenses. Not so long ago I sold off some waste land – a whole meadow. I did it as a partial trade-off really. I bent over backwards to do the fellow a favour, to be benevolent, God help me! He was my best man, a member of the family from long ago who has worked for me for years, which is the only reason why – may he have bad harvests! – I have a soft spot for him! The understanding was that I'd receive the balance in cash. Don't ask me why they trust in my benevolence, all these wily peasants and my supremely wily best man. Who they trust is not my business! Anyway, after that I was at least able to sort out some of my affairs, to plug the leak. But now? You may well ask! And what am I to tell my wife, the good Signora Maria? God, what bad luck she's had! People will be saying her husband is a total reprobate! But it's easy to sing when you're not trying to keep up with the dance! And my daughters? Poor wretches! And my sons? Who knows how they'll turn out one day! But they too... they too...'

He paced up and down the room for some time, fretfully mulling over the same problems, then raising his hand as if to mop his brow he continued: 'I wrote to all of them, I did everything I could. I left no stone unturned. But not one of them responded, not one! Not a peep! To expect a peasant to pay up – an absurd idea! He'd have to be stupid. Greek law is on his side nowadays. It's his government and he can do just what he likes! Certainly, just what he likes! Once upon a time the law obliged him to pay up and with a bad grace he did so. Now the devil's taken up his cause! Tithes, corvée contributions, outstanding debts, one can kiss them all goodbye! Prison terms have been reduced, the cost of going to law is frightening, and in the end the verdict isn't worth the paper it's written on. How is the landlord supposed to chase after the peasant? Under this monarchy they'll gradually get rid of all our liberties. That's to be expected – thanks to universal suffrage. Nothing one can do about it.'

With these and similar reflections he continued unconsciously to nurse his grievances, and this made him nostalgic for the British protectorate which as a young man he had known in all its glory. 'In those days, we shabby-genteel noblemen still counted, even if we were up to our ears in debt! A letter from my father would set a whole village trembling in those days. Things were a thousand times better! And yet some demon possessed us to expel the British – those refined and courteous people, a government like that! Serves us right now, under Greece. Serves us damn well right! And yet we were already in decline by then, with the cost of living soaring and the liberals curtailing all our privileges... A curse upon them!'

In the old days, he remembered, his father, who could set a whole village trembling with a single letter, lived in unimaginable splendour yet spent very little, and could even fritter money on politics without impoverishing himself. So that when he died at a ripe old age he had left his son a sizeable estate, which might have flourished had he looked after it but for the fact that it was encumbered with a substantial debt the old man had not had time to clear – and that had proved the initial cause of their financial problems.

Even so, Alexandros Ophiomachos had not been completely stupid. He had astutely contrived to marry the heiress of an ancient (and for the times affluent) family – an innocent young girl in those days, neither wilful nor demanding – and had paid off his father's debt out of her dowry. With prudent husbandry he could then of course have put his house in order, but even as a married man Alexandros Ophiomachos continued to live in the manner his forebears had been accustomed to. He gambled and frequently lost. He always kept two or three horses in his stable and periodically would trade them in – invariably at a loss – as they fell sick or he got bored and hankered after a better one, and all the while his family kept growing and his expenses mounting. Then one day he found himself with no money. He was shaken, became fretful and impatient, then alarmed and for the first time in his life was obliged to borrow. He did so secretly, avoiding banks so that his name would not be talked about, calling instead on a money-lender of his acquaintance, who eagerly provided all he asked for, indeed offered him more, at once scenting the profits that would slowly line his pockets. The money-lender was not risking anything, indeed he knew he would be repaid two or three times over, provided he managed to take advantage of the situation, because Ophiomachos's property was thriving and basically sound.

This had been the beginning of Ophiomachos's downfall. Once he got into debt, he quickly started slithering towards the abyss. He paid off the first bill of exchange punctually when it fell due, but to get out of another little difficulty – he had been obliged to trade in an expensive horse bought for his gig, having disregarded advice that it was unsuitable, obsessed as he was with training spirited animals – he again borrowed a much larger sum which the money-lender produced with equal readiness, but this time he had not managed to pay it back by the due date. The money-lender, now scenting his quarry drawing closer, eagerly agreed to renew the bill, indeed, guessing Ophiomachos's financial predicament, offered him more money still, pointing out that come the harvest he would be able to pay him back at leisure out of his gambling winnings. His entire debt would then be trivial, a mere bagatelle. Meanwhile the rest of his income was used up meeting everyday expenses. And then the seasons had gone all haywire. The earth seemed to be under a curse. For a long while the agrarian properties yielded nothing, while Ophiomachos's debts were growing exponentially. They doubled, tripled, increased fivefold, and during the unproductive years they went on multiplying. All this time the Count was growing older, without being willing to sacrifice any of his self-indulgent habits, any of his vices, even though his fortune was declining year by year, concerned as he was only to avoid selling off his land and to make sure no one heard about his ruin.

Meanwhile his children had grown up. Two young men and two young ladies, none of them earning and all requiring money. Indeed the eldest, Giorgis, whom he had sent to Paris, had inexcusably squandered a small fortune. And now he was unemployed, as was his second son, Spyros, an indolent and unambitious youth, who had barely made it through secondary school and showed no inclination either to study science or to see the world. Both his daughters were now of marriageable age, they too needed pocket money, and in a year or two when someone sought their hand they would be a cause for further worry, since he would not be able to provide them with a dowry.

All these concerns made him irritable and disturbed his peace of mind. Pondering, he paced up and down his gloomy study which exuded the odour of decay. He glanced at the time again, shivered and adjusted his ancient overcoat as if trying to keep warm, and just then heard a faint ring at the front doorbell. Guessing who it was, he resolved to answer it himself. He went out of the study, descended the short flight of damp wooden stairs, hesitated a moment, looked up nervously to see whether he was being observed from the floor above, adjusted his overcoat again and at last opened the door.

'Come in,' he said to his visitor in a serious dignified voice, closing the door quietly behind him.

'My compliments, Master,' replied the stranger, bowing humbly.

He was a pale lanky man of about fifty who looked old already, with his bald head, shaggy eyebrows, vacant eyes and large hook-nose above a trim, badly dyed reddish-black moustache. His hands were huge and his legs knock-kneed and bony, and he was dressed in a black jacket and necktie and dirty threadbare dark grey trousers.

'Let's go upstairs,' said Ophiomachos, lowering his eyes and nervously adjusting his old overcoat.

Just then the voice of the old Countess rang out from the top floor: 'I say, Where-Are-You?' – his wife always addressed him in this manner, because ever since she was a girl she had been too much in awe of him to call him by name – 'Who is it?'

'Nobody,' he shouted from below, flushing red with anger.

'How do you mean, nobody?'

'Nobody for you!' Then grinding his rotten teeth he shouted: 'Mimis Hadrinos has come to see me, he wants to talk to me, not to you. Not to any of the rest of you.'

The two of them went up to the study and, having locked the door and seated his visitor next to him at the table, the old man asked him unceremoniously:

'What is it you want?'

The other man gave him a wry look out of the corner of his eye and smiled ironically under his badly dyed moustache. 'Have you forgotten, Master?' he said. 'One of your bills falls due tomorrow and I've come to collect the money. A trivial amount, a trifle! A mere bagatelle! I came to collect it today because I didn't want word to get around!'

So saying, he reached into his inside jacket pocket, as if ready to produce something. But the Count did not reply immediately. He looked thoughtful for a moment, his fine rosy complexion turned a shade paler, and finally he replied in a low embarrassed voice:

'To tell the truth, I don't have it just at present!'

Hadrinos of course was expecting this response. It was not the first time their conversations had started off like this. He withdrew his hand from his pocket, looked questioningly at the old man, whose gaze was now riveted to the floor, and pretending to be displeased said sternly:

'Master, as you know I am here to serve you, I'm devoted to your family, I'm a kind-hearted person, exceedingly kind-hearted, and every day my kindness costs me dearly. Yes, that's the truth, so help me God. But Master, your creditors are asking for their money!'

'I just told you I don't have it,' the worried old man repeated apologetically. 'Well then, go ahead and ruin me!'

'What are you saying, Master!'

'It's fifteen hundred this time, where am I to find that kind of money? I've written twenty letters to my tenants in the last few days, don't think I've not been busy. But you know these peasants... Ah, nowadays peasants take but give nothing in return. So I'm going through a rough patch, and the harvest too is late.'

'They won't renew the loan, Master.'

'I haven't got the money, I tell you! Don't you believe me?'

'Me?' protested the money-lender smiling humbly. 'Me, Master? But what are we to do? It grieves my heart to hear all this, and that's the truth, so help me God!'

He crossed himself with a gloomy expression, as if he really were distressed, and continued: 'Because as I said, Master, I've an exceedingly kind heart, a heart of gold. And it grieves me even more to see you going through such anxious times. But it's not my fault. However, out of affection for you, Master, I'll go and beg them to let us defer repayment for six months, though I doubt very much they will oblige me. That way, Master, you'd only have to pay the interest.'

'I can't manage even that just now,' the old man admitted gloomily. 'I don't have a thing to give you.'

'Not even the interest? Not even that? In which case there's nothing to be done. Oh, my God!'

'Not a bean!' repeated Ophiomachos with a despairing sigh. He thought with horror of the precipitous path he was careering down, the certain destruction that was looming ever nearer and encircling his ancient family. The money-lender looked at him gravely, and as if feeling genuine sympathy for him and having second thoughts, continued warily:

'Since that's how matters stand, Master, and I have every sympathy, you'll just have to begin selling!'

The old man changed colour. The veins in his forehead bulged and he suddenly felt himself seething with anger, but he managed to control himself. 'Selling?' he exclaimed bitterly. And as the word passed his lips it stung him like a whiplash on his bare flesh. He had of course already realized that things were bound to come to this pass eventually, since, for the present at least, he was not expecting help from anywhere else. But on the lips of the money-lender the word dishonoured him, kindling feelings of affection for the paternal heritage he wished to preserve intact and safeguard against seizure, of attachment to the tumbledown old pile deep in the country, in which his forebears had lived as lords and masters and which only lack of resources had obliged him to let go to wrack and ruin, and finally, of appreciation for the revenue the family had enjoyed for centuries, which it was his duty to pass on to his children just as he had received it from his father. No, he did not want to sell, he couldn't – at least not today, he would postpone making the decision, even though he knew necessity would soon catch up with him. Ah, he could see it all! His mortgaged houses would be forcibly impounded to pay off the interest on them, they were as good as sold already. Next would come his fields and pastures one after the other, the peasants, his serfs, would get their hands on them, his magnificent estate would be split up. Yes, all this would inevitably happen, but not today at least, no, not today.

'I won't sell!' he said decisively.

'So what now?' asked the money-lender with a questioning gesture, a frown on his pale brow.

'Well, if you were willing...' Ophiomachos replied sweetly. 'After all you've earned from doing business with me... well, you could renew this damned bill out of your own pocket! With me you certainly wouldn't have anything to lose. And who knows what will happen tomorrow, what turn events might take, Fortune might suddenly raise one back up to where one started. But instead you create difficulties for me!'

The money-lender suddenly turned deathly pale. He gazed at the Count with his vacant eyes and said: 'I'm completely devastated, Master! And that's the truth, so help me God! My heart is positively melting with kindness. Do you think I wouldn't have offered without your mentioning it? Do you still not know me, Master? It's just that I'm a poor man and don't have anything myself. Do you think humble folk like us have your kind of resources? It's not my fault that I have nothing! And that's natural enough, because to acquire money one needs to be dishonest and unjust, whereas I on the contrary... but we've been over this so many times... Myself, I am the epitome of honesty and justice. The very epitome... and that's the truth!'

On this occasion the old man did not laugh at the money-lender's garrulous disclaimers and anxiously replied:

'I could give you an IOU for the interest.'

'For the interest?... The interest, Master? Yes, but against what security?'

'Security? The same as you've always had. My signature, what else!' And he looked at him with curious pride. 'I can sign for two thousand. I can sign for however much you like, provided we can end this whole sordid business right away!'

He was getting angry.

'Two thousand, Master?'

'Why yes, you scoundrel! How much more do you want? Tell me, tell me at once!'

The money-lender smiled humbly. He took a sheet of paper out of his pocket and gave it to the Count to sign. Ophiomachos sighed, unfolded it feeling sick at heart, took up his pen and scrawled a few figures, then shamefacedly handed the paper back to the money-lender, who looked it over carefully, folded it and put it away complacently.

The final act of the catastrophe had been postponed.

But as was his wont, the good Mimis did not depart immediately. Once business was concluded, the two of them would always continue chatting about other matters. The old Count, who never read the newspapers because he couldn't fully understand their language, liked to pick up the international and local news from those he talked to, and the money-lender, who was always well-informed, made a point each time of reporting something that would pique his curiosity.

Having calmed down, Ophiomachos now asked casually: 'Any interesting news lately, by the way?'

'They say, Master,' the other replied, his vacant eyes widening, 'they say all the crowns of Europe are again banding together to wage war on Russia.'

'The way they did during the Crimean War?' asked the Count indignantly, his father having belonged to the Russian party during the British protectorate and having always sided with the Russians himself because they didn't have a constitution. 'Ah yes, but this time the Russians will wreak havoc on them all. Mark my words. Things are not the way they were!' And after a moment he added apprehensively: 'Ah, yes! The world is going to the dogs! Prices will soon rise. That Crimean War was the mother of all calamities. And what is to become of us?'

'They also say,' the money-lender went on earnestly, 'that pampered government of ours in Athens will call up the reserves. General mobilization again, all because it intends to carry out some border operation! More troubles, more upheavals. That's why anyone with money has to be very careful with it.'

'Why can't they leave us alone, I say,' muttered the old man, flushing angrily. 'What do we owe them, to justify their rounding up our sons whenever they fancy? Why not let the Greeks poke their own eyes out? Their interests are not our interests! The treaties declared us neutral and Greece has no right to recruit soldiers from us over here. Yet our precious MPs never say a word against it, because of course they don't want to face the music back in Athens. And I'll tell you another thing: we should never have gone ahead with the union, never! If only our signatories had agreed conditionally! Then we wouldn't have these troubles every other year. Confound the despot who brought it all about!'

'Confound them all!' sighed the money-lender. 'Hard times, Master! They say the officers, the top brass, they're going to topple the government in Athens. They don't consider it efficient, nor are they happy about ours locally. But then the Greek kingdom is used to such rebellions.'

The old man did not reply. His own worries now prevented him from talking. Normally he would always have remembered some analogous incident from his times, or recounted some past family glory, some martial triumph of his ancestor in armour, who under the Venetians had fought against the Turks in Crete and the Morea, and who even now was looking at him proudly from his tarnished frame. Or else he would have quoted some High Commissioner of his acquaintance, who had maliciously predicted the island's woes, or even taken the opportunity to dig up some long-forgotten scandal that had caused an uproar in his day – but today he remained silent.

'And all the time,' continued the money-lender gravely, as if the matter were preoccupying him, 'money is becoming scarcer. Let's hope the country holds out courtesy of the wealthy foreigners who come here every day and spend their money, build houses and provide work for all those masons, so at least some cash is circulating, otherwise we'd surely have a revolution on our hands. As surely as you see me and I see you, Master. Woe betide us! And yet we live with that fear all the time, the people only have to realize their power to have us dancing on hot coals. Only God has prevented them uniting, and so we've been able to muddle through so far. Now there are even teachers who bring them lessons ready-made from Europe, and go out into the villages to teach the peasants all their newfangled ideas and urge them to unite. But so far God's been on our side, Master, and always intervenes because they are His enemies, they're atheists who war against Him as He does against them. That friend of your son's, Alkis Sozomenos, he's one of them.'

Ophiomachos scowled at him. He was fond of Alkis – a young man after his own heart. He wouldn't hear a word against him. He refused to believe everything they told him about Alkis out of envy, jealousy or spite. He was no fool, that young man, he was well read, had travelled and without a doubt would be successful, provided God granted him his life. How could such a splendid fellow stray from the straight and narrow path laid down by centuries of human history?

'He's such a fine young man!' the money-lender corrected himself at once, realizing that he had made a faux pas. 'Pure gold! The only thing one can find fault with is his health. He's not well, he's very thin and frail, and yet he takes on the burdens of the world... He's not one to keep his head down either, to live quietly at home and get a cushy job the way his father did. He doesn't have much property and will have to work if he wants a decent life. He's wasted a lot of money travelling. As you know yourself, Master, it costs a fortune to send one's children overseas. And he's studied a subject not much in demand back here at home. What's he going to do with his philosophy? All he can do is become a teacher – a lame duck teacher plagued by the world's children and heading for an early grave.'

Ophiomachos gave him another odd look and, as if to put an end to his garrulity, told him curtly: 'Alkis is an exceptionally gifted person.'

'Who's denying it?' the other man exclaimed at once. 'I too admire him, just as I admire your noble offspring, who are like my children as I don't have any of my own. I'm very fond of all of you, Master, and that's the truth, so help me God! I've been devoted to your family from the outset, and I have a heart of gold, and that's the truth! You speak highly of Alkis – was I not the first to do so? Pure gold. And who said he's in dire straits? He's single and living with his elderly mother. Two people can get by with less. All the same, if I were him I'd rather not get married, unless I were lucky enough to secure one of those fat dowries – then I'd change my tune. But such strokes of luck are scarce as hens' teeth.'

'What are you getting at?' Ophiomachos interrupted rudely, now starting to get bored with his long-windedness. 'Why are you telling me all this?'

'Forgive me, Master,' he replied submissively. 'You know I'm very fond of all of you, and that's the truth! You can see into my heart and you know I am your man. That's all I want, to be your man. And if your affairs prosper, I benefit as well. Come what may... isn't that so? And I'm telling you all this because I too, a man of no significance, have heard the rumours and can see they're true and am delighted. Miss Eulalia, eh? So your darling noble daughter, long may she live, is inclined to favour Alkis. She'll accept him, no doubt... I mentioned it only to congratulate you on the match. That is, with your permission, Master! Long may you enjoy both of them!'

Here he lowered his eyes and stared at the floor in embarrassment. Ophiomachos looked at him haughtily, went red in the face, and after a moment's pause said:

'My daughter will not do anything without my express permission!'
Then suddenly changing expression he continued, unable to keep the secret
any longer: 'I don't really know how it's all come about... Some fanciful
idea of my son Giorgis, apparently. He let his mother into the secret, and
his mother half-confessed it all to me... I can't remember exactly what she
said. And as usual I lost my temper with her. No doubt that was unfair
of me. But frankly I don't think anything will come of it. Just airy-fairy
talk! Like all Giorgis's little schemes! Perhaps Alkis imagines Eulalia will
receive a solid dowry. But if that's what he thinks he'll be disappointed!
What can I give her in the pickle I'm in just now? You've no idea how
ashamed I feel. To have to marry off my poor girls without a dowry!
Alas, I've frittered everything away, and without realizing it! Without
intending to, I have impoverished them.' And he rested his head in his
hands dejectedly.

'Hard times, Master,' sighed his companion. And for a few moments
they both remained silent.

After a while the money-lender continued quietly: 'I'm a humble
and illiterate man, Master. So I shouldn't presume to have an opinion on
these matters. But my affection for you as your man prompts me to tell
you something too. Think what you will of me, but you know my heart
is in the right place. The only reason I'm offering you advice, Master, is
that I have another idea regarding Miss Eulalia, one that would be much
to her advantage.'

'Oh hang all this matchmaking!' said the old man in sudden exasperation. 'I'm not planning any marriages this year!'

'Hear me out,' replied the money-lender patiently. 'What if the groom
were wealthy, extremely wealthy? What if he were a fine young man, living
in a palace fit for the king? What if he were also a man after my own heart,
a paragon of honesty and justice? What if he were like... what if he were
the doctor, Aristidis Steriotis, in person?' Having said this, he heaved a
deep sigh, as if he had just got a load off his mind.

'What, him?' said Ophiomachos contemptuously, his hackles rising.
'Him? You mean Demos's son for my daughter?'

'He has untold wealth, Master,' he replied, smiling strangely and closing his dull eyes. 'Wealth that could benefit her immensely! And wealth
these days is everything! Isn't that so, Master? I don't mean to say – it
would never cross my mind – that your daughters are not noble, worthy,

polite and well-brought-up young ladies, indeed a more virtuous and
homely pair it would be impossible to find these days. Where could one
find their like? Ah, nowhere, I can tell you! But today everyone bows
down to wealth. Wealth, Master, covers every fault. And after all, what's
the late Mr Demos got to do with anything? What, I ask you? Is Doctor
Aristidis or isn't he a thoroughly decent fellow – honest, good-hearted
and... and... Even if he had no other means besides his profession, with
a clientele like his he'd still be doing very nicely... What was that? But
of course not, Master, he doesn't know I've broached the subject with
you. It was entirely my idea. Indeed, he told me not to breathe a word to
you about it. But how can I keep something that would benefit you all a
secret? And what a benefit! All he told me was that he'd seen Miss Eulalia
somewhere, been very much impressed and would like to be the man to
make her happy. And it's true, she really is a beautiful young lady! The
poor man complained to me that he's tired of being lonely and has lost
his appetite for living it up away from home. The years slip by, you know,
he's only human – and as respectable as you or me! And now he wants to
settle down and have a couple of children to leave his ample fortune to.
He's tired of running around. But in his time he has enjoyed life to the
full, more even than you, I dare say, Master.'

He chuckled, wagging his ugly head a moment.

'So he's a reprobate, eh?' said Ophiomachos thoughtfully.

'Yes and no. Depends on how you look at it, Master. Now that's all
over and he has matured... Once the matter is settled, Miss Eulalia will
become a queen! And that's the truth, so help me God! He'll be thanking me every minute of the day, Master, and saying: "Good for him!" He
told me his heart was set on Miss Eulalia. The wealthy all have their little
fantasies, and why not, since they can afford them! Of course he'll also
be thinking of the bond he will be forging with the better families – no
mean consideration. He'll be establishing roots here without losing
anything, he'll be acquiring precisely what he lacks at present. In this,
as in all other respects, he seems to be a prudent fellow. He's not some
callow youth, Master, but a mature man with a mind of his own, he must
be forty if he's a day.'

The old man had been listening to him sadly and thoughtfully all
this time. Yet he didn't dare reply. More than once he became enraged
at what the money-lender was suggesting, and his heart would prompt

him to dismiss the shameless fellow, but he restrained himself, sighing and pondering what best to do. Then, growing weary, he would look about and his eye would be caught by his family tree: there inscribed in its little blue medallions were the names of his illustrious kinsmen, who for centuries had been the noblest in the land, the very noblest of the noble, and now here he was, one of their descendants, obliged to submit to every imaginable degradation, to sit and listen patiently while a money-lender propositioned him about his daughters. Then he would look at the darkened portraits on the walls – the knight in armour, the beautiful ample-bosomed ladies smiling disdainfully from their gilt frames, the noblemen with their powdered wigs and gold brocade – and had the impression that all those dead souls felt the insult too and shared his sorrow, that the portraits were actually becoming darker, as if they wished to disappear after hearing the ill-considered and insolent proposals of this rogue whom he, an Ophiomachos, was obliged to listen to because he had fallen into his clutches, because the man could now play with him as he saw fit.

In the end however he merely sighed and scowled at his visitor with the fierce look of a man in revolt against his unjust destiny. And while the money-lender went on talking, the old man brooded bitterly on how times had changed! The son of Demos Steriotis – the man who'd arrived in shabby *tsarouchia* from Epirus and hawked his *kokoretsi* round the streets, who'd opened a small grocery and slowly built it up, who'd lent to the poor at outrageous weekly rates to get rich quick – the son of that same Demos, a miserable upstart doctor, a decadent reprobate, was seeking to become his son-in-law! All the pride of his ancient race was now seething within him. He recalled the doctor's face with hatred: his faded blond goatee just beginning to turn grey, his unruffled dead-pan gaze, his wide mouth and quivering nostrils. All the signs that betrayed the boundless ambition of a man determined to be accepted and to lord it over others. He recalled his ugly foreign accent, the vulgar way he swung his hips, which always put him in mind of Demos in his dirty *foustanella*, and he couldn't help comparing all these defects with the youthful aristocratic beauty and cultivated charm of his Eulalia.

Meanwhile, as if he had guessed his secret thoughts, the money-lender continued in his soft obsequious voice: 'Times have changed, Master! What can one do? Now society has woken up and the nobleman who has no money loses both his position and society's esteem. That's the way things are. Take your humble servant's advice, Master, and don't refuse, it wouldn't be to your advantage!'

The old man still didn't answer immediately. Alkis, he reflected, wasn't anyone important, nor of course would he ever become rich and famous, but at least he wasn't a Steriotis! Alkis wasn't the bridegroom he'd always dreamed of for his daughters either. But the poor girls were unlucky!... Frankly, he couldn't see anyone in town truly worthy of Eulalia's hand. But when all was said and done, Alkis was a good fellow whom he'd known since he was a child, and he had a good figure, courteous manners and a kind and noble heart. He was a different proposition. Of course, they might have been lucky enough to meet better suitors – a foreign aristocrat, let's say, with millions to his name, like the Venetian nobleman who had been found for one of his grandfather's aunts a hundred years before. He himself would never have married locally had it not been for the presence of a wealthy young heiress to a noble family, the lady who today was his old Countess. But now her fortune too had all gone down the drain. And yet people still paid tribute to her kind and honourable nature, and would always do so.

'It would be to the disadvantage of your family,' Hadrinos continued quietly, rubbing his hook-nose. 'Take it from me, your humble servant. The doctor has taken a fancy to Eulalia, he wants to make her happy and naturally he won't wish to see you go to the wall. The doctor is the one who has most of your IOUs in his pocket. Take my advice, don't say no when he asks you for her hand.'

'What?' exclaimed Ophiomachos, suddenly flaring up and flushing red. 'What? So he is trying to twist my arm, is he? Him, him?... So now these foreigners who've grown rich sucking the blood of the poor, they think they can tyrannize us too? So that's it, eh? Well, even if he takes the spoon out of my mouth, I won't bow to his will! Who asked him to interfere in the lives of my poor girls? Who suggested it? You lied to me, you rogue! He sent you round and you won't admit it! And he's trying to force my hand, he, the son of Demos, whom my father would have disdained even as his slave! You remember him yourself, don't you, old Demos with his hawker's tray!'

'As you wish, Master,' replied the money-lender calmly, familiar of old with Ophiomachos's harmless rages, and knowing that real power lies with those with money. 'As you wish, Master. But it would be best for you to think about these things at leisure. There's no need to give an answer right away. But as you see, Master, your various debts have multiplied and you're having difficulty repaying punctually, indeed as things stand it would be impossible for you to clear your debts completely, even if you did decide to sell. We would still be on the rocks. I tell you this out of the kindness of my heart... and that's the truth, so help me God!'

'Ah well!' said the old man, adjusting his overcoat as if feeling the cold and mopping his brow sadly. 'I might as well sell everything. It's going to happen anyway sooner or later!'

'But buyers can't be found overnight, Master, and you know it. If on the other hand you were to become relatives, Doctor Aristidis would look around when he came over, assess the situation and give you time, he'd see to all these chores himself. To tell the truth, Master, I don't see what you have to lose.'

'Well,' said Ophiomachos, now much calmer and feeling that the man was not giving him such bad advice, 'I suppose I'm not the one who's going to marry him.'

'Wisely spoken!' said the other man at once delightedly, raising his long forefinger to his temple. 'Anyway, Miss Eulalia is an educated and sensible young lady, so how could she fail to agree? Everything is being done for her benefit. How can she scorn such good fortune when it comes her way? Do what you can, Master, to make her see sense. To tell the truth, in the times we live in, some sacrifices must be made! Let her consider the difference for herself. Alkis is a poor lad, Doctor Aristidis is affluent! Alkis would merely take, Doctor Aristidis is prepared to give! Alkis is a wreck, Doctor Aristidis is as healthy as an ox. And after all, Sozomenos is not of princely lineage like you, and other young princes won't be easy to attract from overseas. So let her assess things for herself and then you can all do as you please. But take the advice of a kind-hearted man who's fond of you, Master, more kind-hearted than you realize!'

By now Ophiomachos's anger had subsided completely. He was painfully aware that money matters were crushing him and he sighed pathetically. With a defeated air he said in a low sad voice: 'I'll do my best.' The money-lender smiled with satisfaction. He rubbed his large hands, got up, bowed humbly to the Count and left, while Ophiomachos went back to pacing up and down his gloomy study which exuded the odour of decay.

4

'Nowadays,' Ophiomachos was reflecting to himself, 'the wealthy lord it even over us! They are the ones who do as they like, not us!'

Suddenly he paused in his walking and listened. On the stairs he could hear footsteps, and a moment later he saw the door open and his wife came into the room, a tall earnest lady with impeccably combed white hair, in a long faded slightly threadbare yellow dress, with the woollen shawl she had knitted herself about her shoulders. Her eyes just now were restless and suspicious. She closed the door noiselessly behind her, sat down on a chair near the table, and in a soft but determined voice addressed her husband, who, as if anxious to avoid this conversation, continued to pace up and down in silence:

'Where-Are-You!' – she always addressed him like this because she couldn't bring herself to call him by his name – 'What did that man want?'

He glared at her fiercely, ready for a quarrel, and answered curtly: 'Nothing!'

'How do you mean, nothing?' she persisted, looking at him anxiously. 'Nothing, all this time together?'

He glared at her again in some perplexity, not knowing what to say. Why couldn't his wife settle down today, he wondered, instead of pestering him with questions? Hitherto she had put up with all his extravagance, all his infidelities in silence, uncomplainingly submitting to his will. Had she finally lost patience with him? Was her heart about to overflow, now that he could no longer put things right?

'How do you mean, nothing?' she repeated. 'I see him here every other day, and I'm sure he makes off with something every time he comes. Why are you like this? Do you think I didn't realize long ago that our affairs are going downhill? Just because I've not said anything? Do you think I don't know that all those bills are still unpaid and you haven't had any ready cash for days? Alas!...' And the tears welled into her eyes.

'So now,' he replied maliciously, halting in front of her, 'I suppose you're going to take charge of things in your old age? An heiress like your good self, and from a family like yours, how could you not be personally concerned about your assets! Now look here,' he continued, changing his tone and suddenly losing his temper, 'so long as I'm alive, I remain master in this house. The law too says so! When I die, it'll be another matter. You can all do what you like then! But for now, I'm accountable neither to your good self nor to my children! Do you understand?'

'To *our* children,' she corrected him plaintively. 'To *our* children, whom you're ruining!'

His anger abated for a moment, because he suddenly reflected that she too needed to know their situation if he wanted her help over Eulalia, and he continued in an aggrieved tone:

'You've all been giving me a hard time recently, Maria. How is it you've suddenly all woken up? Why didn't you wake up earlier? There would have been some point to it then!' And flaring up again, he added: 'For the last time, he didn't want anything, I tell you, anything at all! Not from you, at least. He wanted to see me. Since you wish me to, I'll spell it out, I'll tell you exactly why he wanted me. You said you know what's going on. Well then, you'll know I owe him money. Has that sunk in? I'm in debt to him!'

'I knew it,' she replied bitterly. 'But why go to him, when he's destroyed so many families? Alack the day! So now you're in his clutches?'

'His and other people's! You're not happy about it, all of you? Well, so be it! I'm delighted! How was I supposed to provide for you all during so many years of poor harvests? Can you tell me that?... One of your sons alone wasted thousands getting that packing-sheet degree in Paris, which has been lying idle in a drawer ever since. Do you hear me, in a drawer! Your other son keeps running up debts, and I have to pay them off to prevent him going to jail and disgracing all of us! And yet I've never said a word! He keeps on spending like a lord to increase his chances with Asteris's daughter, but he too will be left licking his wounds. That's how things stand, Maria, as you'll soon see! Furthermore, the household expenses are no trifling matter, and then there are the servants' wages both here and in the village, and the occasional horse that dies, and you women who are always squandering money!'

'Oh, we are, are we!'

'Yes, you are, and where's it all to come from? And our vineyards aren't producing, and the houses are not rented out because there's no money to repair them, I've no money for anything! Ah, today everything's

conspiring to upset me! First that confounded Hadrinos, now you! You've
never been like this before! What do you expect me to do? Tell me, if you
believe in God! I've fallen into debt. One thing has led to another – and
now I'm drowning!'

'And what about my money? And my property?' asked the Countess,
pale from the shock of realizing that the damage was greater than she
had assumed.

'You're referring to your personal possessions, your jewellery, your
five-drachma pieces and all that! From all those years ago! Did you think
they were inexhaustible? Don't you remember, they went to pay off the
huge debt my father left? All that remained were your miserable houses
and your wooden shacks, but what have they brought us all these years?'

'My father saved all those silver fivers for me one by one and kept them
in bags of a hundred in his wardrobe, just the way he handed them to you.
Ah, God help us!' And she shook her head sadly and crossed herself. 'Do
we really owe that much?'

'I don't know myself. But the interest keeps increasing. Debt, says
Hadrinos, is something alive and self-generating. It grows, gets heavier
and scuttles one. Now I've told you everything… so leave me alone! I
don't know what to do!'

'Alas, Where-Are-You,' cried his wife loudly, 'do you have no conscience! Didn't you give a thought to our children? The boys are all right,
but what about our two girls you'll be leaving in the gutter unmarried and
defenceless? All this time and you haven't said a word, not a word! – either
to me or to the children so we'd at least know where we stand, instead
you've fallen into the clutches of that usurer who's going to fleece us! But
I shall tell the children everything.'

He looked at her furiously: 'And they'll cut off my allowance, I suppose!' he replied churlishly. 'I'm really frightened of your sons, you know!
Oh dear me, yes! Look, Maria, I've told you already, as long as I live, I
remain the master! I won't tolerate anyone else in charge, so understand
that!'

The Countess, looking pale and distraught, rushed out of the study
and hurried up the stairs. But the old man had become even more irate,
and running after her he shouted furiously: 'I'll tell them myself! Indeed
I will! I'm not afraid of any of you! I'm not handing over the reins, even
if you all conspire against me! Do you hear? Do you hear?'

Both now found themselves upstairs in the large dining-room above the study. That too had four windows and was furnished with shabby walnut pieces: a huge long table in the middle with several chairs around it, two glass cabinets filled with porcelain and crystal, a leather sofa and two deep leather armchairs. On the walls hung several photographs, one or two pieces of embroidery done by Ophiomachos's daughters, and two old paintings – one of some fine white grapes and assorted fruit set out on a table, the other of a brace of woodcock strung up by their feet.

Now both Ophiomachos's sons arrived on the scene, disturbed by all their parents' shouting.

'Calm down!' said Giorgis, the one who had studied law in Paris, with a genial smile. He was a young man of twenty-eight who looked very like his father, though taller, slender and well dressed, with dark curly hair, lively brown eyes and a trim little moustache. 'Calm down! We've never seen you in such a state. Your quarrels provide royal entertainment for the neighbours though.' And he smiled.

'Pharisee!' shouted his father with hatred, angered even more by his son's jovial manner. 'No doubt it was you who sent your mother to confront me! I'm spending my own money, damn it! My own money! You're giving yourself airs because you think you're somebody, now you're back from Paris with your law degree. Get out, go and talk to that woman who's reducing you to skin and bones! Get out! You with your lavish spending over there, you've ruined our family! You've wasted sixty thousand drachmas, for God's sake! I've kept a strict account and watched your progress... And now you condescend to me! But I'll sell off everything, every last damn thing!'

He had gone bright red and the veins in his face protruded as he kept on shouting ever louder, making strange histrionic gestures. Giorgis frowned sadly but made no reply.

'What's this all about?' Spyros, Ophiomachos's other son, now asked.

He was a young man of about twenty-five who looked more like his mother and was shorter, swarthier and stouter than his brother. He too was well dressed, had a sweet face, thick lips like all the Ophiomachos clan, and slightly sleepy eyes.

The old man gave him a sidelong glance, but exhausted as he was, did not start cursing right away. His wife promptly seized her opportunity:

'Well, I like that, he even has the face to swear at us!' she cried. 'There isn't a fiver in the house, my children. Oh God, oh God! And he keeps on signing IOUs to pay the interest. What are we going to do now? You should think about it too. He's put us on the street!'

'Ah, so that's it?' said Giorgis with a smile of indifference and yawned. 'I've known about all this for ages. But there's no solution, at least not for the moment.'

The old man calmed down a little and looked questioningly at his son, as if he were suffering qualms of conscience for having done him an injustice.

'What's to be done?' said Spyros, glancing at himself in a large mirror. 'Who's going to get involved in such a tangled mess? Best for him to try and untangle it himself. Myself, I think I'll be able to muddle through somehow. Asteris's daughter has taken a fancy to me lately. It all started two or three days ago... And now she even strikes me as pretty, I even think I might be able to fall in love with her perhaps. And my father-in-law-to-be will provide a dowry and a job in the firm to boot. A little patience and I won't be a burden to you any longer. Quite the contrary.' And he laughed, again glancing in the mirror.

'And my property?' said the mother, more desperate than ever. 'What's going to happen to my property? Will that be lost as well? My poor parents left it me so that I wouldn't be dependent upon anyone, neither husband nor sons and daughters nor their spouses, not to have it scattered to the winds and gobbled up by money-lenders. Well, am I going to lose it?'

Just then Ophiomachos's two daughters, Eulalia and Louisa, also came into the dining-room, alarmed by the commotion and the sobering words they had overheard from their room. Eulalia was the taller, a fair-haired light-skinned young lady, with arched eyebrows, sapphire eyes, full attractive rosy lips, and in general appearance and complexion very like her father. Louisa on the other hand did not resemble any of her family. She had small pretty hands, tiny feet, and her features had a charm of their own, a rare indefinable quality that everybody found attractive.

Spyros meanwhile, responding to his mother, said: 'You'll get whatever's left of it, mother.' And he continued to admire himself in the large mirror.

'And these two? Oh God!... What about them?' cried the old lady, indicating the two girls.

'Legally,' said Giorgis, adopting the grave manner of one of his Paris law professors, 'Mother can secure her dowry and be paid out, but family honour dictates that she just take what's left. After the debts have been paid off.'

The old man had by now calmed down completely. He realized that his suspicions had misled him and were quite unjust. Moist-eyed he gazed at his first-born son appreciatively and said in a quiet benevolent voice:

'You are clearly not as I imagined, children... Hitherto I hid the truth from you because I was afraid you might disagree and not let me pay. But Giorgis said the debts come first. That's what I want too, absolutely... to avoid my name being entered in red letters by the court of first instance in my old age. As for the rest, God will provide, dear children. You too can see that an Ophiomachos doesn't want to live on borrowed money. No! Sell everything, but pay up. Sell the horse even! Everything, everything!'

'We, poor wretches, are the ones who'll have to pay!' exclaimed Louisa suddenly with a bitter sigh. 'We'll end up on the shelf at home, because who's going to marry us without a dowry these days?'

Eulalia was not unaffected but kept quiet. Inwardly she commended the decision taken by her brothers.

'Ah, pig-headed man!' exclaimed the Countess finally and started weeping, now resigned to the latest catastrophe.

For a few minutes no one spoke. The old man adjusted his old overcoat again, as if feeling the cold, and suddenly stretched himself out on the sofa, tired and reflective. The two young men sat silently at the table, and the mother, pale and anxious, wandered restlessly about the room finding little things to tidy up. The two young ladies remained standing side by side, looking at their father.

Finally the old man observed quietly: 'It's just as well that things have come to this. All of you can help me now and give me your advice. In fact, Giorgis, being a lawyer...'

'I want my property!' cried their mother, aware that she was wasting her breath and, as it were, chanting a lament.

Ignoring her, the old man continued: 'If I start paying up today however, as matters stand even with your mother's assets we'll still be left without a bean, because buyers are hard to find and the money-lender will only accept cash. This is quite apart from the shame... which is no small matter and which so far has led me to postpone filing for bankruptcy.

I've been waiting, my children, for the rents to come in. But they've cheated me. And the worries keep increasing... But there is just one way that everything could be sorted out!'

The old Countess suddenly stopped shuffling about, crossed herself and looked at him attentively, biting her lips.

'It all hangs on your decision, Eulalia,' the old man went on, 'if you so wish, the whole family will be saved. Yes, Eulalia, if you so wish we'll all be saved!'

'Me?' exclaimed his daughter fearfully.

The old man didn't quite know how to proceed. He looked at the floor, adjusted his overcoat as if feeling the cold, flushed, coughed, fidgeted and finally said thoughtfully:

'You all know Aristidis Steriotis, the doctor...'

He again fell silent for a while. 'Well,' he continued nervously, 'he's got most of my IOUs in his drawer. I don't know how he has come by them. But that's not what I'm getting at. The point is, he's wealthy and will give me time to pay, provided... You see, Eulalia, he got in touch with me today. Hadrinos came round and talked to me for hours. The fact of the matter is, Eulalia, he wants you as his wife! If we accept him as our son-in-law, he'll sort out our affairs as he thinks best. Naturally, I've not committed myself in any way. Ah, Eulalia!'

'Never!' cried Eulalia crossing herself. And her face flushed crimson.

'As you wish, Eulalia,' replied her father gently, adjusting his overcoat again. 'You've every right to object, Eulalia. Do you think I'd force you? Oh, my child... never. But necessity, the circumstances... That's the only reason I even bring it up. Do you think I would want the son of Demos as my son-in-law, Eulalia? Me? But at the same time, he's a fine young man. No? There we are then... But in our present predicament, don't you all think... we perhaps ought to accept?'

Eulalia was by now tearful and trembling with agitation: 'No!' she said in a firm voice. 'No!'

'Necessity rules the world,' said Spyros with a smile of indifference. 'Do you imagine, Eulalia, that I'd want to choose Asteris's daughter? There are other girls I'd much prefer. And yet... after all, a man must live.'

At this point their mother suddenly smiled amid her tears. All these people gathered round her filled her with hope. In an instant the oppressive gloom of their calamity had lifted from her heart, things were being put right, her worries were all vanishing. It crossed her mind that Eulalia would now be providing her with security for life, and as in a dream she pictured her daughter splendidly dressed, radiant, free, adored by the whole town. The wealthy man making the offer was after all a scientist and genuinely had the wherewithal to help the stricken family. He had the power to prevent her property from vanishing completely, something very dear to her heart, and for all this she was prepared to forgive his faults, if indeed he had any, and to forget about his vulgar origins.

But Giorgis shook his head moodily and said: 'Isn't it a bit unfair to expect her to sacrifice herself for us?'

'I would have him!' exclaimed Louisa excitedly, her hopes soaring.

She didn't care a fig about the man or about his origins, all she knew was that she was poor and with his wealth would be able to live among people who enjoyed life, without having to struggle, without irksome necessities and constant worries. She knew money bestows power on those who have it, and so she would accept him without a moment's hesitation, without brooding overmuch about what she was doing.

'My poor Louisa...' said her mother sympathetically, a fresh tear in her eye, 'but he wants Eulalia. Now I understand why all this time he's been observing us. It was never his intention to make fun of us. Oh, Eulalia, listen to your mother, don't treat your good fortune with contempt! Today indeed... I shall no longer have to worry about you when I close my eyes. You'll be lightening our burden too!'

'Never!' said Eulalia resolutely, twisting her fingers and staring at the floor. Her heart swelled with indignation. She felt that she was a human being with certain rights in life, that no one should try to control and prostitute her body, subject her to his will and demand she sacrifice her love! What right had she, for such sordid motives and with two young men in the family quite capable of working if they wished, to embitter the man who loved her? Oh, better never to have loved at all!

Yet oh, how happy she would be if he were now asking for her hand, the man who whenever he spoke, whenever she recalled his voice, made her quiver! How great her happiness would be if her fondest dreams were to come true!

'Never!' she declared again. 'I won't marry that man. I can't.'

Her fine moist eyes sparkled more than usual, her cheeks were hot and flushed and she felt as if her heart would burst. The two brothers

glanced uneasily at one another, and Louisa laughed sarcastically, looking at each of them in turn, surprised by her sister's defiance and distress,
while their anxious mother, looking at the floor, said nothing. Finally,
Ophiomachos asked Eulalia shamefacedly, adjusting his old overcoat
again as if feeling the cold:

'Is it Alkis that you're thinking of?'

'Yes!' she replied without hesitation, tears streaming down her face.

'Poor thing,' murmured her mother, looking at her sympathetically.

She remembered the days of her own youth. The world was changing
very fast, yet the human heart always remained the same! She now saw
her own story reviving before her mind's eye. As a young girl, Countess
Ophiomachos too had fallen in love, but timidly, in secret and in silence,
preserving in the warmth of her maiden heart that innocent flower of her
maidenhood, destined alas to wither... The young man she loved had been
handsome, honest and good-hearted, but unfortunately not wealthy. She
had been convinced that she could find happiness with him alone, and for
a moment thought she might obtain him, it seemed so perfectly natural
to love him, then suddenly her parents had given her to Ophiomachos
without even consulting her, as was the custom in those days. They had
preferred him because he was wealthy and a nobleman. And she herself
had found neither the strength nor the will to oppose their decision, and
so her humble passion had remained forever a secret, buried in her heart
of hearts. The young man she had been in love with was Alkis's father,
Ayisilaos Sozomenos, now peacefully slumbering in his tomb, having died
before his time, defeated by life's struggle. Even he had never learned of
her love from her own lips, either while she was still single or later after
she had married Ophiomachos, since the well-bred Countess had lived
respectably all her insignificant life, shut up in her house, caring solely
for her husband and her children. And gradually she had adjusted to her
fate. She had commanded her heart to be still. She had closed her eyes,
strengthened her resolve and uncomplainingly suffered all life's sorrows
and later death and grief, just as she was now ready to accept the anxieties
of poverty.

'How could I betray him?' Eulalia cried again after a lengthy silence.

'You didn't consult us, Eulalia, and so you are not bound to him,'
observed Ophiomachos gravely, his distress at the weeping all around him
bringing a tear to his eye. 'And I'm asking you today, Eulalia, to sacrifice

yourself for us and not throw us out onto the street. Why are you crying? It's for your own good too. Come now, that's enough!'

'You didn't consider us, Eulalia,' said Spyros, smiling indifferently and reflecting that women are quick to change their minds. 'Now if I had already married the daughter of Asteris, if poor Valsamis had finally passed away and Giorgis were now free of worries... at least we could have helped. But as things stand?... What if the doctor loses patience? What if he puts us out onto the street? In that case... in that case... We can kiss our golden dreams goodbye! Asteris naturally won't let me have his daughter, Louisa will never get to marry, and Giorgis, who knows... Only you will survive, Eulalia, and perhaps not even you, as Alkis might not even want you given his bad health.'

'Poor thing!' murmured the mother again with a sigh. 'Sooner or later Eulalia will pay for everyone's pig-headedness. But even so, I'm sure she'll enjoy life with Steriotis. He has my blessing from now on!'

Giorgis, whose illicit affair was well known to his brother, looked down in embarrassment, comparing his own lustful passion with the virgin sensibilities of his sister, whom the others were preparing to sacrifice unjustly to preserve their social standing. Then he turned to his brother and said: 'Why are you muddying the waters like this, when our situations are so different? Surely there are distinctions to be made! Let's just see what needs to be done.'

And he laughed sarcastically.

In his mind's eye Giorgis pictured his friend Alkis depressed, discouraged and embittered at being made a pawn in their collective game. They were all conspiring to blight the couple's innocent love before it could take root, before it could put forth boughs and blossom, sacrificing it to so many base considerations. Money was what was poisoning and choking off their happiness. He asked himself whether it might not be better for them all to accept the need to hold out against Steriotis, restrict their spending and start a fresh and more productive life. The old man, of course, would rather die than face bankruptcy, especially since the wealthy doctor offered him an easy way out. And now their mother agreed with him and thought it right to accept the solution so providentially being offered them. The old man did not of course consider the doctor, a man he deemed vulgar and greatly his inferior, worthy of his daughter, and was only giving his consent to escape the intolerable burden of so

many corrosive daily worries, and to prevent further gossiping about
his downfall. The wealthy doctor was toying with the Ophiomachos
family as he pleased, gradually earning the right to be regarded as their
saviour. Bitterly Giorgis reflected too that the old man had reached this
catastrophic and humiliating crisis without spending even half what
he now owed, because of course the interest had been accumulating
exponentially. And Alkis, Eulalia, their feelings for one another, their life
together, all had to be sacrificed to this outrageous profiteering!... But
was it really a sacrifice? Wouldn't it perhaps be more rational, and better
for both Alkis and Eulalia, if the marriage with the doctor proceeded and
they got over a passion that perhaps might never bring them happiness?
After all, shouldn't they too submit to the customs and expectations
of society? And didn't Alkis need a social life independent of the one
Eulalia would provide if he wanted his ideas to make any progress and
his health to remain strong?

Bemused by all these contradictory reflections, Giorgis looked affectionately at Eulalia, who had now raised her tearful face again, and he
couldn't help admiring his sister's rare beauty.

'You're a free agent,' he said.

'I love him!' she replied proudly.

'Don't let our family be destroyed,' pleaded Ophiomachos. Wearily he
got up from the sofa. 'A simple "yes" from you will put everything right,
Eulalia. My hair is white, Eulalia. You won't let me be disgraced. I must
go to hell as I have lived!'

The mother had by now recovered from her emotion and was reflecting that she too had gradually become accustomed to her husband.
Later she had genuinely grown to love the father of her children, and
apart from the sorrows that had been her lot, her whole life within
the Ophiomachos family had been tranquil, respectable and pleasant.
She said:

'I can't see, Eulalia, what harm it would do you to listen to your
father. You can still love Alkis. For the rest of your life his love will be a
cherished memory.'

Such indeed had been her own first love. A dried flower preserved
between the pages of some book of yesteryear. A flower that had retained
its modest fragrance all these years...

'Nor would Alkis himself,' she added, 'wish such a disaster to befall us.'

'We'll see,' said Giorgis finally. 'We'll see...'

They continued talking at some length, and meanwhile evening had set in.

It was already late when Petros Athanatos appeared at the door of the dining-room. He was an ugly, swarthy young man with a large head, but beautiful lively black eyes. He always looked a bit unruly, as his clothes were worn and shabby, and he stooped as he walked, his head bowed, and clutching his old soft hat in both hands as if uncertain what to do with it. He halted at the door, greeted the family awkwardly, and looked curiously about the room.

Old Ophiomachos was sitting comfortably in the deep sofa gossiping with his sons, and Petros observed them with faint irony. By now all three had fallen silent and the old man, mechanically adjusting his old overcoat as if feeling the cold, reciprocated Petros's greeting cordially and invited him to sit down next to him.

Petros however stayed where he was and said to Giorgis with a sarcastic smile, without even looking at him:

'Mrs Aimilia Valsamis has sent me to invite you round this evening, Giorgis. She says they are expecting guests.'

And he laughed unpleasantly.

'Very well,' replied Giorgis, evidently embarrassed.

'How is Valsamis, by the way?' Ophiomachos suddenly enquired curiously, as if emerging from a dream.

'Even aristocrats are like ordinary people,' replied Petros with the same unpleasant laugh, 'they too die, just like the poor. Charon makes no distinctions, he takes everyone alike. Valsamis? Well, Valsamis is dying! There's no doubt about that. Just that he's not in any hurry. So what? Rather like an ant! Good luck to him... he won't survive the summer. He spits blood every day now. What would you say, Giorgis?'

He laughed again maliciously.

Giorgis remained silent, shaken by his friend's manner. But Petros Athanatos continued in the same sarcastic tone, as if talking to himself:

'Money, money! It's the root of all evil! Without it I would not occupy my current lowly station in Aimilia's household – part slave, part friend, part go-between.'

He laughed again angrily. And still laughing, the eccentric fellow then bade them an awkward farewell and hastily left the room.

They listened to him clumping down the stairs. The three of them looked at one another and laughed. But Giorgis half-imagined that amid the heavy footsteps he had also heard a sigh.

5

That year Dionysios Asteris, the wealthy industrialist, was giving a ball in the palatial villa he had built himself a few years earlier in a seaside suburb of the little capital.

By ten in the evening the carriages had begun to draw up at the grand front porch, where a tall dark-bearded lackey well known to everyone and shivering with cold in his resplendent uniform welcomed the guests and ushered them courteously into the house. Warm air emanated invitingly from the brightly-lit vestibule. On either side of the first flight of marble stairs were two dazzling candelabra supported by half-naked wooden blackamoors, each bright-eyed and smiling, each wearing huge gold earrings, a red and golden turban and a blue and silver sash.

The tiled floors and ash-grey walls gleamed like polished mirrors. Strips of red carpet muffled the sound of footsteps and palm-trees in large pots displayed their stately fronds.

It was now eleven o'clock and the music and clatter of dancing could be heard out on the road. Passing through two opulent, high-ceilinged anterooms, one red, the other blue, each brightly lit and crowded with people chatting merrily or playing cards, visitors eventually reached the ballroom, where numerous couples were dancing in a fine haze of golden dust. It was a spacious room, with four windows draped with pendulous red velvet curtains and four white gilt-trimmed double doors. The yellow ochre walls were adorned with bronze and marble statues and paintings of various sizes in freshly gilded frames. Occupying pride of place among them was a copy of Dürer's *Christ*, which Mr Dionysios Asteris had purchased on his last trip to Munich, and which appeared to be gazing down contemptuously on the grand ballroom and the dancing couples. Clustered round this sacred image were four lively smiling watercolours, the work of a famous local artist and self-proclaimed supporter of traditional techniques, who sold his works of photographic realism to courts and foreign dignitaries.

More pictures adorned the other walls, vying with a collection of eastern weapons – Mr Asteris's true passion and said to be worth a fortune. A large marble fireplace with a blazing log fire and a colossal mirror over it, two lighted crystal chandeliers twinkling with reflected colour, and an assortment of heavy gilded furniture – tables, armchairs, sofas upholstered in red silks and satins and elaborately carved and turned – all combined to imbue the hall with rare magnificence.

Comfortably ensconced in these chairs and sofas were gentlemen in black tailcoats and white shirts and ladies in low-cut silk gowns of various colours, while in the middle of the room a dozen tightly embracing couples were waltzing across the waxed floor to the strains of the piano and the violin, the dust rising continually to form an aura round the electric lights and crystal chandeliers, which seemed transformed into incandescent alabaster.

Through an open door the brightly lit dining-room with refreshments could be seen.

Dionysios Asteris, a handsome, well-nourished man in middle life, his auburn hair just beginning to turn grey, had received every one of his numerous guests with aristocratic courtesy, finding a word of welcome for everyone, or giving a friendly nod or flattering smile, and once the dance was underway his face positively glowed with pleasure at his party's lively atmosphere.

Now he was dancing for the first time himself that evening with the wife of a foreign consul who was honouring his house, a little white-haired old lady with girlish ways who leaned her head on his shoulder as often as she could. After them came Archangelos Daphnopatis, also middle-aged, a tall inflexible insipid fellow renowned for his political defeats, his arm round the waist of his successful rival's daughter, a shy and beautiful young lady dressed in white, who was making her début that season. They were followed by her father, a gentleman well past his prime who occasionally would still become a minister, tall and immaculately groomed with an aristocratic air and ready smile, and now waltzing spryly with the radiant and still youngish hostess of the evening, Mrs Euterpi Asteris, a plump and pretty woman in blue satin décolletage, with a quantity of diamonds in her auburn hair, a pearl choker round her alabaster throat, and gold bracelets set with sapphires round her slender wrists. Next came the three Kallergises, haughty impoverished noblemen, two of them living off their wives, the third and youngest on a modest sinecure from the Asteris firm, a gentleman with waxed moustache and ugly teeth, now dancing energetically with one of the host's daughters, a gorgeous nimble bright-eyed little creature in a plain white dress, as if bent on making her fall in love with him by force; while his brothers, who strikingly resembled one another, both small and insignificant and prematurely aged, one dark, the other fair, had taken charge of two tall, expensively dressed foreign beauties who had married locally. Then, dancing with Giorgis Ophiomachos, came Mrs Urania Daphnopatis, another rich foreigner who pawned her jewellery periodically to support her husband's shoestring politics, and who in her diamond tiara and sea-green silk dress embroidered with white roses scarcely looked her thirty years. Other couples followed, including finally a triumphant Spyros Ophiomachos dancing with Asteris's other daughter, whom he had long been chasing without the least smile of encouragement, a slender dull-eyed girl with a turned-up nose wearing a plain pink dress and a rose in her coarse black hair.

Having withdrawn to a corner of the ballroom, Countess Ophiomachos sat in silence, looking about her nervously. Social gatherings always overwhelmed her and she never went to balls or other people's houses, except to accompany her daughters in fulfilment of a duty that weighed heavily upon her. She was wearing a high-necked black silk dress, evidently altered many times, and an antique diadem that everybody recognized, a last remnant of the Ophiomachos days of glory. Beside her sat another elderly woman, a widow, similarly clad though with no jewellery, who had also accompanied one of her daughters to the dance, and Eulalia, who had not yet danced that evening and seemed pale and preoccupied in her plain white dress.

For a few moments the Countess followed the progress of her younger son, who seemed to fly past among the other couples, and with a shy smile said to Eulalia:

'Our Spyros is enjoying himself immensely, just look at him!'

Eulalia shrugged indifferently.

'So many foreigners here tonight,' remarked the widow, gesturing with her fan towards the crowd.

'It was like that in our day too,' replied Countess Ophiomachos shyly. 'Society needs to be replenished as the old families are in decline.'

She sighed. Then she fell silent for some time, watching the lively progress of the dance before her.

'What's happened to Louisa?' she asked her daughter after a while.

'I haven't seen her,' replied Eulalia smiling. 'She should be here somewhere.'

Countess Ophiomachos cast her eye about the room between the whirling couples. Enthroned on a sofa like a queen beneath Dürer's *Christ* was a robust middle-aged lady, still young-looking but wearing a heavy black silk gown and no jewellery at all. This was Mrs Theophano Chrysospathis, a well known character about town. Seated reverentially on either side of her were several other ladies, in the midst of whom, half-buried among their flounces, was the banker Andreas Arkoudis, a thin bald man of average height with a dark goatee and crooked legs, who squinted a little as he tried to make his ugly smile seem charming, and chatted in his whining voice now to Mrs Chrysospathis on his left, now to another lady on his right, or leaned back to have a word with someone else behind them, bringing his pallid face as close as possible and sniffing the aromas emanating from their silk dresses.

Mrs Chrysospathis was herself a foreigner, but she was extremely wealthy and had acquired considerable influence in town. Her husband was a banker who had gone bankrupt, withdrawn from business activity and now lived off her dowry. Earlier she had lived in some town in Europe, where in the course of her travels she had met a local aristocrat, also travelling, and – without leaving her compliant husband – had a passionate affair with him, afterwards returning with him to his native island, husband and children in tow, where she had continued to live happily with him for several years. That, it was said, was the only misconduct of her life. But her lover had died and Mrs Chrysospathis, unable to forget him, had thereafter always dressed in black. And now, having married off her daughters, she spent her time and money on charitable works as a memorial to her beloved, causing people to remark that she was like a sister to the queen, and every day for years she had put flowers on the tomb of the great romance of her life.

'Exactly twenty-eight thousand and seventy-three drachmas and twenty-eight cents,' the banker was saying in his whining voice, bringing his face close to Mrs Chrysospathis and deliberately squinting to increase his charm, 'is the amount left in the orphans' account with my bank. This year's withdrawals from the first aid account have also left a substantial surplus. We have recorded the Duchess Castelnuovo as a benefactress for her donation of a thousand drachmas to that charity. She left town yesterday.'

'All in accordance with the charter,' added Mrs Chrysospathis gravely, heaving a little sigh as she remembered her dear departed lover.

'And the St Bartholomew Benevolent Society,' continued the banker, leafing through his notebook, 'has exactly four hundred and thirty-five drachmas and fifty cents in its account. I think perhaps those two accounts could be merged.'

Seated further on beside the marble fireplace was another lady. She was a tall buxom good-looking woman, with blond hair interlaced with diamonds and sapphires, sensuous red lips, sparkling blue eyes and a neck as white as marble. Her pleated brown silk dress left part of her handsome back and alabaster bosom showing. This was Mrs Aimilia Valsamis. Restless and a little pale, she was watching Giorgis Ophiomachos, who as he danced past with Urania Daphnopatis happened to whisper something in his partner's ear and smile. Irritably Aimilia tapped her knee with her fan to the rhythm of the music, feeling it was high time this dance came to an end, and turned to address Petros Athanatos, who had been sitting just behind her in his frayed tailcoat without venturing to speak and gazing with a sad abstracted smile at the couples whirling past intoxicated by the dance.

All around, small groups of people were laughing and conversing quietly.

In the adjacent anteroom, which though by no means large had a resplendent red, white and green Persian carpet and yellow Oriental curtains covering the two windows, four gentlemen were seated round a table absorbed in a game of cards. On one side was Alexandros Ophiomachos Philaretos, sitting hunched in his ancient discoloured tailcoat, which he adjusted now and then as if feeling the cold, and looking old as he stared glumly at his cards. Opposite him sat the bankrupt foreign banker, Mrs Chrysospathis' husband, thin, elderly and bald save for a few wisps of hair, his eyes dull behind his heavy gold-rimmed spectacles; on his left sat Periklis Valsamis, a pale likeable gentleman, still young but coughing intermittently and looking exhausted from his hopeless illness; while on his right was another grey-bearded gentleman with gold-rimmed spectacles, well over seventy but still handsome, robust and immaculate in the royal livery he wore with pride.

Just then the rubber had come to an end and a sharp altercation had suddenly erupted concerning the game.

'Trumps decided that round!' Ophiomachos, who was losing, remarked to his partner angrily, flinging his last card down.

'Not so, sir!' replied the bankrupt banker coolly, and proceeded to analyse his partner's game, demonstrating that their opponents had made an error, even though they'd won.

The old man in royal livery also rehearsed the entire game, without however apportioning praise or blame to anyone, while Periklis Valsamis avoided taking part in the discussion, busying himself with totting up the score.

In the ballroom meanwhile the waltz had come to an end. The violinists were tuning their instruments. Giorgis Ophiomachos had escorted Mrs Urania Daphnopatis to the small red anteroom and lingered with her for a moment, whereupon Mrs Aimilia Valsamis had flushed and grown angry and impatient, then laughing at herself had looked away to where the old Countess Ophiomachos was still sitting placidly across the room, but when there was still no sign of Giorgis returning she had bitten her pink lip with frustration.

'Go and tell Giorgis,' she finally said acidly to Petros Athanatos, barely turning her head, 'to come here immediately!'

Petros gazed at her soulfully in silence for a moment, as if worshipping an icon, then got up at once, crossed the brilliantly lit ballroom to the adjacent room and went up to Giorgis, who by now had been joined by the two Kallergis wives and Goulielmos Arkoudis, the melancholy banker's son, a lanky twenty-two-year-old with unattractive clean-shaven features, whose cold eye, unsmiling mouth and dry demeanour proclaimed his pride in his English breeding.

'She wants you,' Petros said to Giorgis quietly, staring at the floor.

By now the whole town knew of and accepted the affair between Giorgis Ophiomachos and Aimilia Valsamis. The gorgeous woman could not love her sick husband, had never done so and had only known love in young Ophiomachos's arms. She was passionate and tender-hearted, and love tormented her, making her restless, causing her deep anxiety and suffering, dominating her entire life. At dawn each morning when she awoke in her bedroom where she slept alone, he would be the one whom in her drowsy state she first remembered clearly from among the thousand images that crowd in upon a person's consciousness in those first moments. In her mind's eye she would picture him before her, tall and handsome with his well-bred smile, fine eyes and that fleshy lip of the Ophiomachos clan, and this image would bring back all their blissful moments, the indescribable refreshing power of love, the times when she would tremblingly surrender to him, forgetful of the world amid their breathless fiery kisses, amid the intense embraces she could still feel like a voluptuous pain throughout her tender body.

Later she would suddenly be seized by bitter, tormenting anxiety. What was Giorgis up to at that moment? Was he alone? Where did he spend all those hours she couldn't see him – most of the hours of the day and night? She wanted him constantly beside her breathing the same air, wanted to feel his admiring gaze upon her, to participate in all his woes.

And then when she rose late, she would be seized by a fever of impatience which would dominate her utterly, leaving her mind in disarray, until finally Giorgis would come round at the appointed hour. Yet the long-awaited moment was always a bitter disappointment, because when he arrived he would never be as she had imagined, never fired with the same ardour and tenderness she felt herself. She never saw his eyes – ah! – overflowing with tears of delight, he hadn't suffered, he hadn't dreamed about her, he wasn't yearning to surrender his whole body to her passionate embrace.

And every day would bring the same brooding thoughts, the same burning desires. Her impatience would again increase by the moment, she would again career from sweet remembrance and sweeter hope to black despair, and her rioting brain would contemplate some harsh punishment, some terrible revenge – eternal separation, or her own destruction on fanciful and spurious grounds – or urge her to overcome her amorous weakness for him and give him a taste of the poison of jealousy, or better still, do something irrevocable that would plunge him into bleak dejection and linger in his heart forever.

Brooding thus, she would pace up and down her cluttered room, pale, edgy and on the verge of tears. Suddenly she would feel the blood surging through her body like a tidal wave. What was that noise on the stairs, in the passage, outside her room? A maid coming upstairs, someone looking for Valsamis... some visitor she didn't care two hoots about?... Ah, wasn't that his step?... Then at last she would see him in the little parlour next to her bedroom, and immediately all her trembling anxiety and yearning would evaporate. Suddenly she was palpitating with joy, she would forget all the bitter reproaches she had resolved upon, the malicious vengeance she had been plotting – all this would vanish like a nightmare within a dream that was just then beginning but – alas! – would last no time at all...

Thus her life was consumed by constant insatiable longing, by an unquenchable desire which didn't leave her a moment to think calmly about anything that was not connected with her lover. She was made positively ill by the terrible suspicion that Giorgis, ungrateful dog, might be seeing other women, tasting with them the delights that they had enjoyed together, wasting his kisses gratifying them. Oh, he would earn her deadly hatred if it turned out to be true, she would rather die than prove incapable of keeping a man, despite all the ardour of her passion! And yet, Giorgis might well be philandering behind her back. Shame, self-respect and her social position deterred her from running after him and finding out what he was up to, and – alas! – it was beyond her power to read all his transgressions in his wayward heart. She was obliged to believe what he told her between kisses, what he chose to tell her, and who knows whether he was telling her the truth!

Such was Mrs Valsamis's passion for Ophiomachos, and her passion failed to find the same response in his heart. She could not feel satisfied unless he too were to suffer the same torments, unless she could see him ignoring society, convention and even the law for her sake – for the sake of a gorgeous young woman positively throbbing with desire, who was able to surrender utterly to the blissful intoxicating moments that obliterated her identity. Then her mind would switch off and all she responded to from the depths of her being was the voice of erotic passion. Her eyes would sparkle more than usual, her nostrils seemed to be inhaling a more invigorating air, her burning mouth would kiss with furious abandon and her awakened body would quiver in oceans of unending bliss.

Her suffering on the other hand was as intense as bitter poison, the waiting like a frenzied madness, when the hours would tick by minute by interminable minute, exhausting her with doubts and resentment. Why did he do it? What was keeping him? When would she see him again? She had no answers and would simply torment herself, cursing the mad passion she lacked the strength to root out of her heart and couldn't even hide so as to bring the thankless wretch to heel.

Mrs Valsamis frequently tortured herself like this, which despite herself made her long for the speedy demise of the man who was her husband and who was the only real obstacle to her erotic life, because only thus could Giorgis become hers for ever. Yes, he was the only obstacle!... Fate seemed opposed to the rapid deterioration of this man, who despite everything was kindly disposed towards his wife and tried to be self-effacing confronted by her indomitable will, acknowledging, poor fellow, that he had already forfeited his rights in life and was himself to blame for his own misery. He let her have her freedom, watching with stoic understanding the violence of her latest passion, the life-giving urge his illness had denied her, and with bitter-sweet patience awaited the end.

Mrs Aimilia Valsamis had accepted this dark sacrifice, the humble self-denial of this man marked by death, who observed life from a world no longer his. But what really terrified her was her vague suspicion that the torments of love might come to an end, that even her love might with time lose its initial fervour, might weaken, flicker and go out, no longer kindling the uncontrollable desire that intoxicates one's soul and transports one's whole being.

But now, here at the ball, knowing that he was in the company of another woman, and imagining him being gratified by someone else, she was again experiencing intense anxiety, could feel her heart pounding restlessly, was conscious that her eyes were sparkling unusually, and for moments at a time forgot that she was among so many people, so many prying eyes. Meanwhile her mind was racing. How could her heart be burning with desire, her thoughts constantly preoccupied with him, while he was avoiding her like this, amusing himself with other women, even perhaps seeking new conquests? How could he want to enjoy himself anywhere except with her, except thinking about her, revelling in her all-consuming love for him? And why was Eros so unjust? Why didn't he hand out love impartially, bestowing on two hearts the same longings and desires, the same willingness to sacrifice, where as it was one lover always gave and the other merely accepted love, one suffered hell while the other emerged unscathed, able to cope rationally with all eventualities because for him love was merely one aspect of a well-balanced life in a harmonious universe? Ah, why was Eros so unjust?…

With this thought she felt a secret pang in her heart, making her blink and bite her lip. Was he going to come or not, for goodness' sake, she asked herself angrily. Oh, of course he'd come. And for the rest of the evening she'd make sure she punished him. She would refuse to dance with him if he asked her, but would not let him escape, she would prevent him dancing and ruin his enjoyment. She again became impatient. Why couldn't he come quickly? Would she be obliged to go across to him in front of all these people? Why at least couldn't Petros report back at once? Or might Giorgis have resolved that from tonight he would not submit to her, jealous of his independence and ready to begin some other idyll, could he perhaps be attracted to Archangelos Daphnopatis's lovely wife, who had had more than one affair already?

With a distracted air she brusquely declined a courteous gentleman's invitation to dance, unable even to smile at him graciously, preoccupied as she was with watching the door to the small red anteroom. Giorgis, she suspected, was just inside the door. How dare he be unfaithful! How dare he go around smiling at anything in skirts! Just let him try!…

But now Giorgis had appeared. He was talking casually to Petros and looking cheerful and relaxed. What were they discussing? For a moment Mrs Valsamis thought Giorgis was about to reclaim his former partner, who had reappeared beside them, and launch into the dance with her again. The blood rushed to her head. She felt a painful reflex action in her legs prompting her to rise, but she managed to control herself, merely reflecting with bitter resentment that this was the first time Giorgis had rebelled, the first time she had seen how little he really cared for her.

But the music was striking up again. Several couples had started dancing, swaying rhythmically in one another's arms, and Mrs Aimilia Valsamis suddenly noticed that the other woman was gaily joining the dance with Petros Athanatos, and saw Giorgis sauntering towards her.

Secretly she smiled.

'Shall we dance?' Giorgis asked amiably, approaching her and smiling too.

'No,' she replied looking him in the eye, 'but come and sit beside me!' And she motioned to a chair.

Giorgis made no reply and obeyed submissively. He met her gaze and they both smiled, each seeing their own reflection in the other's eyes. Giorgis was in a good mood and at once told her the news he had heard that evening, which was causing a sensation about town: a wedding had been held somewhere, at which the two brothers-in-law had danced together the whole night.

But Mrs Valsamis pretended not to hear. She looked at him again searchingly and said: 'But why with her? Oh, I won't have it, I won't have it!'

And her eyes blazed.

Giorgis gave her a protesting look. For three years she had held him in thrall and his bonds seemed to be getting ever tighter… yet he felt powerless to rebel against his servitude, even though she was neither his first nor his only mistress. He was captivated by her rare beauty, her passionate intensity, her ardent, insatiable love-making, the magic of her moist red lips eager for more kisses, her beautiful blond hair, her marble neck, her god-like bearing, and he was dominated by her strength of will which had made him wholly hers, depriving him of his free will and often of his reason. He saw the effects of this imperious will of hers everywhere around her – on her sick husband who submitted uncomplainingly to his pitiable fate, as if this were only natural, as if the poor fellow were publicly confessing that he alone was to blame for his misery; on Petros Athanatos, that strange eccentric who agonized over the meaning of existence and yet accepted her heavy yoke as something transcending ordinary human will, just to be able to admire her angelic figure and breathe in the myrrh exuded by her body, reduced to beggary by a hopeless passion that was destroying his existence; and finally on society, rich and poor alike, who revered her passion, readily forgave her what they would find culpable in others, and looked upon the lovely woman with much sympathy, no one daring to condemn her, as if they all acknowledged that she really was a superior creature exempt from the moral laws and hypocritical virtues that enslaved everybody else.

Giorgis sighed and she, much calmer now he was beside her, glanced at him affectionately, a hint of a smile at the corner of her moist lips. Their eyes met. For a moment she was the only person in the ballroom Giorgis had eyes for, all the others simply vanishing. His warm blood surged to his head and his eyes watered with the intensity of desire again coursing through his veins as powerfully as the first time he had felt the magic warmth of her glorious body next to him.

She was well aware of this.

Then she remarked sweetly: 'I sent Goulielmos Arkoudis over to dance with Louisa.'

And she pointed with her ivory fan to where the young people were twirling gracefully.

'We'll present him to your mother afterwards,' she continued. 'He's a splendid fellow, just right for Louisa! But why is Eulalia sitting out dance after dance like this?'

'Alkis isn't here yet,' he replied with an appreciative glance at her. 'She's upset because Doctor Steriotis is very persistent and she is not to be persuaded.'

'She must accept him though,' she replied, shaking her head sadly. 'Don't let her suffer the same fate with Alkis that I've had to with Valsamis.'

Giorgis reflected that Aimilia's love for him really was disinterested. She empathized with all his family's troubles, suspecting them without ever asking him directly, she showed discreet concern for their declining fortunes, and she worshipped him for his own sake. What more could a man ask of a woman, and such a woman too? Why couldn't he surrender unreservedly, without its weighing on his conscience? Why did he always consider their bond temporary? And how could he do better? He was now twenty-eight and had wasted the best years of his life blindly following a natural and hereditary aversion to any kind of gainful employment involving tasks and obligations. And so his fine diploma from the centre of learning where he had studied and enjoyed himself immoderately, contributing to the ruin of his family, remained forgotten in a drawer. Yet he always remembered those madcap adventures fondly and readily made excuses for them, showing great forbearance towards himself. After five years abroad he had returned triumphant and full of grandiose dreams, but when fate stopped him short at the first hurdle they had quickly evaporated and now he could no longer even remember what they were. At the time he was still used to the pace of life in the great city and felt restless in his small home town and unable to appreciate its beauty, and just at this critical juncture he had got to know Aimilia Valsamis and her beauty had immediately enchanted him. He would see her on the street escorted by her husband, already pale, sick and stooping, and by Petros

Athanatos, who accompanied them just to inhale the balmy fragrance
of her body, and he had been deeply impressed by her moist lips, her
exquisite poise and her golden hair under her plumed hat. He had also
heard that she had never loved her sick husband and that, in her yearning
for a deep and genuine relationship, she had already been deceived several
times, dismissing a succession of men who either could not or were not
prepared to love her.

He had first met her at a dinner party given by the politician who
would periodically become a minister and always celebrate by gathering
the town's young educated elite around him. They had seated him next
to her. Giorgis had never forgotten the black velvet dress she wore that
evening, which displayed her marble throat down to her cleavage. It was
discreetly pinned together with a diamond broach, and her golden hair
was adorned with sapphires and sparkling sequins, exactly as again tonight.

The dinner party however had ended like some Roman orgy. Everyone
was excited by the exhilarating speeches and the wine. And the host,
without losing his sangfroid or interrupting his charming conversation,
had received his fair neighbour's leg onto his knees, thereby initiating yet
another fleeting idyll. The lady in question was Mrs Urania Daphnopatis,
the wife of his political opponent, renowned for his indolence and
electoral defeats, who was seated at the same table flirting happily with
the daughter of the house, a lively little minx who at fifteen already felt
relaxed in that heady atmosphere. Opposite him the hostess, a slender
lady of about forty, was talking freely to the handsome old man in royal
livery and pretending to listen to some court scandal he was recounting in a low insinuating voice, while her husband's brother, an elderly
gentleman with faded whiskers, who had also tasted Mrs Daphnopatis's
favours and understood what was happening, looked on with jealous
eyes. Two or three other ladies were also present, along with the sick
Valsamis silently philosophizing, Petros Athanatos with his melancholy
ecstatic gaze, and the doctor, Aristidis Steriotis, who rarely managed to
hold forth on his subject. But Aimilia had been as it were the goddess at
the banquet – tall, proud, radiant, worshipped by all, and resembling a
statue of the Pandemos Aphrodite.

Giorgis himself had indignantly realized what was going on when
he bent down to pick up the napkin Aimilia had deliberately dropped,
and looked around unable to believe his eyes. The whole company just

then seemed to be under the sway of some scarcely controllable desire, some erotic urge transmitted from one guest to another and manifest in every eye. The hostess gave him an odd look, as if to say that she was well aware of what was afoot, and from that moment on Giorgis ceased to listen to the host's panegyric lauding his last ministry for purchasing ships intended to establish their wretched little kingdom as the chief naval power in the region, and looked Aimilia in the eyes as she leaned back bored and silent, and when she smiled encouragingly he felt a little thrill as desire overcame him too. They began an animated conversation and when his knee brushed hers another shiver ran through him. Little by little he grew bolder, and by the end of the evening he realized that sooner or later this beautiful woman must become his, perhaps for ever.

There followed a period of expectant waiting. Her erotic appeal had completely conquered him. He lived only for her, had eyes for no one in the world but her. Then at her residence one day, amid tears and sighs and palpitating hearts, Mrs Aimilia Valsamis had finally surrendered her ardent body, she too vanquished by desire.

Since then three whole years had passed...

'She should accept him,' Mrs Aimilia Valsamis said to Giorgis again. 'Only the rich are free to do as they please.'

Just then Mrs Theophano Chrysospathis approached them grandly, her silk gown rustling. Two other ladies followed in her wake.

'Will you be coming to the foundling hospital bazaar?' she asked. 'It starts next Sunday. These dear ladies are on the committee too, you know.'

Mrs Valsamis shrugged her bare shoulders, not wishing to commit herself, and after a moment Mrs Chrysospathis sat down beside her and, looking first at Giorgis then at her, asked with a patronizing air:

'How come you're not dancing this evening?'

'Perhaps after supper,' replied Mrs Valsamis, smiling at Giorgis archly. 'I did have a bit of a headache but it's gone now.'

The music had stopped and there was a pause in the dancing. Smiling gentlemen clad in black and perspiring slightly perambulated round the ballroom with their opulently dressed partners on their arm. Then Petros Athanatos reappeared at his patroness's side, humble, melancholy, shy, hoping only for a smile from her.

'Alkis is here, in the small red anteroom,' he remarked.

'Ah, so he's come!' replied Mrs Valsamis, finally rewarding him with a smile that made him lower his eyes.

Giorgis stood up, explaining that he ought to go and join his friend, and she let him go without protesting.

'It's unfortunate,' Aimilia said to Mrs Chrysospathis after a pause, 'It's most unfortunate. His sister is deeply in love with Alkis, but she can't marry him.'

'Can't marry him?' repeated Mrs Chrysospathis patronizingly. 'Might one ask why? Are there financial difficulties? But those are the only ones that can be remedied, provided Alkis is sufficiently determined. Soon our dear friend and fellow citizen will be minister again and he won't of course be unjust to Alkis. The country, as those gentlemen never tire of telling us, needs able employees in every field. In fact I could take the matter up myself, provided he wants me to of course.'

'There are other problems too,' replied Mrs Valsamis thoughtfully.

Suddenly Petros Athanatos laughed sarcastically.

'Alkis... Alkis!' he said. 'No point in trying to change the situation! He's not going to do what he wants either, he won't find the strength, any more than I can do what my mind urges. Oh Aimilia... The mind, ha, ha! The mind is no more than a parasite inside a larger organism. The mind isn't life. Life is something more primitive, more real, something that desires and suffers. We lack the strength and we lack the money, and so time and our lives slip by, ha, ha!...'

Mrs Chrysospathis, who found his eccentric remarks thoroughly unsettling, was getting up to go. But Aimilia detained her, taking her hand.

'There you go again!' she scolded Petros laughingly. 'Don't you realize such remarks are out of place in polite society? Haven't I told you so before? Next time I won't let you escort me.'

Petros lowered his eyes sadly and said nothing.

The dancing had begun again. The musicians struck up a lively tune and the couples whirled past in front of them, their silk skirts rustling, their pattering steps gliding over the waxed floor, their jewels glittering in the lights. Just then the two ladies noticed Doctor Steriotis coming their way, his smile revealing his large yellow teeth as he strode across the room, swinging his hips in the curious way he had.

Mrs Valsamis greeted him affably and made him sit next to her, saying: 'Will you be taking part in Mrs Chrysospathis's bazaar, Doctor?'

'As a matter of fact, I've already contributed a little something!' said the doctor, smiling shyly, his dull eyes staring at the ceiling.

Mrs Chrysospathis gave him a friendly nod, confirming this was so.

'How wonderful!' replied Mrs Valsamis, seeing that he expected to be praised, and after a pause she asked: 'Has the dancing tired you out already?' And she smiled at him.

'I'm not much of a dancer,' he said a little peevishly. 'Anyway, Miss Eulalia... you'll no doubt have heard. She has refused me categorically. Can't be helped! In this world one has to arm oneself with fortitude. Survival of the fittest and all that. Darwin was quite right.'

'She's not too well at present,' said Mrs Valsamis hastily. 'She's had no appetite for days, poor thing.'

Petros Athanatos laughed again.

'But that won't stop her dancing,' he murmured in an aside to Mrs Chrysospathis, 'you'll see.'

Mrs Valsamis glared at him angrily and this shut him up. The doctor meanwhile responded to her comment, stroking his little goatee that was beginning to turn grey, and looking slyly at Petros with his dull eyes:

'A husband would cheer her up at once, a husband who of course couldn't be a beggar! Beautiful women have a duty to be the ornament of a rich man's home. That is the only way for a family to improve its stock. And indeed, a beautiful woman is in no way disadvantaged by such a preference, since the purpose of life is happiness and seventy-five per cent of happiness consists in economic prosperity, which is the privilege of the few.'

'Who often don't deserve it,' remarked Petros to annoy him.

'Society,' continued the doctor, looking at him coolly with a sarcastic smile, 'society,' he stressed, 'is fortunately built on very firm foundations. Social laws are laws of nature, and no amount of irrational behaviour can overturn them. Let us observe what occurs in nature, the great teacher. She treats individuals unjustly, not only in the case of humans and the lower mammals, but with all animals and plants, and even with molecules of inorganic matter. Who knows what the laws that govern what we call destiny might be!'

He laughed.

'He's quite right,' said Mrs Chrysospathis, who was well known for her conservative convictions.

Just then Goulielmos Arkoudis, the clean-shaven young banker's
son whose whole air betrayed his adulation of the British, came up
and after deferentially greeting the ladies said in his awkward foreign
accent:

'Don't forget, Mrs Valsamis, you were going to introduce me to
Countess Ophiomachos. You promised.'

'Of course,' she replied with a happy smile, and rose at once. Nodding
to the doctor and smiling at Mrs Chrysospathis, she moved off towards
where the retiring Countess was still sitting modestly and talking to the
widow about issues of their day that younger people were happy to forget,
while Eulalia sat silently beside them. Louisa too was there now, having
only moments earlier left Arkoudis's side.

Petros Athanatos promptly vanished into the red anteroom, and
Doctor Steriotis continued talking to Mrs Chrysospathis.

Mrs Valsamis proceeded to pay her respects to the elderly Countess
who reciprocated warmly, as if she too considered Mrs Valsamis's liaison
with her son quite natural and were grateful for her patronage. Then
Mrs Valsamis said:

'This, my dear Countess, is Goulielmos Arkoudis, the banker's son, a
very sound, respectable young man!'

'We've heard a lot about him,' replied the elderly Countess, smiling
as Arkoudis made her a deep bow and indicating a chair next to Louisa.
'My sons are acquainted with him. Do sit down Mr Arkoudis, please
take a seat Aimilia!'

They both sat down and the pleasantries continued.

Louisa was now chatting with Goulielmos a little to one side, while
the Countess was asking Aimilia about some gentleman both knew who
had just strolled past.

Soon Spyros Ophiomachos hurried over too, looking distractedly
about him:

'You don't happen to have seen Andromache?' he asked them anxiously – this was the name of Asteris's ugly daughter.

'No,' replied his mother guardedly and Aimilia burst out laughing.
'No, but come and join us for a little!'

'I don't know where she can have got to,' he continued, on the point
of moving away. Then as if suddenly recalling something, he added: 'Old
Iustinianis has cornered Alkis in the red anteroom and is driving him

crazy with his ranting. He won't let him escape.' He laughed and looked around, still keeping an eye out for Asteris's ugly daughter.

'Ah, so he's come!' said Eulalia, smiling sadly and restraining an impulse to get up at once.

'What's your father up to, Spyros?' asked their mother anxiously.

'He's playing cards,' he replied with a laugh and looked about again.

'He'll lose, I know he will,' said the Countess frowning, as Spyros moved away.

The music had stopped and the dancers were again perambulating round the hall in pairs. Meanwhile, tired of their game, the four card players emerged from the gaming room – the diminutive Alexandros Ophiomachos Philaretos, a sad smile on his thick lips and evidently feeling cold in his worn discoloured tailcoat, the handsome full-bearded elder proudly wearing royal livery, the bankrupt banker Chrysospathis, and the ailing Periklis Valsamis, sunken-chested and exhausted, a sweet smile on his pale lips.

They all stopped beside the sofa under Dürer's *Christ*, where Mrs Chrysospathis was again majestically enthroned. She was now flanked by Mrs Euterpi Asteris and the two Kallergis wives, while Doctor Steriotis and the aristocrat turned minister sat facing her.

Her husband looked at her with pride and gave her a happy smile.

'The Russo-Turkish disagreement,' the minister was saying with a smile, 'will put the government in a very difficult position, and it will be reluctant to discharge the reservists. There will certainly be serious friction with the great powers. Moreover, the country needs peace and tranquillity, it needs robust and serious government. The king will indubitably call on the current administration to resign and invite us to take over governing the country, in which case, it goes without saying, dissolution of parliament will follow! So let me ask you therefore, Doctor Steriotis, will you consent to be my deputy?'

'A splendid choice!' exclaimed Mrs Chrysospathis approvingly.

The other ladies smiled and nodded, thinking ruefully of their own husbands.

'We shall have to see,' said Doctor Steriotis, trying to hide his joy which was positively overflowing.

'I'm the only one that won't be invited by His Majesty,' said the old man in royal livery, bitter and aggrieved. He sat down beside the two

Kallergis wives and in a low voice started telling them about the scandal that had forced him to leave the palace.

'Lucky fellow, that boorish doctor!' thought Alexandros Ophiomachos, involuntarily recalling Demos with his hawker's tray as he looked first at Steriotis and then at his wife. When he noticed her gazing across at him expectantly, he adjusted his tailcoat and made his way to where she was sitting with their daughters.

'Fate, the miserable hussy,' he said to himself with a sigh, 'has always persecuted me!'

He was accompanied by the bankrupt banker Chrysospathis, while Periklis Valsamis headed for the red anteroom.

'How did the game go?' the old lady asked her husband with a forced smile.

'He lost!' declared the banker, laughing heartily as he greeted her. 'He lost two hundred and fifty points!'

'Fate!' said Ophiomachos gloomily.

The old lady gave him a pained look, rapidly calculating that twenty-five drachmas had just taken wing from their already depleted kitty, but pretending not to care she asked with a little smile:

'So who won then?'

'I did, of course!' said Chrysospathis proudly. 'Bridge is a tricky game, you know, ha, ha! But perhaps Mrs Chrysospathis will be dispensing alms tomorrow!'

He laughed again.

Meanwhile Goulielmos Arkoudis was engaged in more intimate conversation with Louisa, and with feigned humility and downcast eyes was saying to her softly:

'If only things today were as in Dante's and in Petrarch's time! Every civilized young man should be entitled to his idol, to his Beatrice or Laura.'

'There's nothing to prevent it,' replied Louisa, laughing coyly. And a moment later she added, gazing at him with contrived emotion: 'Perhaps Petrarchs and their Lauras still exist, except they're not all poets who can write beautifully about their feelings.'

Their conversation continued in this vein, always revolving around love.

Now the voice of Doctor Steriotis could be heard booming across the room, holding forth to several gentlemen.

'Life,' he was saying, 'is a form of warfare too. *Bellum omnium contra omnes* as some English philosopher has put it. It's a struggle for dominion! The phenomenon of purposeful design is merely the result of this process. It in no way proves the presence of intelligence at work in the universe, but it is something that could not have been absent from any universe without leading to complete collapse. It is the mechanical consequence of physical forces. This has been proved by two more recent disciplines, biology and its sub-branch sociology, and it has also been demonstrated by research at institutes in Lille and Paris conducted by Le Dantec and others...'

6

In the small red anteroom an elderly aristocrat, Marcantonio Iustinianis, small, erect and red-faced, with gold-rimmed spectacles, faded brown hair and a trim beard, had for some time been delivering a fiery oration. He gesticulated a good deal as he held forth, taking his listeners by the hand or arm and shaking them, his whole body galvanized like some marionette.

'Our native land,' he was saying, continuing his speech, 'admired by all cultivated nations, this island of ours, this unhappy island, this bastion of civilization... And not one of you young people gives a fig about your heritage, about the brilliant history of this glorious land, or cares to remember those great illustrious years under Venetian rule.'

'Don't shout so much,' remarked someone looking nervously about the room: it was the tall stout grey-bearded old poet renowned for his musical settings of courtly and patriotic verse, who proudly sported a Greek medal and whose patriotism was invariably ruffled when he heard his beloved Greece maligned.

'As for you,' Marcantonio replied sarcastically, thrusting his thumbs into his lapels, 'they'll soon be worshipping you on bended knee. You know they will! But history never lies.'

He laughed.

Giorgis Ophiomachos, who was standing next to them and often found the old eccentric entertaining, laughed as well, and Petros Athanatos pulled a face in an attempt to stifle his unpleasant laugh and turned to where Alkis had been waiting for some time.

He was sitting in a large velvet armchair with his feet up looking tired, and just then was thoughtfully smoothing back his hair. A faint smile played on his lips and his eyes under his long lashes were gazing vacantly across the room. He was pale and still a little thin after his latest illness, but he felt strong and buoyed by a new lease of life.

Fragments of the others' conversation reached his ears but he tried not to listen, as it always put him in a pessimistic mood which tonight he wanted to avoid. Not altogether successfully, however. The fatuous old rhetorician frequently glanced in his direction, as if hoping to continue his insufferable prattling with him. Alkis however had not come to the dance to listen to him but to see Eulalia, who doubtless had been waiting for him in the adjacent ballroom all this time. But because crowds made him feel dizzy, he had lingered in the red anteroom with a few acquaintances until he could bring himself to mingle with the larger crowd. Finally, deciding there was no escaping the disagreeable experience, he got up, shook his legs, adjusted his tailcoat and rubbed his hands together from irrepressible anxiety. Just then he heard loud laughter all around him and saw Marcantonio Iustinianis shouting strangely and incoherently and making histrionic gestures first with one hand and then the other.

He moved towards the ballroom door and as he looked in felt dizzy. The music was in full swing and the couples were dancing with great zest. He cast his eye round the room, taking in the milling crowd of people one by one. They were all familiar.

Suddenly he asked himself what he and Eulalia were doing there tonight, amongst all these people whose sole object in life was enjoyment and facile merrymaking, whatever could be obtained without effort or serious endeavour, what was he doing among them when his life was governed by a different aim, a demanding and difficult ideal, the creation of new beauty. Hadn't he been convinced he'd been cured of his grave illness to pursue this? And hadn't he vowed to continue battling against his physical debility? But now life was suddenly confronting him in all its seriousness, with all its pressing needs. And it was insisting that he adapt his own existence to the lives of others, willingly accept what the moment had to offer, and moderate his anguish, his sorrow and his passion if he didn't want to be stricken from the book of life. He had brooded over all these demands and found them impossible to resist, but his heart found it equally impossible to deny the bonds of love, if the price of retaining his

independence was to sacrifice them – to sacrifice Eulalia! He had come to
this ball because he had realized that he too must bow to the inevitable.

Hadn't his father done the same? Hadn't he also been a man of
enlightened views and hadn't he also been obliged to bury his most
cherished ideals deep within his heart, seal his innocent lips and submit
to necessity, with no option but to scorn the wretched struggle for
advancement and his ignoble contemporaries, while privately clinging
to the precious hope of some distant future triumph? Shouldn't he too
now follow his father's example and choice of career and settle for what
happiness was within his reach, the happiness of love in a sequestered
home where peace would reign?

He always remembered his father fondly and with reverence. He
and his mother had been his only consolation during his bleak childhood – bitter years of serious illness that had left an indelible impression
on him. He often recalled how his father would take him on his walks,
constantly talking to him and trying to teach him things, and how while
still a lad he would sometimes fail to understand his father's meaning.
Despite this, however, his words had left their imprint on his mind,
and in retrospect he had come to appreciate his elevated concepts and
cultivated views.

One of those walks he remembered especially vividly. He was sixteen
at the time, it was spring and restless desires had suddenly begun to waken
in his youthful heart. Leaving town, he and his father had followed the
peaceful verdant shoreline until they came to the ancient remains of a
Venetian fortress, the golden reflection of its ruined towers mirrored in
the sun-drenched bay. Everywhere the trees and shrubs were blossoming,
imparting a delightful fragrance to the cool breeze descending from the
mountain. And everywhere tender new shoots were springing up and
birds chirping as they chased each other through the branches, responding
to the secret urges that incessantly reveal the will of all creation. Whole
trees had taken root inside the deserted fort and were sprouting from its
towers, their green branches thrusting up through the intricate masonry
and ruined windows, sucking life from its decay, while ivy enveloped the
entire fortress, clinging to it tightly as if trying to hide all signs of death
within its green embrace. Larks had built their nests inside its disused
embrasures, and the clear air enveloped it as in a shroud of silence and
oblivion.

The ruin had plunged him into such deep and heartfelt sorrow that he no longer heard what his father was saying about the unforgettable past glories of the fortress, so often fought over by both Franks and Turks, and tears had come into his eyes. All that evening and the following day, and for many days thereafter, he had been unable to forget this melancholy scene, and his youthful imagination kept conjuring it before his eyes and making his mind race. Then little by little he saw the old fort emerging from the vegetation, which mysteriously fell away, and rising up in all its former glory, a huge bizarre structure standing there with no useful purpose above the azure mirror of the sea.

And now the memory of that awakening revived in him a dream of liberty and justice, the dream secretly worshipped by his father, the old admirer of the Carabinieri. He could still picture the rejuvenated Venetian fortress, but now it seemed heavy, massive, terrifying, at once a bastion and a prison. Its fixed cannon seemed to intimidate a subject people, the bond-slaves of his island... untold generations that had lived obscurely, watering with their sweat a land they did not own, a vast hoard of wretched souls incessantly tormented by their overbearing rulers.

Ignorance had led those sons of the soil into servile subjection and still held half the world in chains. A desire for liberty would never flourish in weak, ignoble, small-minded souls. And yet Alkis remembered how suddenly and for no apparent reason universal liberty had become imminent and pressing. In the chaos of recent times many shackles had already been thrown off, shackles forged by tyrants down through the ages. And now in the West a tempest of creative destruction had arisen, unpredictable new forces were awakening and in the terrifying gloom the Idea shone like a beacon. The alarming yet consoling impetus of these upheavals was now reaching his small island, which stood like a bridge between East and West. It too should now begin to stir. He imagined that he himself, the sickly lad who had wrestled all his life with death, was destined one day to sound the trump of insurrection, or with steadfast heart and indomitable courage to follow the liberator who would sound it.

The heady Idea had inspired such unshakable conviction in him that bringing it about actually seemed to him a relatively simple matter. How could any of the oppressed fail to respond enthusiastically to the new gospel of love? Would any of his childhood friends refuse to follow? Surely not the two sons of Ophiomachos? Surely not Petros Athanatos, that eccentric loner racking his brains trying to solve life's momentous issues? Surely not the wealthy Valsamis, who worshipped beauty and steeped himself in ancient poetry? Nor was the island short of venerable poets who could themselves extol the rebirth of liberty. How could their souls remain untouched by the honest work they would see before them?

They were all there this evening at the ball, the Ophiomachos brothers, Petros Athanatos and the sick Valsamis, dragging his tired body round among fit and healthy people. But who among them all would be prepared to forget about himself and the pursuit of life's trivial advantages to devote himself to a cause ruled exclusively by the Idea?

Then his eye fell on Eulalia, still sitting quietly beside her mother. The sight of her suddenly rekindled all his youthful hopes, made all his dreams appear more tangible. It was as if a fountain of life were again flowing from her beauty, a wellspring of immortal water which once before had wakened him with its refreshing coolness from the deep slumber of oblivion and death.

Was there anything the man could not achieve who was assured of her love, who would have her as his life's companion in happiness and sorrow?

As this thought crossed his mind, he again felt lonely, frail and insignificant among all these carefree people untroubled by anxiety. How could one ever hope to find a man among them endowed with the gigantic strength, heroic courage and prophetic gifts needed to begin the task ahead? And what if the Idea were merely an irrational craze, doomed to give rise to laughter and derision? Wasn't it obvious that dedicated comrades were not to be found among this light-hearted assembly? Oh, if such there were, he would be ready to overturn and trample on all obstacles, even resorting to extreme violence if necessary to drag society down the path of its historic destiny and liberate it from all this sterile barbarism! She too would be beside him! The incessant battle with death would give way to a new struggle which, together with his faith in victory, would grant him health and strength and fresh life-giving courage. No matter if the dream appeared irrational, if the means and reasons for imposing it were far from clear, results in life were always unpredictable: didn't the most considered human actions always have incalculable consequences totally at odds with what was intended, as if the world were indeed ruled by some mysterious providence that made use of human thought to fulfil its hidden plans?

Then suddenly the whole edifice his reason and imagination had concocted seemed tenuous and ill-founded, something the slightest hesitation would at once transform into a pile of rubble – destroyed by harsh realities. He himself was merely another of these ordinary people milling round him, indeed weaker, more unhealthy and inept, and if this were so his life had no purpose and he had no right to enjoy it.

He cast his eyes around the room again. Men and women were dancing, chatting and enjoying themselves without a care in the world. He was struck by their triviality and insignificance and deep down was convinced that his soul, for all its doubts and imperfections, was incomparably superior. He at least could see a distant light amid the chaos in which the others were adrift, unconsciously following their hereditary pursuits and thus collectively giving a rhythm to the society they created. And the people followed uncritically and blindly where they were led, down the inglorious path of submission, marked by slavery, privation and the harsh laws of necessity. How was it that from so many wills with no common objective, so many individuals united by no single idea, so much undisciplined commotion, it was nonetheless possible for a harmonious social order to emerge, such that it appeared immutable, as if its laws had been established by the mind of the Creator?

He noticed Doctor Steriotis, who had just approached the aristocrat turned minister again and was chatting away to him. The doctor's face was still radiant with the intoxication of success. His gaze swept the room triumphantly, as if he were looking for someone in the crowd, and lighted with a happy smile upon Eulalia, who however refused to look at him.

Alkis reflected with heartfelt bitterness that he was perhaps destined to sacrifice his love as well, vanquished in the social struggle by those who collectively drew up its laws. No special decrees would intervene on behalf of someone as insignificant as him, and he couldn't rise above the circumstances he had to face because he lacked the material means to do so, whereas others had more than enough at their disposal to secure their happiness.

He was still brooding over these matters when he became conscious that Marcantonio Iustinianis was again beside him, shaking him by the shoulder and shouting in his ear:

'How can you have your head in the clouds in times like these, in distressing times like these? This place still expects something of all the

younger generation, if it's not destined to go under. Why have you studied
all these subjects, why have you visited so many places of high culture,
why are you blessed with so many talents? Just so you can behave like all
the others, I suppose, and follow all the newfangled ideas and skuldug-
gery now current, while forgetting all about our history – the glorious
history of our island! Are you listening? This place is very dear to me,
dearer than my family, dearer than myself. And I'm deeply saddened
because I see men like myself dying out, I see the place degenerating by the
day, forgetful of all courtesy, and no one profits from all this except the
peasants, those enemies of virtue! This is the result of universal suffrage,
general conscription, mobilization, Great Ideas, false patriotism, and I
don't know what else assails my ears like cracked church bells. Everyone's
out to profit from the state of things: the politician flatters the wretched
peasantry to secure their vote, the merchant and industrialist are busy
getting rich, others are after medals and awards, and everyone looks out
for number one. And yet... and yet...'

He spoke as if in a rage, making grand gestures, fired by genuine feeling
and his insatiable appetite for oratory, fixing his listeners with his blood-
shot eyes. Now he had suddenly fallen silent and was waiting for somebody
to praise him, ready to refute any objections. But Alkis remained silent,
looking at him for a moment with some sympathy, and only the elderly
poet responded, lowering his eyes in annoyance at his last remark.

'No one can deny that the country's making progress, albeit at a slow
pace, but that's because the state is small and its responsibilities are heavy.'

Marcantonio Iustinianis laughed aloud, immediately getting hot under
the collar: 'Oh yes, oh yes,' he exclaimed with a dismissive gesture, 'fairy
tales to keep little children happy!'

'Nothing like a quarrel!' Petros Athanatos remarked sarcastically to
Giorgis Ophiomachos. 'But don't forget, Aimilia doesn't like to be kept
waiting.' Then reassured after glancing through the ballroom door, he
added: 'Ah, she's in good company, I see.'

Attracted by Marcantonio's shouts, the aristocrat turned minister had
entered the red anteroom, lighting an expensive cigarette, closely followed
by Arkoudis the banker and Periklis Valsamis, pale and emaciated in his
loose clothes, his hollow eyes and fleshless brow portending death.

'Social problems,' observed Valsamis smiling faintly, 'can neither be
created nor resolved by individual initiative. They arise of their own accord

and are resolved collectively through trial and error. Consequently, the only thing the individual can do is cultivate himself by means of learning and the arts. The problems of life and death are so many and so complex that even the longest human life barely gives one time to touch on them, let alone investigate them fully. But in studying them the soul achieves a measure of serenity. And we are in the greatest need of such serenity.'

He shook his head with the same sad smile.

Marcantonio Iustinianis glared at him and was on the point of replying, but suddenly he was so touched by the man's gaunt appearance that he merely shrugged his broad strong shoulders, glancing despairingly at Alkis, who noticed a tear behind the old eccentric's gold-rimmed spectacles.

Just then a flustered Spyros Ophiomachos appeared at the door, still searching for Asteris's ugly daughter, and greeted everyone with a quick smile, while Arkoudis the banker, smiling his most baleful smile and squinting hard, was saying in his whining voice:

'The only progress that can be made via legislative means is through economic prosperity. And the prudent policies of our distinguished fellow citizen, the minister, who has been at pains to encourage industrial development, both here and on the mainland, are especially laudable. Thanks to his efforts, the largest factory in the East is now thriving here today, and this does credit both to our island and to the genius of Mr Asteris, our generous host.'

He looked round, pleased with his pretty speech, and at once continued, resuming his sorrowful expression:

'Economic prosperity is civilization.'

'Who would deny that?' said Alkis, who suddenly felt the urge to speak. 'Economic prosperity may be civilization, yet equally, the economic affairs of a country prosper as it becomes more civilized. But is it ever possible for such cold material objectives to replace eternal faith, and does it help if the Idea loses momentum simply because initially its implementation is not easy, calls for sacrifices and may even appear conceptually irrational today?'

The aristocrat turned minister smiled knowingly to mask his irritation. It had immediately flashed through his mind that if word got about that he favoured a policy of sacrifice and even civil war, his popularity would plummet. And continuing to smile, he said with his usual air of indifference:

'A nation's sacrifices are of two kinds: sacrifices of blood and sacrifices of money. Who doubts the bravery of the Greek army? But for money to be sacrificed requires, or at least requires business confidence in, foreign markets. The policy of our party in no way undermines nationalist aspirations, it simply confines them to what is practicable and postpones their execution by a generation. I put it to you all, is it not achievement enough for our generation to accumulate wealth and bequeath to our immediate successors the economic means that will guarantee them military victories? At present, our country needs total peace.'

The elderly poet smiled approvingly and winked at him, as if to intimate that he perfectly understood the subtlety of his calculating tactics, then glanced down at his medal as if to remind himself of what was closest to his own heart.

The banker nodded his agreement, murmuring:

'Absolutely, if the country is to make economic progress, that is the only way.'

Suddenly Alkis felt the urgent conviction that he at least must protest against the interminable lies on the lips of those governing this indolent society, who were hastening its downfall merely to indulge their own petty cravings, callously indifferent to the fate of an entire community that trusted them like children. He felt his soul suddenly expanding, overcoming his natural shyness and his sickly constitution, which even at that moment was reminding him of his own frailty. His eyes shone and his face became serious and formal as he looked round at his friends, who watched him curiously at first and then with strange intensity, and he realized that in their souls these people were all seeking liberty and only needed confirmation of their thoughts and feelings to yield and follow him. And that same instant his whole being was flooded with preternatural light, he no longer felt that the coming days held any mystery, a host of quasi-prophetic assumptions deluged his mind, one following the other in ill-assorted haste, compelling his belief and generating an imaginary world that could only be tomorrow's reality, because events themselves would necessarily give birth to it.

He began addressing the room in a quiet voice, his eyes downcast:

'Our friend Marcantonio is doubtless prompted to speak out by his yearning for a higher civilization. And it is that which makes him look back on former times and become angry because he can't

fulfil his dream, not some self-serving motive unworthy of his age
and station.'

'Ah, gone are the days!... Gone are the days!...' shouted Marcantonio,
without being able to continue because by now he was quite tired.

'Why should we conceal the fact,' continued Alkis, 'that our native
land is backward and the burden of its ancestral heritage weighs heavily
upon it: ancient Greece, the light of which went out, then the obscure
Middle Ages which attempted to see a vision of its regeneration, not of
course one impossible to implement...'

The aristocrat turned minister grimaced with displeasure and glanced
towards the door, anxious to escape a futile discussion, but then noticing
that other gentlemen who had entered the red anteroom for a smoke were
listening attentively to Alkis, he decided he ought to stay and if necessary
defend his political agenda. For the moment he was content to smile with
wary benevolence, glancing at the elderly poet who winked and nodded
back, as if to intimate that he too had sung of the glory that was Greece.

Marcantonio Iustinianis again became so angry he couldn't say a
word: his face went red, the veins at his temples bulged and he shook a
menacing finger in the air.

Petros Athanatos stared at him and, laughing unpleasantly, shouted
in annoyance:

'The people are no longer fooled by all that stuff. Nationalist dreams
are all a fraud because the truth lies elsewhere! Where Karl Marx saw it
from in exile.'

And finally Periklis Valsamis, smiling sweetly as he recovered from a
bout of coughing, said:

'To the philosopher, past and present are one and the same. Himself
remote from the struggle, he examines them with the same detachment,
simply as phenomena of life.'

'But that's why,' Alkis promptly continued, 'error and superstition
in this country reign supreme. Science doesn't aim at truth, grammar
attempts to control art and state religion withers faith.'

'Oh!' exclaimed the aristocrat turned minister in alarm, while several
others looked one another in the eye.

'Our country however,' continued Alkis, 'cannot remain this backward
for ever, nor can it wait for things to unfold slowly and naturally, so the
awakening must be both short and swift. What's the use of people looking

back, dazzled by their irrational devotion to a tiny corner of our land, or out of hereditary pessimism remaining indifferent to everything, when the times are constraining us on all sides and demanding a united effort, a common task of great significance, a work of liberation? In times like these, when everywhere stormclouds are looming over a world grown old, how will this land be able to remain aloof? Small, impoverished, unruly and enslaved, our country is like some shapeless chaos where everything has yet to be created. Who will be the man to begin this creative task, even using extreme violence to lead the people, if necessary against their will, along the path of their deliverance?'

He was speaking with rapture and conviction, with a rhetorical forcefulness he didn't know he possessed, and he noticed that his words penetrated deep into the hearts of his audience, swaying their will, kindling ideas dormant in them, or making them flush with rage. Only the aristocrat turned minister looked at Alkis with a smile of feigned indifference, but even he didn't manage to conceal his perturbation.

'Greece,' Alkis continued, 'will soon be a military camp.'

'And the people will end up paying for these wars with their own blood, sweat and tears!' shouted Petros Athanatos, laughing his unpleasant laugh.

'War!' exclaimed the minister, smiling contemptuously, while the elderly poet also smiled and winked at him.

'There's no other way,' Alkis continued, 'there's no alternative to war and revolution!'

For a moment everyone remained silent, looking at one another as if a thunderbolt had struck there in the middle of the room; then everyone started talking at once, gesticulating, eyes bulging, forgetting where they were, most of them remonstrating against Alkis. Then someone burst out laughing. Suddenly the laughter became general, spreading infectiously round the room, clear, resounding, unconstrained. But the aristocrat turned minister, flushed with indignation, had by this time hurried off into the ballroom to avoid hearing any more, while amid the general laughter a voice could be heard shouting: 'We are a constitutional monarchy! The constitution makes no provision for a revolution!'

At last the tumult died down. Marcantonio Iustinianis had turned his back on Alkis and was again haranguing those close to him, cursing Greece, the French Revolution and the very idea of an insurrection, predicting famine and disaster for the island. Petros Athanatos was smiling sarcastically, while relishing the idea of a popular uprising that might perhaps take a different direction from that intended by its organizers. Periklis Valsamis was standing in a corner coughing and looking on compassionately at all these people whom words and ideas had the power to throw into such turmoil. The banker and the poet had followed the minister into the ballroom. Yet a few young people, among them Giorgis Ophiomachos, were actually clapping and shouting 'Yes! Yes!' with happy smiles on their faces. They were by now the only ones still standing around Alkis. There were about ten of them, all still very young, and a curious elation was visible in their innocent eyes, as if they were longing to become constructively involved.

Alkis was strangely moved, his lips trembled, a fine sweat stood out on his brow and shivers ran down his spine.

'A revolution,' he said to them quietly, 'which will purge the country, consign the old world to oblivion, and silence all opposition using salutary threats!'

'Yes! Yes!' replied his young admirers.

In his mind's eye, Alkis could see clearly that the revolution he was proclaiming here tonight was already under way and would swiftly overcome all opposition. This was apparent from the general dissatisfaction, from the widespread apathy and disillusionment, and from the hopes of those who looked nostalgically back to bygone eras, or expected some futile intervention from abroad. All it would take was a few bold high-minded workers, in whose hearts denial would be replaced by faith, despondency by hope, sorrow by zealous inspiration, and once they set off as apostles of an Idea and emissaries of a religion they would undoubtedly succeed in transmitting the flame of their enthusiasm to other hearts, everyone would unite in a single sustained effort and without too many problems the revolution would finally succeed, ushering in a new era and opening the way for a new civilization.

'Who will be our leader?' Alkis went on in a quiet thoughtful voice.

'You! You!' shouted everybody rapturously.

'No, no!' he replied in great alarm and his face went pale. 'I'm just an aspiring writer!'

Stunned, he stepped back a pace, his mind in turmoil. He was obviously not the man to set such a massive enterprise in motion, to take on such a huge responsibility, to see through a course of action that was so onerous it would inevitably crush him. He could only be a follower devoting his modest talents to the immense task, a faithful but insignificant worker in the cause of a Great Idea.

'You! You!' they again cried jubilantly.

He thought about his poor health and the years that had been one long struggle against death, he remembered his passion for Eulalia and the misery it had caused him, and he reflected on the unjust power of wealth, and he realized that each day he was losing a little of himself and a little of his happiness.

'No, no!' he repeated, still frightened.

Turning his head towards the ballroom, he exchanged glances with Eulalia, who was showing signs of impatience. He hurried through the door. His ears were buzzing and his head spinning as the young people tried to detain him, stretching out their arms and shouting:

'You! You!'

When he entered the ballroom, all eyes turned and stared at him and he realized that everyone was talking excitedly about him. The aristocrat turned minister was standing to one side, still talking animatedly with Arkoudis the banker and gesturing oddly. They were soon joined by Doctor Steriotis, the banker Chrysospathis and the handsome old man in royal livery, and together they set about denouncing all revolutionary ideas, all movements that might disrupt law and order.

Further along, seated under Dürer's *Christ* and surrounded by a bevy of ladies, Mrs Chrysospathis herself was in a flap, as if the revolution had already erupted on the streets and the royal statutes were in danger, which she considered the ultimate guarantee of social order, because as she said she was like a sister to some queen. Among her entourage was Mrs Aimilia Valsamis, impatiently toying with her fan and mulling over the harsh words she would shortly blast her lover with, since he had chosen to listen to Alkis's nonsense all this time instead of keeping her company. Count Alexandros Ophiomachos himself was sitting sadly and silently beside his wife, trying not to listen to Marcantonio Iustinianis, who was standing before him flushed with anger, denouncing the folly of all radical utopian ideas and waxing eloquent about the ancient glories of the land.

Meanwhile the music continued and several couples were dancing a quickstep, while Spyros Ophiomachos, all alone in the crowd, watched incredulously as Asteris's ugly daughter surrendered blissfully to the arms of Mrs Chrysospathis's nephew, recently recalled from abroad, for that very evening word had got out that they were to become engaged.

And Alkis, still elated, moved and worried after his speech, hastened towards Eulalia, asking himself whether in his heart he really believed everything he had said this evening would one day come to pass.

He had reached the Ophiomachoses by now. Eulalia, looking pale, gazed at him with her eager smile and a wave of happiness surged through his heart. His eyes shone and his cheeks flushed red. He greeted everyone courteously and remained standing in front of Eulalia. A comforting serenity came over him, like that of the sailor who casts anchor in a sheltered port. He wondered what to say but could think of nothing and so continued to gaze into Eulalia's eyes. Suddenly the depressing thought flashed through his mind that Eulalia was not destined to be his, and that another, Doctor Steriotis, would soon be claiming her. The very idea was utterly abhorrent.

'Alkis,' said the elderly Countess with a vaguely hopeful smile, 'the good minister was telling us earlier that he'd be delighted to see you in a government position. We will be very happy for you!'

Alkis smiled without replying. Then extending his hands and nodding to Eulalia, he invited her to dance.

In an instant she was in his arms. And together they flung off into the dance, rapturously surrendering to the rhythm of the music, turning gracefully as if on wings, feeling gloriously free at last, like birds first leaving the nest, as if a new life were opening up before them.

'Alkis,' whispered Eulalia, faint with her first taste of bliss.

'You *shall* be mine!' he replied, squeezing her waist a little.

As in a dream she thought about her father, her home, Doctor Steriotis, the terrible disaster looming over them, and was conscious of tears welling in her eyes. On she danced, now clasping Alkis's hand more firmly, as if seeking his protection, while he kept tightening his grip around her waist, as if to prevent her from escaping. His heart was pounding and her body trembled in his arms, her bosom swelling with tender feelings new to her. He felt a deep ecstatic joy pervading his soul. His whole being seemed to be expanding. With her beside him he felt he was cured of all his ailments and at last breathing fresh invigorating air, giving him new strength, free will and energy, he now believed that everything which without her support had seemed impossible and only moments ago had frightened him, everything which his young listeners had urged him to take on and would become the great venture of his life, was suddenly no longer either a pipedream or a burden so onerous it was bound to break him. With the same guileless joy he saw all the most significant moments of his life before him: his father on that lonely shore showing him the old Venetian fort, his latest illness and resurrection from the dead, his passion for Eulalia, and now this evening's events that had shaken him so deeply. The value that his life was now acquiring made him careless of all consequences. Eulalia must be his, everything else was meaningless, contemptible, indifferent. Only then would he be able to set to work.

Suddenly he became conscious that the music was about to end. He again squeezed Eulalia's waist and, watching her out of the corner of his eye, said passionately:

'You *shall* be mine!'

She sighed shyly, her breast overflowing with indescribable happiness, and as if surrendering to his arms forever she smiled and, lowering her tearful eyes, declared: 'Yes, yes, whenever you wish... however you wish...'

PART TWO

I

I T WAS STILL EARLY. That day Alexandros Ophiomachos Philaretos, thin, elderly and stooping, wrapped in the ancient overcoat he always wore about the house in winter, restlessly went down to his study once again. His mind was troubled. Reality seemed to have become a nightmare, a burden so colossal his emaciated old body was bowed down by it.

He had never before imagined that life could take such a tragic turn, so suddenly departing from its normal rhythms. He considered that fate was dealing harshly with him, because he had reached the latter part of life without ever suspecting that such moments might await him. The old man had never truly understood the world, he had not wished to understand it as it really was. And so far he had overcome its difficulties with a minimum of effort. But now the problems looming up ahead seemed like an impassable mountain, a huge immovable obstacle that frightened him and sapped what little will he had, so that again today, after so many deliberations and prevarications, he hadn't made the slightest progress. His daughter wouldn't consent to marry Doctor Steriotis, Periklis Valsamis was not about to make a timely exit from this world, so far his son Spyros had had no success with the ugly daughter of Asteris, and even Goulielmos Arkoudis, the banker's son, did not seem in the least enamoured of his daughter Louisa, despite his wife's opinion to the contrary.

The present situation was truly alarming. It gave them no time at all. There was no money, the house in the country he was fond of had gone to rack and ruin, his horses were dying, every blessed thing was going wrong. Soon Doctor Steriotis would begin to get tired of being put off. Eulalia though aware of all these misfortunes was inexplicably obstinate about submitting to necessity. She refused to listen to him. She seemed insensitive to the effect her obstinacy was having. And their needs were becoming pressing!

Involuntarily he thought of his two long-standing mistresses. He still kept both of them. They were both a bit past it and inclined to whinge, but he hadn't had the courage to get rid of them. He had been neglecting them of late and saw them only briefly now and then because they too were getting troublesome. Indeed the old man was afraid of them! He was afraid of their incessant cursing and bad temper. They had sensed he had fallen on hard times and were becoming more demanding by the day, almost as if they were in league, even though they weren't acquainted, lived in separate neighbourhoods and hated one another. Each wanted to be the one to salvage the last remnants from the shipwreck. Both condemned him in the harshest terms, cursing him angrily because, they said, they could now see themselves dying in the gutter, and they hadn't sacrificed their honour and wasted their lives on an old man just for that. They had put their trust in a wealthy man precisely to escape the opprobrium that now inevitably awaited them. Had he, Ophiomachos, had any qualms of conscience while he was well off? Why hadn't he secured their future then, as he could so easily have done? He should now give them a house, or a bit of land if he hadn't any money. Yet everybody knew they were lending to the poor at a usurious rate – money they owed entirely to his generosity.

The anxiety now choking him brought his peasants to mind as usual. They were the ones who had ruined him by never paying up. He suddenly became furious with them. They would have his blood on their hands... he had been far too lenient. They were consuming his entire revenue, everything that his land, his ancestral farms produced. They had become his father's true inheritors, they alone! Unjust laws protected them. But he must go after them with every means at his disposal, some of them at least, and make an example of them. As soon as a bit of money came his way, he'd show them! Even though the law courts were so cripplingly expensive!

Meanwhile, for something to do he took down a large ledger from a shelf, as if intending to start preparing his case against them straight away, and putting it on the table he sat down and started leafing through it.

He pored over the names, making calculations on his fingers and jotting down numbers on a piece of paper. He knew all these people – some he had known since his childhood, others he had seen being born and growing up, others still had grown old with him. He knew the history, family and circumstances of every one of them. Some he was on friendly terms with, considering them honest loyal vassals, many he had done favours for and socialized with, or helped in times of need, and there wasn't one among them that he hated. These peasants owed him an absolute fortune, the very shirts on their backs, and according to this ledger the richest of them appeared to be the least reliable. If only he could collect half of what was owing to him, or even a quarter, he'd be saved! But who was going to square all those accounts for him, who would prepare so many cases, how could he unravel so many entanglements? He himself had never done a serious day's work in his life. Old contracts, judicial verdicts, certificates of baptism and wills would have to be located and transcribed, the mortgages and ledger entries would have to be brought up to date – a whole host of tasks he had never bothered with because he had been content simply to accept what the peasants had brought him, and he had never in his life found the courage to treat anybody harshly, except when he got angry. But even his anger never lasted very long. And now he realized that most of the debts he was counting on would have to be written off, as many wasted years had passed since they had lapsed.

Here, as often happened, old Ophiomachos became angry with himself. He got up, violently pushing his chair back, and began cursing himself: 'Alexandros, you old fool,' he said, 'you unmitigated scoundrel. I should pluck your eyes out, I should have you put down, you old dog! Look at the mess you've made of things! How could you do it, letting your fortune go down the drain like this? Why didn't you have your wits about you all those years?'

He started pacing angrily up and down the spacious room, cursing his own kind-heartedness, his indolent life, his hereditary negligence, the physical weakness that prevented him from working hard and being efficient like others whom he envied, for instance his present confounded creditors who were charging him a fortune. What was he to do? The pages in his ledger going back many years were blank, his two hundred or so retainers had been defaulting and he hadn't said a word. And now his creditors were at his heels, harassing him, intimidating him, demanding that he sell his daughters to avoid sullying the family honour and his aristocratic name.

These reflections made him laugh sarcastically. Occasionally he would stop and gaze at the ceiling, as if to ask the heavens what had become of divine justice. For he really did consider all the torments that were dogging him unjust, after a life of forbearance and charity towards so many humble people whom, had he so wished, he could once have ruined himself. Where was the justice in all that?

He was overwhelmed with despair. His mouth felt dry and acrid, his chest was so tense he had difficulty in breathing and his whole body kept on shivering. He went to the window and stared through the dingy panes for a moment at the street, returned to his desk and again stood still, racking his brains for some inspired idea that might help him, looked down at the street again through the other window, and the whole time he could feel his agitation mounting. Of course he couldn't simply sit there passively and do nothing at a time like this. Then he took down several thick bundles from the shelves, each carefully secured between thick boards covered with dust and full of old contracts, case histories and other legal documents. He shook the dust off, sighing and looking away, then untied them one by one and started examining the papers, cursing the names of the deceased he found in them.

The work, however, quickly tired him. With trepidation he realized how pointless it all was, since current necessities of course were hardly going to wait. Where was he to find the capital to start proceedings? Where? And even if he did, the courts would take months, years to reach their verdict – at the rate they were operating these days. And assuming a favourable verdict were finally arrived at, it would remain unenforced like so many others on his hands, a mere piece of paper no peasant would ever be afraid of. So he folded his arms and sat motionless for an hour, staring at the plastered beams in the smoke-stained ceiling. His heart wept.

So what should he do? He had to do something, make a move, find something he could do to try to save himself. Why were his children not helping now, why had his wife become so silent lately? Had everyone forsaken him? Everyone?

He tapped his foot on the floor nervously for several minutes from sheer worry, then drummed his fingers on the wooden armrest of his chair, a wry expression on his mouth as if he were feeling pain in some

vital organ. Then quite suddenly, indignant at his family, who were uncon-
cerned because they never thought of anyone except themselves, while
he was going through agonies embroiled in all these hopeless matters, he
decided not to bother about anything but just relax and forget about it
all. He would never receive the money-lender again, ever, and his affairs
could take care of themselves, never mind where they might end up. They
could go to hell for all he cared! One way or another, there was nothing
he could do about it.

But almost immediately he felt dissatisfied with this decision. It was
no solution but a knee-jerk reaction which would have precisely the
consequences he wanted to avoid. But how to avoid them, how?

His worries returned, preoccupying him completely, making him turn
his head this way and that distractedly. But how? But how? He could find
no peace, he no longer knew himself what he wanted and he couldn't
get his troubles off his mind, they would not let him rest. How could he
sit back with such a disaster hanging over him? And as for Eulalia, she
couldn't care less! Unbelievable! Unheard of! She must make the first
move. There was no other solution. None!

Without being conscious of what he was doing, he struck his head hard
with both his fists. It hurt. And it occurred to him that at such moments his
body should feel pain, since his soul was in such distress, wallowing in such
black despair. He dug his nails into his palms, held his breath, tried to gash
his thigh and hit his head with his fist again. Better death than the disgrace
awaiting him! No, he was not going to wait around for that! No fear!

Suddenly he stood up, violently pushing his chair back. An idea he
could scarcely acknowledge to himself had just flashed through his confused brain. Without being fully conscious of what he was doing, he took
off his ancient overcoat, put on his frayed frock-coat, seized his hat and
descended to the street. He was pale, tired and out of breath. He felt cold.

His steps brought him to the broad tree-lined square. He exchanged
greetings with one or two acquaintances out strolling at that hour in the
still wintry light, but he could not shake off his restlessness. He couldn't
bring himself to stop and chat with people, the way he had always done
almost daily since his youth. His feet seemed to guide him of their own
accord. He followed the wide street that descended all the way to the
sea, looking at the familiar shops and acknowledging the shopkeepers
as they greeted him with deference. It was the street that Alkis's house

was on. That was where he was heading, where he was being driven by his desperation. He had to talk to him! He would tell him he must give Eulalia up, explain all his troubles to him, insist that he relinquish her and save her family from disaster through his sacrifice. That was what he'd say. He'd lay his cards on the table, yes, he'd find courage enough for that at least. Even if it meant admitting he wasn't master in his own house. No need to feel ashamed. He wouldn't even be ashamed of admitting he knew his daughter favoured Alkis. Hard times had turned everything upside down. And besides, young girls these days found the man they would marry for themselves.

Just then he ran into his two sons, who were out for a stroll together in their fashionable clothes and stopped him. Giorgis, noticing his pained expression, asked him anxiously what the matter was. The old man responded with a bitter smile that conceded he was in deep trouble, and looked the young men in the eye as if asking them for hope and consolation. But he realized that they had decided to remain aloof from what was happening at home. And with a wry expression he asked Giorgis:

'How is her husband today?' He smiled unpleasantly.

'I don't know,' Giorgis answered irritably, 'but nobody should expect anything from that quarter.'

'I see!' his father said, his eyes widening. 'I was angry with you at first,' he went on. 'I didn't like the whole affair and I didn't like that woman, but as things turned out the way they did, I told myself that at least you would be safe!' Then suddenly, as if something else had occurred to him, he looked Giorgis thoughtfully in the eye, then stared at his feet and said with a curious smile: 'Who knows! Perhaps you're doing the right thing, my boy. Who's to say otherwise?'

At this Spyros laughed derisively. He glanced about uneasily. His baby face had a peculiar look today, because his heart, unaccustomed to feeling anything at all, was suffering bitterly. And pain was something he found quite intolerable, something he would make any sacrifice to avoid. Just then his narrow soul condemned his brother for despising so much happiness, the tranquillity of a rich life free of care, while he himself was suffering as he watched the shattering of the dream that he had pinned his hopes on and worked for all this time!

Giorgis looked at him, sympathizing with his distress, and remarked to their father:

'Spyros is going through a rough patch too today. We just saw Asteris's daughter in a motor car, driving out into the country with her mother and that young nephew of Mrs Chrysospathis's – she's summoned him from abroad after prearranging the marriage.'

'I see, I see,' said the old man stupidly, looking from one son to the other. So fate had decreed the destruction of all their hopes in a single day!

Fearfully he wondered whether destiny might not have some further calamity in store for him, amid the general shipwreck now changing all the circumstances of their lives.

He didn't say another word, and without further reflection turned his back on the two of them and made off in the direction of Alkis's house, resolutely going straight in through the door.

Mother and son were sitting together in the same room. Photini was by the window silently bending over her work, her large spectacles on her nose; Alkis was thoughtfully leafing through a book. Both looked up at Ophiomachos with genuine pleasure and Photini smilingly proceeded to enquire after his health and that of his wife and children.

The old man, who had entered the house determined to speak out, now suddenly found himself defenceless faced with the friendly smiles of Alkis and his mother. He seemed to have forgotten all the arguments he had come prepared with, and the ideas that entered his mind were confused and incoherent. He stared stupidly now at Photini, now at her son, responding mechanically with his natural courtesy, yet ill at ease and in evident distress. He looked around at the clean, simply furnished room, the brightly coloured curtains, the little pictures adorning the greenish walls, the large desk, the handsomely bound books in the new bookcase, and tried to recover his initial resolve, though he knew he would now not even dare mention his daughter's name. He sat anxiously fidgeting with his clothes, embarrassed at being there at all, looking for an excuse to leave again without doing anything, his conscience telling him that what he had contemplated was just not done, and that if he must impose his paternal authority it should not be at the expense of those who had done him no harm. It would be a different matter of course if Alkis were to make the first move and ask him, or write to ask him, for Eulalia's hand. Oh, then he'd have no difficulty in responding... But in the present situation what could he say?

Meanwhile Photini, carefully putting away her spectacles, was saying politely with a sweet smile:

'How could I forget such kindness during our terrible ordeal! Eulalia raised him from the tomb!'

Alkis laughed. The old man sighed dejectedly. A despicable idea that had been preoccupying him involuntarily flashed through his mind. He dismissed it with a shudder and looked about nervously, fearful that the others might have read it on his blushing brow, and in his agitation he thought for a moment he might actually find the strength to speak. But not a word passed his lips. A timid smile was his only reply. He became angry with himself, remembering how often that strange timidity – which made him irascible and rude as the only release when he was tongue-tied – had caused him to forgo his rights or appear inferior in the company of others. Even today, the same fault dogged him everywhere he went, and it would be with him till the day he died.

Meanwhile Photini continued:

'Who would have said so then! And now our children have even danced together. Ah, everyone enjoyed themselves so much at the Asterises' ball! What a splendid mansion... How hospitable those people are...'

Suddenly Ophiomachos scowled at the floor, then looked wildly about the room and, as if freeing himself from a heavy burden, blurted out:

'That's the reason I've come.'

And just for a fleeting moment his restless gaze rested upon Alkis.

'What's the matter?' the young man asked him gently, conscious that his heart was pounding.

'What's the matter!' echoed Ophiomachos in the same agitated voice, shaking his head. 'What's the matter! Alas! I must speak out, but I don't know how to because something inside me makes the words stick in my throat. They only get so far and I have to swallow them again. I've always been like that... a miserable coward! But even so I must speak out, I know. Because there's no other solution. None at all. And don't imagine I'm not master in my own house, quite the contrary! I'm the one who gives orders there, I've always done exactly as I please, no one dares oppose me. I could see it again in the present situation, my word is all that counts – you do believe me, don't you? But why am I telling you all this? Why can't I say what I came to say and have done with it. I don't know what's wrong with me. But you see, I'm being obliged to respond to something I wasn't asked, to say something on which my opinion wasn't sought. Yes, Alkis. I know, I know everything! Back to the day you claim she raised you from the dead like Lazarus, yes, I know everything. And that's what I've come about, that's precisely the issue. Oh, leave her alone, Alkis. She only gets more tearful and depressed – ever since the ball it's been the same old story. And when she weeps I get angry and become obnoxious and tyrannize the entire household. And then I feel a pang here in my chest, just as I do talking to you now – right here, deep down in my heart! Yes, just as I do now, because you've no idea how much it hurts, really hurts me to see her suffering and making her own life a misery, and not be able to oblige her, simply not be able to. Yes, that's the real reason I've come. And now, Alkis, I am suffering because I know I'm going to upset her yet again. Yes, I tell you, I know everything, everything! But it's not to be... it simply can't be done. Hear me out a moment, then you can have your say. You can tell me anything you want to. But be patient just a moment, or I'll become tongue-tied again. Just one more minute. It simply can't be done, that's the real reason. And as I say this, I feel that same sharp pain again inside me. Yes, I know, I know, she'd have been happy with you, here in your lovely little home alongside your mother. And I'd have been happy seeing you both and blessing you as my children every minute of each day. Ah, why did such a good thing have to end like this? You too would have been happy, Alkis, because my Eulalia has a heart of gold, pure gold! And she has a great capacity for love, she's the best of our four children. Take my word for it! And you too are a good person, Alkis, I know that, just like her. But what can I do? Don't ask me any more. It's not to be, I tell you... that's the real reason.'

He took out his handkerchief and dabbed his eyes.

Photini, now very pale, was looking at him sadly and uneasily. She was afraid the old man might have lost his wits. Alkis was impatiently waiting to speak to him, he too had gone pale and his soul was in turmoil, since the old man seemed intent on extinguishing his fondest hopes – assuming that was indeed the point of all his rambling. He suddenly felt utterly dejected. The world as his erotic passion had created it was being shaken to its very foundations. He reflected that he would have to start the struggle with life afresh and he felt tired and weak.

The old man had stopped talking, as if expecting his reply already, and he kept looking at him uneasily, his face very red, occasionally casting a plaintive glance at Photini, as if begging her forgiveness.

'But how come? How come?' Alkis asked him.

The old man didn't give him a chance to go on and replied impetuously:

'That's what I came to explain to you... precisely that... and to your worthy mother. Leave the hapless girl alone while things are still just beginning, let her go, I tell you, otherwise all of us are doomed!'

'But why? Why?' Alkis asked in a hurt voice, leaving his chair and going over to the window.

Outside, life was following its normal rhythms. In the small café people were gossiping as usual. A bird was singing on a branch of the lilac tree, already anticipating spring, a coachman was flogging and shouting at his horse. And with bitter melancholy Alkis reflected on creation's indifference to the suffering and death of the individual. He might be in pain and unable to sleep, his thoughts might be dark and bitter, but in what way did that alter the overall harmony around him? Nature would always answer with her silence, or with the merry laughter of life that never ceased regenerating.

'Why?' asked his mother too, shaking her head.

The old man looked at them fearfully and his lip began to quiver.

'Mr Ophiomachos,' Alkis said, approaching him respectfully, 'perhaps I was wrong not to have asked you for her hand earlier, but I swear to you, that was always my intention. I'd like to do so formally here and now. Agreed, mother?'

Photini wiped away a tear and smilingly took her son's hand.

'But that's just what can't be done!' exclaimed the old man in distress. 'That's the one thing that can't be done, that's all I came round here to tell you. No, Alkis, you're not going to insist! You wouldn't want me, her father, to go under surely! Isn't that so? How can I explain everything to you? I feel so embarrassed, when I try to talk about it my mouth won't open, my throat tightens, my shoulders tense up and I hang my head in shame, I blush even thinking about it all when I'm alone. How can I go into it with strangers? Anyway, that's the situation, what more can I say? You wouldn't want us to be ruined, would you, Alkis, isn't that so? Eulalia, ah, my sweet Eulalia, she is very fond of you too, you know how much! She'll do anything you ask! But you're not going to ask for what you just said, which would have pleased me too, which all of us would have wanted. You're not going to ask, for the sake of all the rest of us, for an old man's sake. You'll be able to find another girl, anyone you choose... I'm asking a sacrifice of you as well!'

He fell silent, by now quite out of breath. His eyes glazed over, his face went pale and his thick lips trembled uncontrollably. His fingers kept fidgeting with his clothes and he frequently adjusted his old frock-coat as if feeling the cold.

Alkis's face darkened. What sort of sacrifice was this the old man was asking of him?

A sacrifice it was not in his power to make, a sacrifice of his whole being, of everything most deeply rooted and unique about him, everything that for him made up the world, his identity, his faith. A sacrifice that while he lived was simply never going to happen, one of those that no one ever makes. He looked with bitter curiosity at the pitiful old man who was silently and nervously awaiting his reply, his gaze fixed on the ground, his knees opening and closing rhythmically.

A thousand ideas passed through Alkis's mind, and he kept wondering what lay behind Ophiomachos's gloomy remarks. What was the old man trying to conceal in all that verbiage? And what in fact was the real obstacle that frightened him so much?

'But why?' he again asked the old man ardently, glancing at his mother. 'Is it that I'm not worthy of Eulalia? As long as I live I swear I will look after her, her happiness will be my own! I can't imagine it any other way.'

'Besides,' said Photini with a sigh, 'why should a promising young life be shipwrecked, just as it is being launched with Fortune's smiles! Alkis isn't rich, I know, but he is educated. Isn't that a form of wealth? And what do all your titles, wealth and high society amount to, compared with love? People don't give a fig about such things when they're in love.'

Alkis gave his mother an appreciative look. Because she loved him, she was defending something precious they were trying to take away from him, something he feared might slip from his grasp through no fault of his own, simply because blind fate had ruled against him. And for an instant he thought with alarm of Eulalia's feminine weakness and soft-heartedness: perhaps she would not be able to hold out until the end and he would lose her!

His pale face took on an agonized expression at that moment, which didn't escape the anxious gaze of Photini. She too was deeply moved and concerned for her son's health. Ophiomachos meanwhile remained silent, his forehead resting on his hand, and gazing about and sighing sadly, as if his conscience were tormenting him over what he had just done. Twice he raised his head and exclaimed: 'No, no!' and not another word.

But now the mother was talking anxiously again.

'Ever since that evening,' she was saying, 'the evening she revived him, I could see that it would end like this. We could all see it, I suspect! Alkis was her destiny. And since she loves him too, why shouldn't she have him? I know what Alkis wants out of life, and that's why he deserves to have the best of girls.'

'Life...' said Alkis sadly, lowering his eyes and again going over to the window.

Life, he reflected, that was the great mystery, that was what man sought to conquer. A mystery full of suffering it constantly strove to cover up, a will that would not consent to annihilation, something eternal and immortal within a realm of chaos, of interminable random strife, a system plucked, as it were, from universal anarchy.

Meanwhile after a pause Photini continued:

'As his ageing mother, I want to see him settled with someone who will cherish him as much as I do. I've met Eulalia, and I've got to know her. All we are waiting for is your consent, Mr Ophiomachos. Just your consent!'

'No!' the old man repeated sadly. But now at last he felt the need to explain, to reveal his family's secrets, as if duty-bound to abase himself before these good-natured people. His perturbation gave him courage, and he started rambling on confusedly, painting the gloomiest picture of his desperate finances, his imminent ruin and the fatefulness of this dark hour. He could see no possibility of help from anywhere. No one cared about him any more. His sons, his wife, Louisa, all gave him black looks, and who could blame them. Only Eulalia, his poor Eulalia, was different. Even his death would not make any difference to the situation. Except that his daughters would end up on the street and his aged wife have no protection.

So the only salvation in sight was still Steriotis the doctor, provided Eulalia didn't obstinately continue to refuse him. That was the reason he had come, that was why he was asking this of Alkis, that was the only reason he could not consent. Nor should he insist, women hadn't simply vanished from the earth, either on the island or elsewhere. Just so long as he released the unfortunate Eulalia, since then of course she would realize that her duty was to make this sacrifice, however harsh, however much she was bound to suffer!

While the old man was speaking, Alkis's feelings were in turmoil. Such were the social conditions of the island and his times, organized, regulated and protected by so many laws and statutes, upheld in all their manifold tyranny by the unconscious will of an oppressed submissive people. There were three men in that family, yet the only solution to their problems they could find was the inhuman sacrifice of Eulalia, all three of them being condemned by their ignoble class prejudices to the idle insipid life that was their undoing. According to the old man, Alkis himself ought to yield to prevent the Ophiomachos family being dislodged from its hereditary position in society! The crazy old fool imagined that Alkis too respected all that nonsense – he who proclaimed and ardently desired revolution, liberty, independence and a dignified existence for all human beings – and asked no less of him than the sacrifice of Eulalia and his whole life's purpose. But that sacrifice he had neither the power nor the least desire to make. And now, hearing the name of the man who with his wealth was conspiring to undermine his happiness, he cried out:

'Doctor Steriotis? But he's no longer young! He's certainly not going to make Eulalia happy!'

Worn out by all his talk, Ophiomachos did not reply, merely shaking his head sadly, as if to tell Alkis that it wasn't a question of love and happiness but of sacrifice. Eulalia was no more than an innocent victim, because wealth could trample on the rights of love and had the power to stand opposed to all human feelings until they withered.

For a few moments all three of them remained silent. And then in a humble voice, with eyes downcast, the old man began again. Pleading and complaining, he went over the same ground again in different words. Alkis was overwhelmed with anguish and impatience. His countenance grew ever darker and a cold sweat drenched his palms. He would never accept this sentence! And with his soul in turmoil he again vividly recalled his father on the lonely shore by the old Venetian fort, that first awakening to a higher spiritual life, then later his miraculous resurrection from the dead, and finally that inspired and joyous moment which had revealed

to him his own rare spiritual strength, restored his confidence in himself
and his fellow human beings, and made him yearn for deliverance through
struggle in a constructive common cause.

His assurance of Eulalia's love had made him believe in victory.

But now, how could he renounce all this as well as his beloved? How
would he survive as a fractured soul unfit for action, a sickly fellow thrust
aside with no right to life or happiness, an unbalanced mind that for a
brief moment had conceived an impracticable dream?

Again no one spoke for a few moments. His mother looked at him
sadly and attentively. Ophiomachos was impatiently awaiting his reply,
though his soul felt easier now that he had expended all his energy. Now
Alkis was standing in front of him, and told him resolutely:

'No! I refuse to sacrifice her!' And he looked down contemptuously at
this pitiful old man whom such petty concerns were driving to distraction.

Photini came over and stood beside her son. She placed her hand on
his shoulder anxiously, concerned about what effect such intense emotion might have on his weak heart, and gazed pleadingly at the old man.

Ophiomachos was trembling, and looked pale despite his naturally
ruddy complexion. With downcast eyes, he adjusted his old frock-coat
and tried to pull himself together. He was overwhelmed with shame. In
the depths of his soul his conscience condemned him, telling him that he
himself was responsible for his calamity and that Alkis was quite right to
insist. And once again he found himself completely tongue-tied. He felt
his life might come to an end there in the armchair he had been sitting
in for some time. But he forced himself to get up and, hanging his head,
made for the door, murmuring an awkward farewell and sighing as he left.

'He won't let her go, he won't let her go!...' mother and son could hear
him muttering confusedly.

When he had finally gone, Alkis said to his mother:

'I'm afraid... Eulalia won't be able to withstand the pressure.'

'Life, Alkis, is never like it is in fairy tales,' she replied with a sad smile.
'All the Ophiomachoses are expecting Eulalia to save them. It's a great
pity, but what can she do?...'

She caressed his shoulder affectionately again. She had no one else
to love besides her son, and she saw life as it was, drawing the strength to
cope with adversity from within herself.

'Leave me alone, mother,' Alkis replied, utterly dejected.

'Do you think I can forget such an unpleasant scene? I don't want you to get sick again.'

Alkis looked at her tenderly and again went over to the window. In the little café people were gossiping and enjoying themselves as usual, a coach was going by, a bird was singing on a branch already anticipating spring. Even at a time like this everything was full of life and the indifferent rhythm of creation had not paused even for a moment.

2

As soon as Ophiomachos reached the street he raised his hand to shield his eyes and looked at the sky. He felt his mind was giving way. His conscience weighed heavily upon him: Alkis's words rang in his ears and he could still see Photini's sorrowful expression.

He was now walking with eyes downcast along a narrow street. He was oblivious to the passers-by, many of whom greeted him, and his anxiety was rising steadily because he had no idea what to do. All he knew was that Eulalia would not see reason, and it was now clear that Alkis too would oppose his plans and eventually find a way to attain his goal. It was all too easy for them to deceive a frail old man like himself, especially as Eulalia would be abetted by her mother. That confounded mother of hers, ever ready to oppose his wishes and support her children's rebelliousness! She had spoiled them so much from the beginning that his house had now become ungovernable. They and they alone were to blame for the catastrophe.

But the voice of conscience deep within reproached him for this last thought, and he tried in vain to persuade himself that it was just.

Meanwhile he proceeded on down the narrow street and without his being aware of it his steps led him to Doctor Steriotis's house. He raised his eyes and gazed attentively at the handsome villa with its cheerful façade, its splendid, well-trimmed trees, its marble steps and iron palings, and realized instinct had led him there to make one last desperate attempt.

Doctor Steriotis – alas! – held their fate in his hands, he could toy with them all as he saw fit. But sometimes the people who show the most forbearance are those one might least expect it from. After all, Steriotis was a human being and a man of education; so what if he was Demos's son, that didn't mean a thing! On the contrary, he was quite capable of being carried away by a generous impulse, indeed if he loved Eulalia he might even withdraw his suit and still not leave them in the lurch.

Such were his baselessly optimistic thoughts as he knocked on the door. The doctor however was not at home. Momentarily the old man felt relieved at this mischance, reflecting that at least for today he would now be spared some very awkward moments. But then on impulse he decided he would wait. The doctor would not be long, as it was already past midday. Or so he was informed by a smartly dressed maid, who ushered him into the airy study and bade him take a seat in one of the comfortable leather armchairs.

Now Ophiomachos looked admiringly around the room with its plush new furnishings – the ornate desk, the thick-piled carpet, the books with gilt-tooling in their handsome slipcases, the wall pictures in their expensive frames, the fine lamp suspended from the lofty ceiling, the numerous objects dotted about which all attested to the doctor's affluence – and he compared the opulence before him to his own bleak study with its antiquated furniture exuding the odour of decay.

How many young ladies, he reflected, would consider Eulalia lucky, how many would envy her and begrudge her her good fortune! What could such a place fail to provide to make her happy? Where could she be better off? And didn't Hadrinos the money-lender have a point when he assured him the doctor's wealth, education and present social status more than compensated for his vulgar origins? Eulalia was doing herself a disservice, that much was obvious to him as her father, but she was not to blame, she had simply lost her head.

The old man went on ruminating thus and before long the doctor returned. He came into his study with a smile, swinging his hips in the curious way he had, and greeted his visitor with easy courtesy, concealing the fact that he had not been expecting him. He sat down at once in the round-backed chair behind the heavy desk, rubbing his bald patch, offered Ophiomachos an expensive cigarette and started making small talk, scrutinizing his guest with his languid gaze and trying to look into his obstinately averted eyes.

He had just come from the minister's residence, he told him. The minister had tried to detain him for a meal, but he had wanted to get away because he always received his patients immediately after lunch, even in summer, as he never slept during the day. It was now certain that the minister would support his candidacy at the election, and no less certain that he would win, as people were tired of hearing about wars and conscription all the time and naturally wanted peace. Besides, the election would cost him nothing, a point he had stipulated with the minister, or next to nothing! – just the cost of polling booths, travel expenses and a few other trivial maters. He'd no idea what others would be spending. But he was not really concerned about winning, not at all really, all he wanted was to see the island prospering. He would lose money going into parliament, because many of his patients would desert him. And anyway, what need had he of political accolades, he was a man of science. As it happened, a foreign doctor, a former student of Pasteur's, had just arrived from Paris to study various diseases common in the East. And he was keen to open a microbiology lab with him, the very latest of its kind; he too intended to conduct various experiments on pigs – not rabbits or muskrats, he did not accept that method. Absolutely not! Even the ancient Greeks, our wise ancestors, had noticed that of all the animals the one most closely resembling humans is the pig. Yes sir, the pig! Galen had pointed that out, or was it Aristotle, he could never remember which.

So there it was, if he did not get into parliament, so much the worse for the island. Not of course that he wished to refuse to serve the place he had been born and raised in, the place where he had his modest property and small business interests, where the community with which he was acquainted lived. What did he care if they called him a foreigner! He knew he was more of a native than the natives. He was conservative by nature, more so even than the old aristocracy, and his party's principles were conservative as well. Of course, a certain flexibility over the peasant issue was essential, otherwise the party would never have survived. That way it could avoid agrarian reform. After all, those excellent laws benefited the masses considerably, only affecting a few unimportant individuals adversely, and they gave the government the powers necessary to carry out its programme.

Ophiomachos listened attentively to everything he had to say. For the moment he had forgotten what had brought him to the doctor's house and he smiled blithely back at him. Then in a low voice and with downcast eyes he replied that he of course was a staunch supporter of the minister's party, as he considered him a great man and a credit to their island. He too was a conservative of course and over the years had been opposed to union with the mainland, universal suffrage, general conscription and separation from the Patriarchate, and he was certainly no friend of anarchy or what nowadays they called the people's rights. They were yet another source of trouble. He didn't want to hear about any of that... that was why he preferred to live under a foreign protectorate... that among other things. The people must know their place, work hard and be submissive, though of course they should not go short of bread. It was only his two sons who did not support the minister's party, Giorgis because he was friendly with Sozomenos and Spyros because he was influenced by his brother. And this displeased him greatly, like so much else that had been happening to him lately...

These words brought him back to reality. They reminded him of the purpose of his visit, but he was at a loss as to how to begin. He fell silent. His soul was again thrown into turmoil as he recalled his daughter's sacrifice, his talk with Alkis and Photini's reactions... He again felt sorry for this mother who wanted to provide her son with a support in life and showed such affection for his daughter, and his mind suddenly went blank. He looked about him in a daze, conscious only that Doctor Steriotis was looking at him with embarrassing curiosity and smiling as if he wanted to encourage him. Finally, when he was least expecting it, he heard him say with the same easy courtesy and earnestness:

'I've not yet asked to what I owe the honour of your calling on me here at home.'

Ophiomachos became flustered. He realized that he must now either speak out or leave, as it was getting late. His face changed colour more than once and his lips murmured something he couldn't hear himself. He held his breath for several seconds, opened his tired eyes wide and closed them, and finally making up his mind like someone about to fling himself into an abyss, he said in a trembling voice:

'I've come... I've come because... Yes, because Hadrinos... you know, Doctor, the fellow with the' – and he made a gesture suggestive of the money-lender's hook-nose – 'well, you see... he had a word with me. He seemed to be speaking on your behalf. I don't know if you prompted him... well, not actually on your behalf, but that was the general impression, shall we say... after all, I wasn't born yesterday! Anyway, he told me everything.

And so I've come. Of course, it's a great honour, you are too kind... This Mimis fellow also told me that you've enslaved us, that I, Alexandros Ophiomachos, whom you see before you, owe you a fortune! We are in your hands and you can do what you like with us!... But...'

The doctor, smiling, interrupted him:

'The purpose of life is happiness! And my purpose in life will be Eulalia's happiness. That is to say, my principal purpose, my first priority. And of course for me that will be the more easily accomplished as I am firmly convinced that I shall be happy with her. All I ask is that you give us your blessing. You see, Mr Ophiomachos, I speak my mind because you have broached the matter.'

And as he said this, he opened the adjacent double doors for him and with a proud smile showed him the splendid new drawing-room, with its gleaming gilded furniture, ornate mirrors and large black grand piano; then he invited him out onto the wide veranda and, through the windows, showed him the fine master bedroom, where though it was still unoccupied the beds had already been made up; then he showed him over the bathroom and the dining-room, adjusting the furniture, praising the worthy carpenters responsible, commenting on the style and where the models had been found; and finally, having escorted Ophiomachos back to the ample leather armchair in the study, he said with a smile:

'Wouldn't you yourself agree that, from the material point of view at least, our happiness would seem assured? Well then, give us your blessing!'

'My blessing?' murmured the old man, once again at a loss how to begin, 'I can give you my blessing easily enough, it doesn't cost me anything. But what's it worth? What's it worth without Eulalia? And Eulalia, good Doctor... Ah, the poor wretch! She's not the woman for you, here in this splendid house... She's not quite right in the head, you see, even if she seems like a nice girl. So consider carefully what you ought to do. But if you love her, don't ask for her hand, good Doctor. Let her go, she's not in her right mind! I'll let you have my other girl, Louisa. She's also my daughter, and she's more beautiful... younger too. No? Well, as you wish... But if I may let you into a secret, my Eulalia was in love with someone else before you appeared, ever since her childhood. Not so my Louisa, she's as free as a bird. Long before you appeared... so let her go!'

'It's Alkis,' exclaimed the doctor with a harsh smile, 'Sozomenos! Am I right?'

'How did you guess?' replied the old man, startled. 'Ah yes, Hadrinos, that Mimis fellow... the man with the' – and with his finger he again suggested the money-lender's nose – 'he must have told you. He knew about it, of course, from his visits to my house. Every young girl, you see, has someone she fancies. And Eulalia happens to fancy Alkis! What can I tell her? She says it's her right. She has a will of her own, you see... And she's the one who's getting married. Alkis, she says, is the man she wants. What can I do?... But you, Doctor, you may have Louisa, if you want... my other daughter... She won't make any difficulties. Ah, you are magnanimous, I know, and you're worthy of possessing all this wealth! And I know you won't squeeze a poor old man like me... Whatever I owe I intend to repay with time, or by amicable settlement. You're not going to destroy my family, even though we are all slaves in your hands. You said you were conservative by nature. Then you will respect my family's glorious past. And you won't force Eulalia against her will.'

'Life,' replied the doctor, offended and adopting the dispassionate air of his profession, 'is an incessant battle, *bellum omnium contra omnes*! We see this everywhere, throughout nature, in animates and inanimates alike. Conflict is ubiquitous. The survival of the fittest! Why should it be any different when it comes to human love? I was the one who spared no pains to cure Alkis. But now I find he is my rival, so why shouldn't I want to win? I intend to make use of every means at my disposal. And so I should! I can't believe my proposal has been scorned; if it were so, I should feel the insult both as a human being and a man. But I must inform you that I'm not going to withdraw. Certainly not! Now I am aware that at present Miss Eulalia does not feel the same fondness for me that I do for her. Would it were otherwise. All true enough! But I am equally sure that she will develop such feelings later. Why wouldn't a woman come to love me, when I intend to be utterly devoted to her?'

'If only you would be magnanimous, Doctor,' repeated Ophiomachos trembling, 'if only you would leave her to her fate and accept my other daughter!'

'So you intend to refuse me?' replied the doctor, frowning. 'You intend to give preference to Alkis? Very well! As you please. Who can force you?'

And his face assumed such a cold, harsh expression that the old man suddenly found himself quaking with fear.

'No!' he said, 'I was merely begging you...'

'In that case,' said the doctor triumphantly with a bland smile, 'all I ask is your blessing! Two weeks after the wedding you must come round again and visit us – and then you should ask Eulalia if she's happy. She will say yes, I promise you!'

Ophiomachos looked him in the eye submissively and adjusted his old frock-coat. The doctor smiled at him complacently. The old man reflected that what the doctor was doing was perhaps only fair, or at least he believed what he had said. He was a man who had faith in himself, in his power and destiny. One of a new breed who now ruled the world. How could the old Count hold out against him any longer? A sad smile appeared on his lips and two tears rolled down his cheeks as he rose from the deep armchair in distress, shook the doctor by the hand and took his leave, now quite clear in his disoriented mind that only Eulalia's consent could remedy the situation.

Hastily he made his way home. His tired brain kept imagining all kinds of wild fantastic scenes. Because of him a whole world was going to rack and ruin, and he himself was sitting amid the devastation lamenting and awaiting death. Doctor Steriotis was laughing triumphantly in the Greek Parliament, the bartered Eulalia beside him, half-naked and with her hands bound, while he, Alexandros Ophiomachos Philaretos, was escorting numerous strangers to his ancestral home, where his other daughter was waiting to entertain them.

He realized he must be going mad.

By the time he re-entered his gloomy study, his head was splitting. Involuntarily he gazed at the portraits of his ancestors one by one – the knight in armour, the clean-shaven noblemen with their white wigs, the ladies with their opulent bosoms and sweet smiles – and laughed sarcastically. Then suddenly he was overcome with rage. All this ancient glory was of no use to him at all, it was just one more intolerable burden in the general collapse, further embittering his life and nullifying his individual identity. He glared at the portraits furiously and spat at them. Then he opened a small cupboard containing his family papers, accumulated over five centuries and many generations, took them out and flung them on the table – diplomas on parchment written in calligraphy, letters to his ancestors from the Venetian authorities, appointments to high office, yellowing ledgers – where he proceeded to examine them one by one, spit on them, tear them up and trample on them, becoming more and more angry as he did so. Then he seized the huge ledger he had been leafing though that morning, still open on the table on top of all the dusty legal documents, and one by one tore out the blank pages, cursing the peasants' names inscribed at the top of each. All these records were useless, absolutely useless, in this hour of crisis!

It was already afternoon and he had not yet had lunch. Concerned, his children now ventured down to the study to see if he was there. He was still raging, still wrenching documents from the thick bundles, tearing them up and throwing the pieces on the floor.

With a savage threatening look and ready to curse them, he stopped his sons short at the door and, red in the face, sweating and muttering under his breath, went on with what he was doing. Suddenly he shouted at them:

'I'll burn the place down!'

At this his sons rushed towards him, intending to secure his hands.

He gave them another savage look, flung a bundle of papers at their heads, scattering them everywhere, then spat in Giorgis's face and shouted at the top of his voice:

'You're the ones who've ruined me! Now I'll sell you too, not just the girls! Yes, both of you!'

The two young men were pale and trembling. Giorgis cast an eye around the room as if seeking some assistance. Spyros's baby face assumed an idiotic expression. Just then the old Countess herself came down to the study, alarmed by all the shouting, her face pale and frightened. The old man suddenly calmed down, ashamed in the presence of his wife. He shuffled his foot a little, as if trying to conceal the torn documents under the table, but glared at her a moment too, as if considering whether to attack her suddenly. The Countess took one despairing look at the scene of devastation, gave a piercing scream and collapsed weeping into the arms of her two sons. But now the old man began to tremble. With two large tears rolling down his cheeks, he approached his wife and shyly and sadly stroked her head, then sitting down exhausted in the old wooden armchair at his desk, he buried his face in his hands and wept. He felt like an orphan on this earth. Where could he now turn for help?

While this was going through his mind, he heard the wailing voice of Eulalia as she came running into the study. He raised his head and looked at her. She was weeping desperately and clutching at her blond hair with both hands. For a moment she stared at the chaotic scene...

'All right, I'll have him!' she suddenly declared, clasping her hands to her bosom with a sob. 'I can't bear to see you in such misery!'

The old man rose from his armchair, trembling and tearful, wrapped his old frock-coat closer round him as if feeling the cold, and with head lowered slowly went over to his daughter. Silently taking both her hands, he kissed them repeatedly, bowing before her and finally kneeling at her feet, where he again began to weep.

His two sons and Eulalia quickly helped him up and the aged Countess, coming over to him, herself in tears, said gently:

'At the Second Coming, God will remember your broken heart...'

'At the Second Coming!' muttered the old man stupidly as he steadied himself and, calmer now, shuffled over to his dusty sofa to lie down. 'At the Second Coming!' he exclaimed again and laughed sarcastically.

Late that evening, Hadrinos the money-lender reappeared at the study door. Ophiomachos was now trying in vain to piece the torn documents together, noting the numbers on the deeds and other legal contracts, looking gloomily at the torn bits of parchment and regretting what he had done, but he was slowly recognizing that the task was hopeless and exhausting.

Noticing his visitor, he tossed aside the fragments he was holding, as if he felt embarrassed, and conscious of the money-lender's sly look of curiosity, remarked casually:

'Today I've been sorting through my papers and getting rid of what's no longer needed.'

Then he smiled and winked at Hadrinos, nodding his head. The money-lender understood at once.

'Ah, so she's consented?' he exclaimed, his eyes widening.

Again Ophiomachos nodded.

The money-lender rubbed his hands gleefully and began to chuckle, exposing his large teeth.

'I can't tell you, Master,' he said, 'how my heart rejoices, because she's a good girl, pure gold, and that's the truth, so help me God! Miss Eulalia will be the first lady in the land. What riches, Master, what mansions!...

How delighted I am!... And all this bounty, Master, she owes to me your humble servant, me the louse!'

'Yes,' replied Ophiomachos seriously, adjusting his old frock-coat which he had not taken off all day, and added in a constrained voice: 'What now? We're in urgent need of money. All these expenses to be met!'

'Name your sum, Master,' replied Hadrinos with a laugh. 'We'll raise any amount you wish. We'll get the backing of all the banks now, every single one of them! Since we have access to the Doctor's strongbox, and for the love of Miss Eulalia, I shall make the impossible come true! Ha, ha!'

And he went on chuckling for some time.

3

Mrs Aimilia Valsamis had slept fitfully that night and woke up very early, unusually so for her. She opened her tired eyes, turned over in the red silk sheets, adjusted her white pillow, arranged her thick braids over her bosom, and suddenly became conscious that another oppressive day of worry was just beginning for her. She looked across at the window. The sunlight coming through the shutters formed a pattern of pale yellow dots on the drawn white curtains, so many lightless little suns. But the lamp was also still alight under its bell-shaped red glass shade.

By now she was fully awake. The world was re-forming in her brain, just as it had vanished the moment she had drifted off to sleep. She was in her bedroom, looking at the window, conscious of the warmth of her bed and the flickering of the lamp. Her husband too would be lying in bed just then, sick and alone in his own room. He hadn't made a sound all night. And Giorgis?... Yes, Giorgis – where might he be now? Where else? – Asleep of course... but might he perhaps be... no, undoubtedly he too would be in bed. Did he think of her when he awoke? Who could tell... If so, how did he remember her – fondly or with indifference? Which of their moments together first came to his mind? Which ones especially? Those when their individual wills and reason were eclipsed in the ecstasy of their souls and commingling of their bodies, or those when hostility and hatred would flare up between them, a sort of malicious frenzy, some aggressive force determined to destroy and obliterate the mystery that had united them? Something between them would then seem to snap, something that could never be put right, rage would consume them and their words would become bitter, poisonous and unrestrained. Yet it only needed a look recalling earlier tender moments, or a tear or sigh during a lull in their quarrelling, for hostilities to end in a warm and passionate embrace, ravishing their lacerated souls. And this was how these scenes had invariably ended. But they had now become so extraordinarily intense that her love no longer managed to prevail, they were like ruthless slave revolts sweeping all before them, and the bitter words that they exchanged as they raked over past deeds they now regretted, or spelled out long-forgotten grievances, seared them to the very quick. Why was this? Because he was now chasing after other women, one of the Kallergises – ah, how easily those two surrendered! – or Mrs Urania Daphnopatis! The Asteris ball wasn't the first time she had suspected him. And more recently when he'd not been coming round and she'd not seen him at all, he might easily have begun again. But then of course, he was that sort. He just needed a woman, like all the rest of them. Ah, why did she have to remember them too at this moment, confound them!

She felt stiflingly hot in bed and kicked her legs, shifted her position, wiped her mouth with a hanky and gazed across at the sunlit window, trying to expel the images of her past life that came flooding uncontrollably back into her mind – all brief extravagant affairs she preferred not to think about. Her heart beat more quickly and so violently that she could feel her temples throbbing. Giorgis came into her mind again. It had been three or four days since they had quarrelled – an absolute age! Petros Athanatos had been run off his feet going to and fro between them. Yet he had refused to come. But now she was no longer going to send for him, and Petros could just stay at home. She too had her pride, he need never come again if he didn't want to! Let him chase after Mrs Daphnopatis and the Kallergis girls! He'd soon see if he had anything to gain by the exchange. That's how the Ophiomachoses were, the lot of them. Useless! Yes, useless!

How had their row started last time? Over nothing, over some trivial matter. But she couldn't simply sit there listening to his curses and interminable whingeing, and he had become so touchy lately. After all, was it her fault if his family affairs were in a mess, was it her fault? And she was not, like him, going to be so stupid as not to see that Doctor Steriotis

was a thousand times preferable to Alkis! Why should Giorgis hold that
against her? The doctor was rich, healthy and had a position in society. The
other fellow didn't have a thing, not even good health! At least she herself,
in marrying the sick Valsamis, had married someone rich – moreover, if
things had turned out badly for them, they would turn out much worse for
Eulalia. Giorgis's reply had been impertinent... Not everyone was tarred
with the same brush, he had told her, his sisters were well brought up. Oh
yes, a fine upbringing, out there in the Ophiomachoses' country house,
that mouldering pile! Pride and penury! But she was not going to put
up with insults. Insulted for having yielded to him, for having been weak
enough to love him! And yet he was the one who had gone off in a huff!
Well, let him stay away then, let him go and find Mrs Daphnopatis and
tell her everything he had confessed to her – he could tell her anything
he liked. He'd soon see if another woman, and supposedly a lady, would
put up with it!

She had raved at him of course. She had said some pretty harsh things
and certainly touched a raw nerve. She had called him a beggar and
accused him of wanting to marry her for her money when her husband
died because he and his debt-ridden family had no other option. That was
their ideal solution, that was why his mother was always sucking up to
her. The Ophiomachoses were a crafty lot, she said, like all down-at-heel
aristocrats. So much for his lofty ideals, so much for his love. She had
been carried away by fury, of course, but she was right, yes, she was also
right. Finally she had threatened to throw him out because, she claimed,
she couldn't stand his begging. But that was a lie, Giorgis had never
broached the subject of her wealth or endeavoured to find out about her
circumstances, nor had he ever mentioned his financial worries to her,
not once. In that respect too she had been unfair. Perhaps she had done
something irreparable, because he certainly hadn't taken it lying down.
She had seen him blanch and his eyes glaze over strangely and watched
him foam with rage, and she recalled that his fury and the damage she had
inflicted on him had given her great pleasure. That was the way people
were when their blood was up! They ruined everything in an instant, they
destroyed themselves as well as others. And she was so quick-tempered,
that was the way her sad life had made her, though as a young girl she had
imagined life quite differently, full of happiness and laughter – certainly
not tied to a sick man's bed.

But there wasn't much Giorgis hadn't accused her of as well... Spitefully he had brought up all her former lovers. How on earth did he know each of them by name! He told her he had never even thought of marrying her, because in spite of poverty at least he wanted to preserve an honourable name. He said such hateful things!... Then they had cursed each other in coarse unrelenting language, both speaking in undertones in case the rest of the household heard them there in the drawing-room – language one wouldn't hear in taverns, whispered with grotesquely smiling faces, so that anyone entering would not realize they were quarrelling. Finally, quite beside himself, Giorgis had stormed out with a parting curse, and since then Petros had not managed to persuade him to return.

But did her love really mean nothing to him? Surely she would eventually manage to win him over? How else could she demonstrate her love if not by letting him see all her weaknesses? Did he not know how tender, how strong her passion for him was – something as essential to her as life itself, like the heart's warmth, like breathing? Would he not come to her today at long last? Would he never let bygones be bygones? Would Petros bring him over? – No? Then she would go round to his place today herself and find out what was going on. How tired she was of that entire Ophiomachos clan, all those women! The old Countess who was for ever anxiously expecting the worst, yet so tough in the face of adversity. A soul steeped in misfortune yet utterly devoid of malice, so much so that she found her quite exasperating. Then there was that Eulalia girl, a servile insipid creature, a wooden saint! What could anyone expect from her... Something about her reminded one of her father, but what was it? As for the old man himself, he was mad as a hatter, with his humble greetings, forever shivering in his old frock-coat. And finally that brainless Louisa, whose head could be turned by anyone and who thought she was the only person on the planet, just like her idiotic brother Spyros. As for him... what a joke he was, he had really come a cropper over Asteris's daughter. And how that old house of theirs exuded the odour of decay... Oh, she was fed up with their whole clan and all the stupid things they talked about! What did she care about any of them? Giorgis of course was different, she would never tire of him. She hated him sometimes, but her hatred was just as passionate as her love. What she wanted was for him to be more like her, but he never was like that and now difficult days lay ahead.

Her lamp had started flickering and spitting, and she heaved a sigh. She found the rhythmic dancing of the little red flame annoying. Restlessly she readjusted her position in the bed and, after watching it a moment, looked away again towards the window...

Often her imagination would weave fantastic scenes, her mind refusing to accept life as it was – as it really was. What was wrong with the lamp now? How tiresome!

And before she knew what she was doing, she had leapt out of bed and put out the lamp. Then glancing round the room, she drew the curtains, opened one side of the window and the shutter and looked out into the street. Her eyes were not accustomed to the light of dawn or its characteristic solitude. The sun was still weak and a chilly wind was blowing. But it was going to be a fine day. She closed the window again and went back to bed, adjusting the bedclothes and white pillows.

For so many days now, she reflected, she had been waking up this early. And even during the night she wasn't sleeping. Those early morning hours were the worst, when she just could not get off to sleep again. Previously those moments had always been among the sweetest. The mind and will by then had not yet gathered enough strength to banish the creatures of imagination, and so many things, so many wonderful things seemed possible... Reason did not ask how... And the days that followed had seemed rosy in the radiance of her new-found love, after she had first got to know Giorgis. What more did she want from life besides a man, just one, to whom she could devote herself wholeheartedly and who would in turn be hers and hers alone? And that man could not be anybody else – Giorgis was the one who must love her with anguish in his soul, with feverish jealousy, with passionate intensity, he was the one who must hang upon her every look, her every smile, her every word of harsh reproach. Her charms must keep him in a state of permanent unease, permanent emotional excitement, she must make him weep before her, just as he had filled her with elation, just as he had now plunged her into such terrible anxiety she could think of nothing else.

Previously in these early morning hours she had always thought of him with such delight. She would recall his handsome face and the gracefulness of all his movements. Even in their moments of passion he could never entirely forget himself and always retained his self-control. Then she would remember yesterday's encounter and relive each embrace, each kiss, savouring every moment, trying to decide just when their hearts had throbbed to the same beat, when their two souls had become one while the world around them slipped out of sight. Daydreaming thus, she would half-close her eyes until sleep again reclaimed her. When she reopened them it would be time to get up! She would dress hurriedly because the man she adored would be arriving any minute.

And today? Alas, today she had nothing to look forward to at all. But she couldn't help remembering those bygone days. Would they really not return? Would Giorgis really be able to bury the memory of her love for ever? Would he remain unshakable in his resolve, especially now when her husband would very soon be dead? Yes, he was going to die at last, poor man! He had lived longer than anyone expected. He was still clinging on, a sad invalid suffering patiently and never once complaining about what was going on behind his back. Giorgis always felt sorry for the poor fellow. Who could tell whether he reproached them behind that mask of calm endurance which he never lifted for a moment. He himself knew he had lived longer than he should have, and awaited his own death with fortitude. She too pitied him, as her love for Giorgis had expunged all gloomier feelings from her heart, she was no longer able to hate anyone, and it was only when she herself was suffering that she resented him. Now his hour was approaching. Soon a new life could begin for her and Giorgis. Her fortune and his ancient name would acquire fresh merit in society, enhancing their unclouded happiness and the beautiful enchantment of their love. Yet now, at the eleventh hour, that dream was under threat.

A shiver ran through her whole body and she opened her eyes wide. Then she shut them tight as if afraid and huddled under the bedclothes. Now things were very different. He was neglecting her, he never came, he no longer wanted to be with her and her wiles were insufficient to bring him to heel. But no, no! She wouldn't let him go, she couldn't bring herself to do that, she wanted him so badly, she simply couldn't live without him! Why wasn't her love, such boundless, such devoted love, enough for him? Why didn't he want them to be happy?

He had told her why in no uncertain terms. The aristocrat turned minister had been her third – no, her fourth lover before Giorgis. He too had played his cards astutely. He had exploited all his prestige, all the wiles of the politician's art to win her. And she had believed him too, just as earlier she had believed all the others. She had been convinced that he really was prepared to sacrifice his ministerial position and his privileges for her sake. That's what he kept telling her but she couldn't let him do it. High office was no obstacle to love! And so she had surrendered to him, yet all the time he had been chasing other women and telling them the same thing, and they had fallen for it too. And so she'd kicked him out! He had only laughed as he departed, having known from the beginning that their relationship would never last, as even then the pretty Mrs Urania Daphnopatis was already flirting with him. They had all been together at that dinner party he had given at home the evening when Giorgis Ophiomachos happened to be seated next to her. From the dull glow in Mrs Daphnopatis's eyes, from her nervous gestures and her silly giggle, she had guessed what was going on. She had deliberately dropped her napkin and so the scandal had erupted, becoming common knowledge all over town the following day.

But that very same evening, furious at the minister's treachery and determined to show him her indifference, she had smiled encouragingly at Giorgis, who had been making eyes at her repeatedly, and their affair had taken off from there. Never before had she known true love. It was quite different from anything she had experienced before.

He had told her why in a fit of anger. He was afraid of her fiery temperament, of her decisive will, her wealth. In his rage he had told her that she was never deterred by moral principles. He had told her that society was always watching and judging other people's conduct and knew all about the minister and her other lovers; moreover, it knew about the Ophiomachos family's decline and would be unlikely to view things charitably and concede that love, not money, was involved; on the contrary, to avoid censuring him people would say he was a clever fellow who knew how to get his way with women and discreetly turn a blind eye to their affair. That was what he had told her. This had precipitated their exchange of terrifying curses, whispered with grotesquely smiling faces lest anybody entering should see that they were quarrelling.

But such clear-sightedness was evidence that he could still think rationally and calculate his every move. It revealed that his love for her was temperate and half-hearted, a common, mean-spirited, contemptible affair compared to her grand passion, which filled her life and determined everything she did.

Then before delivering his parting curse he had said something even more vicious, uttered in all earnestness, without tears, in a hoarse but steady voice. No man, but no man, was a completely free agent, an autonomous anarchic spirit, he was also a social being. People might readily accept their affair, as others in society lived the same sort of life and the man's name protected them. But he would never want to use his illustrious name to cover up such things, he would feel too ashamed. He, an Ophiomachos, wanted to be proud of his poverty, he wanted to be able to proclaim it with his head held high.

And she, poor wretch, had put up with this humiliation too. Even after he had cursed her, as she saw him leaving, she had relented and in the heat of the moment forgotten her dignity, so anxious was she to avoid a final breach, but his resolve had remained unshakable. How pale his face had been and how dull his eyes! And he had shown amazing determination in scorning her amorous advances, in resisting her body which even then was yearning for him with tremulous desire, in dashing her hopes that all their bitterness might dissolve in a passionate embrace. Ah, she had been wounded to the quick.

But she would not give up, she refused to submit to her harsh fate without a murmur. She, Aimilia Valsamis, was not that sort of woman! Perfidious wretch that he was, making her suffer like this with his cold dispassionate reasoning – just when she was on the point of surrendering her whole being to him, becoming the handmaid of his desires, his slave! – oh, in her fury she too would find the strength to punish him, and the more distant he became the more fiercely she would hate him. She was no longer a slip of a girl to be taken in by lies and lose her head over a love affair! She was quite capable of hitting back hard, decisively and without mercy. Her revenge would be as harsh as her love-making had been passionate.

She turned over two or three times under her silk sheets, but just couldn't get herself comfortable. One minute she was shivering, the next too hot. She kicked her feet restlessly, hid her face in the down pillow and wept...

Meanwhile her mind was active. How long had that bitter duel with the man she loved gone on? A long time, she could no longer recall how many hours; all she could remember was that she had glanced in the mirror and seen an alien face. Her hair was dishevelled and her forehead swollen, her eyes were dull and strangely vacant, as if bereft of sight, her nostrils were quivering, her lips were pale and cracked and her cheeks inflamed. And ultimately, he was the one who had left victorious that day. Afterwards the room had suddenly gone so appallingly quiet that she could hear her own ears buzzing, and she had looked about idioti- cally, checking to see if the furniture were still in place and the walls still standing. In that moment of despair, her mind refused to function, her heart pounded violently and her whole body trembled uncontrollably. Oh, the hour of death couldn't have been harder. Never before had she experienced a moment of such bitterness, such sorrow and dejection. And all because of that distant, that heartless, but – ah! – so utterly adorable young man...

But what was she going to do now for the rest of today, a day which had begun with all these preoccupations and still had many interminable hours to go? Petros Athanatos would be run off his feet again, she would send him off to find out what Giorgis was up to, where he was going, how he was spending his time... And she would not put up with his lecturing her in that sarcastic way of his about the disadvantages of wealth which sometimes became a heavy yoke on the shoulders of the wealthy and destroyed their happiness.

Nowadays she found Petros's sententiousness and that laugh of his annoying, and there were moments when she felt ready to hate the loyal fellow for devoting himself so single-mindedly to Giorgis. All she would ask of him was that he get his friends to keep an eye on Giorgis – at home, in the street, on social calls, or at the theatre if he went – then at least she would know if he were suffering too or did not care, if he were pursuing one of the Kallergis women or Urania Daphnopatis, or enjoying himself in other ways. Now he would gad about independently when and where he pleased, while she was languishing in the misery he had so cruelly inflicted on her.

She herself would also be spending many hours out and about, as she had done the day before. Perhaps that day she'd catch a glimpse of him... or maybe she'd again hang about in vain for hours on end. She would sit alone in the café under the trees that were once more in bud. She would wait and he would not appear. She would pretend to be reading some newspaper or novel, while listening intently for his footsteps, and her eyes would wander in the fond hope that she might suddenly see him. She would wait and again he would not appear. And the longer she waited, the chillier her heart would grow, the more frequent the icy shivers down her spine, and the more firmly she would be gripped by grief and black despair. And still he would not appear. It would be sheer martyrdom again...

The second day after their row however, she had caught sight of him. He was with several others. He had greeted her courteously, too embarrassed to do otherwise in front of his friends and the promenading crowd, but she had again noticed that same glazed look which had so frightened her and was not him at all. She had beckoned him over and he had come to her side at once, extending his hand limply without gripping hers, and this lukewarm greeting had frozen her completely. He had smiled and been polite, exercising perfect self-restraint, while she had hung on his every word and gazed at him reproachfully, but he had refused to raise his eyes and look at her, so that she felt like bursting into tears, pleading with him and reminding him of all their happy times together. But there were people all around, so she had simply stood there trembling. He had stayed with her only a moment and then asked if he might rejoin his friends to listen to a speech that had just begun. Alkis was among them and she sensed that he was gratified by this. She had not seen him since. Perhaps today, if he saw her coming from a distance, he might try to avoid her.

It was sheer hell, worrying like this under her silk sheets...

But she couldn't just wallow in her misery. Shouldn't she try to get over her wretched infatuation?... Don't be absurd! she said to herself with a hysterical laugh. How could she ask that of herself? Life would be dark indeed without his love, and what else was the pain she felt but love – something that she treasured in her heart, that meant more than life itself to her, that ennobled her and helped her to see beyond the ugliness of human nature in its incessant sordid decline and feel pity and compassion for the human soul's timorous attempts to escape from pain and the fear of death. Love had something of the moral force of a religion, and Mrs Valsamis was a believer. How could she go back to her wretched former life and the savage hatred she had been nursing in her heart?

Here it occurred to her that it was precisely her former life that was to blame for her current misery. If she had remained virtuous and never strayed, if her reputation had remained unsullied, she would now be worthy of him, there would be no obstacles to overcome and she would be embarking on a genuinely happy life.

She hid her face in the down pillow and again burst into tears.

Suddenly she roused herself and leapt out of bed. It was already late. She put on her slippers, wrapped a red silk dressing-gown around her, anxiously adjusted her braids in front of the full mirror and hastened to her husband's room.

Periklis Valsamis was lying in bed. Against the white pillows his like-able waxen face, with its fine large patient eyes and good-natured smile, looked even paler. Petros Athanatos was by his side and reading poems written in calligraphy to him.

The invalid welcomed her with silent joy, his eyes thanking her for coming, and Petros Athanatos at once stopped reading, stood up and turned a little pale, as always in her presence. She greeted them with a sad smile and approached the bed. A feeling of infinite compassion for this bed-ridden man, who had spent his life uncomplainingly beside her, suddenly came over her, heartsick though she already was. Kindness was prevailing. Her body trembling slightly, she bent over her sick husband, and as she kissed his translucent brow tears came into her eyes.

He looked at her curiously. Joy suffused his waxen face, his eyes glowed, and clasping both her hands he gazed into her eyes with his unfailing smile. But then a gut-wrenching fit of coughing overcame him.

Petros Athanatos remarked sarcastically with his characteristic unpleas-ant laugh:

'Ha, ha! There are some things money can't buy! One of them is love!'

Aimilia gave him a furious look. But she could see that he too was moved. His entire bent body was shaking inside his shabby clothes and he raised a finger to the corner of his eye.

'A speck of grime has brought tears to my eye,' he said maliciously, 'but a little water should get rid of it.'

And as he began to leave the room he murmured:

'The eye, the eye... can't tolerate the tiniest speck. Yet the world is full of grime!'

4

'Revolution, ha, ha!' laughed Alkis Sozomenos cynically, as he sat in his little study. 'Revolution! In a place like this, in a society like this... How could he ever have imagined it! Ha, ha!' So even Eulalia had bowed to necessity! She had lost her nerve, she had rejected him and refused him her support. Everything that his heart, brimming with vitality and joy with her beside him, had seen unfolding in a new creative dawn was now dissolving like an unreal phantom before the ugliness of the actual world – barren, futile, unjust and harsh, its very foundations no more than sorrow, pain, disease and death. And yet it had all been true! Elsewhere a new faith was guiding the human race through difficult and tumultuous struggles. Indeed in some places these struggles were already coming to a head. Clear-sighted minds had seen signs of imminent deliverance, and soon an unprecedented joyous cry of freedom would ring out. Sozomenos had considered himself one of the clear-sighted, a leader of his peers on the road to freedom, and had thus found a meaning to his existence in keeping with the creative spirit of the times. His entire life had been one long struggle against physical debility and spiritual inertia, and he had emerged triumphant over suffering and weakness, as if destined by some providence to further its enigmatic ends.

But now he too was just another member of the downtrodden masses. Even he, whose spirit had been liberated. And his own bonds were veritably choking his life's blood, separating him from the creature he held dearest, the creature who had raised him from the tomb and inspired his dreams of a higher humanity in a regenerated world. Fate, alas, was condemning him to the role of mere spectator, bearing witness to pillage which his whole being rebelled against and wanted to prevent. But that was quite beyond him!...

And this weakness, which he recognized so clearly, now deprived him of his courage, blighting his soul, making him consider all his efforts futile, life itself with all its struggles absolutely futile. It left him in a state of silent misery, melancholy apathy and pathological indifference to everything around him, making him bitterly contemptuous of everything he had hitherto respected and admired – human wisdom, human art and human virtue.

In this world virtue was no more than a word devoid of meaning. Even Eulalia was not the woman he had fashioned in his dreams, a woman who would rise above adversity. She too had bowed, solely because she was not a true woman and her spirit was weak, because her mind was incapable of reflecting deeply and considering the baseness and ugliness of what she was about to do. No, hers was not a sacrifice at all! Surely she must have realized that if she weakened she would be throwing herself into the arms of Doctor Steriotis, a virtual stranger, and the very idea should have told her that such a sacrifice was out of the question, a fate worse than death. Ah, why should he alone be tortured by this thought, why did it make his heart beat violently then falter as if about to stop, making everything go dark before his eyes? And why did she have to submit so easily?

He realized his thoughts were now becoming incoherent. Disconnected images passed through his mind as in a dream, and his lips murmured her name sadly. He felt utterly dejected. Ah, her mind had failed to guide her wisely and she had yielded to base considerations which never should have swayed her, while sacrificing those that were genuinely meaningful and sacred, and she had broken a commitment to him unilaterally that he expected her to honour and would never willingly release her from. He wanted what he had an intrinsic right to in this world, wanted it from Eulalia, and she had now denied it him, depriving him of the very air he breathed, stifling his soul, wringing his poor long-suffering heart. Shouldn't Eulalia have been prepared to sacrifice something, perhaps everything, for love of him? Yes, for love and love alone! Ah, how much anxiety, how many wretched hours he had endured since then. His entire life had become a misery. His grief, far from abating, was as oppressive and harrowing as ever and his soul's assumed indifference was merely a pretence, an attempt at self-deception. He felt embittered and worries would erupt that led to indecision and despair, so that he longed for death and railed against life and his own human frailty, unable to find peace because worrying constantly renewed his grief and grief brought further worries.

And if Eulalia was so frivolous, irresolute and weak, what could be said of all the other women that he saw around him? He only had to think of the two Kallergis women, or Urania Daphnopatis, or Aimilia

Valsamis, or Louisa... All these respected ladies in the front rank of society went from one round of enjoyment to the next, with laughter on their lips, evading life's difficulties whenever possible, and Eulalia was simply one among them. Just another society belle, even if she was the best of them. She had yielded to the desperate pleas of a weak, timorous old man stupefied and blinded by misfortune, whose two sons were of no support to him because they were just like him – defenceless against life, weak in the face of adversity, defeatist to the core. He recalled all the other figures he had seen at the Asterises' ball – the haughty and inflexible Mrs Theophano Chrysospathis; the aristocrat turned minister, a mendacious demagogue quick to condemn any independent view or novel undertaking; Archangelos Daphnopatis his weak-willed ineffectual opponent, a bankrupt banker unashamedly living off his wife; Arkoudis, the treacherous squint-eyed financier, sly and hedonistic; and Marcantonio Iustinianis, that passionate absurd old man for whom times never changed, mesmerized by an inglorious bygone age of ignorance and superstition. And then there were his own friends, the Ophiomachos brothers, weak and useless individuals adrift in a meaningless world, Petros Athanatos, a lost and restless soul, a living enigma, and then the sick Valsamis, resigned to his bodily affliction, with his smile of sympathy for others. But wasn't he just as ineffectual? Last to appear before his mind's eye was Steriotis the doctor, of a new breed of men, a conqueror in a society that was in its death-throes. This was the man who was now triumphing over him too, shattering his dreams, plucking love out of his heart, the man who was about to take Eulalia away from him...

How different his father had been from all these people, the old Carabiniere with his venerable appearance and steadfast faith. With a thrill, Alkis again recalled the old Venetian fort and his father's words when showing it to him. Since then times had changed, since then Alkis had briefly believed in his high destiny, in the happiness of a love-match that would anchor him in life, and now he saw these hopes lying dashed before him, his whole existence superfluous and worthless.

'Revolution... revolution...' he reiterated bitterly, 'in a society like this, in a place like this...'

He shook his head and went over to the window. In the little café people were chatting and enjoying themselves as usual, a coach was passing, a bird was singing on its branch, already anticipating spring. Even at that hour everything was bustling with life, and the indifferent rhythm of creation did not pause even for a moment.

His mother called him in her gentle voice, looking at him anxiously and sighing.

'Alkis,' she said, 'Ophiomachos is in the next room waiting for you.'

Suddenly his heart leapt and his eyes lit up. He was surprised at himself, because an absurd irrational hope was welling up within him. Perhaps society on the island was not quite as indolent and hedonistic as he had censoriously concluded earlier. Eulalia was not going to surrender after all and Doctor Steriotis, being a gallant honourable man, was not going to accept her sacrifice or pressure Ophiomachos, everything would be put right and Alkis would regain his Eulalia just as he had left her, and with her his identity.

But as he finished this train of thought he laughed sarcastically, realizing how baseless it all was, and followed his mother into the little sitting-room.

Ophiomachos was standing waiting among the spotless light blue furniture, holding his sun-bleached hat in one hand and adjusting his old frock-coat with the other as if feeling the cold. There was a sad smile on his thick red lips and he stared fixedly at the floor in evident embarrassment. He greeted Alkis warmly, but avoided looking at him, then sinking heavily into the nearest armchair, bade the young man sit down opposite him, sighed and tried to smile.

Photini looked on, then sat down near them and for some moments all three remained silent.

Mother and son waited for Ophiomachos to speak first. But he was again at a loss for words and his distress was clearly discernible in his face which kept changing colour, his heavy breathing, his quivering lips and the way his tired eyes kept twitching. And now and then they noticed him clutching at his old frock-coat.

Full of apprehension, Alkis tried to guess what the old man had on his mind. Suddenly Ophiomachos started talking, opening his eyes wide and making an expansive gesture.

'Alkis,' he said, 'everything at home with us is topsy-turvy!' and he sighed, as if he had just removed a huge load from his mind.

But then smiling again sadly and suddenly relaxing, as if he had had second thoughts, he went on:

'I mean, the furniture and so on are all topsy-turvy. The women have taken all the curtains down and are trying to repair them in the dining-room, but they're so old they keep on tearing. They've been oiling my old leather chairs, and today they're beating our ancestral carpet – which is still in very good condition, by the way. What a to-do! How else can I describe it, everything is topsy-turvy!'

He fell silent, evidently disconcerted, not knowing what to say next, and stared now at Photini, now at her son.

Alkis gazed at the old man sadly with a look of pity. That senile worrying reflected in his petty garrulousness, that pathetic weakness which Alkis considered so degrading, made him reflect on the utterly trivial, sordid factors determining his happiness, his life's purpose, all that might be achieved in a life of vigorous endeavour. Just then he felt like shaking the frail old man to make him see the justice of his claim and change his cowardly attitude, yet he knew this would be expecting him to be a different person, indeed he himself would have to be a different person, someone who could inspire his comrades to follow him unswervingly, make their hearts beat in accordance with his will, maintain his authority unchallenged. He could not then be this sickly youth, who nurtured infinite desires without the strength to face reality and overcome its obstacles. Alkis knew that if he were stout-hearted he would by now have ceased to brood over his lost love, it would have been a minor setback and would not have deterred him.

Photini was still watching him anxiously, trying to guess his thoughts, then finally to relieve the tension smiled and remarked politely:

'What a lot of trouble it must be for your dear wife!'

'Oh,' said Ophiomachos, curling his lip contemptuously, 'you should see her revelling in it all, you really should! Her daughter couldn't have made a better catch, she says. Good luck to her, now she's made up her mind! It won't do her any harm and her family will be rich. She goes on and on, telling her all this to boost her courage. Courage is what our family lacks. None of us has it and we have to get angry to decide things, in fact sometimes we get angry deliberately to do so. Yes, Mrs Sozomenos, that's how God has made the Ophiomachoses. It's a quirk we've had for generations. And my wife too is aware of it, since she's known all about our family affairs for years, as if she herself were a member of the clan. But the poor woman is a bit dim-witted. Yes, she

was never very bright. And she talks a lot, her tongue never seems to
stop wagging these days, indeed she says whatever comes into her head...
just for the sake of something to say, without any idea what others might
be thinking. And that annoys me, even just thinking about it now. You
know me... Why should the girls wait to get married, she says? Let them
leave home early, Louisa too, let them marry young. Who knows what
life has in store for them, their parents are getting on and could die at
any moment, and then where will they go? Meanwhile their youth is
fading and after that they won't turn heads so easily. Everything she says
is quite sensible and proper – but even so she's pretty dim! And now
she's always buttering up her future son-in-law, the doctor, to ensure
that he will love her daughter, and that's the way things should be since
she'll be his wife.'

'His wife!' exclaimed Alkis with revulsion, getting up abruptly and
going over to the window.

The old man pretended not to have understood. He started trembling
with agitation, adjusting his frock-coat two or three times, and for a while
said nothing.

'It's only natural,' he at last continued. 'Any mother would do the
same. She regards him as her son already, even calling him son. But not
me, never... And now she's remembered all the pomp and ceremony of
our marriage, and – stupid woman! – has herself taken to working like a
coolie, sweeping, dusting, sewing, mending all day long. Her daughters
and a woman they've engaged are helping and they cut and sew, cut and
sew morning, noon and night. God help us, what a to-do!'

And he gave a forced hearty laugh, nervously adjusting his old frock-
coat as his eyes rested now on Alkis, now on his mother.

'I can well imagine,' said Photini understandingly, looking at the old
man with curiosity.

Alkis suddenly felt his resentment rising.

Did the old man really not appreciate what he was saying? Did he
not realize that his conduct was quite unseemly?

Why couldn't they leave them in peace. No one was asking them for
explanations. And yet his heart was urging him to ask about Eulalia, he
just wanted to know how she was, whether she still thought about him,
having betrayed him so contemptibly.

But Ophiomachos began rambling on inanely once again:

'They don't trouble me however. Of course, I wouldn't let them. In my study they aren't allowed to dust even, no one's going to create confusion among my papers. And now visitors are calling on us one after the other, the whole blessed town! I see them coming from my window and hear them on the stairs... Where on earth do they receive them with everything in such a mess?'

He gave a forced laugh and got up as if to go, upset because he couldn't bring himself to tell them why he had come round.

But now Photini asked him, smiling sadly:

'And Eulalia?... What about Eulalia?'

The old man slumped back into his chair, his legs outstretched as if he were on the point of passing out, and fiddling with his hat he said in a faint voice:

'That's what I came about, but... but... Do you understand? Eulalia, ah, Eulalia... She weighs on my conscience like a millstone because it's all my fault. I obliged her to say yes, I frightened her. Otherwise she'd never have agreed, poor thing... And now? Ah, now she won't even speak to me... She has to force herself to do so. And I, her old father, love her dearly, because she's the best of all my children. But what can I do about it? She looks at me with fear in her eyes, as if I were her enemy, which I can't bear, because it was you she loved, my boy, she said as much, indeed she shouted it!'

Alkis looked at him again sadly and was about to respond, but Ophiomachos didn't give him a chance:

'There was no alternative,' he continued, 'you know that, Alkis. Anyway, it's a good thing she has had such luck. I wouldn't say this to the doctor's face, but he's a sensible and honest man, he knows what he wants and he's wealthy, very wealthy! He knows life from a different angle and he makes no bones about what he aspires to. Us, for example! The man impresses me. And yet her heart is grieving, and she won't speak to me... That preys on my mind. Her mother simply laughs at me. She's accepted it all and sees only the positive in whatever comes our way, not like me, she says, who now see only the worst. All this is poisoning my life, poisoning Eulalia's too, and... and...'

He again fell silent, dabbing his tired eyes with his handkerchief, but then as if he were ashamed of this weakness, his face assumed a hard expression and he continued hoarsely: 'And I wanted...'

Alkis had stood up and was looking at him with a pained expression. For a moment he had hoped the old man might have repented and that Eulalia was now free again, and he was impatient to hear it from his lips. Photini was also looking at the old man apprehensively. Alkis was overwhelmed with compassion for the young woman who was suffering on his account. All he wanted now was to know that she at least would be happy, even if it were not a happiness the two of them would share. He saw himself as weak, defenceless and defeated by life, no longer equal to the struggle. In some respects he now resembled Ophiomachos himself, who was unable to put up any resistance to calamity and accepted the most expedient solution, Eulalia's sacrifice. And yet it was true that he too loved Eulalia.

Again Alkis heard him say: 'You see, Alkis, I wanted...'

'What do you want from my son?' asked Photini, anxious and impatient.

'I want her, Alkis,' continued the old man, 'to hear from your lips that there was no alternative... that it was not my fault. I want her heart to be at peace and not bear me a grudge. Besides, I'm constantly afraid for her, afraid the doctor might become impatient with her attitude and that we'd then find ourselves back at square one. He'd be quite within his rights, of course, and then, my God, things would go from bad to worse!'

'Why should he?' Photini promptly replied in the same anxious tone, and looked at Alkis as if asking whether she shouldn't end this scene there and then herself. For her the case was now closed, Eulalia could not marry her son. Alkis should come to terms with it, however much she pitied him. What was the point of all this talk, all this raking over the past? It could only affect her son's health adversely, turning the knife in a wound that ought to be allowed to heal.

'He really shouldn't come!' she said.

A lengthy silence followed. Alkis looked at Ophiomachos with the same contempt, his anger and resentment mounting. How craftily the senile old man had managed to disguise the true cause of his anxiety! Beneath his tender sentiments, his queer affection for his daughter and his grotesque emotionalism, there was no mistaking his cowardly egotism and his fear of economic ruin which stripped him of all humanity, all self-respect, while failing to win Alkis's sympathy, indeed obliging him to deny his own identity. All Alkis was certain of was that he was in love.

He had suffered unbearably and been plunged into depression when he heard that Eulalia had rejected him, and even now he risked his sanity when thinking about her, only too aware that he had become a broken man, paralysed and bereft of hope, now the light of love had been snuffed out. He had never expected her to be so timid. Bitterly he told himself that she too had submitted far too readily, offering no resistance, bowing to the family's determination to make her the victim. So she had sunk in his esteem and he thought of her with irony, almost with spite, and while this stifled his love and hardened his heart against her, it did not really ease the pain. And now he was hearing from the old man that her decision was not so firm and unshakable, because she had consented in a moment perhaps of inner turmoil and was now regretting it, making her father fear she might retract. And in his unrivalled naivety the old dotard believed his rationalizations were so true that anybody would be moved, so logical that no one could refute them, and that Alkis therefore would naturally be obliged to accept their consequences. This was the only possible explanation for his visit, for his making such an unreasonable request. But Alkis was not at all obliged to listen to him, and was quite capable of telling him bluntly what he thought of his reactionary ideas and outrageous request. He would give him a piece of his mind and reproach him as he deserved.

With his soul in revolt he was ready to reveal his indignation there and then, and the venerable image of his father and his dream of a world liberated from the tyranny of wealth came into his mind. He remembered the young people so eager to follow him in the just cause, and again imagined himself leading a splendid active life full of dreams and ideals that one by one were being fulfilled. His fellow islanders, children of the soil, were abandoning their traditional errors, emerging from the blind ignorance that held them captive and opening their eyes to a happier, more enlightened future. He himself no longer feared his ailments, the weight of his task no longer daunted him, because his heart was overflowing with love for his suffering fellow creatures, a love inspired by his passion for Eulalia.

And now a faint voice of hope again began to cry out within him: Eulalia was not yet definitely lost to him for ever. He would be able to find her once more, to speak to her again very soon, the old man himself was offering him the chance.

He was intoxicated with unsettling joy.

'I'll come,' he said quietly and his face went pale.

Ophiomachos leapt to his feet at once, his small body trembling, and after glancing suspiciously at Alkis and muttering something as he adjusted his old frock-coat, he shrugged his shoulders as if finally making up his mind, courteously took his leave of Photini, who continued to watch them apprehensively, and said her son: 'Let's go then.'

'Ah well!' exclaimed the mother with a sigh.

Whereupon the two men left the room.

5

They walked along the street in silence until they reached Ophiomachos's house. The old man conducted Alkis into his gloomy study, bade him sit down and as usual began pacing nervously about the spacious room. Alkis watched him impatiently. The old man continued striding up and down for several minutes. Suddenly he said:

'I'll go and fetch her,' and his face flushed scarlet. Then without another word he left the room.

Alkis's heart was by now pounding as if about to burst out of his chest. With a thrill he looked forward to the moment when he would first set eyes on her, tried to think of what to say and guess what she might reply, and struggled to recall her face. At last he saw the door opening and Ophiomachos came in first, his head bowed and looking gloomy, slowly followed by Eulalia.

She was very pale, her willowy figure stooped a little and her downcast eyes were on the verge of tears. She paused at the door a moment, uncertain what to do, then clasping her hands to her breast she raised her eyes. There was Alkis standing gazing at her. Suddenly she felt dizzy, her eyes went dim and, feeling as if the floor was about to give way beneath her, she clung for a moment to the door to steady herself. Then unconscious of what she was doing, she rushed forward on the point of throwing herself into the young man's arms, but stopped short in the middle of the room, while her father locked the door behind her. By this time Alkis was standing in front of her, his face pale, his lips trembling. His tongue felt dry and the tumult in his heart prevented him from speaking. For a moment he felt he must be dreaming. A thousand vivid images flashed through his mind and vanished before he could make sense of them. He gazed at her as if turned to stone. He realized that at this moment his life would be decided. Her eyes were still downcast. Finally the couple looked at one another, a thrill ran through them and tears came into their eyes. Trembling, he took her hand and held it silently for several moments. She was weeping.

'Alkis! Oh, Alkis!' she murmured.

'Eulalia!' he answered with a sigh.

Involuntarily he turned for a moment towards the old man, who was staring at them in a daze, and observed that his eyes too were brimming with tears. He watched him attempting to conceal the fact, embarrassed at being noticed, by gesturing impatiently and buttoning and unbuttoning his old frock-coat, before hastily opening the door and leaving the room.

They were now alone. For a long while they both stood there in silence, as if rooted to the spot. Their hearts were beating violently and their breathing was rapid and uneven as their minds wrestled with the self-same thoughts. Eventually, their lashes fluttering almost simultaneously, they burst into floods of tears. And before they knew what they were doing, they suddenly found themselves trembling in one another's arms. His lips sought hers in a long and fervent kiss, which sent the blood surging through their veins and shivers down their spines and brought warmer, more passionate tears into their eyes. Again and again they kissed, forgetting where they were and surrendering to one another heart and soul.

A slight rattle of the doorknob startled them, bringing them to their senses and making them draw apart. Instinctively both thought of the old man, who was doubtless keeping watch outside and reminding them of his presence.

Alkis's face had now become sullen and dejected and he was staring at the floor.

'Ah,' sighed Eulalia, overwhelmed by the depth of her feelings, 'I know love is invincible and always triumphs! But...' And she looked about as if appealing to the walls to bear her witness.

After a few moments she continued passionately: 'I don't know if it is love that makes my heart so restless. I don't know what it's yearning for that I can't give it, any more than can my wretched father or my mother.

But when I hear your name, it leaps up inside me and I can't control it! And then what's about to happen seems impossible, that I should become another man's wife seems utterly impossible, and I lose my head and everything around me seems completely desolate and wretched! I don't know if love is something higher and more sacred, but you've made me see things about life that I'd never seen before, even though they were there all along. And now? And now?...'

Her whole body had been trembling as she spoke, and she wondered how she had found the words she wanted. She was perspiring lightly and her palms and brow were moist as she gazed tenderly at Alkis, her eyes suffused with tears.

In a quiet voice he said to her:

'It's in your hands.'

She smiled sadly and for some moments said nothing, as if afraid.

'What's in my hands?' she suddenly replied.

'Didn't you say so yourself?' he exclaimed. 'What's to prevent us being happy? Can't you see that a life is in your hands – my life? Can't you see that it's only with you and because of you that I have the strength to carry on living in this world? Oh, Eulalia! If my heart still expects something from life, still wants me to make something of myself, is still capable of faith and worship, it's only because it still lives in hope, still has tender feelings for you. Can't you see that?'

'Ah,' she replied, 'why should you believe that, Alkis? How can such a life as yours lie in the hands of a weak woman, even if she loves you with all her heart and soul... Our love is doomed, Alkis! My old father is desperate and frightened and he has turned to me in his hour of need – am I to refuse him? The road is opening up before you, follow it alone and leave me. Go, go!'

'I refuse to leave you!' Alkis cried. 'While I draw breath, no one else shall have you! You say you love me, then you shall be mine! Why ever not? How can I throw away such rapturous happiness? How can I pluck out of my heart the very thing that warms it and sustains its faith in life? No, no! Anyway, why should everyone in this family imagine that the calamity is going to be so great, and even you yourself be quite prepared to sacrifice me? Don't worry, none of them is going to die; let your brothers work for a change, let necessity put a bit of life into them. Why should they expect everything to be settled through an injustice, through your sacrifice, Eulalia, through such an outrage? Retract your promise, Eulalia I beseech you! My love beseeches you! Look into my eyes... yes, like that... look at me... Take courage, later things will quieten down, you'll see, the old man's imagination is exaggerating everything. You'll see, you'll be vindicated by everybody, even by your father! The poor old fellow is weak but our happiness will strengthen him, because happiness bestows courage, and ours is no ordinary happiness, Eulalia... Oh, don't look away!'

'Alas, if only it were so!' sighed Eulalia, her eyes brimming with tears.

'Well, isn't it?' replied Alkis, trembling from head to foot. 'Doesn't your heart tell you it is so?'

'Oh!' she exclaimed, yielding to him.

Again they found themselves in one another's arms exchanging long and ardent kisses and weeping copious tears, as if intent on surrendering their souls to one another.

Here the door began to open slowly, giving them time to draw apart and let go their hands. The old man re-entered, pausing on the threshold for a moment and leaning his shoulder against the doorpost. He looked pale despite his ruddy complexion and his body was shaking inside his old frock-coat. He looked at them timidly. And in his gaze, that dead, shamefaced, wretched gaze, all the anxiety of his soul appeared, all his dread lest their lips should now pronounce his doom. He longed to know what the young people had said privately, what they had decided, and his abject expression seemed to beg for mercy.

The three of them looked at each other with mounting emotion, until finally Alkis said to his beloved in a trembling voice, all too aware that his whole life was about to be decided:

'Eulalia, you speak to your father.'

But she didn't move or say a word. She was shaking.

The tragic spectacle of the old man, his cowardly despair, that look beseeching her to have pity on him, completely undermined her courage. In her mind's eye she again pictured him insanely tearing up their family documents in that same bleak room, carried away by a frenzy of destruction, and tears came to her eyes. No, she could not deny him the help that he was asking, she could not refuse to have pity on this wretched old man who was her father!

Suddenly she made up her mind.

Meanwhile Ophiomachos had come hesitantly into the middle of the room, looking fearfully now at Alkis, now at his daughter, and with head bowed said in a low tremulous voice:

'Forgive me, Alkis, I've kept you waiting a long while, but I had business to attend to. Such is life. One doesn't do what one would like... Such is life.'

And as he said this, he again looked at Eulalia with the same humble, plaintive expression.

'Oh, speak to him!' Alkis urged her in a despondent anxious voice.

But she shook her blond head, still not uttering a word. Then, her face pale, she took the old man's hand and kissed it repeatedly, drenching it with tears.

Ophiomachos, his whole body shaking inside his old frock-coat, turned his face aside to avoid looking at her and began to laugh, as two large tears rolled down his cheeks.

The despondency within Alkis's heart increased. He was no longer conscious of his surroundings. Greatly affected, he took the old man's other hand and tried to add a word, but could think of nothing. He just stared sorrowfully at Eulalia's head.

'I am parting you!' said Ophiomachos weakly, squeezing his hand.

Now however Alkis felt it was time this distressing scene came to an end. All was now lost! It was already late. But just then Eulalia raised her eyes and, as if she had guessed his thoughts, seized his hand and held it for a moment. He was by now so overwhelmed with grief that he felt he might lose consciousness: his chest heaved, dizziness blurred his vision and there was a buzzing in his ears. All at once, as if suddenly reaching a terrible decision, he let go of both their hands and staggered towards the door. There he paused a moment, looked back at the bleak study and Eulalia still standing beside her father, then opened the door violently and left the room.

At the front door he paused a moment to wipe away his tears. As he came out into the street, still badly shaken, he caught sight of Goulielmos Arkoudis, the banker's son, who happened to be walking past, clean-shaven, erect and nonchalant in his fashionable dark English clothes and twirling his stout cane. Alkis tried to avoid him, but Goulielmos greeted him with a bland smile. And curling his lip ironically he said:

'What's this I hear? Is it true that Doctor Steriotis is going to marry Eulalia?'

'Yes,' replied Alkis faintly, trying to smile as the blood rushed to his head.

Goulielmos gave an unpleasant laugh and looked at Alkis curiously.

'I see!' he said. 'Well, that's something that will never happen to me! No fear! Why? Well, Louisa will be at my disposal any time I please. So how should it?'

'And when's the wedding?' Alkis asked politely, with a sigh.

'When?... I've no idea. All I know is that Louisa will be mine!' He laughed again.

Alkis glared at him contemptuously a moment. His cynicism irritated him, particularly just then.

'How could you be so dishonourable!' he exclaimed.

The other man flushed, without however losing his nonchalant air, and shrugging his shoulders remained silent for a moment. He had adopted this glib tone because he assumed that Alkis would have left the Ophiomachoses in a rage and would relish the malicious scheme he had in mind. He was unsure whether to laugh or take offence, or perhaps jestingly return the insult. He decided on the last option and laughed again.

'At least women don't slip through my fingers,' he said and gave a peculiar whistle.

Almost immediately a window opened. Alkis hastily withdrew into the doorway and heard Louisa's voice replying softly:

'I'm coming, I'm coming!'

'You see?' exclaimed Goulielmos Arkoudis triumphantly, and burst out laughing.

Whereupon Alkis emerged from the doorway and dejectedly proceeded down the narrow street.

6

He had no idea where his feet were taking him. Every so often he would quicken his pace, as if he had suddenly reached some decision, and then slow down, look back and heave a sigh. He had a splitting headache and there was a buzzing in his ears. Every word that Eulalia had said came back to him, the intoxication of her kisses, the tumult in her soul, he could picture how she had stood before him vacillating, how her face had changed colour, how her eyes had filled with tears and how her love-sick heart had yielded to him, overwhelmed by this first taste of happiness that she was powerless to resist. He was also haunted by the image of the pitiful old man – frightened, bewildered, unable to think rationally, lacking the will to face up to any of his troubles – who, scarcely aware of what he was doing, had contrived to part them, there in that large dark study with its documents and dust, with its antiquated furniture exuding the odour of decay.

Bitterly he brooded over the way the old man had subjected them to his weak will, and over his own failure to dissuade Eulalia and save her from being dishonoured and bartered in the shameful way she had consented to. How could he have been so inept? Why hadn't he weighed his words more carefully while they were alone together? Why had he followed the impulse of his heart, just when he should have been summoning all his powers of reason to plead his cause, come up with irrefutable arguments to overcome Eulalia's hesitation and persuade her to go back on her decision – a decision that was now plunging him into such suffocating anxiety and despair that he could neither breathe nor weep nor grieve nor acknowledge his resentment nor begin to remedy the situation. Ah, why hadn't he explored every avenue while they were together? Why, but why?...

His heart felt unbearably constricted and he scarcely noticed his surroundings... He had now reached the broad, tree-lined square and mingled with the crowds, which at that hour were still strolling casually up and down, as if life contained no sadness. The day had ended and in the little cafés the lamps were being lit.

Suddenly Alkis halted, stood staring at the ground stroking his little goatee a moment, and in a tumult of emotion said to himself: he simply must find a solution. Not to do so didn't bear thinking about, because life would become intolerable. He couldn't believe that he would not be able to sway Eulalia's resolve, because Eulalia loved him too, and he alone was to blame for not having spoken to her more resolutely; had he done so he was now convinced he would have won her over, she would have been unable to resist. Yes, he had only himself to blame. It was up to him to try once more, he must turn back, pay her another visit and talk to her again. He couldn't lose the love of his life like this, he couldn't just surrender her to someone else. He must turn back at once...

With all these thoughts running through his mind, he turned round and slowly retraced his steps up the street he had come down earlier. As he proceeded however, he began to doubt he could ever bring himself to knock on the door, ask to see Eulalia and find himself alone with her again in Ophiomachos's gloomy study; yet despite this he continued on, every step buoyed by some fresh irrational and delusive hope. He would approach Eulalia on the street when she was out for her evening walk and argue passionately until he finally convinced her, or at least arrange a later assignation so that she could hear him out, as it was hardly natural for anyone to throw away their happiness. Or perhaps he would see her at her window, as Eulalia would be expecting him herself, unable to believe he could relinquish her without a fight and surrender her to someone else. A look would suffice to re-establish their rapport, the look would be followed by a smile, the smile by a quickening heart-throb, the heart-throb by overwhelming joy, and a golden world of promise would open up before her once again.

He was becoming more and more irrational. On reaching the Ophiomachos residence, he surreptitiously glanced up at the windows but all of them were shut. All was quiet in the street. As he passed their front door his courage failed him and instead of knocking he continued on to the end of the narrow street. He looked about to see whether he had aroused the curiosity of the neighbours, then, anxious and irresolute, he retraced his steps. But this time he didn't even raise his eyes and quickened his step as he passed the Ophiomachoses' house. His dejection increased as he realized that further attempts were futile and he racked his brains as to what he should do next. The most bizarre ideas were running through his mind. He must put an end to his miserable life! No point in going home, he would take some road out into the country and walk through the night and all the following day without a break, until eventually he collapsed from sheer exhaustion. What else was left for him to do on earth! All his dreams now lay in ruins and he himself was done for...

He had walked some distance out of town, following the road along the shore. Night had set in and not many people were about. The sea was calm and a few stars were mirrored on its surface. In the darkness under the trees he noticed the chairs and tables of a little café still out,

and went over and sat down. He ordered a bottle of spirits from the
disconcerted waiter and settled down to drink. After the first couple of
glasses he began to feel a little dizzy. He suddenly felt light-hearted and
his sorrows disappeared. Gradually an irresistible desire to laugh came
over him. All he could remember was that he had dreamed a ghastly
dream which now had vanished and that he was blissfully happy in his
current circumstances. It was just that his head was spinning a little and
there was a strange buzzing in his ears, but that would soon pass no
doubt, he felt absolutely fine, he was not in the least concerned about his
health, it wasn't at all chilly this evening. So, bottoms up! Eulalia was his
and he would marry her, she had consented at her home – those other
worries that had plunged him into such irrational grief were all part of
that hideous and unnatural nightmare, which was neither consistent
with Eulalia's character nor with ordinary human kindness! All human
beings were innocent and decent! They did not enjoy tormenting others.
Ophiomachos had relented, he had seen how unjust his request had
been and given them his blessing, he too was innocent... After all, he
too had been afraid of something non-existent. He was not consumed
by worries, he too could live as he pleased, happy in his old house, yes,
yes, untold happiness and pure joy reigned throughout the world. How
glorious life was! Drink up!

But why was his head spinning like this, especially when he closed his
eyes... and yet his eyes did seem to want to close. At the same time, he
had never felt better than he did this evening. Never in his life! Nor had
he ever been so certain that he would not fall sick again. He had grown
stronger and his health was now robust, just what he needed for the great
task that lay ahead. And how splendidly all that was now progressing...
The peasants were hungry for education and the island's youth had no
higher ideal, no greater duty than to elevate the people's consciousness.
Everywhere a cry of joy resounded, which his soul eagerly embraced. The
revolution was at hand, it was meeting no resistance, soon it would reign
triumphant over a happy jubilant world. Drink up!

He himself would now like to address the crowds, to fire them with his
enthusiasm, oh, he already knew what he would say. He would use songs!
Nobody would laugh, the words and meaning didn't matter, people would
know the reason he was speaking, whatever he might say, and would sing
along, that was what revolution was about, and they would pour into the

streets reeling with laughter. He couldn't help laughing now himself. Ha, ha! Life! But he had never understood it quite like this before. Ha, ha! Another drink!

Just then a group of peasants came along the road singing. It was some ordinary popular song. He heard them in the distance and started listening intently. The voices drew nearer. To his ears they had the resonance of celestial harmony, enhancing his euphoria. He beat time with his foot and joined in the singing in a low befuddled voice. The handful of peasants seemed to him an inestimable crowd and his heart leapt up for joy, the song was the triumphal Hymn to Liberty, the crowd the island's workers returning from their victory, and he was bent on joining them. But why must his head start spinning just at this important moment, why were his legs refusing to obey? Perhaps he should settle the bill, as he really ought to join them – after all, wasn't he their leader? Hadn't those young people hailed him as their leader? They were there too now among the workers. Ha, ha, ha! One last drink! He himself had led them brilliantly in their victory today. They would all run to Eulalia's house together, and he would weep for joy…

He tried to cry out and tell them to wait for him, but his tongue got tangled in his teeth and this made him double up with laughter. He considered this too the effect of his solemn joy. Yes, his joy was truly solemn, full of dignity. And of course he must set an example. He had to struggle to get up from his chair. This also made him laugh. He realized that he was having difficulty moving his legs and was stumbling along, then he noticed that he was lurching from left to right and from tree to tree at an escalating pace. Even this made him laugh and he said to himself that his legs must be in a hurry to join the workers and the young people up ahead. He went on a little further, staggering and bumping into trees and lamp-posts in the dark and laughing all the time, until finally he broke into a run and, unable to keep his head up, fell flat on his face in the dry grass, then after trying in vain to get up again, suddenly lost consciousness and fell into a torpid sleep.

Late the next day he woke up in his own bed. His mind was a blur, his head felt heavy, and he had no recollection of how he had found his way back to his room. He looked about and saw his mother sitting in her armchair at the foot of the bed. He realized she had been keeping watch beside him the whole night. A sigh escaped him. He felt ashamed.

'I'll emigrate,' he said to her quietly, after greeting her with a sad smile.
'Not a bad idea!' she replied in earnest and embraced him tearfully.

7

Spring was almost over, the hot weather had set in already and midday
was approaching.

Petros Athanatos, ugly and stooping in his shabby clothes, had been
wandering all over town. From the tree-lined square he descended to
the sea and walked along the coastal road, then past the market and
the harbour, calling in at all the cafés and making enquiries among the
common people he knew and often fraternized with, and twice already
he had ascended to the Ophiomachos residence, but all in vain, Giorgis
was nowhere to be found, no one had seen him or had any idea where he
might be. Poor Petros was exasperated.

He was just returning to the square when suddenly he saw Spyros in
the main street up ahead. He decided to ask him too. He watched him for
a moment and smiled sardonically. Spyros looked tired as he ambled along
in his impeccable white suit, looking about him with his usual slightly
inane smile. Petros greeted him and asked if he had seen his brother, as he
needed to get in touch with him at once, but Spyros was of no help either.
They had left home together, but much earlier. He had bumped into him
again later on the street, but Giorgis had not mentioned where he was
going, and he of course had not enquired. There was an understanding
in their family that no one ever asked such things. But he would take a
turn with Petros, since he was at a loose end: Petros would know just how
that felt! No doubt Giorgis was wanted at the Valsamises' residence. Of
course, that would be why Petros was looking for him. How was the poor
fellow anyway? Had he finally resolved to die? People said he was getting
much worse. Ah, Giorgis seemed to be having better luck than himself
in that regard. Even though Giorgis was stupid to insist that he would
never marry Aimilia Valsamis. Who was the smart one now! But then it's
invariably the stupid whom Fortune favours. Ha, ha, ha!

He laughed and rambled on like this, trying to keep pace with Petros
who, finding his garrulousness tiresome, walked rapidly ahead, glancing

into shops and keeping an eye out among the passing crowd. Suddenly Spyros's face clouded over and the inane smile vanished from his lips as a painful thought tugged at his heartstrings, though without distressing him too deeply as he was incapable of serious thought.

'Did you know?' he said. 'Asteris's daughter, the girl I was chasing, will be getting married shortly to that fellow from abroad – but I suppose you've heard already!'

'No!' replied Petros abruptly and, glancing at him superciliously, laughed his unpleasant laugh.

'It's true though,' insisted Spyros. 'Money follows money. Asteris got wind of us, I'm certain of it from the hints he dropped. My father, you see, has made a complete mess of his affairs, and everyone expects him to be completely ruined. I tell you this in confidence, of course. All my plans have been shot to hell simply because my father didn't have the wit to conceal our situation for a few days longer. Just a few days!'

Petros looked at him again and laughed sarcastically.

'You think it's funny, eh?' Spyros went on gloomily. 'But I'm the one who's lost her and she just slipped through my fingers!'

'What does it matter,' laughed Petros.

'How do you mean, what does it matter? At the ball I thought I had everything sewn up and she'd be mine – but then Mrs Chrysospathis... No chance of finding another girl as rich as that now!'

'But for God's sake man, are you really afraid of poverty? One needs so little to keep body and soul together. Amazingly little! What would I do with heaps of money? Of course, you Ophiomachoses are a proud lot and you don't want your poverty to show. That's natural enough. I know how it is with the old aristocratic families, but at least the others show some initiative, by accepting sinecures for instance – your family could do that too. Ah, you Ophiomachoses! You know how to go about making requests like that, or having others make them for you. So you shouldn't just rely on dowries. Especially with your future brother-in-law Steriotis running for parliament. The government is bound to change and the present lot will be sent packing. There's your opportunity! Get Eulalia to request a place for you as well, of the kind they give to ruined aristocrats, in a pawnshop shall we say.'

Spyros's small face lit up. A smile appeared beneath his trim little moustache and his whole body seemed to move more gracefully as he

looked about. He liked the idea. He must pursue it. He would consult
Giorgis right away. There was no longer any reason not to join the minister's party like all the other landlords now that their future brother-in-
law was going into politics! Even Giorgis could have no objections and
would agree to it. Especially now that Alkis would no longer be around
to lead him astray.

Petros was tired of listening to this glib chatter. He replied in mono-
syllables, looked at Giorgis irritably and quickened his pace as if trying
to shake him off. He glanced at his watch and with an impatient gesture
muttered:

'That Giorgis, that Giorgis, it might almost be deliberate! Mrs Valsamis
doesn't like to be kept waiting and she'll take it out on me. We're supposed
to be there by eleven!'

They had arrived back at the square. Underneath the trees, ladies and
gentlemen were sitting in the shade. Mrs Theophano Chrysospathis,
seated between the two Kallergis sisters like a queen, was discussing
charity shops with Arkoudis, the banker with the mournful face who
squinted to make himself more charming. Further down, surrounded
by a group of young people who kept bursting into laughter, an angry
red-faced Marcantonio Iustinianis was again holding forth with histrionic
gestures, cursing the Greek nation, the new administrative structures and
the peasants' immorality, and eulogizing the era of Venetian rule. Also
out for a stroll in the square that morning was the stout, serene-faced,
white-bearded old poet, renowned for his musical settings of courtly
and patriotic verse, accompanied by a small ugly pale-faced elder, with
glittering eyes and trim white beard, who seemed mere skin and bones in
his black suit. He too was one of the island's celebrities, but the common
people hated him...

At last Petros Athanatos caught sight of Giorgis up ahead. He was
talking to a friend, a tall blond man with dreamy blue eyes, another writer
and enthusiast for Greek patriotic causes, who regarded the nation's
ambitions as virtually achieved already and was impatiently awaiting the
hour of war to throw himself into the struggle too. Petros took his leave
of Spyros and hastened towards them. He watched the visionary poet
curiously a moment, restraining his impulse to burst out laughing as he
waited for him to finish his critical assessment of the political situation in
Europe. Things were unmistakably leading to war, and this would afford

Greece too a unique opportunity to 'vindicate' her rights, her sacred and 'indefeasible' rights. It would be a fatal mistake should courage fail her when the time came!

Finally, Petros said to Giorgis, looking at him peevishly:

'I've been looking for you for hours! Where on earth have you been? I went round to your place twice and have been traipsing all over town with your brother looking for you, but by now Valsamis may well have died on us. The fact is, he has become much weaker. He'll soon be on his way... And Godspeed! He has arranged for the lawyer to come round today to hand over his will to him; he's leaving everything to Aimilia, because, he says, a woman like her should be able to maintain the social position she's cut out for. The lawyer will be there by now and Valsamis wants you as a witness.'

'Me?' replied Giorgis in a curious tone.

They took their leave of the poet, who was smiling at them ironically, and hurried off together.

'So it looks as though he won't live then?' remarked Giorgis sadly.

'No, don't worry,' replied his companion, laughing sarcastically. 'And the worst of it is, he never knew how to live. Now we'll see whether he knows how to die. There's an art to that too, as perfidious nature has endowed man's soul (animal that he is) with a strange persistent love of life even if it resembles death. Why ever did he wish to live in high society! Aimilia wasn't meant for him, absolutely not! She was right not to love him. A woman like her... But I can see that she's now deeply saddened. As she's been for some time in fact, and it's the one thing I can't bear – her sadness! – but I can't help her. How could I help her? All I know is that she's a creature who should never be allowed to suffer, she is made for happiness and joy, and if others have to suffer because of her, so what. Ah, Giorgis, even you have failed to appreciate the true value of that creature, even though she's granted you her favours! You don't know the treasures in her heart. And love is not a crime, Giorgis! Don't make her suffer...'

Giorgis looked at him puzzled, but did not reply. The eccentric fellow was an insoluble mystery to him too. Where did he find such tenderness in that savage heart of his? By now they had reached the Valsamis residence and made their way upstairs. The maid who let them in informed them that the lawyer was already there, and that he and Mrs Aimilia Valsamis were waiting for them in the sitting-room.

When Aimilia saw them enter, she went pale and had difficulty in restraining her emotions. As she rose from the sofa she realized that her whole body was trembling. The presence of the man she loved eclipsed all other considerations, and the only thing she was conscious of was her love for him, a love he had scorned for so many long days now. Would this death finally unite them? Would the days of misery, the ugly moments they had lived through, be forgotten once and for all? She raised her hand to her brow and her eyes caressed him as she sighed and shook his hand.

Giorgis responded courteously enough, bowing politely but without raising his eyes. His expression betrayed no emotion and he did not squeeze her hand. She felt as if her heart would break. She realized that this meeting was crucial for their relationship and that she must do something. She glanced towards the door.

But by now the lawyer too had risen, tucking his large file under his arm, and Aimilia, realizing that he had no time to waste, escorted the three men into her husband's room.

The sun was shining through the open window, the light falling on a large walnut table strewn with books and papers in the middle of the spacious room. The sick man was sitting beside it in a large leather armchair facing the door, his legs stretched out before him. He was pale, gaunt and so emaciated that his bones showed through his translucent skin, and his tired eyes, withdrawn deep into their sockets, looked larger than usual and seemed to be yearning for rest. His colourless lips, though barely visible, smiled with an indescribable sweetness. A red silk shawl was draped over his knees. No word of complaint escaped him and the whole room had a cheerful appearance, with its handsome pictures on the ash-grey walls, its plush red carpet, its elegant furnishings and its brass bedstead gleaming in the sun.

Periklis Valsamis was clearly delighted to see his wife entering the room with the three men, and he tried to get out of his chair to receive them, but realizing the effort would exhaust him he smiled and allowed Aimilia to dissuade him, after which the others approached and shook his diaphanous hand.

The legal formalities were concluded unsentimentally and swiftly and the lawyer stayed only a few minutes longer, then murmuring a blessing over the sick man departed, while the other three remained seated by his side.

Periklis Valsamis looked at each of them in turn with the same sweet smile and all of them remained silent for a few moments.

Then Giorgis noticed a book lying open on the table, which the sick man had evidently been reading recently. His curiosity did not escape Valsamis, who smiling serenely remarked in his sad feeble voice:

'It's Lucretius's great poem. I've been translating Book Three lately, where he talks about the soul. I've always had a weakness for translating foreign texts that I admire into our vernacular. It was just a rough draft for my own gratification, my sole claim to being a poet...'

He smiled his tragic smile again and, picking up a notebook from the table, continued: 'Listen...'

And he started reading in his faint voice:

'And so death is nothing to us, nor can it affect us in the least, since manifestly the essence of the soul is mortal...'

And closing the notebook he continued, as if he had prepared what he was about to say:

'That's what Lucretius tells us. It's what others too have claimed before and since and I myself am convinced that it is true, even though no incontrovertible proof exists. Yet, even though I've arrived at this conviction through rational thought, on other occasions, both in the past and now that death is stretching out his hand toward me, I find a vision of another world arising spontaneously from the very deepest recesses of my soul. Something tells me that the soul does not perish with the body. Why?'

'Because,' said Petros Athanatos with his sarcastic laugh, 'you hope to carry on living after death!'

'To tell the truth,' said the sick man with a smile, 'far from hoping any such thing, I dread it. Not me, but my soul itself! And I suspect that even if men could prove with mathematical certainty that the soul really does die with the body, or even before it, nevertheless that voice, which apparently comes from the depths of our being, would still not remain silent. If this is true for the rest of humanity, how many impulses of the soul must have their origin in this uncertainty, and where else does this uncertainty lead if not to religion?'

'What rights does a man have in eternal life?' asked Petros angrily.

'I don't know,' he replied, 'nor am I a believer. But listen, my friends... As a child and even I'm ashamed to admit as an adult, I've always been afraid of lonely nights and dark places near cemeteries and charnel houses, but even when I was quite terrified, my reasoning mind has always mocked such irrational fears and with an effort of will I've been able to shake them off – but never the uncertainty. And the same is happening in my wretched soul today, my mind rejects all metaphysical belief and all religion in the same way, and I've continued to seek evidence endorsing that rejection, yet the uncertainty doesn't go away. So now I've decided to subordinate my mind to this uncertainty, and it has been all the easier because I am so weak. I want to redeem my bond from life, as the poet says, and repay all my debts, because, my friends, that will stand me in good stead if death's loud knock should wake me shortly in another world, be it a better or a worse one.' He paused, exhausted, and looked at each of them in turn with his endearing smile, trying to gauge what impression he had made on them. Then in a weaker voice he continued, weighing his words carefully:

'Let me therefore receive remission for my sins from everyone, starting with you, dear friends, and especially you, Aimilia. And afterwards permit me to do as others do in their last hour, as something tells me I too should submit to society's decrees.'

He sighed and looked for a few moments at Aimilia, who now lowered her pale face. He watched Petros Athanatos get to his feet, glance at him mockingly with a tear in his eye, and cross to the window overlooking the street, evidently to conceal his face. Finally he gazed at Giorgis Ophiomachos, who sat resting his head on his elbow, his eyes covered with his hand. Then he continued:

'Will you find the road to happiness, Aimilia? You searched for it, and rightly so! But from that point on I perceived the world differently. I realized I had to submit uncomplainingly to a fate I was powerless to change because I was an invalid, an outcast from life who could no longer either give or receive happiness. I sublimated the sorrow in my heart by making life itself the object of my study, even though I learned nothing and life remained a great mystery to me too. As a result, however, today I am ready to depart this world without a heavy heart, without sighs or lamentations. Will I see you again, dear friends, either in this life or the next? But now I wish to be left alone while my mind is still clear, because as the ancients recommended in their writings, man should depart with blessings on his lips!'

Giorgis was by now in tears, overwhelmed with remorse. He was reflecting that he more than any of the others had wronged this man, who had taken up so little space on earth and was dying as modestly as he had lived. His heart was devastated and just then he was entertaining unusually noble sentiments. He would willingly lay down his life to be able to cure the man whom he had wronged, or at least throw himself at his feet and beg for his forgiveness. But the near approach of death disarmed him. He noticed that Periklis Valsamis was looking at him from his armchair, as if he had guessed the reason for his turmoil, and that his pallid lips were smiling at him sweetly.

Now however Aimilia too was gazing at him anxiously. Her husband, his illness and his imminent death all paled into insignificance in the face of her grand passion. That alone was living, she alone had a right to life and she didn't want to lose it!

'We should go,' she told the others, getting up. And the two men, deeply moved, bade the dying man a last farewell and followed her out of the room.

Both of them had donned their hats. She looked at them with mounting apprehension. No, she refused to let him go, she simply couldn't, she must talk to him now, tell him how devastated she was feeling, offer him everything, her life if need be. Why was he evading her like this, how could he go on treating her love with such contempt? But – alas! – they were on the point of leaving, they were already getting ready to say goodbye. Oh, she must think of some way to detain Giorgis, if he stayed back perhaps there might still be some hope of a reconciliation. And pale from another wave of emotion and with a tremor in her voice, she asked him pleadingly:

'Oh, do stay, at least until Petros gets back. I don't want to be alone!'

Giorgis looked at her questioningly, shuddered, uncertain what to do, then followed her into the little sitting-room adjacent to her bedroom.

He sat down on the soft divan and she stood in front of him, overcome by her emotion, gazing at him with uneasy fervour, yearning for a kind look, a compassionate smile from him. She was in deep distress. He remained silent and kept his eyes averted the whole time, preoccupied with his own thoughts.

Finally he said with a sad smile:

'He's leaving quite an ugly shadow...'

'Life,' she replied, flaring up, 'is not death, that's why it's not afraid of shadows.'

Suddenly she sat down beside him. Her cheeks were flushed and her heart felt about to burst. She looked him in the face, but he was still absorbed in his own thoughts. She seized his hand. Alarmed, he attempted to withdraw it.

'Oh, Giorgis!' she sighed.

They both remained silent for a while and she gazed at him almost tearfully, with longing in her eyes. Was she going to lose him? Would he leave her? How would she ever find him again? Why did he keep avoiding her eyes so stubbornly? Did he have no feeling for her any more? Didn't he understand her?

'Oh, Giorgis!' she repeated passionately, 'how can you torture me like this, when I love you more than anything or anyone in the whole world? Oh Giorgis! How can you?'

He looked at her embarrassed. His brow clouded. He found this woman's passion thoroughly disturbing, it weakened his resolve and insinuated itself into his heart. Did he still love her? At that moment she was certainly making a deep impression on him.

'But don't you see?' he replied. 'He's just next door!'

'How can you do this to me?' she persisted with the same intensity. 'To my love for you? Can't you see what this love means to me? Do you think it asks who might be next door, do you think it chooses time and place? Oh, don't be so heartless... I've waited for you here, I've waited on the street to tell you everything, and now I'm tongue-tied and don't know how to tell you how much love has made me suffer, the love you've scorned! But why? You've rejected me so long – you've wilfully refused to let me love you as much as I should wish, with no regard for anything beyond your happiness! Oh, Giorgis! Why, but why?'

He listened to her bewildered by the depth of her feeling, his face pale and conscious that he was on the point of giving in. Suddenly he recalled their former flaming rows, her cruel pride which had only temporarily disappeared, and the deep humiliation of her sick husband, willing to efface himself murmuring a prayer, and he still managed to resist her feebly:

'Don't you see?' he said. 'Now's the time for things to end between us.'

'No!' she cried, as if she had been stabbed. 'You talk like that,' she continued, 'because you don't know what I feel for you here, deep inside – yes, for no one else but you, now and always. You don't see it because you don't love me! And if I don't speak now, when will I get another chance? It's easy for you to keep avoiding me, Giorgis, because you don't love me. But even if you don't, at least have pity on the woman who adores you, who regards you as a higher being, as the master of her destiny. Do you hear me, Giorgis, do you hear?'

She was talking rapidly with ever-increasing emotion and her voice sounded husky on her burning lips. Her eyes were blazing. She kept turning her head nervously and adjusting her position. Suddenly she began to weep, letting her tears trickle down her cheeks unchecked, for in her distress she was not conscious of them. He listened with growing trepidation. Her words dripped molten lead into his heart, kindling his sympathy for this suffering woman whom he could make happy with a word, he recalled all their moments of ecstasy together, the sweetest he had ever known, and thought of the elation he would feel were he to surrender, finally vanquished by her fiery passion. But instead he made a move to get up and go. She seized his hand and held him back by force, her pale face transformed into the picture of despair.

'So you're going?' she said fearfully. 'But where to? Has everything I've said, all my anguish been in vain? Oh Giorgis, can't you see you're the only person in the world I care for? And are you determined even so to make me suffer? Oh, I refuse to let you go!'

She flung his hand away and continued, wiping her eyes:

'No, no, I won't oppose your wishes, I know you'll do the right thing, a man like you can only do what's right, what kindness calls for, but I'll never stop adoring you, Giorgis, as only I know how. Oh Giorgis!'

She fell to her knees before him, seized both his hands and kissed them, wetting them with her tears; and raising her face occasionally, she searched his eyes for the least spark of love.

Suddenly he sighed and leaned towards her. She flung her arms around his neck. He embraced her fondly, drawing her head close to his chest. An immense serenity came over him, flooding his heart with pure joy, making everything that had kept them apart seem utterly trivial and the whole world beyond their love irrelevant. He raised her and made her sit beside him, clasping her around the waist. She was still trembling and sobbing in his arms and went on kissing both his hands, until at last a smile of happiness blossomed on her lips. Now she kissed him on the cheeks and brow and he returned her kisses.

'Can this be true? Isn't it all a dream?' she sighed. 'Are we really together again just as before? Oh, oh!'

She went on kissing his brow, his cheeks, his lips and he returned her kisses with an ever increasing ardour that took possession of his heart. She caressed his head, gazed deep into his eyes and planted fiery kisses on his lashes, then pressing him to her breast she murmured rapturous endearments that sank deep into his heart, making him feel giddy.

Suddenly their embraces became more intimate, their kisses more frequent and intense, lips parted lips and flesh sought quivering flesh with primitive desire. Their hearts throbbed violently. By now reason, memory, time and place had lost all meaning and nothing in the world existed save their two souls intoxicated by desire and love.

He had lapsed into despondency again. She had nestled close to him and was gazing at him full of gratitude. He was appalled by what they had just done, so unseemly in the circumstances with the awful mystery of death hovering above that house. Aimilia again felt content with life as she now saw it opening up before her, full of hope for innocent love and tranquil happiness. She threw her arms around his neck and kissed him tenderly. He tried to escape her grasp, but she wouldn't let him, whispering to him sweetly, caressing his face with her cheeks and kissing him repeatedly. Suddenly he said impetuously:

'And Valsamis...'

'Oh,' she smiled, 'love is not afraid of shadows. Life is all before us! And things will always be this way between us.'

Suddenly she remembered Eulalia, and giving him another kiss she asked:

'And Eulalia? Is she getting married?'

'Yes, soon,' he replied with a sad smile.

'Ah,' she said, 'she can't be too happy! And yet Alkis was a sick man.'

'She's sacrificing herself,' replied Giorgis with a sigh.

Aimilia lowered her eyes, thought for a moment and then said shyly:

'Couldn't I have helped? I'd have been only too happy to. But perhaps it's not too late.'

Her words cut Giorgis like a whiplash across the face. He started up, crimson with shame, and replied bitterly:

'Do you know something, your money is the real obstacle to our relationship. That's why... that's why...'

'Oh,' she insisted, 'no one would ever get to hear about it! Would you leave *me* to my fate if *I* found myself destitute some day?'

He didn't reply at once but remained thoughtful. She didn't know what more to say and looked at him as if appealing for sympathy. At last he smiled and said sadly:

'It's my fault, I shouldn't have said anything.'

He now wanted to get away, reflecting that this woman's wealth would be a daily humiliation, and perhaps more of a burden than her love, as his pride was offended even by her good intentions, which was why he felt himself duty-bound to leave her. He was now quite certain of it... Suddenly he reflected how different his life would be, how true his happiness, if he could earn his right to her by the sweat of his brow, if Aimilia Valsamis were not the wealthy lady everybody envied, but a poor unknown young woman like Eulalia. That was the way life was for most ordinary people, for the entire working population, an utterly different world teeming all around him and capable of believing in a brighter future. He looked about with contempt at the rich silk furnishings, the embroidered curtains, the expensive carpet, the fine pictures on the walls and thought how miserable life in that mansion had been for the man who now lay dying there, anxious to end his life with blessings on his lips after asking forgiveness for the wrongs done to him by others. His wife meanwhile was satisfying her insatiable thirst for life there in that room with him, and he recalled the poor fellow's last words, dripping with the honey of benevolence.

'Ah, money...' he murmured plaintively.

She looked at him strangely, fearing he might have taken leave of his senses. She couldn't understand how anyone could be happy when they were needy, where would they find the time for contemplating love?

As she pondered these matters, old Ophiomachos nervously entered the room, huddled in his old frock-coat, a sad smile on his lips. He looked around enquiringly, as if uncertain what was going on, greeted Mrs Valsamis with solicitous politeness and remarked oddly:

'It was my son Spyros who got me worried. He came home in a great hurry looking for you, Giorgis. He wanted to tell you to come here at once, so thinking something might have happened I left the house and came over to find out... How is Valsamis?'

'All he's done is make his will,' said Aimilia indifferently. 'He's much the same as yesterday and the day before, if anything a little better.'

'Oh!' said the old man. 'I thought... I thought... And so I came to find out...' And he smiled sadly as he looked about.

Flushing, Giorgis listened in embarrassment. He signalled to his father behind Aimilia's back to hold his tongue, but the old man was already prattling on and he didn't take the hint.

'No need for all this talk,' Giorgis finally told him in exasperation, 'there's nothing to be concerned about. You're becoming feeble-minded it seems. Let's go!'

He seized his trembling hand, made him bid Aimilia goodbye and firmly led him towards the door. But the old man kept muttering: 'I thought... I thought... And Mrs Valsamis is so wealthy...'

'Let's go!' repeated Giorgis, beginning to lose patience.

Together they descended to the street and walked along in silence. They were now passing along a narrow side-street on their way home. Suddenly a rotten lemon came hurtling from an upstairs window and splattered at their feet, and looking up angrily, Giorgis caught sight of a fat ugly middle-aged woman, her hair dishevelled and her ample bosom on display, who started screaming at them furiously:

'That's what you deserve, you scoundrel! You're bankrupt, that's why you're leaving us to starve to death. A fine Count you are! Shame on you, shame!'

And she spat at him, gesturing obscenely with both hands.

Giorgis looked at his father gloomily. The old man hung his head. He had recognized the woman's voice and now remarked:

'But that ogress doesn't even live here! She must have come on purpose, knowing I come down this street.'

The woman was one of his old flames. They did not reply to her, and quickening their step soon arrived back home.

8

The island's social elite were ascending and descending to and from the Valsamis residence. All were doing their best to appear grief-stricken.

Valsamis had died. Inside the house Aimilia, already dressed in black and clutching a white handkerchief, was welcoming her guests in the large drawing-room. The shutters were closed and a melancholy gloom pervaded the room. Seated beside her were the silent elderly Countess Ophiomachos and Mrs Theophano Chrysospathis, the lady generally considered to be like a sister to some queen, who frittered away her time on charities in memory of her late lover and just then was whispering to the two Kallergis women, who were smiling and listening attentively. Also present, all clad in black and sitting round the walls, were Mrs Urania Daphnopatis, the wife of the idle politician, the pretty Mrs Euterpi Asteris and several others, including Alkis's mother, Photini Sozomenos, a small sad figure clutching a white handkerchief and sitting quietly next to the Countess, whom she knew best.

It was afternoon and the weather was hot. The men were arriving dressed in black and each of them paused before Mrs Valsamis for a moment. Some would shake her hand, bowing their heads and offering a word of consolation or praise of the deceased, others would kiss it silently, displaying unusual emotion. Still others would pass by her just murmuring a greeting. Close friends then went on to kiss the corpse in the airy bedroom, where all the windows stood wide open.

The corpse was already laid out in its imposing coffin, as if buried among the roses, fresh flowers and other sprigs of vegetation, the blond hair and fleshless waxen head just showing and looking as if in a light and dreamless sleep. The deceased's fine mouth was still smiling sweetly, since he had met his end quite fearlessly, as if surrendering to a real eternal peace, and his whole face had retained an incomparable serenity beneath the yellow and frighteningly transparent skin.

A thick lighted candle had been placed beside him, and a plethora of garlands and bouquets adorned the room, giving it the fragrance of a flower garden. Standing in attendance by the coffin were Petros Athanatos, stooped and smiling ironically in his shabby black suit, and Giorgis Ophiomachos, solemn and genuinely grief-stricken.

People entering the bedroom would approach Giorgis, as if to offer him condolences as well, some even shaking his hand. This annoyed him.

Now the poet renowned for his musical settings of courtly and patriotic verse appeared, tall, stout, his affable white-bearded face serene. He was followed by the elder with the long white beard who had worn royal livery for years and the ugly emaciated gentleman also considered one of the glories of the island because he dabbled in philosophy and occasionally wrote songs. Behind them came an older boy in his smart school uniform and clean white gloves, carrying a small bushy laurel wreath. Many ladies had also come through from the drawing-room and the bedroom was quickly becoming crowded, as other gentlemen had followed the elderly poet in, among them Alexandros Ophiomachos Philaretos, wrapped in his old frock-coat and smiling, Dionysios Asteris the rich manufacturer, Doctor Steriotis, the banker Arkoudis, his sad face looking positively tragic for the occasion, as if he were the only one grieving in that indifferent crowd, Archangelos Daphnopatis the languid parliamentary candidate along with his political rival the aristocrat turned minister, whose hauteur betrayed his indifference to the proceedings, and finally all together in a group the three Kallergis brothers – two living off their wives, a third still chasing one of Asteris's daughters – Spyros Ophiomachos, tired but as always on the look-out for a pair of pretty eyes that might fall in love with him, and Marcantonio Iustinianis, ever restless, ever ready to expostulate, but reluctant to cross the threshold as he feared the countenance of death.

Now the widow in her black weeds came into the bedroom and stood beside her dear departed husband, her eyes resting sadly on his smiling waxen face, her pained expression the picture of inconsolable grief. The elderly poet cleared his throat and, lowering his eyes sadly, took the laurel chaplet from the schoolboy and placed it on the dead man's clammy brow, then in a quiet voice began to recite a memorial ode.

The poem told how the wreath was woven from the laurel trees of Helicon, indeed from the very ones the Muses had themselves planted by the Castalian springs. Now however the Muses were in Helicon no longer, as they were escorting their chosen devotee's departed soul to the feet of his Creator, and at this very moment his blessed soul was beseeching the Almighty to pour the balm of consolation from on high into the bosom of his grieving widow, and to comfort his dear friends by persuading them that their parting was but temporary and his fate one to be envied, since he had inherited a better place in everlasting peace.

The audience was overcome by emotion. The ladies were weeping, some on the verge of fainting away, and the men also looked distressed, only Petros Athanatos glanced at the old poet with a derisive smile and then looked angrily about the room, muttering something nobody quite heard.

Meanwhile the priests had arrived. Mrs Valsamis kissed the dead man's brow without a tear, and standing a moment longer by the coffin, gazed at him with a thoughtful, troubled look and her lips whispered the words:

'With you into the grave!'

What she was wondering was whether he might indeed be taking her happiness with him. But those among the crowd who heard her thought this called for fresh displays of emotion. The two Kallergis ladies held her hand consolingly, another woman praised her for her heroic devotion to her ailing husband, and only Petros Athanatos cast his eyes ironically around the room again.

By now the gentlemen were descending to the street, the pall-bearers were hastily covering the coffin, the priests started their monotonous chanting and soon Valsamis's mortal remains were being manoeuvred awkwardly down the broad staircase of his mansion.

Out on the street the aristocrat turned minister had secured a place at the head of the procession, as if he were the principal mourner, well aware that no one would want to take precedence over him, while everyone would want to be seen beside him. He was flanked on one side by Doctor Steriotis and two or three more gentlemen, and on the other by Chrysospathis the banker with his political opponent Archangelos Daphnopatis. They were talking politics and the minister was saying in a fairly loud voice:

'There is no longer the slightest doubt that the election results will amply confirm our predictions, because indubitably the government is facing a defeat in parliament. But I put it to you: will it be possible to accept the opposition's proposal to form a government, given the anomalous external relations with our neighbour? The situation is critical indeed! The opposition is committed to a policy of peace. But I put it to you: will it be able to enforce it? Will it be able to adopt an irreproachable position? Aside from that, the idea is being mooted in opposition circles as to whether it might support the present government, on condition that it agree to give way on the issue of employees. It is therefore imperative that we appoint a number of our own people straight away!'

'You'll bear my brother-in-law in mind, of course, Your Excellency?' said Doctor Steriotis.

'Could there be any doubt?' replied the minister with a smile. 'As you know, I hold the illustrious Ophiomachos family in the highest regard! I've already taken steps to...'

Close behind them came the elderly poet and the pale emaciated gentleman who was the island's other glory, and in the same row Giorgis Ophiomachos and his blond poet friend, whose blue eyes dreamed incessantly of wars of liberation, who believed unshakably in the Great Idea, national rights and their swift implementation, and who meanwhile was preparing himself for bloody conflict. Then came the small wiry red-faced old Marcantonio Iustinianis, restless as ever and looking angrily about him, ready to curse the Greek nation, the new system of administration or the peasants' immorality and praise the glorious Venetian past. Others followed, including Alexandros Ophiomachos Philaretos, wrapped in his old frock-coat and smiling sadly, and next to him Arkoudis the banker, with his tragic expression, just then explaining the nation's economic situation to a few rich friends.

'The fall in the price of gold,' he was saying dejectedly, 'is a very natural phenomenon in my opinion. Gold is a commodity, now that mandatory circulation is in force, and not a currency, that is, a means of exchange. At the same time there is a shortage of paper money. So we are going to see the paper drachma exceeding the value of the gold frank, though only temporarily. I say temporarily, because the political situation is extremely volatile. Many clouds obscure the diplomatic horizon in the East, and diplomatic events are bound to have an impact on the financial market. This is why I advise all my friends to invest in gold.'

And he laughed dolefully.

'Commerce, on the other hand,' he went on at once, 'is getting healthier. The island is making great commercial progress, always comparatively speaking of course, but enough to inspire confidence.'

And squinting at Ophiomachos he added even more gloomily:

'We, the banking house Arkoudis and Son, for example, have just been obliged to open a new branch in London. For obvious reasons, I shall be appointing my son as manager there. Yes, of course.'

And he laughed again lugubriously.

'Ah!' someone exclaimed, nodding in admiration.

Someone else remarked casually:

'Rumour has it that he's about to get married. Will he be taking his bride with him then? What marvellous good fortune those...'

With an even more anguished look, the banker interrupted him:

'Parents,' he said, 'are duty-bound to create career opportunities for their children. If my son wants to get married, that's his business, who can prevent him? Marriage is entirely up to him. I will never force him into it, nor will I ever advise against it.'

Again he smiled his baleful smile.

Old Ophiomachos adjusted his frock-coat as if feeling the cold, and looked at him with hatred. What new disaster did fate have in store for him now? He sighed and shook his head dejectedly as he stared at the coffin on the shoulders of the four pall-bearers. The man who had just departed from this world was young and might have been happy, since he had no financial worries. But in fact his life too had been a torment, only now had he finally found peace. His fate was like his own. Why was he himself, now grown old and feeble, still clinging to this world? Was he blessed with a robust constitution merely to withstand these many poisoned chalices? This time it was Louisa, barely launched into society and now destined to suffer its opprobrium and so become embittered. It would be hell again at home, more unbearable than last time, just as he thought he might get a chance to catch his breath!

But at least this time the one to blame would be Louisa, he was not responsible, he was not standing in her way. She herself had chosen the fellow, completely of her own accord. He had turned a blind eye at first, afraid of the responsibility and persuading himself that this cocksure young upstart wasn't going to cheat her. Louisa, poor thing, was in a hurry to escape the poverty of their home, which was stifling her with its heavy odour of decay. They had become even poorer lately... But then, whatever happened they'd still say he was the only one responsible because he had ruined the family. What a burden daughters were... All they wanted was to get married – and at a time like this! Couldn't they imagine any other future for themselves?

Suddenly the old man had a more consoling thought. Fortune certainly seemed to be smiling on the Ophiomachos family with this death. Giorgis at least would now be wealthy! Why shouldn't he marry Mrs Valsamis after all? Giorgis was an educated, enterprising young man, well respected on the island, and now he'd be well off as well. The family was on the rise again. Eulalia too had managed to console herself. And there was still hope that something might turn up for Spyros, if not today then some time soon. So many people were anti-aristocracy these days, upstart foreigners who didn't know the origin of their own fur coats, yet determined to marry their daughters into noble families. So were the old titles really not worth anything, just because the Greek constitution had abolished them? Pooh! Let him go to London if he wished, that cockscomb son of old Arkoudis, *Mister* Arkoudis! Let him go anywhere he liked! There'd be plenty more suitors for Louisa, provided he left town at once. Old age wasn't exactly hounding her as yet! But he must inform his wife tonight. She would give Louisa a good talking to.

By now they had reached the church and he was obliged to stop and wait at the door. Spyros came up to him smiling stupidly and in his sleepy voice informed him that Doctor Steriotis had already spoken to the minister about a job for him, for the second time in fact, there at the funeral, and the minister had given his word. Surely he wouldn't lie over such a matter, particularly since he knew the Ophiomachoses had some influence in their village, especially Spyros himself, whom the peasants were so fond of.

But the old man looked at him in disbelief. He was far from gratified to receive this news. The idea that his sons should have to take a job out of necessity did not please him one bit. Work seemed to him degrading. But then he reflected that times had changed and one must adapt. It was just that he didn't approve of the particular job his son was after: the responsibility was far too great, the administration far too onerous. Notebooks, jewellery, valuables – all too easily stolen. Spyros might be duped some day, might put his trust in the wrong person – who could tell? After all, he didn't have much strength of character. He must explain all these things to Spyros. He ought not to take on such a burden. But then again, let him do as he pleased!

They had by now entered the lighted church, and father and son remained side by side. Ophiomachos entered a pew. The choristers were beginning their monotonous chanting. Spyros looked at his father, awaiting his response, anxious no doubt to thank the minister on his behalf. But the old man merely shrugged, looking him in the eye and making a wry face.

Then putting his hand on his son's shoulder, he nodded in the direction of Arkoudis the banker and whispered in his ear:

'He says his son Goulielmos is going abroad. He's off to London to set up a branch there.'

'What of it!' replied Spyros. 'I've known about that for days! He's taking Louisa with him.'

'How do you know that?' asked his father, glaring at him angrily.

'He wrote and told Louisa. She showed me the letter herself. Why are you getting all het up in front of people? He's such a splendid fellow, Goulielmos, such an honourable chap!'

'Just wait until we get home!' his father said threateningly, becoming livid with rage because he couldn't give vent to his frustration. 'You'll see! I shall do outrageous things. You'd be masters in my house, would you? Before I'm dead and buried, eh?'

All through the service he was restless. People began to stare at him. He couldn't sit still, kept looking round impatiently and fidgeted with his old frock-coat. The one thing that he couldn't stand, that enraged him, drove him mad, made him evil-hearted, caused him to forget all bonds of affection, all responsibility, his self-respect and his position, was for anything to happen in his house without his knowledge! When he got home that evening, he would either have to let off steam or he'd explode! He hardly knew himself what he might do!

At last the service came to an end. He followed the crowd of mourners out of the church, but didn't feel like accompanying the coffin to the cemetery and hurried home. He wanted to speak to Louisa and his wife. What was all this he had been hearing!

No one was at home. They had not yet returned from the funeral. He began pacing up and down his gloomy study, casting angry looks at the knight in armour, the lords with their white wigs, and the lovely ladies smiling sweetly from their frames, and as he did so he kept mulling over all his grievances, bewailing his current dire poverty, the bitter pills he had been obliged to swallow, and the fresh calamity awaiting him over Louisa. He would now have to count every penny before spending anything, because Doctor Steriotis, who would be managing his affairs until all his debts had been paid off, would not be handing out more than absolutely necessary for their subsistence. The catastrophe was far worse than he had ever imagined. It would take years of hard work and good management

to put things right. Or so Doctor Steriotis had told him. He had ordered
new ledgers, started to give written notice to the peasants, and begun a
dozen court actions without considering the cost or the people he would
be offending. Having none of the Ophiomachos weakness, or hereditary
sympathy for the peasants, he set resolutely about his task. He was well
aware that life is a struggle and that the weak must submit to the strong
and work for them.

At last he heard their footsteps on the stairs. They were taking their
time coming up. He heard Louisa's laughing voice, listened with distaste
to his wife sighing as she battled up the stairs, and once again losing his
temper gestured obscenely at her through the closed door. It was all her
fault, of course it was. How could she and her daughter put so much
faith in the assurances of that young jackanapes, who was still a boy and
doubtless had nothing more in mind than to amuse himself? Why couldn't
his wife have a little sense for once? And why had she kept her daughter's
affair secret from him? He felt a malicious urge to bring up every scandal
about his wife's family he could think of, all those aunts of hers, the sisters
of her mother and her grandfather, each with her disreputable story. None
of that had been forgotten with their passing. The British governors, their
officers and many locals had had a rare old time with them. The old man
knew all about this ancient gossip. And now Louisa was showing signs
of taking after them, of keeping up the family tradition.

It was already late. He took another turn around his gloomy study
where it was getting dark, giving them time to go upstairs and change
their clothes, then unable to restrain himself a moment longer he hurried
up the stairs and burst into the dining-room. Now he had them where he
wanted them, under his control, now they'd see who was in charge! His
old eyes emitted sparks of rage as he looked around. He had lowered his
head more than usual and there was spittle at the corners of his mouth
as he adjusted his old frock-coat.

The two women realized something out of the ordinary was happening again and looked at one another apprehensively, both simultaneously
fearing that perhaps he had gone mad. Meanwhile the old man, coming
straight to the point, began shouting:

'What have the pair of you, mother and daughter, been up to behind
my back? What's going on? Good God! How dare you bring disgrace
on my white hairs! All I had left in my old age was my reputation, it was

in your hands, and you have made me blush with shame! What d'you mean by it, eh?'

'What on earth's the matter?' said the mother softly, looking frightened.

He did not answer her, but started striding up and down the spacious room, flushed to the gills and breathing heavily, the veins bulging at his temples. He was again at a loss how to begin reproaching them for their shameless conduct, for keeping all their shameful secrets from him, the whole family conspiring to deceive him. Eventually he thundered:

'It's your daughters, Maria, your daughters! They've turned out just like your ancestors, like that aunt of yours who disgraced herself with the High Commissioner and eloped with him to England, the Indies, Persia, I've forgotten where! Such are the glorious memories you pride yourselves on! Everyone knows about your family history. And now you're trying to launch your daughters on the same path! How dare you!'

'Are you out of your mind, Where-Are-You!' his wife exclaimed, stung to the quick. 'Don't shout like that! Don't make your family a laughing-stock for nothing, people can hear us in the street!'

Her voice quavered and she kept clasping and unclasping her hands in her lap.

'For my daughters to be receiving love letters while I'm still alive,' the old man shouted, 'and for none of you to know a thing about it! I can't believe it! And for you to accept them, Louisa! Why, for heaven's sake? Who gave you permission? Your mother? Without consulting me? Do I count for nothing in this family? Without her saying a single word to me? What's the meaning of it? Are you all determined to disgrace me?'

They made no reply and the old man ranted on, raising his voice:

'Well, if that's what you're up to, here's what I intend to do! I won't give you a single penny for your dowry, because he dared to seduce you in my house, behind my back – that village lout. And he even plays the English gentleman, what, what!' Here he swayed his whole body in imitation of Goulielmos's swagger. 'Just let him show his ugly mug round here again, and we'll see if he ever gets to London. I'll give him what for! And anyway, his father doesn't want you! D'you understand? That's why he's sending him to London. But if he sets foot in this house, he'll soon see! I'll give him something to remember, old though I may be. And he won't marry you, even if you swallow the cutlery to please him! D'you understand?'

He shouted these last words so loud that the cutlery rattled on the table. He was about to continue his tirade when suddenly he realized that anger was choking off his voice and he became quite desperate. His rage turned to frenzy.

Louisa standing there pale before him made no reply and her mocking smile seemed to declare that she would jolly well do what she wanted and marry Goulielmos Arkoudis if she pleased, that she was her own mistress and nothing whatsoever was going to stop her. He understood at once. Flinging himself upon her, he tried to grab her by the hair, but he wasn't quick enough and she easily slipped from his grasp, ran off and locked herself in her room.

Quite beside himself, the old man now collapsed onto the ancient sofa. His eyes filled with tears and he sobbed aloud. But now his wife approached him, a smile on her lips and a tear in the corner of her eye, and said to him gently:

'It's no use getting all upset like this, Where-Are-You, and making yourself ill. Do you think I haven't been keeping an eye on them? Nothing's happened, Louisa's innocent. He wrote to her, that's all. She's not replied, nor will she. Why should I keep your family's secrets from you?'

'She's deceiving you as well,' he replied, glaring at her. 'Louisa has your family's blood. She'll come to a bad end!' Then, completely shattered, he got to his feet, adjusted his old frock-coat and prepared to go back down to his study.

'How can you be so unjust, Where-Are-You?' replied his wife.

PART THREE

I

SEVERAL MONTHS HAD ELAPSED and spring had again returned. Inside Doctor Steriotis's splendid villa, in a small high-ceilinged recently redecorated room, Eulalia was playing the piano. Ensconced in a deep settee, his eyes half-closed, Giorgis Ophiomachos was listening attentively to the harmonious melody as its complexities unfolded. Pellucid light and a cool balmy breeze came in through the open window. Their minds just then were wholly absorbed in the music, forgetful of their everyday concerns.

Eulalia was wearing a thin green dress with flared skirts and sleeves that showed off her alabaster neck, and her youthful face looked radiant as her fingers glided over the ivory keys, now swiftly now more slowly, now flying apart now reuniting, coaxing out the rhythmic harmonies, her rings flashing now and then. The lengthy sonata, which had opened with a simple tune, suddenly began to open up like some spacious apartment, weaving several disparate melodies into a single poignant soulful harmony, which steadily ascended, trembling, clamouring, weeping, then quite suddenly subsided. And progressively it became more complex, striving to overflow into the human heart and overwhelm it with its pathos, with this tragic tempest that had no need of words, and then at last after a portentous pause it closed with a majestic funeral march, rolling on sedately, questioning, answering and so leading into the anguished compassionate closing section, as if it too wished to show that existence upon earth was meaningless and harsh.

'How beautiful that sonata is!' said Giorgis, its rich melodies still ringing in his ears.

'It was one of Alkis's favourites too!' smiled Eulalia shyly, carried away by her emotion and repressing the sigh that had arisen in her breast.

'You still haven't forgotten him!' remarked Giorgis sadly.

'Still not!' she replied, and a long chilly silence followed.

Innumerable past events came flooding back to her. How long ago it seemed since she had played that sonata to Alkis! It had been at her father's house, no longer her home, now that Doctor Steriotis really was her husband. And the thought reminded her of all the things she was obliged to do but resented deeply, of her intolerable new life of slavery, which weighed upon her day and night because she was no longer her own mistress and constantly had to give in to a husband whom she did not love and who was not like Alkis, wasn't Alkis! Ah, now it seemed to her that he had been the one who had taught her to feel and appreciate the language of that music. A language from another world that had no need of words or specific meanings to make sense of life, love and passion, or kindle pity and fear in the heart. The music was the dreamlike embodiment of all the love and harmony that were missing from her life, all the thirst for a passion that would unveil the mysteries of existence, all the grievous pain that she had suffered; it was a reminder of this other world, created by a dream of infinite felicity that was doomed to vanish in the real one.

'Is Alkis writing these days?' she asked suddenly, closing her eyes.

'He's been ill ever since he left the island,' Giorgis replied. 'At the moment... he's struggling with some book.'

A dark cloud passed before her eyes. She remained motionless for a moment, holding the closed score on her knees, then sighing and shaking her head sadly she gave a little shrug and gazed dreamily ahead.

Eventually she propped the score open on the piano again and her fingers rippled over the ivory keys. She played the same sonata through once more. The whole room filled with its passionate melodiousness, moving her intensely and sending shivers down her spine, harmonizing at the deepest level with her sorrow, as if the rhythm of the music were granting her another life, as if the plaintive tunes were making it more tangible.

'How beautiful that sonata is,' Giorgis exclaimed again, 'and what a heart-rending conclusion...'

A moment later he added with gloomy irony: 'The musicians were supposed to play that funeral march to see Valsamis off, but they never turned up!'

'Valsamis!' mused Eulalia sadly.

'The man,' said Giorgis thoughtfully, 'was a finer person than his wretched life suggests. He really loved Aimilia and accepted everything she did without a murmur. He adored her!'

'He wasn't the only one!' she retorted smiling. 'Look at the way she toys with Petros Athanatos, who worships her! She uses him as a go-between in her other love affairs. And you too... you too!'

That woman frightened her. Lately she often heard her husband too singing her praises. Steriotis was her personal physician and admired her. He considered her a woman of strong character and formidable will, as if born to exert her power over others, and so he sympathized with her faults and felt she wasn't obliged to submit to what in the case of other women was their duty. This, the doctor believed, was the prerogative of superior people and of them alone! Eulalia by contrast felt nothing but antipathy towards the woman who trampled upon love, making anyone she fancied fall in love with her. She felt an insuperable aversion for the power of her lovely body and her ardent soul, and she did not want to see her married to her brother and have to imagine him enslaved like Periklis Valsamis, nor did she want it to get around that her brother had turned a blind eye to Aimilia's past because she was a wealthy woman. And Giorgis was well aware that these were her feelings.

'And now, brother,' she continued, 'what's going to happen?'

'What's going to happen?' he replied irresolutely. 'Who knows? Take yourself, for example. Don't you see that our wishes never really determine anything? Events pursue their own relentless course, they don't consult us, they subject us to necessity and carry us where they will.'

'But what do you intend to do?' she persisted, sitting down beside him and taking his hand.

'Too much thinking's such a bore,' he replied. 'Won't you play another piece, it will relax us both!'

She smiled sadly but did as he requested and rose without another word. Resuming her seat at the piano, she flicked through the score and played the first chord of the new piece. But then, as if determined to make one last point, she turned her head towards him with a sad smile and said:

'You've again become her slave. That's what I think anyway.'

Then she went on playing.

Giorgis did not reply. He looked at her affectionately. How very much he wanted her life to be a happy one. She could talk like this because she didn't know the passionate intensity of the other woman, whose shady past made her reprehensible in her eyes, the eyes of a woman sacrificed. He contemplated her in silence.

Eulalia was now playing a fantasia, an exciting, lively piece. She played on and on. Her fingers flew over the keys, her face smiling and radiant with emotion. Then the door behind her slowly opened and in came Doctor Steriotis, who not wishing to interrupt her signalled to Giorgis to say nothing and stood there listening.

He was smartly dressed and in a good mood, and a beaming smile lit up his face, exposing his large teeth beneath his blond moustache and beard flecked with grey. He waited for the piece to end, and as soon as the piano fell silent strode across the room laughing and shook hands with Giorgis, then gleefully rubbing his hands remarked in his crude voice:

'Aha! Brother and sister enjoying themselves famously, I see!'

Eulalia turned round and smiled at him. Kindness always made an impression on her. Then he added thoughtfully:

'It's a regular paradise in here! But I, alas, am a working man, a man of science, and don't have as much time as I should like to enjoy the comforts of my little nest. One I built myself, I might add!'

They both laughed.

'But back here I'm a different person!' said the doctor.

'Where have you been?' Eulalia asked him with a friendly glance.

'Oh, you know,' he replied, looking down while nervously watching Giorgis out of the corner of his eye, 'I was summoned yet again by Mrs Valsamis! God, what a hysterical woman she is. Now she's afraid of Death herself and wants a doctor at her pillow all day long to ward him off. By the way, I was standing outside listening to you play for quite a while. But I didn't want to interrupt. Won't you now play something for me too, Eulalia. The serious stuff goes straight over my head, you know. But then of course music is not my business! All I want is music to relax and entertain me after work. Why not play something light, a song from *Madame Angot* perhaps.'

Eulalia closed the score with a shrug and began to play a well-known song she knew by heart. Approaching the piano, the doctor gazed at her with genuine admiration. He was proud of her and congratulated himself on being the husband of this beautiful young woman. Suddenly, in his atrocious French accent, he began singing the last verse, laughing uproariously the moment the piece came to an end.

The others laughed too.

After a pause, Steriotis remarked complacently:

'Getting married was the best thing I ever did. As I say, it's a regular paradise in here.'

And he closed his eyes with a self-satisfied look. Then the three of them went on talking about everyday matters for some time.

When Eulalia left the room for a moment, Giorgis asked the doctor anxiously:

'What's the matter with Mrs Valsamis?'

'Oh, nothing,' he replied with a smile and winked at him, 'I prescribed a little bromide for her.' And after a pause he continued thoughtfully: 'A gorgeous woman though! My word, yes! There are only two women in this town, one is my wife of course, the other Aimilia Valsamis, ha, ha!'

Giorgis gave a forced laugh.

Steriotis himself laughed heartily, watching Eulalia as she resumed her seat at the piano.

The music began again and both men now listened pensively.

After a while, a smartly dressed maid came in and announced that Mimis Hadrinos was waiting in the study. The piano fell silent.

'Show him in here,' said the doctor and once the maid had left added:

'Nothing confidential, we'll be discussing your affairs. So why should he deprive me of your company?'

Eulalia looked at him offended, but didn't say a word.

A moment later Hadrinos was greeting brother and sister with respect, and having cordially shaken hands with the doctor he sat down beside him and began his little speech at once.

'I've brought along your documents,' he said with an unpleasant smile, taking a large envelope out of his inside pocket, 'and by the way, Doctor, the Count's signature is now acceptable. The magistrates became more compliant the moment word got out that you'll be paying.'

'Let's leave them to their business,' said Giorgis, much displeased and like his sister blushing, 'we'll be in the drawing-room.'

'Fine!' replied the doctor airily, immersed already in the documents. 'Fine, I'll call you.'

And as brother and sister left the room, they overheard him saying to the usurer sternly:

'Don't imagine you're still dealing with my father-in-law. You can't cheat me, Mimis, even if you have a mind to!'

'Me?' said the money-lender laughing. 'But you're like a son to me, my dear Aristidis! Me? I'm a paragon of honesty and justice. But what can I do? As regards the other three promissory notes that are now due, they want all the interest on the nail. They're making no concessions!'

'Fetch them then!' said the doctor resolutely. 'This business must end. It was a mistake from the beginning. I should never have let myself in for all these headaches!'

'I have them here,' the money-lender replied with a shy smile.

The doctor took them, looked them over carefully one by one, then stared hard at the other man and said to him coldly:

'Mimis, you've come to some underhand agreement with my father-in-law! He's probably in need of ready cash and you've drawn up these promissory notes between you. I can see the ink's still fresh!'

The money-lender did not seem in the least offended by the insult, and merely lowered his eyes and replied coolly:

'Me, my dear Aristidis? I'm a paragon of honesty and justice. I'm stupid and illiterate, and would need your education and intelligence to even think of such a thing. And that's the truth, so help me God!'

'These are the last ones I'll redeem!' the doctor told him resolutely. 'Is that everything?'

'Everything.'

'You may go now,' he said, 'I will look over everything again carefully.'

And while the usurer was getting ready to leave, he opened the door and summoned Giorgis with a shout.

Brother and sister re-entered the little music room.

'There really was no need to leave,' he said smiling. 'Nothing confidential was discussed. I've now got all the IOUs here safely in my wallet. I've redeemed them at a discount. But what on earth has the old man been up to all these years? I'll make you a long-term loan which can be paid off gradually as your revenues increase, because with Mimis's help I'll be chasing up those peasants who are in arrears, mark my word! So things will soon be sorted out!'

He laughed.

'You should talk over all these matters with my father,' replied Giorgis in a bored tone.

'You see, you see what a kind heart your brother-in-law has?' said Hadrinos with feigned emotion. 'Just like mine, so help me God! And all these blessings, Master, your family owes to a louse like me. Yes indeed, so help me God! And what a shrewd head the good Doctor has, eh! A real scholar! Abler than his father, who built up their fortune. He has the money market at his beck and call with all his schemes, and every one of them running like clockwork!'

As he said this he brought his forefinger and thumb together to endorse the point, and his eyes in his pale face sparkled.

The doctor, gratified by this flattery, surveyed the room complacently. Hadrinos took his leave and hurried out.

Now Giorgis was impatient to be off.

'Won't you take a spin with us?' the doctor asked him.

'No,' he said thoughtfully. 'There's something I have to make up my mind about today.'

And Eulalia added:

'I'd really like to stay at home myself. After all the music I feel quite melancholy.'

'Perhaps you're unwell?' said her husband with a concerned smile, automatically stretching out his hand to take her pulse.

'No, I'm all right, but I'd prefer to stay at home.'

'Come, go and get dressed,' he replied with another smile, suspecting some ulterior motive behind her lame excuses. 'I didn't marry a beautiful noblewoman to hide her from the world. I want everyone to envy me. Go and get dressed, Eulalia!'

Giorgis wished them a good evening and departed.

Eulalia put up no further resistance. And soon the couple were climbing into their one-horse carriage, which at once set off towards the road along the seafront.

The doctor settled back proudly. Eulalia sat next to him with eyes downcast. Crowds of people were promenading up and down enjoying the spring evening. The first of their acquaintances to greet them was the portly old poet famous for his musical settings of courtly and patriotic verse, who was shuffling along beside the bankrupt banker, husband of Mrs Theophano Chrysospathis. Next they saw Arkoudis the banker, sitting in a café with a sad smile on his lugubrious face and squinting. He was seated with the two Miss Kallergises and Mrs Urania Daphnopatis, who just then was talking to them animatedly and laughing. As they drove on they waved to several others, even spotting Ophiomachos in his old frock-coat, stooping and smiling sadly as he made his way home. He was accompanying his elderly Countess, who kept looking about anxiously, as if expecting the worst even on an evening like this, and his daughter Louisa who would glance round furtively without actually turning her head. Close on their heels came Goulielmos Arkoudis, dressed in his fashionable English clothes and holding his straw boater in his hand.

With a shock Eulalia suddenly saw Goulielmos go up to her sister and slip a note into her hand, which she hastily concealed up her sleeve. It was clear that her sister was rapidly heading for disaster. Yet she felt she lacked the energy to intervene, just as she had lacked the will to save herself. So she just smiled and waved to them.

Further on the doctor was the first to salute Mrs Theophano Chrysospathis, the lady who was like a sister to some queen and had devoted her life to charity in memory of her late lover. She was riding in an elegant carriage with Asteris's ugly daughter and the nephew she had brought back from abroad to marry her.

Sadly Eulalia thought of her brother Spyros and his dashed hopes.

Soon the coach brought Eulalia and the doctor out beyond the suburb, rolling swiftly along the well-paved road which followed the low shoreline. The sea was like a vast mirror and the setting sun gilded the mountains in a last embrace, shedding crimson, mauve and golden light across the deep blue sky, the treetops and the sea. A group of half-naked fishermen wading in up to their knees were rhythmically hauling on their nets and singing a melancholy song to ease their thankless task. Just then a spit of land directly opposite, across the glittering expanse of water, became irradiated with reddish-golden light, detaching it from the range of mountains that stretched away behind it. There was the ruined old Venetian fort! Eulalia responded with a shudder to the melancholy beauty of the scene, sighing as she remembered Alkis Sozomenos and the dreams that he had woven gazing at that same ruin, bathed in the same glorious setting sun.

2

Mrs Aimilia Valsamis was in bed, still unable to get to sleep.

Despair had overwhelmed her heart. Outside, dawn was already breaking.

Oh, she could no longer endure the melodrama of her affair, which had been in its death-throes now for months. Couldn't she see that Giorgis no longer wished to be her lover and was doing his best to discourage her as well, that he avoided her eye when speaking to her and seized every opportunity to pour a drop more poison into her heart, regardless of the pain he caused her? And yet he knew very well how much she loved him, of course he did!

She hid her face in the downy pillow and sobbed her heart out, and as the warm tears flowed freely she wished they might never cease and she dissolve in sorrow.

How many times had he been to see her since Valsamis's death? Twice? Five times maybe? She could count them on the fingers of one hand. And oh, how she longed to see him, to have him constantly beside her as before! How could he leave her languishing like this and not take pity on her, when her heart was on the point of breaking? Why? Oh, why?

After her husband had died, for days Giorgis had not come to see her. Perhaps there had been good reason for it then. But time had now moved on, they had made love and she had triumphed once again. Yes, one day he had simply reappeared, the trepidation in his heart quite evident from his uneasy gaze, his pallid brow and the strange forced smile upon his lips. He had come at an hour when she still had company, confident that there would be no time for them to be alone together, but she had managed to detain him and he had not had the strength of mind to tear himself away as he'd intended. She noticed how he kept glancing round anxiously, as if looking for somebody no longer present, and watching the door as if expecting some ghost might enter any minute. He later admitted as much to her himself.

That day he had been half-prepared to find everything in her residence transformed, the plants in the grand entrance wilted, the walls of the house decaying, the smiling portraits in the drawing-room in mourning, and even herself completely changed. But to his surprise everything had remained exactly as it had been before her husband's death, even her heart, her treacherous heart, that loved him with such anguished passion, had not changed a bit.

To encourage him she herself had dragged him to her bedroom, where she had surrendered to him body and soul as passionately as ever, and he had been powerless to resist her, not – alas! – because love had overwhelmed him and his heart ached as fervently as hers, far from it! – but because his spirit was weak and easily defeated and he had become used to giving in to her. Yet he was ashamed of his own weakness and afterwards had spoken to her strangely, saying he despised himself for doing precisely what he didn't wish to and knew he shouldn't, for going back on the harsh but just and necessary decision he had made. So much for his love!

Now, in a fit of rage, she told herself she would do whatever was necessary to bring matters to a head. She had had enough of begging, being endlessly humiliated and exposing her own weakness. She was fed up with hearing him say he didn't want to marry her, after she'd been his mistress all this time – she'd waited long enough. So she herself would throw him out! She would try showing him her anger and contempt! She was more than justified! She would let him know that she could hate him too! But could she bring herself to do it? Would she have the strength? Oh, how very much she loved him! But that was the very reason she must act like this, there was no other option. And again she burst into tears.

What bizarre ideas were passing through her mind! What strange irrational pictures her imagination was creating, as if reason were no longer able to control her sick exhausted brain.

She looked at the flickering lamp which fitfully emitted a red glow, like the breath of someone at death's door, and she compared its guttering flame to their affair. Was it likewise destined simply to fizzle out? And would all their dreams, which now could so easily come true, just vanish down the wind? Was this how her life, her entire life, was to be destroyed and plunged into impenetrable darkness?

The lamp at this point flared up more brightly, briefly eclipsing the daylight filtering softly through the shutters. That was how her love too would be eclipsed, she realized with a pang that wrung her heart. But was a proud audacious woman like herself really going to surrender meekly to sorrow and regrets? No, no, she loved too deeply not to act maliciously in her despair, not to hate. No, she wasn't just going to resign herself to the present situation. She refused to sit patiently and put up with his disdain. No, no! She would set everything ablaze around her, yes she'd flare up much more fiercely than the little lamp now spluttering under its cracked glass. No, she wasn't going to think about whom she might harm, she didn't care how many hearts might suffer – far better if he were to suffer too! She didn't care about the pain her revenge would cause. Why should she worry about anybody else when she herself was suffering such bitter anguish, when her body, her soul, her love were being despised. And by whom? By the man who was her idol, for whom she would willingly sacrifice everything, her life even, were he to ask with a fond look. Oh, how very much she loved him!

She started weeping bitterly and plaintively again.

Her imagination was now running riot, conjuring up harrowing images of murder, conflagration, smouldering ruins. Feverishly she reflected that she would have to find a way to plan her vengeance in advance. She was determined to punish Giorgis, that beloved, hateful man, who had left her to suffer without pity or remorse. Yes, indeed she was... But what was his punishment to be? How would she sow devastation all about her, as befitted a woman like herself, proud and humiliated, spurned in her erotic passion, in all that was noble, true and sacred in her soul, a soul where no lies or sordidness lay hidden?

In her anguish she was momentarily overwhelmed by an unfamiliar sense of satisfaction, her heart beat more rapidly and she opened her eyes. Paying him back for all her anxiety and pain would be sweet indeed to her tormented soul, the only sweetness she would savour if she could no longer command his love.

One by one her imagination conjured up all the dire events in a dream scenario that could so easily become reality, depicting all the characters taking part in a tragic drama that would end in general catastrophe.

Foremost among the protagonists was that faithless, cruel, ungrateful,
adorable – no! despicable creature, who after draining her of her vitality
and youth was now satiated with her love and preparing to abandon her
in search of fresh adventures, easier, more trivial affairs, indifferent to her
though she still yearned for him even as she planned her cruel revenge,
because to her his love was a necessity of life, an obsession wringing her
heart and threatening to suffocate her. Then there was his sister Eulalia,
whom she had disliked from the beginning – indeed she was fed up with
Giorgis's entire family – yes, the one everybody considered an innocent
angelic victim of society, but Aimilia had no patience with the way she
spent her life wallowing in her own chaste martyrdom. Then there was
Eulalia's husband, the strong man with the little blond goatee, the studious
man of energy who always knew exactly what he wanted, bent others to
his will and in the end emerged victorious. Suddenly she paused in her
reflections, recalling with distaste the doctor's physical appearance, which
in the semi-darkness of her bedroom struck her as irredeemably ugly –
large, coarse, corpulent and vulgar – and she couldn't help comparing it
to Giorgis's noble features, charm and grace.

She could feel some sympathy for the unfortunate Eulalia, obliged
to put up with him and share his bed. To her such a situation would be
quite insufferable. His face would be a constant source of irritation and
she could never become accustomed to his ways.

She saw him often these days, because he was her personal physician
and she needed the medicaments that he prescribed for her. She needed
sleeping pills and tranquillizers, otherwise, he told her, her tense frayed
nerves would snap. She saw him every day, or every other day, twice a week
at least. He still tried to appear happy and never tired of praising his Eulalia
and extolling all her charms, but reading between the lines one could
deduce how cold she was towards him, and how vain were his attempts
to make her forget her first love and claim her soul himself. Not that she
complained, quite the contrary, but he often found her looking dejected,
even when she laughed, and at the piano playing her sophisticated music
she always had a wistful smile, which the doctor fondly hoped he might
one day banish through his wealth, his clumsy devotion and his love.
Ah, how comical he was with his little blond goatee, and the droll way
he had of confiding his little secrets to her, where they had not gone sour
already, seated there beside her as if seeking her advice. And how gleefully

Aimilia laughed to herself, as she could never bring herself to like either the doctor or Eulalia.

He had also let her see, while eulogizing the Ophiomachos family, that other little things embittered him. Not one of them, neither Eulalia nor her siblings nor the old man nor the Countess even, considered him their equal, and while they tried to conceal their feeling that he had intruded into their family uninvited because they were in trouble, it showed at every turn, and since he could hardly remain indifferent he felt obliged to stress his own superiority as a man endowed with genuine talents such as the Ophiomachoses could only dream of. This was why he had accepted the nomination the minister had offered him, and why he had submitted all those medical papers to the Academy in Paris: he wanted to show them that he wasn't just some upstart but a productive scientist and a useful member of society, infinitely superior to the local aristocrats, to all those miserable beggars. He despised distinguished names and the Ophiomachoses should understand that. He often talked to her about certain experiments in physiology he intended to conduct. How those monologues bored her... The reason that the fly, he said, shows such remarkable resistance to microbes and to toxins is that it feeds on them, its mouth is a veritable decontaminator. The question was, how might this immunity be transmitted to humans by using some form of therapeutic serum extracted from the fly. He would go on and on interminably like this, becoming really irritating and making himself insufferable company. And yet... and yet... supposing she had to wreak vengeance upon Giorgis, supposing she just had to?

She was overcome by acute anxiety again, and in a moment of deeper desperation she said to herself passionately: 'Even with him! Even with him!'

She shuddered with revulsion at the thought, her eyes widening as she clenched her palms and held her breath in trepidation. It was a diabolical idea, quite outrageous, and would surely never happen. All her perfidious heart was yearning for was love. Oh how passionately she could kiss Giorgis's adorable lips that very moment! And how ashamed of her idea she'd be, were he to suddenly appear. Oh, if only he were here beside her now!...

But her thoughts continued to pursue their desperate course: 'Even with him! Even with him!' Yes, and because she was in love she really would find the strength to start a conflagration! She smiled bitterly as she adjusted her head among the pillows. She too was a strong character – strong in love and hate alike. But again she rejected the idea that was beginning to obsess her, trying instead to recall the most cherished loving moments in her life, her mother's affection, the moment of her father's passing – anything memorably tender. Oh, she wasn't a hard-hearted person, she was always so eager to fall in love, to shed tears of love. But she simply couldn't bear Giorgis's contempt, his malice and unfairness. That was why revenge was sweet and her heart so full of spite, why she was now capable of going down that slippery path. She had taken the first steps already and now only his unconditional love could save her!

She continued to weave terrifying dreams. She tried not to find the doctor's appearance quite so ugly and to appreciate his enterprise and strength of character, his wealth and learning and the promising career ahead of him in politics and high society, and then she would rejoice as in her dream she pictured Giorgis's desperate jealousy and his remorse for himself having brought calamity on the pathetic remnants of his noble line.

Suddenly she distilled her thoughts into a few brief words, which her parched lips pronounced distinctly: she would snatch him from Eulalia! She would destroy the Ophiomachos family. Again she was appalled by her decision and lay there trembling and shivering from head to foot. How feverishly her brain was working! Her whole body was drenched in a cold sweat, and she peered wide-eyed across the semi-darkness of her room, terrified that someone or perhaps some ghost might have overheard her. But from the depths of her soul the question again arose obsessively: how would she contrive it all when the time came? She realized she must have been growing accustomed to the idea, because her mind was already preparing for the unmentionable deed. It wouldn't be hard. She was young and pretty and she knew the doctor fancied her. She would have no difficulty in beguiling him and holding him with all, yes all, the arts of love! Yes, she would snatch him from Eulalia forever and however much this embittered her no matter, the Ophiomachoses would lose the doctor's backing, their debts would overwhelm them and plunge them into poverty again, and they would have sacrificed Eulalia in vain. That would be her revenge. She had worked it all out nicely! Very nicely!

*

Her mouth felt dry and with the lamp now out she groped for her glass of water, but when her hand felt the cold half of the bed she shuddered. Just then some piece of furniture creaked and in a panic she thought she saw the door slowly open and a shadowy figure enter, *his* shadow, then with horror she imagined the shadow advancing towards her, yearning to lie down beside her, and the blood froze in her veins. She started up with a faint muffled cry and lit her bedside candle. The light reassured her straight away. She looked about and saw that day had dawned. All the furniture was in its place and the clock was ticking away relentlessly. She was alone in bed, as she had been when she retired for the night. The door was closed.

She smiled with relief.

But the nightmare gave a new turn to her thoughts. Her smile grew wistful as she leaned back exhausted and thought to herself: he's dead now... And she proceeded to reflect upon the unfortunate man who had been her husband. She remembered their joyless life together and his untimely death. She tried to recollect his sweet face as she had known it during the first days of their marriage, but she had quite forgotten it. Sickness had changed him so utterly that the old photographs of him as a handsome, robust and cheerful man no longer resembled him at all. She recalled his yellowish pallor, his thin translucent face, his scarcely audible voice and his hollow eyes which clouded over every evening as his temperature rose. Indeed, by the end he had been reduced to skin and bones, and his every gesture had expressed the anguish of his soul. Alas, she too had made him suffer. Yet not once did he reproach her for it. She remembered the way he would look at her as if she were some higher being, submissively, without anger or complaint, and he had spent years with her like this, more like her father than her husband, always sacrificing himself, always ready to accompany her to balls and theatres, happy when he could see her blossoming and enjoying life.

His disease however had steadily advanced, gnawing at his vitals, wearing down his body, hollowing his often hectic cheeks. Thus little by little the martyr had faded away, a man who had never managed either to love or hate with passion, and who submitted as if indifferent to the pain, accepting his cruel fate in the conviction that all one could do in life was bear one's miserable cross with fortitude. He regarded strong people like herself and Giorgis as creatures from another world, with more right to life and happiness because they knew how to impose their will on life and seize its blessings. Aimilia remembered his watery gaze following her around the room, the gaze of a defeated man who no longer dared to ask for anything, the gaze of secret love perhaps, because that was how he would also watch his friend Petros Athanatos, who was constantly beside his pillow, often laughing his sarcastic laugh. Then at last the day of his demise had come.

It had been one afternoon in spring. A dry unremitting cough had tortured him and made him fret all night and in the early hours it had become so bad that, summoning all his remaining strength, he had struggled out of bed one final time, still determined to escape death's clutches. Later towards midday he had grown calmer and gone back to bed, and his translucent sweating face had assumed an alien expression no one during his life had ever seen before. Through the open window warm red sunlight flooded into the room. A golden sunbeam lit up his face, weaving a garland of light about his hair, while in the branches of the trees close to the window two birds could be heard twittering, and the fragrance of spring wafted in from trees already in full bloom.

Gathered round the bed were Doctor Steriotis, who was impatient to be off, aware that he could no longer help, Petros Athanatos, grim-faced and unemotional, Giorgis Ophiomachos and herself. With every laboured breath the sick man drew they felt a shiver down their spine, expecting death at any moment; no one spoke and they avoided looking at each other, everyone in awe of the simple terrifying solemnity of the occasion. The man was dying devoutly, as he had intended. Doctor Steriotis held out his hand to say goodbye and gazed at him with a sad smile. Unable to lift his arm, the dying man raised his fingers slightly and said in his faint voice: 'You'll be signing my death certificate tomorrow, Doctor...' And he too smiled sadly. Then he gave Petros a fond grateful look, a large tear welling in his eye as he murmured 'Goodbye, my friend!' He then looked around the room, as if taking leave of the various objects he was fond of, and finally he looked sadly at her too, his eyes expressing an infinite yearning for affection, while a smile flickered on his lips – the last smile of his life. That same instant his whole body shook convulsively and he stared at the door, as if wishing to rush out of the room, as if something were driving him out of that house. She herself had been on the point of saying something and her lips were parted, but then Valsamis's eyes stopped moving and glazed over, just as the sun went in and ceased to play upon his hair...

The candle beside her bed was still alight, but it was now day. Exhausted after her restless night, Aimilia closed her eyes and fell asleep.

She awoke towards midday and learned from the maid that Giorgis had been waiting in the drawing-room for quite some time. He had not wanted to wake her up himself.

She received him in bed. It was quite dark inside her room. The remains of the candle were still burning but did not give out much light. Giorgis, his eyes still adjusting as he came in from the daylight, could only hear her greeting and could not at first make out anything except the brass bed-posts gleaming in the candle-light. Gradually however, as he got accustomed to the gloom, he was able to discern her braided head among the silk sheets and her pale hand in her loose nightgown extended towards him in a gesture of welcome.

She invited him to come and sit on the chair next to her pillow.

He obeyed, smiling as he took her hand and gazed at her.

'What a night I've had!' she exclaimed, tossing her pretty head. 'Somehow I couldn't help my mind dwelling on evil thoughts all night and imagining disasters! And you know why, don't you? It's really strange though, because I love you with all my heart. Yet you refuse to see it!'

She squeezed his hand and gazed at him passionately, her eyes demanding the kiss he was withholding. Why was he holding back, especially now that all their worries should be over and all their ugly scenes and bitterness forgotten?

He smiled as if afraid of her and remarked thoughtfully: 'His last moments were so sad...'

'Yes,' she replied, 'but our life is now our own!' She smiled and flung her arm towards him, gazing searchingly into his eyes. Her smile lit up her face. Had Giorgis come round today repentant, again seeking her love and eager to explain his conduct? Happiness made her heart beat faster. She gazed tenderly at him.

Giorgis kissed her hand and a silence ensued. Then they realized that for the first time in their lives they were afraid of one another, they were hiding from each other. She wanted to tell him something but it died on her lips and she at once forgot it, because he was looking directly at her.

'Will you be mine?' she continued ardently, tossing her thick braids back and sitting up in bed. 'Oh Giorgis! Oh Giorgis!'

Her whole body was quivering under her lace nightgown. She adjusted her hair with one hand and gazed at him ardently with big moist eyes, trying to touch and inflame his heart. And with the same passionate intensity she exclaimed:

'Oh, how I've missed you! You cannot do without me, isn't that true? You've realized it yourself and that's why you've come back, isn't that so, my darling?'

And as she said this she felt a sense of relief and an indescribable sweetness pervaded her heart. How happy she was just then, now knowing she would not need to be cruel, that her life was about to change from that day on, and this guileless joy, so soothing to her agitated soul, was mirrored in her face, her lovely eyes, her smiling sensuous lips.

Tenderly she caressed his head and gazed into his eyes a few moments in silence, as if asking herself whether it really was him beside her, and longing to hear his voice. With beating heart she then exclaimed:

'I'll never stop loving you, never! I'll never let you leave my arms, my side again. Oh Giorgis, oh Giorgis! Do talk to me!'

Suddenly she threw her arm around his neck and pressed his adorable head against her ample breasts, running her fingers through his hair and breathing and sighing heavily. Giorgis, intoxicated by her caress, enraptured by all that feminine flesh quivering beside him and drawing him closer with irresistible determination, began to kiss her naked arm – exposed when a button came undone as she embraced him – and at once realized that even now his desire for this lovely woman was as ardent as during the first days of their acquaintance. Then they found themselves in one another's arms, eagerly exchanging an endless torrent of fierce, fiery kisses. During these brief moments both of them were oblivious to everything – all their past bitterness and brooding... Giorgis could no longer recall what he had resolved to tell her, Aimilia no longer remembered her dark plans, as his hands clasped her ardently around the waist, her passionate lips sought his, their bodies trembled, their nostrils quivered and moment by moment their embraces became closer, their kisses more intense, and their minds clouded over with the intoxication of insatiable desire.

*

He was now seated by her side, and as if concluding some private train of thought he remarked:

'Oh, if only you weren't wealthy...'

She gave him an odd look, suddenly uneasy, and replied with a smile:

'What has that got to do with love?'

And again she embraced his head, as if to prevent him saying any more.

'True, I'm wealthy,' she continued, still smiling. 'And who else for but you? Who else? Who in the whole wide world will be as happy?'

She spoke dreamily, as if thanking him for their ecstatic moments. Yet how could this same man continue brooding and hesitating like this? Why wasn't it as obvious to him as to her that it was up to them to seal their happiness for ever?

'Ungrateful man!' she continued, still smiling.

He did not reply. She gazed at him with clouded eyes, as all the worries of the previous night came back to her, all the recent misery she was afraid to think about and never wanted to go through again. Then her eyes lit up and she said passionately:

'Isn't a woman's love worth anything to you? Not even my love?'

'Of course it is, of course!' he protested warmly.

But the words had slipped out against his will. He reflected ruefully on the weakness of his character. He too was his father's son. He had come round reluctantly, he said to himself, to explain to her what he believed to be his duty. This was going to be the last time he came to see her, because he didn't wish to continue their illicit affair. And one thing was absolutely certain: he would never barter himself in exchange for her wealth. His heart would not consent to it. As long as he was in his right mind he would not do that, and he must never forget it. No, he wouldn't stoop to that. Yet he knew that this parting was going to be difficult, because he actually felt sorry for this woman he made love to and he didn't want to hurt her, but he could see that she was beguiling him and gradually getting her own way, he was conscious of saying things he'd not intended or finding himself at a loss for words, and he was afraid he might be going irredeemably downhill. No, no, that was the one thing he – he, Giorgis Ophiomachos – would never stoop to!

'Well?' she said uneasily.

Despite himself, he smiled, lowering his eyes.

'Oh Giorgis,' she cried with the same passionate intensity, 'you did love me, I know it, a woman is never deceived about such things. And you were the first, you were the one who made me understand what love is all about – made me live through its uncertainties, always with a beating heart, terrified of losing it! Oh Giorgis, you know it's true! And you can't complain about me in bed either!'

'No,' he replied with feeling, 'certainly not.' And he lowered his eyes, annoyed at himself for having again betrayed his weakness.

'Well?' she said again more hopefully.

He sighed without raising his head.

'The number of occasions we've been seen together! People are expecting us to marry. They ask me about you as if you already were my husband. Don't you see, any other arrangement would look distinctly odd!'

But this failed to break down his resistance. It was not what she should have said just then.

Instead it boosted his courage and he replied: 'They talk like that because they judge by their own lights!' She looked him in the eyes, offended by his arrogant remark. Her hackles were rising but she restrained herself, still determined to keep her hopes alive.

He went on more gently:

'You're not a thoughtless person, Aimilia. But get it into your head once and for all, your wealth is an insuperable impediment. How else can I put it?'

Her face went pale and her nostrils flared. Her dark thoughts of the night before revived, and yet she still loved this man whom she was prepared, alas, to hate. She looked into his eyes and forced herself to smile, still hoping to overcome his resistance, ready if so to fall into his arms and purge her love of malice. But he was talking to her again, talking oh so coldly!

'I don't want to hurt you, Aimilia. But think about it yourself. Of course you'd like to be my wife, and there's no reason for things to continue as they are. Of course, I understand all that! But I'm so poor, Aimilia, and my family as you know is in dire straits. Besides, we are members of society and as you know society's not blind. What else will all those people say, who today consider it natural for us to marry, if not that penniless Ophiomachos wasn't so mad as to despise a fortune?'

She looked at him angrily and for a moment thought about her revenge. With some emotion he continued:

'Forgive me, Aimilia, if this is a bitter disappointment. But we'll always remain friends, won't we?'

'So that's how it is!' she said sourly. 'That's how men repay one for loving them! You're not telling me the whole truth, Giorgis, and you're hiding the worst from me. Why should I forgive you, when you're pushing me to despair and madness? Tell me, why should I forgive you?'

He was sitting in the chair beside her pillow, hiding his face in his hands, and did not reply. She was restless and angry. She forced him to uncover his face and look at her. There was a wild look in her eyes and she was trembling with rage. But she still managed to restrain herself and put as much sweetness into her words and tone as possible:

'No, Giorgis, no! I won't let you go, I simply can't, you must continue to be mine, just as you have been up till now, let people say what they like! Take your time and then we'll see. There's absolutely no need for us to hurry. You cannot leave me!'

Her attitude again made him waver. Her cheeks were flushed, her eyes tearful, and when she spoke with so much passion her breasts heaved. Again she looked deep into his eyes and both of them kept quiet for a moment. She seemed to be expecting something. He smiled at her.

She knew the meaning of that smile and was afraid that nothing she could say would alter his decision. Suddenly pride got the better of her, and evidently wounded to the core she said:

'Ah, so that's the way you want things, eh?'

And then she gave full vent to her fury.

'You too are cruel! You've never loved me! You deceived me, you were just after a good time, like all the rest. I know what you wanted. You wanted me to be permanently lumbered with a husband like Valsamis, someone weak and sickly, someone who'd not get furious and interfere – so the two of you could laugh at me behind my back. That's the way you wanted things! And now I suppose you're ashamed of my wealth because you're ashamed of me. That's true, isn't it? Go on! Admit it!'

He looked at her fearfully but said coldly and maliciously:

'It's true, Aimilia.'

She changed colour more than once. So her love was not enough to purify her in his eyes? How dare he, heartless wretch, insult her in that irreparable brutal way! Was that why he considered her unworthy of him, his inferior, was that why he was contemptuous of her wealth? Was that why he couldn't bring himself to love her? But then of course he'd never loved her from the start, he'd been cheating her, he'd cheated her again just now. Love rides roughshod over everyone!

Another wave of fury rose to her head.

'Proud beggar!' she said contemptuously. 'You sold Eulalia, didn't you?'

Her abusive remark made Giorgis blanch. He sensed that something snapped irreparably between them at that moment. He realized that he too was furious.

'Let us part,' he said, trembling and holding out his hand, 'like people who were once in love.'

His words enraged her even further. She had hoped that her anger would frighten him and he would perhaps fall to his knees and beg for her forgiveness, at the very least she expected an outburst of rage from him. She would have accepted his abuse, his hostility, his crude behaviour, because she knew that in the human heart love can sometimes turn fleetingly to hatred, only to be softened later by remorse.

Again she cursed him:

'Ungrateful creature! Beggar! Scoundrel!'

Kneeling on the bed, she seized his hand and shook him violently:

'You scoundrel, Ophiomachos!'

Giorgis wrenched his hand free. His resolve had hardened. His soul was now indifferent. He knew that he should not respond. But anxious to put an end to the unseemly row, he stood up and turned towards the door to leave.

She completely lost control and went on cursing him and uttering piercing shrieks. Suddenly she found herself in front of him, dressed only in her nightgown. Her eyes were dull with fury and there was white spittle on her lips.

'So you're going to leave me, are you?' she screamed.

She seized him by the hand and throat and, no longer conscious of what she was doing, sank her long nails into his flesh. He winced with pain but did not say a word.

'So that's it! You're just going to walk out on me!'

She tried to hold him back, tugging him with all her might, while he struggled to reach the door, leaning forward and dragging her after him, trying to escape from her grasp without hurting her. Aimilia, realizing that all her efforts had been in vain, now started pummelling him clumsily about the head and shoulders with her fists as she pursued him, screaming:

'Go on then, off you go! Out of my sight, beggar! Off you go! I'll cook your goose!'

As he grabbed the door-knob he began to laugh. His laughter inflamed her fury even further. She managed to stop him and frantically redoubled her blows. She tried to tear at his flesh, showing her teeth, pushed him violently into the middle of the room, then back towards the door, beating him relentlessly; then suddenly she opened the door for him herself, spat in his face, bundled him out and slammed the door behind him.

Out on the street he laughed again as he set off, glancing with angry hatred back up at her window. Aimilia, exhausted, out of breath and desperate, paced about her bedroom for some time. Her anger did not subside. She wrung her hands despairingly, her chest felt heavy and constricted, her ears were buzzing, her heart was full of vitriol and the terrifying thought that all was lost kept revolving in her mind, fuelling a raging thirst for vengeance. Finally she collapsed on the bed and burst into tears.

Shaken and dejected, Giorgis did not return home until towards evening. There his father was in a towering rage. His shouting could be heard all down the street. The elderly couple were alone in the dining-room. His mother was seated at the large table, her face buried in her hands. Ophiomachos was pacing up and down the room wrapped in his old frock-coat, and every so often he would again start shouting.

On seeing Giorgis enter, he halted, went red in the face, and glaring at him bawled:

'She's left, she's left!'

His mother raised her head and, her eyes brimming with tears, looked balefully at her son as if seeking his protection.

'Who, who?' asked Giorgis stupidly, looking round the room.

'Louisa!' roared his father at the top of his voice, while his mother sobbed aloud. Giorgis was disconcerted, his brain too tired to think. Was this the day fate would empty everything he had coming to him onto his head? Now what had gone wrong?

'Louisa!' he murmured, going pale and collapsing into the deep settee.

'Yes!' the old man shouted again, resuming his restless pacing. 'Yes! She's following in the footsteps of her mother's family! No one from my family has ever done such a thing before. She's the first. My curse upon her! She's brought shame on my white beard! She's brought shame on her entire clan!'

'But of course he'll marry her, won't he, Giorgis?' said his mother weeping softly, 'Goulielmos is an honourable lad and he has an honourable father too.'

'It's all your doing!' the old man shouted at her again. 'And what's more, behind my back! You turned a blind eye because you thought he'd take her. Well, now he's taken her! You see, you see? That village lout!'

'Poor thing,' the mother continued, 'she couldn't stand it here any longer, with all the grumbling and penny-pinching...'

'And so she chose dishonour!' bellowed the old man, looking round him as if casting about for something he could smash. 'You've created this situation, you, her own mother! And now you try to justify the cursed wretch. It's all your fault, everything that's gone on under this roof's your fault!'

'I'll give her all my property so that he'll marry her,' the mother continued anxiously. 'She can have everything I've got, let her enjoy it with the man she's chosen. Yes...'

Tears prevented her from saying more.

'It was my destiny,' said the father, calming down a little, 'to taste even this bitter cup, even this dishonour. Oh God! But I'm to blame for marrying into a clan that was dishonourable from the beginning. Yes, dishonourable! The most dishonourable in town!'

And with this, pale despite his natural ruddiness, he descended to his study, leaving mother and son disconsolate.

There he paced up and down despairingly for some time. The portraits of his ancestors stared down at him from their antique frames. He glared back at them with hatred. Then he seized them one by one – the knight in armour who had fought for the Venetians in Crete and the Morea, the noblemen with their white wigs, the beautiful full-bosomed ladies with their sweet smiles – and tore them off the walls, tugging at them frantically, cursing each of them by name and spitting on them, then trampling them underfoot, gouging out their eyes and ripping up the canvases with a penknife from his desk.

At last, utterly worn out, he leaned against the ancient sofa and started weeping and lamenting bitterly, and every so often he could be heard calling out his daughter's name and cursing her:

'Oh my Louisa, my Louisa! Oh the cursed wretch!'

After a while his wife and Giorgis went down to the study to check on him. He received them with a look of hatred. His wife, who had heard him weeping and complaining, said to him with a deep sigh:

'In the next life God will remember your suffering and forgive you many sins, because your heart is full of love and sorrow. So forgive her too.'

'Never!' he shouted, turning away his face and pointing to the door. 'Never!' And he went on weeping.

3

In his elegant study, Doctor Aristidis Steriotis was excitedly reading an article he had just had published by the Bulletin of the Medical Academy in Paris. He was reading it out loudly and emphatically, admiring his own style, with its learned convoluted phraseology and its barbarous cacophonous scientific terms, some of them coined by himself, pausing now and then to contemplate its authoritative wording, its logic and its meticulous attention to detail. After all, the Academy had recognized it as an outstanding piece and published it in its entirety, without any editorial cuts at all, just as he had written it, in French. Ah, he had a profound appreciation of that beautiful language, and wrote it as readily as his own, more so perhaps as it was better suited to expressing scientific ideas. His article took up sixteen pages of the Bulletin, with his full name in Roman capitals along the bottom. French had even more appeal because it had no associations for him. Soon he would call Eulalia and let her leaf through his article without saying anything, just to watch her face and see what impression this latest mark of his growing fame would make on her. Yes, fame, certainly! How many local scientists published articles in the Bulletin of the Medical Academy in Paris! How many doctors in the whole of Greece for that matter? He would like to read it to Eulalia himself, indeed nothing would give him greater satisfaction. She would admire it too of course, to the extent that she could follow a work so rich in ideas and scientific innovation, which was precisely why it would make a splash and soon no doubt be debated by the scientific community, especially in learned Germany! His name would be picked up by the press and his discovery discussed around the globe. Of course, he would have to help the process along a bit himself and not just leave everything to chance. He would send copies of the Bulletin to the newspapers in Athens and ask the journalists he knew to write up something. As to the local papers, he didn't care either way, though they of course would print as many commendations as he wished and even proclaim him one of the outstanding luminaries of modern science. He himself was convinced that he deserved the accolade, with an article as significant as this. Others ought to acknowledge his achievement and the press was a means to that end.

He went on reading and stroking his little blond goatee, his head cocked slightly to one side, a smile on his pale lips. Every now and then his usually dull eyes would sparkle or moisten with emotion. 'The animal,' his article began, 'which is pre-eminently suited to biological and micro-biological experiment is the pig. Firstly because, as our illustrious ancestors the ancient Greeks also observed, it bears a close resemblance to man, and secondly because it has a robust constitution resistant to many toxins and diseases, as demonstrated by its thriving on the ptomaines and other substances fed to it, all poisonous to man and other mammals. Further evidence is afforded by the operation for sterilizing sows, a straightforward laparotomy successfully performed in Greek villages under the most primitive conditions without any need for antiseptics...'

Of course, his scientific reputation would also help to advance his other ambitions splendidly. The minister would be able to take pride in the fact that his nominee, Doctor Aristidis Steriotis, was not just anybody, he would be able to boast about it among the peasant voters and even in parliament. There he would be received as a man of distinction, his opinion would carry weight, no one would be able to deny that he was one of the country's leading lights, and above all, he wouldn't have to curry favour because he too was wealthy. And not wealthy in the way that all those idle fatuous society people were. He worked hard and was a useful member of society, and what with his science and his charitable activities,

he certainly did not waste his time. His late father hadn't worked all those
years to leave him with a bit of property in vain! How laboriously, with
what privations and vexations, he had built up his fortune!

But now he really ought to call Eulalia! He was curious to see her
expression when presented with this latest evidence of his success – would
she still remain indifferent to him? What a strange woman Eulalia was.
Nothing whatever seemed to impress her. And yet their splendid house
was free of that odour of decay she was so familiar with at home. And
for his part, was he not solicitous in making sure that she enjoyed herself,
had he not taken time off from his experiments and patients to sort out
the financial entanglements of the Ophiomachos family? Eulalia never
complained of course, not once, but he sensed that she didn't love him
as much as he deserved – as was due to a person of his standing. Perhaps
he would gain prestige in her eyes with this unique achievement and the
ice would break at last. Anyway, best not to brood too much over her
dislike, which really didn't matter. A man should take what a woman
had to offer. Carlyle was quite right that aestheticism is the sickness of
our century, a man of superior achievements should be immune from
all such weakness and accept that woman was a small-minded creature
with peculiar notions, with whom communication was virtually impossible. All a man should require of her was marital fidelity, and the state
should safeguard this through legislation, as it regarded the family as its
foundation-stone and the head of the family as the man. But the doctor
was confident that with Eulalia he had nothing to fear. Her childhood
sweetheart, Alkis Sozomenos, was no longer around, Doctor Steriotis
had vanquished him completely, and according to the general principles
of biology that was the only way their duel could have ended – Alkis had
had to give way to his stronger rival. And how pathetically all his utopian
dreams and tame ineffectual reforms had been slapped back, they didn't
have a hope of succeeding in a town like this, which wouldn't tolerate
them for a moment. And what was Alkis now? A physical and spiritual
wreck, an emigrant addicted to strong liquor, and none of that of course
could end propitiously. But even if Alkis had remained in town, he himself
would have made sure he safeguarded his honour. His doors were barred
to the island's gilded youth, because on that score he needed peace of
mind to focus on his studies, and he had Periklis Valsamis as a shining
example of the dangers. Alas, poor fellow! But it had been his own fault,

he should have considered his illness and declining strength, he should have recognized the kind of woman he was marrying.

Giorgis, his brother-in-law, had had a rare old time with her of course. As a mistress Aimilia was unique, she was enviable. He knew this woman quite well and fancied her himself. He saw her every day now and was intimately acquainted with her entire body. That was a doctor's prerogative, of course, and one that made erotic escapades much easier. Aimilia Valsamis really was a gorgeous woman, and only Giorgis could be such an ass as to let her slip through his fingers. He rivalled his father in stupidity. They were all so stupid, the Ophiomachoses, both male and female. They were drowning in a glass of water all of them. That's why Eulalia couldn't be content with him, she was as brainless as the rest of them. What a different proposition Aimilia was!

She'd taken a liking to him some time ago apparently... A different type of woman altogether. She'd always been pleased by his various social triumphs and even seemed delighted at his marriage. And she was enthusiastic about his nomination and a great admirer of his learning, his articles and scientific work. Her comments flattered him, finding their way to his very soul like a caress. Why couldn't Eulalia be more like her, for goodness' sake, instead of always treating him with cool indifference? After all, he was a human being too and needed some support in his endeavours.

Where could he expect that support to come from? From the Ophiomachoses? Now he knew them, he saw they were all blockheads. He felt that he had done them a favour by marrying Eulalia, with all the sacrifices – not least financial – this entailed. Of course he had no regrets, but this was not to say he might not find someone better suited to him! He wasn't getting the support he needed either from his wife or from any of her family. Old Ophiomachos was so uneducated, so absurd, a garrulous aristocrat without a penny! His mind had gone to mush. How he drivelled on and on about his ancestors, his family's ancient lineage, the exploits of the knight in armour, the nobles in their wigs and the full-bosomed ladies smiling sweetly from their frames. Always the same tired anecdotes which he, Doctor Aristidis Steriotis, for one, was tired of hearing, especially as he was never quite sure whether the old man might not be trying to remind him of his humble origins. One thing was certain, the doctor was very much a stranger in the Ophiomachos household. Even the old Countess, a saintly woman who regarded him with warmth and gratitude for his beneficence, seemed to imply that he'd been accepted as their son-in-law on sufferance, because Eulalia had no dowry and the family was obliged to sacrifice her. This could hardly please the doctor, who had shown he was no ordinary man and in fact had honoured them by becoming their relation.

The best of the bunch of course was Spyros. Poor old Spyros, he was always sidling up to him as if seeking his protection, recognizing him as a strong man with a position in society who tomorrow would be even more important. He was always most obliging but lacked pride, nothing seemed to humiliate him – not a bad sort really, but weak like his mother and such a fool. But a fool who was aware of his own insignificance at least, unlike Giorgis. Ah, he couldn't stand that man, he was the stupidest, the most useless of them all, even more stupid than Louisa. And look what she'd got herself into now! Her elopement detracted from his own marital success – of course it did, if Ophiomachos's daughters could elope with the first scoundrel who came their way. One could only hope the whole affair would at least end happily. Personally he doubted it. Of course he'd be relieved if the Ophiomachoses were the only ones humiliated by her conduct. Serve them right, frankly, the way they looked down on others, they were a stuck-up lot with no respect for riches or high office and talked about everything with the utmost disdain. And in the twentieth century people could see this. Woe betide them!

He would have to turn elsewhere for consolation. And he could think of one woman, a gorgeous and kind-hearted person, who at least knew how to show her admiration for him. He saw Aimilia every day now, and if he neglected to call on her she would summon him at once. She had a certain liking for him personally, and he would be able to spend as much time with her as he could wish now that Giorgis had vacated the seat. Ah, how marvellous, the way she'd kicked him out. The fool thought he could play around with Aimilia, but he had met his match all right! Anyway, he'd be seeing her again today and would take her his article in the Bulletin of the Medical Academy in Paris. Her face would light up with pleasure and she'd congratulate him properly, after all, she was an educated woman who understood these things, not like the others who never read anything except French novels and the odd poem now and then. He of course never read such things, considering them beneath his professional dignity. Even as a boy he'd never enjoyed fairy tales and would fall asleep as soon as his mother started reading them to him.

What ridiculous rubbish all those novels were! Mrs Valsamis would not mind listening to more serious stuff. Besides, the issues he examined in his articles were so wide-ranging and so vital to the human race. The laparotomy performed on sows by villagers, without any antiseptic, proved conclusively that the animal showed remarkable resistance to streptococci, and it followed that serum from such animals could be used to vaccinate against all streptococcal infections. Now that Mechnikov had discovered a link between the ageing process and some kind of micro-organic poisoning, the Pasteur Institute ought to undertake experiments with serum from the crow, the longest-lived creature known to man. Flies too ought to receive more scientific scrutiny. General practitioners in his native land, who were familiar with the antidote for snake-bite long before Calmette, used fly droppings to treat cachexy, and possibly consumption. The fly feeds solely on microbes, on the most potent toxins, its mouth is a natural decontaminator. The problem was how to find a way of transmitting this immunity to humans. That was the whole point of his outstanding article.

But now he really ought to summon Eulalia, after all it was her duty to celebrate with him and by this stage he was impatient for a little praise. Then suddenly he remembered that Eulalia was inordinately upset about Louisa – inordinately, what else! To his way of thinking, Louisa too ought to be celebrating his success.

He rang the electric buzzer beside his crystal inkwell, and a smartly dressed maid appeared at once and went off to inform Eulalia that he was waiting for her in the study. Soon she came down. Her eyes were red with weeping. She felt utterly depressed. Coming just at that moment her husband's summons was most unwelcome, since in her distress she felt ashamed to face this man and would rather have remained alone, not wanting to discuss Louisa with anyone, least of all with him. Alas, now she could see plainly that her father had parted her from Alkis to no purpose, that she had been sacrificed in vain. Her family was continuing down the self-destructive path it had embarked on, she reflected, and no one would have the power to save it.

He welcomed her from behind his desk with the Bulletin in one hand and a smile of triumph on his face, his dull eyes trying to arouse her curiosity. Finally, with a proud little toss of his head he let the pages spring back through his fingers and exclaimed happily:

'Look, Eulalia!'

'What is it?' she asked coldly, glancing down at it.

'My article,' he said. 'The one I mentioned to you a little while ago. Take a look! It has finally been published in the Bulletin of the Medical Academy in Paris – Paris!'

'Ah!' she replied indifferently, a forced smile on her lips, and involuntarily she glanced at him with real dislike.

She found his conduct quite outrageous, feeling that even if he made no reference to her sorrow, at least he should be aware how deep it was. After the sacrifice she had made, he should have been able to appreciate how tenderly she loved her family, especially her weak father, he should have realized what a deep impression his grief, his shame and his despair had made on her, and not be bothering her about other matters when the only thing that could genuinely console her was a little tender loving kindness, but his hollow heart knew no such sentiments. Instead, at this time of crisis, he was again standing over her in triumph, just as when he had forced her to consent to marry him, brutally insisting on her sacrifice. Alas, then he could still have accepted Louisa's hand, granting her herself her happiness, and then everything that had occurred since his refusal could have been averted. But standing there before her now her husband appeared at his most odious, a cruel conqueror riding roughshod over her happiness, indifferent to her pain – and, alas! her life was in his hands, while the man who loved her, the only person who could comfort her, especially in these trying times, might be dying somewhere far away and it was she who had condemned him.

He again said to her with rather less enthusiasm:

'Well, aren't you pleased with our latest little triumph? Don't you realize how much social kudos this will bring us?'

'Of course,' she replied indifferently and sighed.

He looked at her for a moment with his expressionless gaze, stroking his faded blond goatee, then, obviously offended, he laughed unpleasantly and casually remarked:

'Fair enough, Eulalia. I can see Louisa's idiocies have hurt you deeply. You are not responsible of course, but you must recognize that the rest of the world can't be expected to think exclusively about your family. For me at least, there suddenly seem to be far more important things in life.'

He rubbed his hands together, leaving the Bulletin lying on his desk.

Eulalia did not reply and turned towards the study door to go. But just at that moment the smartly dressed maid re-entered with a letter on a silver tray.

The doctor opened it at once as the maid withdrew, read it over quickly and almost jumped for joy. Fortune was positively showering blessings on him today, he would have a great deal to talk over with Mrs Aimilia Valsamis.

It was a letter from the minister, the minister himself! Parliament had finally been dissolved, as everyone had expected, and he was being invited round that evening to discuss who would be on the party ticket. The minister felt confident Doctor Steriotis would not raise further objections to his nomination.

'Read this!' he said to Eulalia, overflowing with joy.

Languidly she took the letter, read it over coolly and handed it back to him. His little social triumphs had no power to move her whatsoever.

'Good,' she said indifferently. 'You'll be going of course. I'll spend the evening with my parents.' She sighed.

He let her go and was left alone, thoughtful and frustrated. So his greatest joys meant nothing to Eulalia, no doubt because she didn't love him. Well, he didn't love her either for that matter! That was only fair. He would find happiness some other way, not being stupid like the Ophiomachoses. He would create his own happiness. Clearly happiness was the goal of life and he was not without resources, but since he was acquainted with Aimilia Valsamis, perhaps fortune would smile on him a second time.

Just then the door opened and Petros Athanatos came into the study, thin, stooping and ugly as ever in his shabby clothes His eye looked unusually fierce and his lips betrayed his bitterness.

Without pausing to greet him, he said to him with hatred:

'Mrs Aimilia Valsamis is expecting you!'

The doctor laughed happily.

'Aimilia, as you know,' Petros continued, 'has finally thrown Giorgis out, and now you're trying to take his place. Don't you have any qualms of conscience? But I know you, Aristidis, I saw through you long ago!'

And before the doctor had a chance to reply he added:

'But I won't be lodging with her any longer, no fear! Valsamis is dead now!'

And with this he left the study.

4

For many days afterwards old Ophiomachos appeared calm, though his smile had become more sorrowful and his stoop more marked. He spent most of the day sitting in his gloomy study, which looked more funereal and seedy without his ancestral portraits on the dingy walls, now marked by lighter patches where they had once hung. He went up to the dining-room only at mealtimes, where as usual though with forced loquacity he would recount amusing stories of his day, the amorous exploits of some lady who had been abducted by a British High Commissioner, or some other whose husband had found her paramour under the bed, invariably ending with a sad sarcastic laugh, prolonged unnaturally until the tears came to his eyes, though no one else was laughing. Everybody was familiar with these stories, having heard them many times, and no one paid attention.

Whenever the old Countess began to say something, gazing at him imploringly, he would turn round and glare at her ominously, ready to fly off the handle should she say anything he did not want to hear. The others understood that Louisa's name must never cross their lips, and that his bizarre behaviour was aimed solely at preventing this, even though he could think of nothing else besides his truant daughter.

He no longer left the house and received neither guests nor peasants, no one except the money-lender, who now was always coming and going up and down the stairs. He would shut himself in his study for hours on end with him, anxiously consulting him about the most trivial matters, until eventually fatigue would overcome him and he would lapse into despondent silence. Then they would go over the old contracts once again.

The money-lender had noticed that the old portraits were missing from the dingy study walls, but did not enquire further. He too knew all those ancient nobles intimately, having often come across them in the yellowing contracts they were sifting through, and would smile and point to them whenever their names cropped up, as if to include them in the conversation, but now, forgetting they were no longer there, he constantly found himself glancing at the empty spaces and couldn't help smiling at the curious illusion.

Old Ophiomachos appeared to be relaxing over these tasks, but his aged wife understood the depth of his grief. She watched him uneasily, full of apprehension. At what point would this artificial calm erupt? In her eyes her husband was a terrifying being – his uncouth behaviour, constant scenes and threats had driven Louisa to the desperate measures she had taken. Why couldn't the unfortunate old man be a bit more easy-going? Didn't he see he was his own worst enemy? Couldn't he see what he had brought about by his own folly? The one happy note in the situation was that Goulielmos Arkoudis loved Louisa deeply and was sure to marry her. He would never forsake her. That much was clear. No one had ever been known to do such a thing, and not a few girls had left home recently, so one would hardly expect it of Goulielmos who was so very much in love. If they weren't yet married, no doubt difficulties had cropped up which she didn't know about. This displeased her of course as it didn't seem quite proper, but then she knew her daughter was a real beauty and Goulielmos was quite mad about her. She had noticed how he would pursue her and try to stay close to her, shadowing them at balls and tea parties and on the street, even coming to church – he was absolutely everywhere. Why would he go to all that trouble if his intentions toward Louisa were not honourable? Why would he waste his time for no good reason? Of course they would be getting married, perhaps this very minute! If that were the case, perhaps Louisa would be thinking tearfully of her dear old mama, knowing that she would always have her blessing! Yes, her unconditional blessing! Let the old man do as he pleased. She would find some way to let Louisa know that everything she owned was hers and that she would sign it over to her at once, and perhaps that would help matters along, as Arkoudis the banker would no longer have any reason to oppose the marriage, Goulielmos would be able to prove to his father's satisfaction that he would be receiving a handsome dowry, and so everything would end as happily as she could wish. What did it matter if she were left with nothing, she really didn't need her money now. After all, her two sons were grown men and Eulalia a grand and wealthy lady, her own needs were negligible and surely her sons would provide them with enough to eat. Her only concern was for Louisa, but once Goulielmos married her the old man would calm down and Louisa would be able to visit her old home as freely as her sister. This tempest in their life would not last long and perhaps she herself would live to see better days. But in her distracted state the old Countess was forgetting that none of her possessions had survived the shipwreck.

She would frequently talk to her sons about Louisa. But Giorgis was sick at heart. His sister's elopement, just when his soul had been rocked by another cataclysmic storm, had shaken him profoundly. He knew Louisa. He knew how little moral strength she had and how terrified she had always been of the family's dissolution, so much so that she had long been prepared to surrender to the first man who came along if she thought he could secure her the life of leisure she didn't have at home. In retrospect Giorgis could see something like an irony of fate in the whole sorry story. The Ophiomachos family was sliding down the slippery slope towards destruction. Nothing could stop it and one by one their hopes were fading, but so far the destruction had been confined to economic matters: their difficulties had gradually increased and bankruptcy had seemed inevitable until Eulalia's sacrifice had prevented it, but that marriage was like the first step in their moral decline, which had now culminated in Louisa's elopement. What more did fate still have in store for them? And what could Louisa expect from the callous youth whom she had chosen?

Spyros by contrast had not lost his apathy and cold indifference even now. Averse to any exertion, his sluggish brain avoided all sorrow, all argument, all friction, anything that might upset him. He was always ready to agree with the person he was talking to and drowned all despondent thoughts in laughter, preferring to remember only the sweeter moments in his life, delighting in building castles in the air and always seeing the smiling face of fortune up ahead. What was the point in his worrying as well? Things would take their course, because he hadn't the ability required to stop them. This thought paralysed any initiative he might have taken. He didn't dare condemn Louisa's action and didn't know if it was wrong. If she had made a mistake, she of course would be the one to pay, it was no skin off his nose. His father too had remained an insoluble mystery to him. As a child he had always been frightened by his threats and shouting, and even now when the old man lost his temper he would become pale and anxious for a few unpleasant moments and think of him as a cantankerous, evil-hearted wastrel. His mother was the only one whom he was really fond of, because she forgave him all his weaknesses.

It was afternoon. That day the money-lender had arrived in Ophiomachos's study early. He greeted him respectfully as always, sat down at the large table and placed a bundle of papers on it. Then he wiped his hands and brow with his handkerchief and as usual casually began telling the old man all the latest news. In the little town the whole community, rich and poor alike, was in a flurry. The government, it was rumoured, had resolved to go to war and parliament had been suspended. Before calling up everyone of military age however, it was asking voters whether they agreed with the decision. And to win over the peasants it was even announcing a moratorium, and some said it was going to write off all their outstanding debts, cancelling them with the stroke of a pen. An unheard-of populist stunt, according to Doctor Steriotis, who like the minister was an opposition candidate, an extremely serious step that would shake business confidence and rattle society to its foundations – and completely unconstitutional to boot! But what else could one expect of the Greek Kingdom, born of revolution and hatching further revolutions every now and then to extend its territory, what else but the persecution of the poor unfortunate landlord, who paid more and heavier taxes to benefit the peasantry. Naturally the doctor now had cause to be concerned. Since the situation was so volatile, he needed of course to secure his money. And he had been wondering whether his father-in-law might agree to have a general liquidation sale of all the landed properties, which had become so intolerably burdensome. He, the money-lender, would see to finding buyers who would pay a decent price, but it would be as well for Master to have a word with his son-in-law too, so that they could find a way to settle things amicably, as between close relatives. Master knew the doctor was a straightforward, good-hearted man, having had a chance to test him, a man moreover who was going up in the world. And Miss Eulalia was truly happy with him. The doctor had not changed his mind about helping them out, to the extent that he could afford to, more would be a crime, nor would Master want it out of consideration for Eulalia. There was one more thing that could be done however, once the debts had all been sorted out. He, the money-lender, could step in as administrator of the property and pay the doctor back his capital at once. It would only be the interest that Master might find a little steeper, as rates in the current climate were naturally higher. Perhaps Master would think it over and give him an answer at his leisure.

The money-lender looked at the old man, expecting him to lose his temper and start cursing him, as invariably happened when they discussed such matters, and wondered why today he remained so apathetic. For some time Ophiomachos had been pretending not to listen and showing his indifference with an occasional gesture of impatience, contemptuously curled lip or muttered interjection. He seemed to be saying that he had washed his hands of everything and no longer cared about his financial ruin, even if the news spread to the ends of the earth, he no longer needed to safeguard the family honour. His daughters!

Suddenly Ophiomachos said:

'Yes, yes, do as you please! Let everything be sold off, I'll have fewer things to worry about. But make sure my wife's dowry is set aside first. That must be seen to today.'

So saying he bowed his head, resting it on the table, and remained silent for several moments. Eventually he raised his proud, ravaged face and said bitterly:

'I've been disgraced beyond endurance!'

'Master,' said the money-lender sadly, 'you are not the first and you won't be the last. She's a giddy lass, our Miss Louisa. She has displeased the doctor too, just when he's riding high on his success. She's behaved badly, but there's a remedy for everything. Only one thing can't be remedied, that's death.'

'Death,' said Ophiomachos shaking his head sadly, 'death is a small matter compared to shame. Death is forgotten, but shame abides down through the ages! I feel utterly dejected now. Who is going to go and tell this fellow and his banker father how aggrieved we feel, how devastated and ashamed? I've thought the matter over. You're the only one who could do this for us. You're the only one I can confide in, because you know my family's humiliating circumstances and were instrumental in the other marriage too. At least we managed that with honour. You know him, don't you, that young scoundrel, that disreputable lout? I can't tell you how aggrieved I am. What have I ever done for him to give me such a poisoned chalice? If he'd asked me, I'd have let him marry her. Why has he insulted me so unforgivably? Why did Louisa act so secretly and unexpectedly, without even consulting? He's deceived her, I know it! What else could that scoundrel have intended if not to deceive her, have his bit of fun and then leave her on the street, forsaken and despised? It was not my fault! But – alas! I'm the cause of this misfortune. Here's what I want you to do for me. Go and find that dishonourable young scoundrel and tell him how deeply he has grieved us all, me, her aged father, her hapless mother and her siblings, who can no longer face going out into the street. Tell him we are all in hiding because of him, ask him why he has scourged us for no reason, when he has no score to settle with us. Go and tell him the whole situation as you see it here' – and he looked round, motioning towards where the portraits used to hang. 'Tell him we are masking our grief with feigned indifference and hideous false laughter, tell him he has only to put matters right at once and her unhappy mother and I will send our blessing, for we love our dear Louisa and it is only her error that has grieved us, we love her and know she is unhappy. Tell him to right the wrong he's done us and all will be forgiven, and if we don't speak to him at once it will be for appearance's sake, though I am willing to call on him in person if he wishes, I, an old man whom he's dishonoured, provided he puts matters right. Surely he'll do so, even if he is a scoundrel, he can't just disregard my daughter's reputation, damn it! Tell him everything just the way I'm telling you. Memorize each point! A thousand times better had she died! And tell him everything I own is theirs, including my wife's dowry, provided they get married. Do you hear me? – Everything, everything! Even if I become landless and at the mercy of my children. We'll end up in the poorhouse, but who cares. Just see to her, see to her! D'you hear?'

Exhausted after this long speech, he hid his ravaged face in both his hands.

The money-lender looked at him with genuine sympathy. Curiously, he felt sorry for the old man whom he had so long regarded merely as a cash cow to be milked. He was about to say something, but Ophiomachos stopped him with a peremptory gesture.

'Not another word about that cursed wretch!' he said. 'Just come back with his reply. Not another word!'

He glared at him almost threateningly.

But the money-lender felt uneasy. The sympathy that had touched his heart was growing, and he suddenly realized that he had become fond of the old man and was willing to do him a good turn, even though he stood to lose by it. For a few moments he remained silent, then finally he said:

'I'll go.'

And immediately he felt as if a burden had been lifted from his heart. Having succumbed to this unfamiliar mood, he suddenly found himself recalling other suffering souls of his acquaintance, Eulalia who lived a permanent stranger in her husband's splendid mansion, unable to empathize with his success, and Alkis Sozomenos long absent abroad and now gravely ill, perhaps because he had failed to bury the memory of his former sweetheart. He sighed, again perplexed by his own weakness, and said:

'Another family, Master, is also going through hard times. Poor Photini Sozomenos's son has fallen ill abroad and I hear will be returning, because he wants to die at home. Lucky that Miss Eulalia didn't marry him, otherwise we'd now have further cares and heartache... His health was never good.'

'Lucky!' exclaimed Ophiomachos without knowing what he was saying. 'Lucky! Oh yes, very lucky, my Eulalia!'

'Alkis,' added the money-lender sadly, 'is a doomed man.'

'But why is he returning?' asked Ophiomachos, suddenly uneasy. 'Why? My heart grieves for the unfortunate young man, indeed it does! He really loved Eulalia, you wouldn't believe how much, but I saw it with my own eyes – and yet I had no pity for them and felt obliged to part them to preserve the family honour – pah, the family honour! – and now Alkis is about to die. I don't know what to say. So young, poor fellow, so capable and good! May he rest in peace! Ah, life, life... A hard struggle... But wouldn't it have been better if the poor wretch had stayed abroad? Shouldn't Mrs Sozomenos have gone over there instead? More worries for my poor Eulalia... My guess is, she's still in love with him! Alas, my poor Eulalia, such a loving creature!'

He hid his head in his hands once more and remained silent for some time. Finally he looked up again. It was late and getting dark inside the study. Noticing that the money-lender wanted to be off, he said:

'When will you be coming next?'

'Tomorrow,' he replied, 'or if not tomorrow, the day after, anyway as soon as possible.'

'Remember, I won't rest easy until you bring me his reply. Well, off you go then!'

On this occasion he actually shook hands with him and saw him to the door.

As he looked at the old man, the money-lender felt a shiver down his spine.

Shortly after, Ophiomachos went upstairs to the dining-room. His son Spyros was there talking to his mother. As he entered, the old man heard Louisa's name. Immediately he became furious and glared at them ominously, his eyes protruding. Ah, so mother and son were talking about her behind his back! They were hatching some fresh scheme he was not supposed to know about! The blood rose to his head and he became crimson with rage, his voice sticking in his throat for a moment. Finally he spluttered hoarsely:

'What's all this! Didn't I say her name was never to be mentioned in this house, didn't I say so? She's no daughter of mine! I don't want to know her, I don't want to hear her mentioned. Ever!'

Spyros looked at him alarmed and then glanced at his mother in silent appeal, while she bowed her head and said to Ophiomachos:

'Don't fly into a rage, Where-Are-You! Wrath is a deadly sin and we are old now. God has inflicted this wound on us. Have a little patience, because there's something you should hear, however much it may upset you.'

'Don't tell me!' he shouted. 'I don't want to know!' And he flung a chair onto the floor. 'I'll break everything in the house, it's mine, isn't it!'

Then, as if suddenly regretting what he had just said, he continued, shouting:

'Well, what is it I should hear, what? Hardly good news, coming from your lips!'

And he cast a spiteful glance at her.

Then in a low voice and with downcast eyes, the Countess continued:

'Spyros happened to pass by their house on his walk this morning. They have rented a place for her out there with a nice garden, and when she saw him she called out to him, and Spyros stopped and went inside.'

'Stopped? Went inside?' replied the old man angrily. 'Who gave him permission to speak to her? How could he speak to her without feeling ashamed? And you, aren't you ashamed of yourself? Have you no consideration for me at all?'

'He went inside,' the old woman continued, disregarding his outburst, 'and she told him they are happy, will soon be getting married and ask for your blessing. He has rented the house for a whole year, she says. Then she sent Spyros into town on some small errand; she was in high spirits, laughing the whole time. On his return she asked how she might put our mind at rest, enquired after me, and said she'd only be completely happy when we were no longer angry with her.'

'What did you buy for her?' the old man asked his son thoughtfully.

'She gave me a crisp new hundred-drachma note and asked me to fetch her some butter, tea and rusks.'

'And the change?' Ophiomachos asked staring at him.

'She let me keep it,' said Spyros, now lowering his eyes, embarrassed. 'I needed money so I kept it.'

For a moment the old man stood there as if turned to stone. He felt as though the floor were about to give way beneath his feet. Then suddenly overcome by an uncontrollable fit of rage, he flung himself upon his son, grabbed him by the wrists, shook him violently, pushing him into the leather sofa, spat in his face repeatedly and, with his tired eyes almost popping out of their sockets, finally bellowed:

'And weren't you ashamed of yourself? You've disgraced me too, you pimp! You kept the money your sister gets from selling her own body? Out of my sight, the lot of you!'

Trembling and sobbing he turned his back on them and, descending to his study, locked himself inside.

Upstairs they could hear him ranting away despairingly for some time.

'She wants to help her penniless father,' he shouted, 'with the money she gets from selling her own body! Oh God! And Spyros has already started living off her!'

At last Giorgis returned home too. Hearing his steps on the stairs, the old man opened his door and called him in. Angrily and plaintively he related everything that had occurred that afternoon, and also told him about Alkis. Giorgis listened in dismay, struggling to digest the depth of the family's degradation, his brother's moral insensitivity and their escalating slide into the abyss. He too now stood there as if turned to stone and could not find anything to say.

Finally, as if ashamed to raise the matter, the old man said to him gently:

'Anyway, my boy, when will you finally make up your mind to marry that woman?'

'You mean Aimilia?' said Giorgis with a sneer. 'By now she'll have become the mistress of your son-in-law the doctor!'

For a moment the old man again stood speechless, then sighing and adjusting his old frock-coat as if feeling the cold, he started pacing about the study, clutching his head, waving his hands about or raising his eyes to where the old portraits had once been, then finally he cried out in despair:

'But why did you let her, Giorgis? You're lying! I can't believe it! Have you all decided to embitter me, unfortunate old man that I am? Oh, far better for you to have married her yourself! Do none of you have any respect for my white hairs? Not one of you, not one? You're lying! This hasn't really happened… Oh my head!'

Then the old Countess too came down and full of trepidation entered the dark study, now dimly illuminated by the only wick burning in the bronze oil lamp, which Ophiomachos had unconsciously lighted himself. When she saw him pacing up and down, completely shattered and close to despair, she immediately started weeping. Guessing that some new misfortune had befallen the old man, she said to him sadly:

'So God has decided to visit all his wrath upon your head… But he will remember you at the Last Judgement, he will remember you…'

That evening people were going in and out of Doctor Steriotis's fine villa in a constant stream. All the rooms were lit up, and even in the street there were crowds of people standing about engaged in animated conversation, many of them cursing or shouting victory slogans. It was the eve of the election. Eulalia however returned to her father's house that evening and, going upstairs to the dining-room, she sat down beside her mother and together they wept…

5

Several days had elapsed and things had finally quietened down in the old house. The money-lender had not returned and the old man's shouting fits had stopped. But he no longer left his study and spent all day tirelessly pacing up and down and brooding. He scarcely touched the meals his wife brought down to him at noon and in the evening. He would sometimes cast a hateful glance at her but stubbornly refused to speak. He had grown as thin as she was, while she looked more fearful than ever. Her face was pale, her eyes seemed always on the verge of tears, her body trembled and she would often glance round as if expecting to see or hear something alarming, while from dawn to dusk she slaved away at all the household chores, as they had not had a maid for quite some time.

But Spyros too was restless now. His appointment still had not come through. He would go up- and downstairs twenty times a day and roam about the house as if at a loose end, disappear into his room for a while, pick up a book and leaf through it for a minute, looking at the pictures or pondering some phrase, then fling it on the table, return to the dining-room, peer into every corner, under the furniture or behind the pictures as if looking for something, irritably dust some object with his hankie or adjust a frame, rush into the kitchen as if to tell his mother something, but then evade her questioning eyes, bolt out of the room without a word and leave the house, only to return a little later and begin again.

The elderly Countess realized that something was the matter and feared the worst. She also noticed that her other son was always thoughtful, as if weighed down by a premonition that calamity was again about to strike, while Eulalia who came to see them every evening said very little and often wept quietly with them.

It was afternoon. The money-lender had been in the study for some time. His ugly face looked as serious as ever. After greeting the ruined Count respectfully, he had resumed his regular seat at the table, taken a thick bundle of papers from his pocket, and started chatting to him about day-to-day affairs, especially local politics. Doctor Steriotis was now a member of parliament. The government had been routed at the elections. The minister was preparing to depart for the capital, but his party had decided to give provisional support to an uncommitted ministry, which in the first place would guarantee peace but would also be held responsible for the sins of the defeated party. The money-lender wished to congratulate the Count on Steriotis's election.

The old man listened with silent indifference, pacing up and down the study, letting the money-lender ramble on for a good while, as if afraid of his proceeding to more serious matters. Finally he came and sat down opposite him, adjusting his old frock-coat as if feeling the cold.

The money-lender fell silent. He pretended to be sorting through his papers, then gave Ophiomachos a friendly look and tried to smile. He noticed how utterly sorrow had changed the old man's appearance. How much his face had aged in a short time: his rosy complexion sallow, his brow more deeply furrowed, his red lips faded and bereft of their sad smile, his pathetic watery gaze uncertain, as if he feared some sudden misfortune might strike at any moment. He felt sorry for him and did not know how to begin.

But with a sigh the old man asked him in a subdued voice:

'Well? What's his answer?'

'None,' replied the money-lender quietly and lowered his eyes, not daring to increase his bitterness. 'None,' he repeated with a helpless gesture. He reflected that everything he had to tell Ophiomachos that day was bitter and there was little point in trying to tactfully conceal the harsh realities he ought to know about. He paused for a few moments and then said cautiously:

'But that's not what I've come about, Master. I wouldn't have come at all if I didn't have some good news for you. As you know, Master, I really do have a heart of gold. However, another urgent matter has cropped up. Ah, life, Master, it brings so many trials!'

'So you didn't see them?' he demanded, glaring at him. 'Or did the scoundrel refuse?'

'Hear me out, Master,' the other replied gently.

Disconcerted, the old man looked at the floor, conscious that his hackles were rising but restraining himself, reminding himself that he still needed this man and would not find anybody else in his present dire predicament. He forced himself to be patient and even tried to smile. Encouraged, the money-lender smiled back and began again:

'However, another urgent matter has cropped up.'

Ophiomachos looked at him enquiringly and the money-lender continued:

'Your son-in-law, the doctor, is getting ready to depart for Athens. He'll be leaving with the other delegates and as he doesn't know how long he'll be away, he says he'd like to sort out his affairs before he goes. He'd have talked to you himself, but with all the complications...'

The old man looked at him indifferently. These matters had been of no concern to him for some time now. His financial ruin no longer made any impression on him now he had got used to the idea, his other worries were far more urgent. He replied:

'Go and find my son Giorgis and come to some arrangement with him, I'll sign whatever the two of you decide. Let him have all the worries now.'

Then after a moment's further reflection he continued, obstinately reverting to an idea he was reluctant to give up:

'If only Giorgis could make up his mind to marry her, he'd save himself so many headaches, our hands would not be tied and at least he would be wealthy. And a wealthy man need never fear contempt. But he tells me he has left her.'

'Aimilia,' laughed the money-lender, 'will be off to Athens herself in a few days.'

Outwardly Ophiomachos remained impassive, but he felt his heart contracting painfully.

'Ah yes!' he said with a false smile. 'Aimilia's been planning that little trip for quite some time. And now the opportunity's occurred, she'll be escorted by her doctor, our son-in-law, what could be more natural! In fact, she'll be consulting various doctors. The poor woman has not been well ever since her husband died. His death affected her profoundly. And now this opportunity's occurred, what could be more natural!'

Hadrinos smiled knowingly and nodded his agreement. Ophiomachos then resumed his restless pacing up and down the study, looking about him uneasily, and after a while he replied impatiently:

'You saw them... you saw her, I'm sure of it! Why, for God's sake, won't you tell me? Can't you see that otherwise I'll have to take matters into my own hands?'

'Yes, I saw them,' he replied with a sigh.

'Well, what do they say? What does he say?' he continued excitedly, pausing by the table.

The other man looked at him with trepidation.

'He says... he says... that he's not really independent yet, that his father must decide. But his father wants him to go straight to London, as their bank has already opened there and is snowed under with new work, and he doesn't feel it would be right for Louisa to go with him right away. He ought to find his feet there on his own for a short while.'

'Ah,' said Ophiomachos without betraying any emotion, but muttering under his breath.

The money-lender noticed that the old man was trembling from head to foot. He thought he had better not upset him any further and was half-inclined to revert to more mundane matters. But Ophiomachos had already heard the worst. So reluctantly he continued:

'He won't allow him to take her off to London and advises him not to marry her at once, because, he says, as a young man living abroad he won't be able to remain faithful to her. But he doesn't insist that Goulielmos follow his advice, he can do what he likes. Except that as his father he had always imagined his wedding rather differently. And Goulielmos now thinks he's found a way to manage the whole situation. He has rented the house by the shore for a whole year for her, and thought he'd leave her everything she needs and return in a year to take her back to England. He'd marry her then, since by that time his father would have softened and he would have acquired more independence and could please himself.'

'And what does Louisa say?' asked Ophiomachos with a lump in his throat.

'What could she say?' replied the money-lender nervously.

'Is that their answer?'

'There's more to it, Master. The father says that if Miss Louisa is displeased at having to postpone things, he'll provide financial compensation making her secure for life. That way, if she so wishes, she will be able to live alone without needing to depend on anybody else.'

'So that's their answer!' said the old man, whose face had suddenly gone pale as death. 'The pimp,' he laughed grotesquely, 'the pimp, the villain, he wants to pay her for their dishonourable conduct! Oh, Louisa! Oh, Louisa!'

He struggled to contain his rage and tears and in the greatest agitation resumed his restless pacing up and down. His heart was pounding. His mind went blank and he kept smoothing down his hair and sighing pitiably.

'I never suspected anything like this,' he said suddenly. 'I was so full of hope... Ah, I never imagined they'd be so dishonourable! This morning I caught a glimpse of Louisa myself. I walked all the way out there because I felt stifled after so many days cooped up here. I couldn't stand it any longer. She was at her window, cheerful and smiling and looking more beautiful than ever. I kept my eyes on the ground so that she wouldn't know I'd seen her. Of course she couldn't have suspected what those two scoundrels, father and son, were up to! But then again who knows? Alas, she accepts life as it comes and never takes anything too seriously, so perhaps she'll make the best of life spurned by society. She's not like us, she takes after her mother's family. She lacks what I have here within me, she lacks a noble heart!'

He raised his head to look at the Ophiomachos ancestors, but the portraits were no longer there. He sighed and remained silent a few moments, then continued:

'I only went out to let off steam this morning and didn't deliberately go past her house, I wasn't even certain where it was and must have chanced upon it. Then as I was passing, her front door flew open and before I knew it she had fallen on her knees before me. But I looked away angrily and tried to avoid her, I don't know how I didn't kill her. And yet at the same time, alas! I realized that all I wanted to do was take her in my arms and hug her, because she was so terribly unhappy... Oh, what has she done, what has she done, the cursed wretch! Then it occurred to me that perhaps she was asking for my blessing and he was going to marry her after all. And I felt prepared to swallow my gall. But no, no, I could never do that for a moment! The bitter taste will remain with me for ever, because she has brought shame on us for ever! And now what? Now what?'

He looked about stupidly as if seeking assistance, then sat down at his desk and closed his eyes. Louisa's elopement was the bitterest blow so far, yet she was his greatest concern and worrying about her left him no peace, thinking about her drove him mad. He had forgotten all his other cares, his financial ruin, Eulalia and her husband, Giorgis and Aimilia Valsamis, and Alkis Sozomenos. He hid his face in his hands and said in a despairing voice:

'Oh God, and now the shameless scoundrels want to pay her compensation!'

He again lapsed into silence, at last letting his warm tears flow freely. But after a while he looked up and struck his forehead. He had had an unaccustomed brainwave. He realized that he hadn't a moment to lose, and that at a time like this rage, cursing and despair were all beside the point. Something must be done, something just and fitting, and it must be done at once. And suddenly he reached a firm decision. He adjusted his old frock-coat, took down his hat hanging in the corner and looked at the money-lender uneasily.

'Where are you going, Master?' he asked in some alarm.

The old man put his finger to his lips, ordering him to be silent.

'And the documents?' the money-lender asked.

'Wait here for Giorgis and discuss things with him, tell him everything we agreed this morning.'

And with this he donned his hat and left the study. Outside on the landing, Spyros was pacing up and down waiting impatiently. His father gave him a fierce intimidating look and said:

'What's up?'

'Oh, nothing...' the young man replied timidly in a faintly hopeful voice, then as if reaching a momentous decision added, lowering his eyes: 'I just wanted a word with Mimis... about an advance on my salary, as I'm in need of cash – urgent need!'

'He's in there!' replied the old man harshly and with a smile of contempt went on down the stairs.

Spyros entered the study. The money-lender too looked at him contemptuously and did not get up to greet him.

'Did you tell him anything?' the young man asked him anxiously.

'I wouldn't have the heart to,' replied the other. 'And after all, what good would it do?'

'So what did you do?'

'Nothing.'

'Nothing? So what's going to happen now? Oh, my God! Oh, my God!'

He stood there as if turned to stone, digging his nails into his palms.

'Who would be mad enough,' added the money-lender sarcastically, 'to make a loan against the salary of an employee who hasn't been appointed? And where is that sort of money supposed to come from? The doctor is fed up with all of you and refuses to endorse any more of your transactions. He doesn't want to set eyes on any of you! And he's quarrelled about one thing and another with Eulalia too, so she can't help you either. He can't let you get away with tricks like that – using his signature whenever you fancy, whether he agrees or not! And he's quite right too! And now he's off to Athens. Tomorrow the bank will be formally investigating your forged cheque, and if there isn't enough to cover it by noon they will put the matter in the public prosecutor's hands. I feel sorry for your father...'

Spyros felt faint as he listened to these chilling words, his face and lips went pale and his whole body broke out in a cold sweat.

'So no hope from anywhere?' he asked, his voice quavering.

'No hope at all!' the money-lender replied harshly.

In despair, Spyros left the study and went upstairs. He had no idea what to do. His mother was sitting on the sofa, only just discernible in the dark room. She too was dejected, her head resting in her hand. Her son sat down beside her with a sigh, and taking her hand burst into tears.

She stared at him in alarm for a moment.

'Another disaster?' she asked tearfully. 'What is it, my boy? What is it?'

He was trembling from head to foot, which upset her even more.

'My poor boy! My poor boy!' she said tenderly, stroking his head.

At last Spyros, as if waking from a nightmare, blurted out:

'Oh, mother, I've done something stupid, I've made a terrible mistake, an irreparable mistake. Even five months' salary wouldn't be enough, assuming I were appointed. And where am I to find that sort of money? Louisa is the only person who could help. She has as much as she wants now. But what about father? The cheque has bounced and the doctor has denied it was his signature, rightly so, since in fact it wasn't. Now he doesn't want to know us either. And by tomorrow lunch-time the bank will forward the matter to the public prosecutor. What am I to do? What am I to do? I'm done for, mother, I'll have to go to prison! I'm finished!'

His mother shuddered, by now thoroughly alarmed.

'Oh, my boy! More disasters, more disgrace... How will your poor long-suffering father be able to endure it... Oh, my boy!' And she burst into tears.

'I haven't anything left for you to sell,' she continued after a pause, 'not a single brooch or silver spoon, nothing at all!... But why didn't you consult us first? And it's such a huge amount! How could you make such a terrible mistake, my boy? I'll go myself and see the doctor!'

'It's no use,' he said despairingly. 'After all Eulalia's cost him... It's no use.'

They wept together, holding hands, both racking their brains as to where to turn for help, overwhelmed by their shared anxiety and desperation. Finally Spyros said:

'Anyway, I'd better go out to the village tomorrow and stay there till some solution can be found. But what? Raising money takes time. I attempted to sort things out myself, but Hadrinos refused to help me. Try approaching the doctor if you want to, but tomorrow when I'm no longer here. I'll call on Louisa too… What else can I do?… I'll stay in our old place out there in one of the rooms still with a roof. I should be able to lie low for a few days and escape being arrested.'

Utterly dejected, his mother made no reply.

Night had fallen. An antique bronze oil lamp with both wicks lighted shed a dim light through the room. Mother and son were still sitting on the sofa, as if afraid of their own silence, when Giorgis came upstairs, gravely turning matters over in his head. He had been talking to the money-lender. A thousand schemes were revolving in his mind, but all of them required money. Preoccupied, he greeted them. His mother sighed and said:

'Oh, Giorgis! If only you'd decided to marry Aimilia earlier…'

'That woman!' he replied contemptuously. 'Tomorrow she's off to Athens with your son-in-law. Aristidis must be out of his mind.'

The old Countess stood up and promptly sat down again, turning her head this way and that, overwhelmed with emotion. Then she hid her face in her hands and her whole body shook with sobs. Finally heaving a deep sigh she said:

'She's doing this, poor woman, because she loved you very much. Now Aimilia too has lost her self-respect. Oh, my poor Eulalia…'

At that moment old Ophiomachos entered the room, small, stooped, adjusting his old frock-coat. His face looked cadaverous and his legs were shaking.

He was followed by Louisa, smartly dressed, beautiful and smiling. She stopped beside the table and looked curiously at each member of her family, displaying no trace of remorse or shame, merely looking a little ill at ease because no one had addressed a word to her as yet and she could see grief etched on all their faces.

With graceful nonchalance she took off her elegant straw hat and tossed it on the table, then adjusting her hair with both her hands she stood silently and waited.

Her grief-stricken mother finally stood up, her eyes overflowing with tears, a torrent of reproaches rising to her lips, but emotion prevented her from speaking, and though she dearly wanted to go over and embrace her daughter and weep upon her breast, she realized that her legs would not support her and so fell back onto the sofa, hiding her face in her hands again.

In a daze, the two young men gazed now at the old couple, now at Louisa. But Spyros was more preoccupied with his own concerns. Louisa's return and Doctor Steriotis's journey had plunged him into the depths of despair.

The old man, choking back a sob that he tried in vain to hide, was now explaining:

'I've brought her back, I've brought her home again to prevent her being degraded any further. And she still hasn't understood a thing, not a thing!'

He could see that everyone wanted to speak, to ask about everything that had occurred, especially the mother who was already mumbling something amid her tears and questioning her daughter with her eyes. Louisa went on smiling blithely.

Suddenly Ophiomachos lost his temper, his eyes went red, and stamping his foot he shouted in his much-weakened voice:

'Not a word from anyone! I don't want to hear any more about all this. Everything is as it always was. No one ever ran away. No one! You've all been dreaming and you just got frightened. Don't ever mention the matter again!'

And he glared with hatred at his wife, whose breast was again heaving with fresh sobs.

Shaking her head bitterly amid her lamentations the old woman exclaimed:

'At the Last Judgement God will remind you of all this... He's the one who has humiliated you. At the Last Judgement...'

Just then Eulalia too came in. She looked round at everyone then herself burst into tears. Ophiomachos glared angrily at his wife and children, adjusted his old frock-coat again as if feeling the cold, and stomping past Louisa spat on the ground in front of her, then red in the face and bowed down with fatigue he left the room and descended to his gloomy study.

After a short while they heard him pacing up and down as usual, and every now and then they could discern a muffled sob.

6

Several days had passed. Eulalia was ensconced in her little sitting-room. The piano was closed. Light flooded in through the open windows with the fragrant breeze, catching the fresh watercolours in their gilded frames adorning the walls. She herself was wearing a plum-coloured house-coat that displayed her dainty feet and was fastened round her pretty waist with a silk tassel. Just then she was sitting on the sofa reading, and every so often she would lay her book aside and gaze out of the window at a fleeting cloud as it drifted across the clear blue sky. Her mind however was preoccupied and she found it hard to relax and enjoy what she was reading.

How amazingly her life had slipped by, like some unbelievable dream… And how differently from what she had expected, or anyone could possibly have predicted… She was stuck in there because one man had wished it and been forceful enough to make her turn Alkis down, because that same man held the destiny of her entire family in his hands. He had demanded that she make that sacrifice. And she, poor fool, had made it – an utterly absurd and futile sacrifice. Moreover, Doctor Steriotis himself had not found happiness beside her. That was only natural. His ambition had been satisfied and he had enjoyed social success, but his love for her was not erotic passion, it bore no resemblance to her own frustrated love for Alkis. She herself had refused to surrender her soul to him, she could never forget that he had forced her consent, while the level-headed, hard-working scholar and distinguished scientist did not waste much time over her either. And finally he had been overwhelmed by a wild obsession, an irresistible infatuation with another woman which left him incapable of rational thought. Now he openly showed his aversion to anything that came between him and the creature he prized above all else, he had restricted his hours of study, and he no longer came to listen to Eulalia playing the piano. Whenever he talked to her, his sole topic of conversation was Aimilia Valsamis, whom he admired with all his heart. Not only was she a gorgeous creature who knew how to use her sexual charms to hold a man, but she was a woman of great spirit. No worthy enterprise escaped her notice. How delighted she had seemed about his articles, how boundless was her confidence in his scientific prowess, how much she had helped by word and deed at the election with her generous donations, how sound her judgement had proved in that situation too... Whereas at home he had to face his wife's icy indifference, and it was not in his nature to put up with this for long, especially now another woman was supporting him so warmly. Why couldn't his wife do likewise? Were she to do so, they'd soon see whether he could make love!

But it was all too late. Eulalia recognized that each of them would have to go their separate ways. Life was parting her from this man too. How base and contemptible his hollow ambition seemed, all that struggle to attain a transient and vain celebrity, how ridiculous she thought his new-found passion for a woman whom a few days earlier her brother had abandoned, and who was evidently acting only out of angry spite – indeed she often asked herself whether she should still call herself his wife, whether in society she should continue to play the part of the wronged spouse, feigning indifference and going about with a false smile upon her lips.

Was this where all her sacrifices had been leading? And what use had they been anyway? Now the doctor, obsessed with his ambitious plans, was completely neglecting the Ophiomachos family's affairs. In fact he made it plain that he couldn't be bothered with them, perhaps because he didn't want Mrs Valsamis to hear that he was supporting the man who had scorned her so contemptibly. It even seemed likely that in her thirst for revenge Mrs Valsamis had turned the doctor against the whole unfortunate family. Some supra-human will seemed bent on the destruction of the Ophiomachoses – not just their financial ruin but their dishonour and humiliation. That power was guiding their every action, every attempt they made to escape their destiny. Mysterious! Each member of the family had been allotted his pitiable role and was blindly playing out his tragic part, and all those who touched their lives more closely were contributing to their downfall. Her husband, Doctor Steriotis, with his boundless ambition, the fiery passionate Mrs Aimilia Valsamis, so ready to forget herself and the opinion of society, Alkis Sozomenos, the innocent soul with his high-flown dreams, who perhaps would lose his life in a last attempt to be creative, all of them were no more than the instruments of that will, all of them were unwittingly obeying that inscrutable power, which was deceitfully leading them on to work the destruction of the Ophiomachoses.

The weak old man had believed that by sacrificing her he could arrest this omnipotent hand and escape disaster, but this first attempt had only brought him closer to the yawning abyss awaiting him. She herself was merely the first innocent victim, along with Alkis, her first love, her true unfading love. Now she appreciated the value of what she had given up, the value of a life spent beside the man she loved. How bitterly she regretted her own weakness! How much better he had understood the world! Why hadn't she listened to him? She had not seen him again since the day they had exchanged those first and last kisses. Oh, how vividly she still recalled their painful sweetness! What transports they had kindled in her heart, opening up before her a world radiant with hope. And by contrast, how deeply she always resented, body and soul, the amorous advances of her husband. How little pleasure she took in that palatial mansion, where the pain of her separation from Alkis was constantly reviving and where she now lived alone and despised by the husband she had not chosen. And she was quite sure that he too remembered her. Ah yes, and with the same melancholy thoughts, with the same fond remembrance of their love, which had merely yielded to necessity and could never be forgotten. Eulalia knew this because he always referred to her with veiled tenderness in the letters he had written to his mother and to Giorgis from abroad. How touched she was whenever she got the opportunity to read them... They helped her understand his life in exile, with all its tribulations.

From the day that Alkis had got drunk his illness had returned, and with it a strange psychological disorder, a torpid pessimism that left him incapable of the least exertion. Faced with any undertaking the difficulties now always seemed to loom large, and he would shy away from tackling them because he was convinced he was incapable of overcoming them. And so his dreams remained no more than dreams that smiled at him occasionally, as from some distant other world. He was depressed, his letters said, and he stayed away from all forms of entertainment, his melancholy enveloped him like a dense fog, obliterating all the joys of life... He was trying to devote himself wholeheartedly to study, because now, under the heavy blows of fortune, he had been overwhelmed by an urge to create, as if his soul needed to soar on the wings of imagination and breathe the free air of art. He was trying to write.

But Eulalia knew that his endeavours would be fruitless. Exhausted by the struggle within himself and overcome by the sorrow that was always with him, Alkis too was bowing his sad head and seeking deliverance, his life a crumbling ruin that the first north wind would level. Indeed, in his letters he referred to himself as a ruin, and Eulalia ruefully reflected that she herself had been the cause of so much suffering and turmoil, and all because she had vainly sacrificed not only herself but this noble soul who had adored her.

She now remembered Photini as well. The hapless mother too was being worn down by the anguish in her heart. She was urging her son to return home, unable to rest easy knowing that he was far away and sick. And indeed she had every right to do so. Oh, how she, Eulalia, herself longed to be at her beloved's bedside, trying to revive him even at the cost of her own life, or at least alleviating his long hours of suffering... Surely that was her duty? Her vainglorious husband, intoxicated by all his accolades and social kudos, was chasing after another woman, so what now bound her to this man for whom she had sacrificed everything? And didn't her duty to Alkis transcend the letter of the law, since it was the product of true love?

She groaned aloud and warm tears welled into her eyes. Even so, she was not completely satisfied with this train of thought. She knew there was another kind of heroism, that of submission to fixed principles, to laws that permitted no exceptions. Why should she fret about what her husband and Mrs Valsamis were up to, or how they were organizing and settling their lives? She herself should follow the straight and narrow path, this was what a voice from deep within was prompting her, she should avoid temptation and lead a virtuous life, however painful. Let her suffer martyrdom. She should never see Alkis again, even if he returned home, even if he summoned her, even if he were doomed to die, poor man. Yes, she must be strong and not allow herself to take that first slippery step, otherwise she knew she would be lost.

But he himself would want to speak to her, were he ever to return, and then his love would overflow, it would be etched in his pale face, betrayed by every word he uttered – and then what would she do, whatever would she do? He would tell her how much he had suffered and was still suffering, how her love could bring about a miracle, how his life was in her hands and he would only be cured if she were by his side. What would she do, how would she react? Was she forever to remain a slave to the irrational conventions of society that had obliged her to ruin her life and sacrifice her love? Would she always be incapable of openly rebelling? What would she do? Whatever would she do?...

But suddenly she felt an insuperable yearning for him in her heart. No! If he really did return, she would be powerless to resist or flee, she would rather die than that! No, she simply couldn't do it! She longed to run and join him, help him, hold him in her loving arms. Yes, she would surely find the courage! And then how her first and only true love, never entirely extinguished, would revive and take possession of her body, heart and soul, and with it her irresistible longing to surrender to him utterly and release all her frustrated desire in his arms. Oh, if only he weren't sick! If only this illness too could be defeated and love again work miracles... No, Alkis was not going to die! He wasn't coming home to die, he would be hers forever, this time she would find the courage to resist the pressures and face the world as she truly was, a woman in love, whose love was capable of miracles.

She was still absorbed in these reflections when the smartly dressed maid opened the door and in a hushed voice announced that Alkis himself was there and asking to see her. She started and clutched her head, and a shiver ran down her spine. Faced with the reality of the situation, her timidity returned. What should she do, what should she do? Had he really returned? Was he really there asking for her? How could she avoid receiving him? Wasn't he aware that he of all people should not have called, that he shouldn't be harassing a poor weak woman? What should she do? Oh, what should she do? The maid was looking at her strangely, expecting some reply, while he was outside waiting – oh Alkis! Whatever should she do? She couldn't just turn him away, though she didn't want to find herself alone with him, there, in the house of her husband – her real husband, Doctor Aristidis Steriotis. What on earth was she to do?... So her dream had actually come true!

She rose from the sofa trembling all over and wiping her brow, then with her hand on her beating heart she looked anxiously about her little sitting-room, as if she feared someone might be concealed there, her pale lips murmuring she didn't quite know what. When the maid finally withdrew she felt relieved, as she found her look distressing. At last she was alone and free to think, free to imagine what she should say. But before she knew it, the door was opening again and this time it was Alkis himself who entered, Alkis, her first and only love. There he was in front of her, no less terrified and tongue-tied than herself after so long! Oh, she couldn't bear the thought of losing him! And how pale and thin he was, how sunken and strangely glittering his eyes! His clothes seemed two sizes too big for him. But why were they both standing there like statues? Why was he so pale? Why were her hands sweating? He was standing so close to her yet dared not cross the space between them. Why was the smile on his parted lips so sad? Was he ever going to speak? This silence distressed her so, yet she was completely tongue-tied, and he was gazing at her so tenderly it brought tears to her eyes, but she didn't want to cry lest he perceive her weakness. But ah, how ill he was! And yet how his love intoxicated her! How it seemed just then to overflow into her heart!...

Suddenly they found themselves in one another's arms and their lips united in a lingering kiss. Still embracing they gazed at one another, their eyes suffused with tears, their looks avowing mutual devotion. He drew her closer and kissed her lips, her cheeks, her throat with unquenchable desire, and she offered no resistance, her whole soul surrendering to his passion as if plunging into a sea of bliss. Her hand caressed his head and as she covered his face with kisses tears streamed down her cheeks.

Their bodies trembled.

'I love you so much!' he told her. 'How well you make me feel! Together after all this time... together once again!'

'Oh, Alkis... oh, Alkis...' she said with growing concern, as his voice sounded dreadfully hoarse.

They lingered in one another's arms, kissing and shedding copious tears, or gazing into one another's eyes with looks that declared their mutual passion.

'Alkis... Alkis!'

'Eulalia, Eulalia!...'

Then she had another shock. Suddenly she noticed that her beloved's eyes had clouded over and she felt the full weight of his body in her arms. Thoroughly alarmed, she managed with some difficulty to get him to the sofa and, lacking the strength to support him any longer, eased him onto it. Trembling, she stared at him. To her horror she saw that Alkis, now lying helplessly before her with his eyes closed, had gone deathly pale and was having difficulty breathing, while red spume was trickling from the corner of his mouth. This frightened her even more – was Alkis about to die on her here and now, here in her husband's house? Oh, how

sorry, how terribly sorry she felt for him! Trembling, she wiped his lips
with her handkerchief, then she fell sighing to her knees before him, her
hands clasped together.

'Ah, how ill you are!' she said despairingly.

Weeping, she seized his hand and kissed and fondled it.

At one point he half-opened his eyes, and whispered her name:
'Eulalia!...' Then he closed them again, as if longing to fall asleep on
this new-found sea of bliss.

Eulalia was still completely overwhelmed by her emotions. Her alarm
over the immediate danger had now receded, but how was it that her
beloved was lying there before her, a man at the end of his tether whom
life was fast relinquishing! She continued to hold his hand, kissing it and
shedding copious tears.

At last he sat up and, making her sit down beside him, again gazed at
her with a look of infinite love, sorrow and concern. There were a host
of things he wanted to talk to her about just then, but he still could not
summon up the strength and so remained silent, continuing to gaze at
her with boundless tenderness.

Finally, smiling sadly, he said in his low husky voice:

'I've heard about everything, Eulalia, everything! And I left my sickbed
deliberately to come to you. I was afraid of dying abroad without seeing
you again. But I feel fine now I'm here beside you, absolutely fine. How
wonderfully your love's restoring me again!'

He flung his arms around her neck, trembling with a fresh surge of
emotion, but in despair she realized that his cheeks were burning hecti-
cally and noticed with horror that red spume had reappeared on his lips.
His love was no longer an unmitigated joy!

'But I feel right as rain, Eulalia!' he said, sensing her anxiety.

With a smile he got to his feet and walked about the room unaided,
as if to show her how much her presence had revived him.

She too had risen and approached him, trembling from head to foot.

He again fixed his deep-set tearful eyes upon her with a look of
boundless love and Eulalia again fell into his arms, feeling that at that
moment she would not be able to refuse him anything, since she too was
intoxicated by a surge of passion.

But before long the door opened and old Ophiomachos appeared.
He seemed more bent and emaciated than ever, as if there were no flesh

and blood inside his old frock-coat. He paused for a few moments by the door and looked at them in silence. Something about his expression suggested he might explode with anger, but sensing that love had not yet won the day, he sighed instead and smiling at them said:

'But what are you doing here, my boy? Why have you come? You're so ill, so very ill...'

'It will all be over soon!' replied Alkis Sozomenos in a weak voice, looking at Eulalia with a sad smile. Then he continued pensively: 'Life is not something easily destroyed. That is why the anguish lasts so long.'

He sighed.

'Yes,' said Ophiomachos sighing too, 'even mine has not yet been destroyed...'

After a moment's silence he went on:

'So ill, so very ill – and I have been to blame! I parted you then and I'm here to part you once again, as I knew you would be here. Yes, I knew it, Alkis! Ah, I don't wish your first chaste love to be disgraced! Nor do I wish to be disgraced any more myself, which is why I'm here! No, you should not have come. And you, Eulalia, shouldn't have received him! That was your duty!'

And so saying he sat down in a chair beside the table, hiding his face in his hands.

'Alas!' exclaimed Eulalia in distress, looking adoringly at Alkis through her tears.

He shook his head with a sad smile and for some time they all remained silent.

Now Eulalia again became alarmed. Alkis was half-reclining on the sofa looking pale as death, red spume had again appeared on his lips and his eyes had clouded over.

'Oh father!' cried Eulalia distractedly, kneeling down beside the sick man and trembling as she wiped his lips.

With anguish she realized that his fever had increased and that he was shivering in every limb.

'Let's get you home, my boy,' said the old man compassionately. 'You must go to bed at once.'

Alkis shrugged indifferently.

*

Father and daughter were now back in the same room, sitting in silence.

She was seated by a little table, her blond head resting in her hands. She was overwhelmed with bitterness and sorrow and the tears were streaming down her cheeks unchecked. The old man now seemed calm and apparently well satisfied. He was leafing through the book Eulalia had been reading earlier, left open on the sofa, occasionally putting on his spectacles to scan a passage. Now and then he would raise his eyes, look at her and heave a sigh.

Suddenly Giorgis entered. His face was very pale and his gaze restless and perturbed. He looked nervously around the room, and without greeting them exclaimed:

'Father, I've been looking for you everywhere.'

His voice was shaking.

'What is it?' Ophiomachos asked uneasily, adjusting his old frock-coat.

Giorgis shrugged.

'You must come too,' he told Eulalia. 'Mother is going to need you this evening!'

'What is it?' she too asked him in alarm, for a moment forgetting about Alkis.

She realized that it must be something serious to have brought her brother round at that hour and looked at him enquiringly, trying to guess what it might be that was worrying him so much, and that the old man should perhaps not know about. She remained silent for a moment and then said with a sigh:

'Very well then, I'll get dressed.'

'Your mother!... Your mother!...' muttered the old man with bitter contempt. 'In that case, Eulalia might as well stay here. When she's alone, your mother's afraid of her own shadow.'

And he laughed sarcastically.

'Come on, hurry up!' said Giorgis and followed his sister to her room.

Soon the two of them returned to the little sitting-room, overwhelmed by their shared emotion. Eulalia was barely able to contain her grief. Her heartfelt anguish was written on her face and her eyes were brimming with tears.

Her father looked at her in alarm, not daring to ask but suspecting some grave new calamity. He adjusted his old frock-coat as if feeling the cold and stared at his children, waiting to be told the worst.

'Let's go, father,' they said to him quietly.

He did not resist.

'Best if you tell mother,' Giorgis instructed Eulalia with a sigh.

They arrived at the old house. Father and son entered the dark study. Eulalia ran upstairs in tears.

Old Ophiomachos, his head bowed, watched his son anxiously out of the corner of his eye. He began to pace up and down the spacious room as usual, waiting to hear what his son wanted him about. But Giorgis could not bring himself to speak. Finally, losing patience he halted in front of his son and looking at him with hatred said in a hoarse voice:

'Out with it! I can't stand the suspense!'

'Oh, father!' said Giorgis, clasping his hands almost in tears. 'It's Spyros!'

'Spyros!' the old man laughed sarcastically. 'Ah, so he's in trouble again! He needs cash, eh? Where am I supposed to find it? He's always been like that. He too takes after his mother. He never could think straight, his mind always was contrary. What a lad!... What a lad!... So it's Spyros, eh?... All right, it's Spyros... well go on then, what's he done this time?'

He was about to conceal his sorrow with another angry outburst.

'He's dead!' Giorgis told him suddenly and heaved a sigh, holding out his arms ready to embrace him.

But the old man gave him a savage look, baring his few remaining teeth alarmingly. And with an angry laugh he said:

'Ha, ha! So you're in league with him, eh, together with your mother! You want to make me feel pity for him first, so I won't resist what you demand, so I'll agree to sell off everything? Ha ha! What artful dodgers! So you need cash, eh? I never thought you could be so dishonourable!'

Suddenly, in an agony of suspense, he looked his son in the eye and, realizing that Giorgis was telling no more than the sober truth, cried out despairingly:

'For God's sake, tell me! Tell me plainly!'

'He's dead!' Giorgis repeated quietly and sighed.

The old man staggered for a moment as if about to collapse on the floor, but struggling to control the violent emotions choking him he managed to stay on his feet and hold his head erect. His tired old eyes were dry and glittered strangely. And in a firm unwavering voice, as if he felt no pain at all, he said:

'Every man is born with his own destiny. Who can escape death, once his hour has come?... Where is he then?'

Meanwhile paternal love awakening within his soul reminded him of all his injustices towards his dead son, his frequent angry outbursts, his failure to show the least affection for this weak child, his sarcastic response to all his worries. He himself was perhaps the true cause of all the young man's failings, his base and craven character and his frequent debauches. And suddenly he burst into tears. A prolonged wail, a low inarticulate lament came from his chest as he gave way to grief and love touched his anguished heart. He mourned for the young man and his still golden hopes. Fate, which had laid him low, might have had many joyous days in store for him, he might have had a happy life ahead!

'My son... my son...' he wailed, wiping his streaming eyes. 'Where is he then? Tell me, Giorgis! How did he die?'

Giorgis looked at him in alarm. He wondered whether he shouldn't conceal the grim reality from the old man, who was evidently sincerely grief-stricken, but then thought better of it and lowering his tearful eyes replied with a sigh:

'He's in the village, in our dilapidated house. He was alone when he took his own life.'

Starting back, the old man glared at the heavens menacingly, his eyes emitting a strange mad light. Then suddenly they clouded over, utterly defeated.

'How? How?' he cried, trembling and wiping his brow.

'Oh God!' groaned Giorgis. 'But as his father you should know! He was found in a pool of his own blood, a pistol was in his hand; the villagers came running and could see him through the broken window. Oh God!'

'But what for?... What for?' asked the old man dolefully, his grief now overflowing. 'But whatever for?' he repeated, sensing that he was beginning to lose his mind.

Giorgis looked at him with pity and replied:

'He paid with his life for his mistake. No one was willing to help because so much money was involved. The doctor, your son-in-law, testified that the signature was not his.'

'He did what?' roared the old man, crimson with fury. 'Wasn't he ashamed of himself, confound him, disgracing both our names like that?'

Suddenly he started laughing hysterically.

'Ha ha! Spyros made the right decision! This way he's given them the slip! How are they going to catch him now? He's managed to shake off this intolerable burden, life, ha, ha! He made the right decision! He found the courage to do it. But the cheque, what about the cheque? It must be honoured! It must be honoured, however large the sum! Even if it's a thousand francs. Let's sell ourselves, all of us. Let Louisa sell herself once more, along with our beds and everything! The cheque! The cheque!'

Giorgis was devastated by the pathetic spectacle. The old man was losing his wits. He had no idea how to calm him down. With tears in his eyes he said:

'Best if Mother doesn't hear any of this, except that he died suddenly. Alas, that will be hard enough...'

His father gave him a savage look that revealed all his hatred. Then suddenly he again became enraged. He clenched his fists, held his head high, adjusted his old frock-coat, looked his son menacingly in the eye, then suddenly bolted out into the hall and pacing up and down started bellowing at the top of his voice:

'He's killed himself! He's killed himself! He's killed himself!'

'How can you be so heartless, father!' Giorgis managed to exclaim, completely shattered.

Upstairs clamorous lamentations broke out at once.

But the old man returned to his study still spluttering with rage. One eye was all puffed up and his lips were trembling. He sat down exhausted in his armchair, holding his head in both his hands, and cried:

'Oh, my head, oh! I'm going out of...' After a while he got to his feet again, no longer aware of what he was doing. His movements were unsteady and erratic, his eye was so inflamed that he could not see out of it, and he jerked his head this way and that, making histrionic gestures. Suddenly he strode over to the window, tugged down one of the faded curtains, shook off the dust and draped it over his threadbare frock-coat; then he put the wastepaper basket on his head, picked up a ruler from the desk, placed a chair in the middle of the room and sat down majestically, propping the ruler on his knee.

Then he shouted:

'I'm the king! Yes, the king! Who doesn't believe it? Here I am, with my cloak of woven gold, my golden sceptre and my diamond crown! Ha, ha! Who doesn't believe it? Off with his head this minute, yes this minute! I shall now decree universal death, because I wish life to be destroyed. Life is the root of all evil! I shall begin with man, and then we'll see. Man is the creature that suffers the most. The midwives must strangle every newborn child. In a few years there won't be any people left, and after that we'll see. Man suffers most because he's endowed with reason. His mind always advises him perversely and that's how God wins him over. Yes, yes, in a few years there won't be any people left, that is what I wish, and my wish is law throughout my kingdom and my kingdom is this miserable world! Spyros made a start today – good for him! He's given them the slip. So first let man be put to death, but then how is the rest of life to be destroyed? The mind boggles at the teeming life on land and sea and air! How can it be done? Everything's alive, even the stones, everything, everything! Life is proliferating everywhere! What kind of mind was it that created so much life, such a variety of life? It was a malevolent mind! Alas, what has it done! My head, my head!...'

He got up and strode majestically about the gloomy study, making the curtain fan out behind him and holding the ruler upright in his hand.

The old man had lost his wits. Upstairs the women were weeping, and Giorgis listened to their lamentations in a daze.

7

Photini was in her kitchen. She was dressed in black, with a light blue cloth apron round her waist; her pale face was very dry and wrinkled, and a tear lingered in her exhausted sunken eyes.

In a corner of the kitchen a rather older woman, her servant, was sitting on a wooden chair in silence, her head in her hand and looking equally depressed.

It was late afternoon. The window was open. Outside, the setting sun had turned the few clouds rosy pink. A light breeze came in, warm and moist, a breath of spring in the heart of winter.

Photini was warming a little soup in a small copper pan. She stirred it with a wooden spoon, let it come to the boil, withdrew it from the glowing coals, broke two eggs into it and as she brought the spoon to her lips to taste, said to herself with a sigh:

'He's in a bad way!'

She turned towards the door and listened, then continued brooding:

'He won't eat it. He can't face anything at all now.'

She shook her head sadly. Her face had the drawn anxious look of a defenceless person numb with fear, who is either unwilling or unable to acknowledge the reality of their misfortune, yet finds the strength to carry on, and the dreaded thought she had been trying to avoid flashed through her mind: this was the end!...

In despair she raised her eyes to heaven and her lips began to tremble:

'My darling Alkis! Surely, surely it won't happen! It cannot be God's will. Why, oh why would He punish an elderly widow like myself? The boy has his whole life before him! Oh!...'

Mechanically she poured the soup into a bowl, stood a moment half hoping, half fearing she might hear some sound, then holding the sick man's meal carefully in both hands she finally left the kitchen. The elderly servant followed her in silence.

The setting sun came in through the window, flooding the spotless little room with glorious light. Outside, the hesitant chirping of a bird was audible, perched on the branch of a lilac in full bloom. From the street came the rumble of a passing coach and the sound of voices from people sitting idly in the little café opposite. Everything in the room had assumed a rosy colour – the walls, the furniture, the sheets, even the pale, thin translucent face of the sick man lying on his back under the sun-warm bedclothes.

His head was propped up on four pillows. His eyes were hollow and half-closed. Dark blotches stained his broad fleshless brow. His cheeks were sunken and his dry lips were scarcely visible beneath his dark moustache and little beard. His whole expression was remote, and his fine features bore the mark of suffering, his breathing was shallow and laboured, like little sighs, and every so often he would turn his head this way and that to suck in air, his long thin fingers clutching at the sheets. He seemed exceptionally long lying there in bed and still extremely young, even though his face looked prematurely aged from the disease.

On a small square table beside his pillow were an assortment of bottles, an unlit candle and two silver teaspoons, and at the foot of the bed was a large wooden armchair, just then unoccupied.

'Here you are, Alkis,' said his mother, approaching the bed and trying to smile, 'here's your soup.'

The sick man made no reply. Resting the bowl on the little table a moment, she tucked a white napkin under her son's chin, then patiently tried to spoon some soup into his mouth. But the sick man couldn't swallow it. His hollow eyes fluttered for a moment, the soup drooled out of the corner of his mouth and he coughed convulsively, his mouth filling with bright red foam. Photini replaced the bowl on the table, turned her eyes to heaven a moment, as if in supplication, sat down in the large wooden armchair at the foot of the bed, and turning towards the aged servant sadly shook her head.

For a long time the two women remained silent. Photini watched over the sick man with patient resignation. He was more restive now. He tossed his head about more violently and rumpled the bedclothes with his feet, while his fleshless fingers kept plucking at the hem of the sheet as he sighed and moaned. A crimson beam of light from the setting sun caught a knob of the brass bedstead, and was reflected in the mother's haggard face, the timid chirping of the bird could be heard more distinctly in the room, as it had perched higher in the flowering lilac outside the window, and the street was now bustling with life.

The sick man whispered something, but they couldn't make it out.

'Still no sign of the doctor,' said Photini anxiously after a while.

'Still no sign,' echoed the other old lady, her face impassive.

Then the two of them fell silent for quite some time.

Finally the mother rose again, went to the head of the bed and felt her son's brow, then glancing heavenwards with a little sigh, she turned to look for something on the dresser and returned to her seat, pressing her tired lids between thumb and finger.

'He's feverish,' she whispered in despair.

After a gloomy pause she shook her head sadly and, indicating the sick man, continued:

'Alas, anyone can see how grave things are. And yet I can't help feeling she will revive him. Oh, what a night, what an interminable night. The two of us shut up in here... It seems an age!'

She carried on like this, sighing intermittently and raising now one hand, now the other to adjust her neatly combed brown hair, which had lost only a little of its lustre with the passing years.

A groan from Alkis suddenly cut her short. She turned toward the bed, but the ray of sunlight from the brass knob dazzled her and she could not make him out immediately.

She smiled at him however, shielding her eyes with her hand and gazing into his pale face for several moments, then she turned fretfully away towards the window.

Down in the street a cabdriver was cursing his horse in a loud voice and other people were laughing noisily. But her eye was caught by the little bird hopping among the branches of the flowering lilac and looking in curiously through the sick-room window, now and then emitting irregular peeps from its tiny throat.

'Still no sign of him,' she said again after a while.

'Still no sign,' sighed the other woman sadly. A lengthy silence followed.

The elderly servant had now approached and was looking sadly at the sick man.

Photini wiped away a tear and said plaintively:

'It's been three days now since he swallowed anything... no medicine, not a drop to drink... His lips are parched and he hasn't slept at all. Three whole days!'

'It's the disease taking its course!' sighed the other woman.

'Praised be the name of the Lord!' said Photini shuddering, 'for He ordains!'

They again fell silent.

By now the sun had set and the sick man's face looked very long and sallow, like that of a corpse. His nose seemed thinner and more prominent and his moustache and beard which covered his pale lips and hollow cheeks much darker, yet his restlessness had increased and his breathing had become more laboured. He struggled in vain to heave a sigh. The attempt choked in his throat and a violent fit of coughing shook his whole frame, his hands clawing at the white sheets and his legs stirring under the bedclothes, which seemed to lie heavily upon his chest.

The daylight continued to fade and the furniture seemed steadily to recede into the ever darkening corners. The air seemed on the point of

congealing and turning into tangible black dust inside the room, where
the two frightened women, though unable to admit as much to one
another, were anticipating death at any moment. With the sad waning
of the day came the extinction of their consoling hopes, and the mother
felt a heavy weight upon her heart which grew more oppressive by the
moment.

'It's dark already,' she said anxiously, 'and still...'

'Still no sign,' replied the old servant patiently.

By now the noise in the street had largely subsided. Only the occasional
shout could still be heard, as the melancholy twilight descended over all
creation. The two women felt even more depressed and restless in the
gathering gloom of the sick-room that seemed to swallow them up, as
they gazed in mute anxiety at the sick man, whose head now stood out
against the white bedding, looking like some eerie shadow from another
world, as only the dark hair and beard could be made out, the face itself
swallowed up in darkness.

Now the elderly servant went out, shuffling her feet feebly, and
returned carrying a lighted lamp. She placed it on the dresser and paused
silently a moment by the bed, her arms folded, then shook her head
hopelessly and with downcast eyes withdrew to her corner with a sigh.

Some time later the doctor finally entered the sick-room. He too
was a man of about forty, with an already established reputation about
town for his scientific learning and ability to work wonders as a doctor.
He too was of medium height, still blond with a little goatee beard
and restless blue eyes, and he too was wearing a new, elegantly cut
black suit.

He paused a moment at the door and his face darkened briefly, then
he smiled and greeted the old lady cordially.

'Save him!' the mother cried immediately, clasping her hands.

'Save him!' the ancient servant also pleaded.

The doctor stood gravely beside the sick man for a few moments, held
one of the bottles on the little table up to the light, pursed his lips and
proceeded to take the patient's pulse.

Photini watched him with mounting anxiety. No one spoke. Finally
the doctor relinquished the sick man's wrist, took a small nickel box from
his pocket, and said with a frown:

'I'll give him an injection.'

'I can't bear to watch!' cried the mother, covering her eyes with her hands. Then suddenly she hurried to the door. The other elderly lady followed.

They went into the parlour. Photini at once lit a candle, sat down at a table and began weeping softly. The other woman remained standing beside her.

'It's all just the same as it was then!' sobbed Photini after a while.

'Just the same!' sighed her companion.

They lapsed into silence, both gazing apprehensively in the direction of the sick-room.

Soon the doctor reappeared at the parlour door, looked in uneasily, and with a sad smile that conveyed his helplessness said:

'Won't you come through.'

The two women followed him to the sick-room in a daze.

Alkis was now lying on the bed without any pillows. The doctor gravely took his pulse again. For a moment the mother thought with horror that the end had come and rushed to kiss her dead child. She was ready to start weeping and beating her breast, but the doctor restrained her with a look and the same hopeless smile, and said quietly:

'He's alive!'

Then correcting himself he added:

'He's still alive!'

Photini sighed mournfully and then, as if remembering something, looked about and said in a hurt tone:

'And she never came...'

'She never came...' sighed the other woman too.

The doctor was now getting ready to leave and bidding them goodbye. Photini did not even attempt to detain him. Fine beads of sweat started from the dying man's brow as he struggled to draw irregular short breaths. The two women looked on with beating hearts. His throat moved convulsively, he opened his eyes wide and started coughing weakly, and a scarlet trickle issued from his pale lips.

Just then, as the doctor was on the point of leaving, there was another knock on the door. Photini leaped from her armchair. A glimmer of hope appeared in her tear-stained eyes only to vanish, although she began to make for the door. Then she stopped, looking at Alkis. The old servant sighed and shuffled out to answer the door instead, and a moment later reappeared accompanied by Eulalia. She was wrapped in a black crêpe gown. Her eyes were red from weeping, her attractive figure moved awkwardly and nervously and her face as she looked around anxiously was extremely pale and gaunt.

She stopped in front of the bed, gazed at the dying man with infinite tenderness, then burst into tears, collapsing into the arms of the distracted mother.

'He's going to die!' the latter whispered to her with a sob.

All of a sudden Alkis opened his eyes again and looked about, surveying the entire room, until at last his gaze met Eulalia's looking down at him in anguish, and he smiled at her with his pale emaciated lips – a farewell smile. He tried to say something but couldn't manage it and closed his eyes again, exhausted.

'Oh, Alkis!' cried Eulalia, falling to her knees and clasping her breast.

The two elderly women looked on dazed and weeping, and a prayer such as people utter who can see no other recourse rose from their lips.

'I too have come to be near you, to be with you!' said Eulalia with a sob.

'Alkis!' the mother said again in anguish, seeing the sick man's bleary eyelids fluttering.

'By tomorrow,' said the ancient servant, 'his suffering will be over...' And she left the room.

'He can hear us,' said Eulalia fearfully.

The mother looked round in a daze. She shook her head and as she raised it toward heaven her eyes overflowed with tears and her chest heaved in a prolonged fit of sobbing. She kissed her son's forehead and stood for several minutes bent over the bed, gazing at the tortured expression on the dying young man's face. He was fading fast. Red spume trickled continuously from his mouth and a deep groan issued from his chest.

The two women now waited for the end, immersed in a silent anguish beyond the power of words. They both realized they had nothing more to say. With their gaze fixed on Alkis, each went over in her mind everything that had happened. In the street all noise had ended. At that late hour, the roar of life had ceased.

The invalid was slipping away...

The end was approaching.

Notes

p. 32, *had studied in Italy.* Since the seventeenth century, Corfiot Greeks had been sent to Italy, particularly to Padua and Venice, for professional training, and the tradition continued even after the establishment of the Ionian Academy, the first modern Greek university, in 1823.

p. 32, *Jacobins.* Originally radicals during the French Revolution associated with Robespierre, but throughout the nineteenth century down to the Bolshevik Revolution of 1917 the term was applied to all radical extremists.

p. 32, *Carabinieri.* The gendarmes of Italy, founded in 1814 by King Victor Emmanuel I to provide Sardinia with a police force, and armed originally with carbines.

p. 33, *Cyprus.* Captured from the Venetians in 1571, Cyprus remained part of the Ottoman Empire, with a sizeable twenty per cent Turkish minority, until 1878 when at the Congress of Berlin it came under British administration.

p. 33, *Greek the official language of the island.* In the 1840s the use of Greek became statutory in Corfu first in the law courts, then in parliament and finally in all public documents, but only came into full effect after the union with the mainland Kingdom of Greece in 1864 (see the last note to p. 48).

p. 42, *universal suffrage.* Otto von Wittelsbach, second son of Ludwig I of Bavaria, appointed to rule over the Hellenic Kingdom by the Great Powers in 1832, finally agreed to a constitution and universal male suffrage in 1844, but women were not to receive the vote until 1952.

p. 42, *curtailing all our privileges.* Even before union with liberated mainland Greece, where noble titles were not recognized, there was constant pressure for reform from the radical or *Rizospastic* elements within the local Ionian parliaments, and the powers of the local upper houses or senates, drawn substantially from the old nobility who were acceptable to the high commissioners, were being steadily eroded.

p. 42, *He gambled and frequently lost.* In his *History of the Island of Corfu* (1852) Henry Jervis-White Jervis remarks on the 'narrow-minded spirit of intrigue' of the place-seeking Corfiot signor and continues: 'Fond of display, although perhaps living in a garret, he will sport his white kid gloves on the Esplanade, and display his person at the Opera. A gambler to the backbone, he will in one night, spent at the nobles' club, lose his income of a month, and thereby further mortgage his small patrimony... The Corfiot signor prefers to waste his years, so long as he can live in the capital, leaving his olives and vines to the care of the farmer...'

p. 48, *couldn't fully understand their language.* As a member of the Italianized Corfiot nobility, the Count is able to converse colloquially in his 'mother' tongue, but finds difficulty reading Greek, especially the archaic *katharevousa* used by the newspapers.

p. 48, *the Russian party.* The fledgling parties during Otto's reign were known as the 'English', 'French' and 'Russian' parties, each maintaining close links with the ministers in Athens of the respective protecting powers. The Russian party was more concerned with keeping the link with the Patriarchate than with establishing a representative government and tended to be conservative.

p. 48, *some border operation.* On the eve of the Great War, Greece fought two Balkan wars (1912 and 1913) in the scramble for Ottoman territory, the first in alliance with Serbia, Montenegro and Bulgaria, which resulted in its annexing most of Macedonia, the second with Serbia against a disaffected Bulgaria that had been beaten to Salonica by the Greeks in the 1912 war by a matter of hours.

p. 48, *should never have gone ahead with the union, never!* After demolishing the massive Venetian New Fortress in Corfu, the British formally handed the Ionian Islands over to Greece on 2 June 1864.

p. 49, *lessons ready-made from Europe.* Young Greeks returning from studies in Germany, France and Italy imbued with socialist ideals played a subversive and progressive role when appointed to teaching positions in Greek towns and villages.

p. 53, *tsarouchia* – rustic turned-up shoes; *kokoretsi* – grilled sheep's entrails.

p. 53, *foustanella.* A white pleated kilt, part of the Greek national costume and still worn by soldiers on palace guard duty in Athens and on festival occasions and parades.

p. 58, *Do you hear?* The many quarrels and occasional moments of tenderness between Ophiomachos and his Countess are clearly based on Theotokis's own stormy relationship with Ernestine. Before they married she had been forewarned by Markos Theotokis of his son's difficult nature, and in one symptomatic incident she apparently returned from a shopping spree having forgotten her husband's requests, whereupon he flew into a rage and flung her purchases onto the fire.

p. 59, *Spyros.* Named after St Spyridon, patron saint of Corfu, to whom the faithful attribute miraculous escapes from famine, plague and Turkish capture, and whose relics were paraded round the city four times a year.

p. 61, *court of first instance.* Above the magistrate's courts and below the courts of appeal, the courts of first instance in Greece handle the bulk of civil and criminal litigation. Ophiomachos is anxious to avoid the opprobrium of being entered in red letters as a bankrupt.

p. 80, *Pandemos Aphrodite.* Traditionally, the 'Aphrodite of the people' was the goddess of carnal love, as opposed to the celestial Aphrodite favoured by the Neoplatonists. In antiquity the Athenian statesman Solon (c.618–558 BC) used taxes levied on the brothels to built a temple to her as the patroness of prostitutes.

p. 81, *purchasing ships.* As naval minister under Charilaos Trikoupis, and later as prime minister, Giorgis Theotokis (from the so-called 'political branch' of the Corfiot Theotokis clan) built up the Greek fleet, ordering three warships, the *Spetses*, *Hydra* and *Psara* in 1887, and introducing measures to professionalize the navy.

p. 85, *'The Russo-Turkish disagreement'*. During World War One the Ottomans waged war against Russia in the Caucasus in a bid to recover Armenian highland territory it had lost in the Russo-Turkish War of 1877–78. In the recurrent conflicts between the rival multi-ethnic empires, the Greeks tended to side with their Russian co-religionists, and Russia in turn encouraged the nationalist aspirations of Greeks and Orthodox Serbs.

p. 85, *The king*. The disagreement between the pro-Entente Prime Minister Venizelos and the pro-German King Constantine over Greece's participation in the war came to a head in 1915 when the king dismissed the Liberals and replaced them with a pro-Royalist government. An Entente-backed northern military coup the following year installed Venizelos as head of a rival provisional government in Salonica – creating the so-called 'National Schism' – which forced the king to abdicate in favour of his son and took Greece into the war on the Allied side.

p. 87, *Bellum omnium contra omnes*. The Latin phrase meaning 'war of everyone against everyone else' was used by the English philosopher Thomas Hobbes in *Leviathan* (1651) to describe man in a state of nature unconstrained by civil society.

p. 87, *Le Dantec*. The French evolutionary theorist Félix Le Dantec (1869–1917) sought to reconcile Darwinism and Lamarckism, claiming that natural selection did operate, but only biochemically on the cells of individual organisms.

p. 90, *the Idea*. The term is left unspecific ideologically to link Alkis as an idealist with the whole radical tradition emanating from the French Revolution, especially the Greek uprising against the Turks in 1821, Garibaldi's Risorgimento and the Corfiot *Rizospastai* active in the cause of union with Greece from the 1840s on. Alkis's call for armed revolution in the red room at the ball recalls Garibaldi's Redshirts and also suggests a specifically socialist agenda.

p. 93, *Great Ideas*. The *Megali Idea* or irredentist 'Great Idea' calling for the liberation and reunion of the Greeks of Thessaly, Macedonia, Thrace, Asia Minor, Crete, Cyprus and the lesser islands within a single state, with Constantinople as its capital, dominated Greek political thinking throughout the second half of the nineteenth century. It ended ignominiously in 1922 with the disastrous invasion of Turkey repulsed by Atatürk, the massacre and evacuation of the Greeks of Smyrna and the ensuing Greek/Turkish exchange of populations.

p. 111, *she raised you from the dead like Lazarus*. Aside from suggesting Photini's piety, Eulalia's Lazarus-like revival of Alkis, if he is seen as embodying the spirit of liberal idealism, may have political overtones. When Venizelos was restored to power by the Allies in 1917, he recalled the June 1915 parliament where he had enjoyed a majority, which was thus dubbed the 'Lazarus chamber.' (See Clogg, p. 93.)

p. 120, *separation from the Patriarchate*. The Church of Greece, originally part of the Ecumenical Patriarchate of Constantinople, was declared autocephalous in 1833 by the Bavarian regents acting for King Otto, who was still a minor, and it was officially recognized as independent by the Patriarchate in 1850, but the merits and long-term consequences of this schism continued to be debated into the twentieth century.

p. 120, *the money-lender's hook-nose*. There was a sizeable Jewish community on Corfu during the Middle Ages, which grew with the arrival of refugees from the Spanish Inquisition, and by 1890 it was estimated that one in ten townsmen was Jewish. Though they prospered they were not fully assimilated but made to wear a yellow badge, and up until the British era the main ghetto was locked at night. Ophiomachos's anti-Semitic attitudes were common among the debt-laden European aristocracy of the period.

p. 159, *'vindicate' her rights, her sacred and 'indefeasible' rights.* Rhetoric associated with the 'Great Idea'.

p. 161, *Lucretius's great poem.* Lucretius's *De Rerum Natura*, or *On the Nature of Things* (the only known work of Titus Lucretius Carus, c.99–55BC) is a philosophical epic in which he seeks to free man from superstition and the fear of death by expounding the materialist philosophy of Epicurus. Theotokis translated Book VI into demotic Greek.

p. 171, *But I put it to you:* The minister's rhetoric is in the *katharevousa* of public discourse at the time, giving it a satiric bite that is lost in translation.

p. 172, *invest in gold.* In 1893 Greece defaulted on its international debt, finally accepting an international commission to regulate its finances in 1898, and the period down to the 1922 Smyrna disaster was one of escalating economic uncertainty and mass migration. Well after World War Two, dowries still tended to be compiled in gold coins rather than paper drachmas as a hedge against inflation.

p. 182, *Madame Angot.* A popular operetta by Alexandre Charles Lecocq (1832–1918), *La Fille de Madame Angot* was first produced in 1872. For two centuries Corfu had a vibrant musical and operatic tradition centring on the Nobile Teatro di San Giacomo (and after 1902 the Municipal Theatre) where the latest Italian, French and Greek operas were staged.

p. 205, *Carlyle was quite right.* The doctor, a self-made man, clearly identifies with Carlyle's natural aristocrats and captains of industry as against the idle aristocrats and dandies he rails against. The reformed prodigal and social activist in Theotokis doubtless relished Carlyle's injunction in *Sartor Resartus* to 'Close thy Byron; open thy Goethe.'

p. 208, *Mechnikov.* Ilya Ilyich Mechnikov (1845–1916), a Russian microbiologist at Odessa University and subsequently the Pasteur Institute in Paris, who did pioneering work on the immune system, postulating a role in evolution for 'phagocyte' cells that destroy intruders, and who in 1908 was awarded the Nobel Prize for medicine.

p. 208, *Calmette.* Albert Calmette (1863–1933), a French bacteriologist and immunologist with the Pasteur Institute in Saigon and later Lille, who developed a vaccine against tuberculosis and the first anti-venom against snakebite.

p. 214, *parliament had been suspended.* Once Venizelos's northern provisional government had declared war on the Central Powers in June 1917, there was a massive and sometimes unscrupulous drive to recruit troops to fight alongside the Allies and repulse advances by the Bulgarians (on the side of the Central Powers) into eastern Macedonia.

p. 231, *Some supra-human will.* Schopenhauer's pessimistic view of life as governed by an irrational cosmic will was congenial to Theotokis; he saw it, like the classical Greek concept of *moira*, or fate, as appropriate to his portrayal of the effete decadent aristocrats of his homeland.

Further Reading

Roderick Beaton, *An Introduction to Modern Greek Literature* (Oxford: Oxford University Press, 1994)

Richard Clogg, *A Concise History of Greece* (Cambridge: Cambridge University Press, 1992)

Douglas Dakin, *The Unification of Greece 1770–1923* (London: Ernest Benn, 1972)

Brian Dicks, *Corfu* (London: David & Charles, 1977)

Gerald Durrell, *The Corfu Trilogy* (London: Penguin, 2006; including *My Family and other Animals*, 1956, *Birds, Beasts and Relatives*, 1969 and *The Garden of the Gods*, 1978)

Lawrence Durrell, *Prospero's Cell: A guide to the landscape and manners of the island of Corcyra* (1945; London: Faber & Faber, 2000)

Spiro L. Flamburiari, *Corfu: The Garden Isle* (London: John Murray, 1994)

Thomas W. Gallant, *Modern Greece* (London: Hodder Arnold, 2001), chapter 5, 'The social world of men and women'

Robert Holland and Diana Markides, *The British and the Hellenes: Struggles for Mastery in the Eastern Mediterranean 1850–1960* (Oxford: Oxford University Press, 2006)

Andreas Karkavitsas, *The Beggar*, translated by W.F. Wyatt Jr with an appendix by P. D. Mastrodimitres (New York: Caratzas, 1982)

Giuseppe Tomasi di Lampedusa, *The Leopard*, translated by Archibald Colquhoun (1961; revised edition, London: Vintage, 2007)

Edward Lear, *The Corfu Years: A chronicle presented through his journals and letters*, edited and introduced by Philip Sherrard (Dedham: Denise Harvey, 1988)

Alexandros Papadiamantis, *The Murderess*, translated with an introduction by Peter Levi (New York: New York Review Books, 1983)

Jim Potts, *The Ionian Islands and Epirus: A Cultural History* (Oxford: Signal Books, 2010)

Michael Pratt, *Britain's Greek Empire* (London: Rex Collings, 1978)

William St Clair, *That Greece Might Still Be Free: The Philhellenes in the War of Independence* (London: Oxford University Press, 1972)

Giovanni Verga, *I Malavogli: The House by the Medlar Tree*, translated by Judith Landy with an introduction and afterword by Eric Lane (Sawtry: Dedalus, 1985)

ANDREY BELY

The Silver Dove

Translated by John Elsworth   978-0-946162-64-2

This first modern Russian novel (1909), by the author of *Petersburg*, whom
Nabokov ranked with Proust, Kafka and Joyce, depicts a culture on the brink, in
the aftermath of the 1905 revolution.

THEODOR FONTANE

Cécile

Translated by Stanley Radcliffe   978-0-946162-43-7

The first English translation of the second of Fontane's series of Berlin novels. At a
fashionable spa an affair develops between an itinerant engineer and the delicate,
mysterious wife of an army officer – to explode in Germany's bustling new capital.

VSEVOLOD GARSHIN

From the Reminiscences of Private Ivanov *and other stories*

Translated by Peter Henry and others   978-0-946162-09-3

Russia's outstanding new writer between Dostoyevsky and the mature Chekhov,
Garshin, 'a Hamlet of his time', gave voice to the disturbed conscience of an era that
knew the horrors of modern war, the squalors of rapid urbanization, and a highly
explosive political situation. This selection contains almost all his short fiction.

JAROSLAV HAŠEK

(author of *The Good Soldier Švejk*)

The Bachura Scandal *and other stories and sketches*

Translated by Alan Menhennet   978-0-946162-41-3

These 32 stories of Prague life, most of them translated into English for the first
time, revel in the twisted logic of politics and bureaucracy in the Czech capital
which was also an Austrian provincial city.

RED SPECTRES

Russian 20th-century Gothic-fantastic tales

Selected and translated by Muireann Maguire   978-0-946162-80-2

Eleven stories by seven writers who used the supernatural genres and
Gothic repertoire to explore the dark underside of the machine age and the
new political order in the first years after the Revolution: Valery Bryusov,
Mikhail Bulgakov, Aleksandr Grin, Sigizmund Krzhizhanovsky, Aleksandr
Chayanov, one of whose stories (included in this selection) influenced
Bulgakov's *Master and Margarita*, and the émigrés Georgy Peskov and Pavel
Perov. All but two of the stories appear in English for the first time.

HUGO VON HOFMANNSTHAL
Selected Tales
Translated by J.M.Q. Davies   978-0-946162-74-1
Seven haunting tales, one of them the nucleus of the author's later libretto for Strauss's *Arabella*, capture the restless, alienated spirit of fin-de-siècle Vienna.

ARTHUR SCHNITZLER
Selected Tales
Translated by J. M. Q. Davies   978-0-946162-49-9
A balanced selection of thirteen of Schnitzler's stories exploring turbulent Viennese inner lives, ranging from the celebrated *Lieutenant Gustl* and *Fräulein Else* to other vintage but lesser-known tales, some of which are translated for the first time.

HENRYK SIENKIEWICZ
Charcoal Sketches *and other tales*
Translated by Adam Zamoyski   978-0-946162-32-1
Three historical novellas by the author of *Quo Vadis?* and *With Fire and Sword*. All have 19th-century settings – the aftermaths of the Polish Insurrection of 1863/64 (*Charcoal Sketches*) and of the Franco-Prussian War of 1870/71 (*Bartek the Conqueror*), and the émigré scene on the French Riviera in the 1890s (*On the Bright Shore*).

ADALBERT STIFTER
Brigitta
with Abdias; Limestone; *and* The Forest Path
Translated by Helen Watanabe-O'Kelly   978-0-946162-37-6
The most substantial selection of Stifter's narratives of the diseased subconscious, richly symbolic and brushed with mystery, to appear in English.

THEODOR STORM
The Dykemaster (*Der Schimmelreiter*)
Translated by Denis Jackson   978-0-946162-54-3
Set on the eerie west coast of Schleswig-Holstein, with its hallucinatory tidal flats, hushed polders, and terrifying North Sea, this story of a visionary young creator of a new form of dyke who is at odds with a short-sighted and self-seeking community is one of the most admired narratives in German literature, and Denis Jackson's definitive series of translations of Storm's finest novellas begins with it. The translator's introduction and end-notes provide commentary on the absorbing background to the tale.

THEODOR STORM
Hans and Heinz Kirch; *with* Immensee *and* Journey to a Hallig
Translated by Denis Jackson and Anja Nauck 978-0-946162-60-4
Three contrasting narratives, two of them translated into English for the first
time. As in *The Dykemaster*, maps and detailed end-notes enhance enjoyment of
fiction strongly rooted in time and place, which has been compared to the work of
Thomas Hardy.

THEODOR STORM
Paul the Puppeteer; *with* The Village on the Moor *and* Renate
Translated by Denis Jackson 978-0-946162-70-3
Winner of the Oxford-Weidenfeld Translation Prize 2005
The first-ever English translation of one of Storm's most popular works, a magical
portrayal of the life of a 19th-century travelling puppeteer family; with two other
vintage novellas almost equally unknown in English.

THEODOR STORM
Carsten the Trustee
with The Last Farmstead; The Swallows of St George's; *and* By the Fireside
Translated by Denis Jackson; Introduction by Eda Sagarra 978-0-946162-73-4
Carsten the Trustee, depicting the decline of a burgher family in the aftermath of
the Napoleonic Wars, is one of Storm's most powerful works. *St George's Almshouse*
is a poignant love story told with dazzling narrative virtuosity. *The Last Farmstead*
and the cycle of ghost stories *By the Fireside* are translated for the first time.

YURY TYNYANOV
Young Pushkin
Translated by Anna Kurkina Rush and Christopher Rush 978-0-946162-75-8 *(cased)*
The crowning masterpiece of one of the most original of 20th-century Russian
writers. This novel brings Russian society in the first two decades of the 19th
century to vibrant life – a dazzling panorama of the leading persons and formative
influences in Alexander Pushkin's early life and first years of adulthood.

MIKHAIL ZOSHCHENKO
The Galosh *and other stories*
Translated by Jeremy Hicks 978-0-946162-65-9
These 65 short stories, nearly half of them translated into English for the first
time, reveal one of the great Russian comic writers in their bitter-sweet smack and
the fractured language of the argumentative, obsessive, semi-educated narrator-
figure, trying hard to believe in the new Socialism of the early Soviet years.